ICHOR

THE ICHOR SERIES
BOOK ONE

ICHOR

THE ICHOR SERIES
BOOK ONE

TRISH D.W.

Ichor
Copyright © 2022 by Trish D.W.

Interior Formatting by: Elaine York, Allusion Publishing (http://www.allusionpublishing.com)

No part of this book may be reproduced or transmitted in any form or by any means, electronic or mechanical, including photocopying, recording, or by any information storage and retrieval system without the written permission of the author, except for the use of brief quotations in a book review.

This book is a work of fiction. Names, characters, places, and incidents either are products of the author's imagination or are used fictitiously. Any resemblance to actual persons, living or dead, events, or locales is entirely coincidental.

ABOUT THE BOOK

This story contains mature topics that may be triggering to some and inappropriate for a younger audience. It includes the following: violence, death, emotional manipulation, emotional & physical abuse, conversations about assault, self-harm ideations, and self-inflicted deaths.

Dedicated to: My mother, Anne, who taught
me a woman's strength, resilience, and persistence.
You are the bravery behind each female character I write.

THE FIRST CHAPTER

My storyteller's ethereal male voice of blanketed obscurity skitters across my skin and whispers four life defying words. "It's time to awaken."

I try to fight my fate, but the Fates laugh at my futile efforts. I try to punch, kick, and bite the creeping sensation of consciousness torturously plucking me from the bliss of my slumber, but I am unsuccessful. Defeat clamors against my bones as I awaken, unable to escape today and all the macabre that follows suit.

Five hundred years ago, the gods of Mt. Olympus despoiled a once peaceful Earth. Where there was once human ignorance and fearless freedom, is now debris upon the gods' feet. Shackles tighten around my races' wrists, replacing the elation that once colored our world with the achromic cries of the enslaved.

Now, our world is of serfdom, sadness, and scarifications.

Every summer solstice, whoever is unfortunate enough to turn eighteen, is taken away from the prison we've lived in our entire lives. Us humans, who have just reached adulthood without a kiss of the outside air, are placed into an arena. Within this arena, the gods responsible for world enslavement vie for our minds, souls, and bodies in a fight of grotesque cruelty.

Devoid of choice throughout our lives, we are sold to the gods. Once made property by the god, they will brutalize us with scarification marks, which they burn into our flesh. These immortal monsters, who rule this world, give us a name that goes with these scars. We are no longer human beings when we are given our marking and name; we are property. Our prison shifts from one behind bars to one within our captors' grasp.

The scar the immortals give us is as close to a name that this barbarous world will ever gift us with; otherwise, we are nameless, disposable humans within the jail cells. Until we are a god's property through blood and fear, we do not exist and are inconsequential. By law, while we grow up and learn to fear our fate, we are forbidden from any identification that'll individualize us. No names, however temporary, are allowed. We are only identified as boy or girl.

Yet, I believe not existing is a grander alternative than becoming a monster's gained prize.

Each year, friends of mine who I grew up beside were taken from the prison and brought into the arena. Once sold, they are to suffer a fate worse than the Underworld. The moment that Lady Hecate pulls them from their cells and propels them into the arena, I am never to see them again.

Today is my egregious day.

As the immortals that govern this prison turn on the lights, I embrace my begrudged truth. I wish I can avoid the inescapable. That I could fall into a splendid sleep, never waking but always drifting. But my story does not continue in a dream world—it strides towards madness.

It gravitates towards the gods.

Two months ago, I turned eighteen. That morning, I awoke to the most volatile storm in existence. The clouds covered the sky in a dark gray hue, while malicious jolts of lightning struck the ground. The thunder yelled, shaking the prison walls with vengeance, and this unforgiving storm did not subside until the next day.

It was then I knew that my eighteenth birthday would bring catastrophic horrors.

Every single day of my life, I have spent inside this prison cell. From sun rise until the inevitable dusk, I'm surrounded by friends as malnourished as me. My feet are as cowardice as my heart, fearful to venture any farther than the showers that we're allowed to use once a month. Throughout my eighteen years, there have been a brazen dozen who tried to escape, and their failed attempts echo the halls with whispers of brutalized torment. The magnitude of their torture was delivered to frightened children as bedtime stories.

The stories were warnings to the rest of us.

Three immortals—Lady Hecate, Lord Phobos, and Lord Deimos—rule this prison in their own pernicious way. They ensure we fear the eventual day we're taken from the jail and sent into the arena. From the stories of our fated deaths they hiss to the children too young to utter a word, and the mutilation they give to the contumelious few who try to escape, these three gods train us to fear each breath we take.

They want me petrified, sobbing until my nose runs, and my cheeks stain with water, but I refuse. My fate with the gods is unavoidable; I will become property to whichever immortal fights and wins me in an arena, but I will not cry. I will not cower in the corner of my cell with aspirations that Lady Hecate does not take me to my destiny because my fate is inevitable. It is as fated as the sun's rise to the sky each morning.

Lady Hecate's nails screech upon the prison bars throughout her journey in the jail. As she plucks inconsolable eighteen-year-old victims from the only home they've ever known; her nails upon the prison cells let the others know when she nears them. My ears threaten to bleed upon the sound, but the closer she nears my station, the more valiant I force myself to become.

I know my time is soon-to-be obsolete when I see Lady Hecate two cells away from mine. Across the hall is my shower-mate's cell. Lady Hecate uses her magic to lift my shower-mate into the air and guide her out of the room. My shower-mate is placed in the line of hysteric people, and her inconsolable weeps grimly reverberate off the prison walls. I am quick to shuffle towards the other prisoners in my jail cell for the last time.

All four of my cell mates, huddled in the corners of the prison, stare up at me with lips quivering in fright. As my time with them slips from my fingers, I cement every face into memory so that when I sleep, I may be with them again. A life within a prison cell is destructive, both mentally and physically, but these four people made it bearable.

Sometimes even enjoyable.

A little two-year-old boy, who I have helped raise, pokes at my leg. I kneel in front of where he sits on another friend's lap. Like all of us, he is a product of two humans. All of our parents, whose sole purpose in life is to sire children, are called the Laborers.

When a god does not choose to fight for a human in the arena, then they're given to Queen Hera. As one of the three goddesses of childbirth, Queen Hera sends the unwanted humans to her labor shops. Those humans don't receive names and they only have one purpose in this world, which is to produce more children who will endure the morbid cycle of human enslavement. The only escape for Laborers is through death by childbirth or execution once they cannot sustain their occupation.

His irises are the brightest blue I have ever seen, and they obliviously stare forward, too young to understand that he will never see me again. Since Lord Phobos brought him into our cell, I have slept beside him each night, but now I am leaving forever. I look at his chubby cheeks and wide gaze, and I wonder if he will remember my face. My chest builds with an intense ache at the thought of exiting his life, all the while realizing he won't recall the nights I stayed by his side.

I bend down and press a ginger kiss upon the young boy's greasy mop of blonde hair. "I will miss you the most," I murmur. When I pull away, I turn to the girl who holds him on her lap. She is only ten years old, but she tightens her thin arms around this boy with the grave realization of her new motherly duty. "Take care of him, okay?"

She smiles, giving way to growing adult teeth. "I'll tell him stories about you every night, so he doesn't forget."

"You both need to forget." I wince once my words fill the air. "It's easier for you that way. To let the memories fall away until I am a distant memory."

With a turn of my heels, I walk away from her and the little boy, and I stand in front of the only seventeen-year-old. She tries to appear strong, just like I am, but I can see through her façade just as easily as she sees through mine. Unlike our other cell mates, she knows I am venturing towards near certain death.

The seventeen-year-old stares at me and foresees her future next year, but she shields her own sorrows and curtly says. "Goodbye."

As if my departure isn't affecting her, she stands stoic. Her chin is raised high, her face impassive, but there is a subtle tremble to her frown. A fracture in her demeanor, but I allow her to appear strong in the face of her future.

"Goodbye, sweet girl," I say.

Finally, I wander towards the last person in the jail cell, who is the boy around my age. Together, we leave our cell today and face our future in the arena, and my heart pangs with sorrowful realization. Out of everybody in my prison, he is my greatest friend. He's been my best friend since I knew what those words meant.

Sensing me, my friend stands up from his spot on the floor, where he slept every night. He migrates towards the front of the cell in silent obedience, and I follow him until we are both at the bars.

We stand side-by-side but are unable to begin our last conversation. There are a thousand words I want to say to him, and I hope he wants to deliver in return because there is a high probability that today is the last day we will see one another. Yet, neither of us makes a noise in fear that this is our last encounter.

He holds out his hand for mine, and I accept the comfort. Our actions speaking the words we are too frightened to vocalize. We stand on the threshold of unspoken thoughts until we see the advancing forms of Lady Hecate, Lord Phobos, and Lord Deimos.

The three immortals striding towards my cell are the most majestic, deadliest creatures I have ever had the agony of encountering. They glide with power radiating off of their blemish-free complexions. At least a dozen solemn humans walk behind them, with their heads down and green cuffs tight around their wrists and ankles, but I can't shift my attention away from the gods' and the energy that emanates off of their bodies.

Lord Phobos and Lord Deimos are twin gods of terror and dread, who are the product of the sordid love between Lady Aphrodite and Lord Ares. They are only a few inches taller than Lady

Hecate, who always wears shoes which stress her height. Their bronze armor amplifies their admirable physiques, while the color heightens the sharpness of their amber eyes.

Lady Hecate—the goddess of magic, witchcraft, and necromancy—is not as muscular as the twin gods, but she is impressive in her own right. She is tall and lean, but the radiance of her outward appearance is a disguise, which hides the vileness that lays rampant inside. Her large blue eyes tell the truth of her malice, as well as the green fire that whorls around the tips of her long, sharpened fingernails. The goddess's plush lips are always red, signifying the blood of the humans, which she uses to create the shade of lipstick.

She is evil incarnate.

My cell door obeys the flick of Lady Hecate's wrist, flying open to welcome my friend and me towards our undesirable date with the arena. While my friend walks out of the cell and joins the dozen other eighteen-year-olds, I assess Lady Hecate's patience and take one measly step forward. I taunt my circumstances, Lady Hecate, and my minimal desire to survive with defiance.

Her red-painted lips snarl with menace, and she asks with a bite of anger. "What are you doing?"

I respond in a steady tone. "I'm choosing my fate."

Her sinister laugh makes me flinch.

"Your fate, you say? You humans and your humorous, unintelligent quips. The Fates have set every inch of your abysmal destiny in stone since a pathetic human woman gave birth to yet another pathetic human." Lady Hecate takes an advancing step towards me, and the green flames on the tip of her fingers scatter around her arms, her shoulders, and creep alongside her neck with an unspoken promise to inflict misery. "Get in line, human."

I only take another small step forward. "Or what?" I taunt. "Are you going to kill me?"

Please kill me, a part of me implores.

With a voice like the stars, each night my storyteller within my dreams tells me tales of a world away from Lady Hecate and the prisons. He says the Underworld is the closest to freedom humans will receive while the gods and goddesses reign supreme. The king and queen of the Underworld do not believe in enslavement. My storyteller informs me that King Hades and Queen Persephone are kind to all the fallen humans who live in the land of the dead.

Once we sail across the River Styx on Charon's ferry, the immortals can no longer harm us; we are free. Death is our release, and I yearn for the feeling of freedom more ardently than anything else. While my fate is destined for the arena, I want to fight it and die by Lady Hecate's hands. To decide my life's path for once.

She breaks the distance between us in three long strides. Lady Hecate is half a foot taller than me, and her hand wraps around the back of my neck. With her grip, she forces my attention up towards the vileness of her fiery glare.

Nails, sharp and unforgiving, threaten to break skin. She teases death as her grip tightens around my throat. Killing me is a promise she will not deliver, even as I silently beg for the mercy of bereavement.

Lady Hecate draws my face close enough to hers, and I can smell the coppery stench of human blood upon her lips. The tip of her nose grazes mine while she stares into the deepest, darkest crevice of my soul.

"Do not pretend that your life is anything more than amusement to us," Lady Hecate snarls.

Her cadence is a dagger, and for a second, I believe she will gift me with death. The vileness of her words teases a vow, but she lets go of my neck, and I stagger backwards in defeat. She remains unfazed by the haggard coughs I release, but she makes sure I can hear her lethal words.

"You do not get the privilege of dying, human," she taunts. "Not yet."

Finally, I stop coughing and level my gaze with hers again. I open my mouth to respond to her, to fight my cataclysmic servitude, but Lady Hecate snaps her fingers and transports me away from the familiarity of my jail cell. My feet land on the line behind the rest of the eighteen-year-olds. Green smoke wraps around my wrists and ankles, serving as the strongest chains, and I am officially property ready to be sold and branded to the highest bidder.

THE SECOND CHAPTER

For eighteen years, I have lived and suffered, yet I have never seen my reflection. Day and its eventual night have come and gone, but I haven't seen what my smile looks like, or if I have minuscule, brown dots on my cheeks like my best friend.

Three or four years ago, when I was venturing away from childhood, curiosity emerged. I asked a girl from another cell to tell me what I looked like. We were shower mates, and she was the only person my age I talked to other than the boy in my cell. I didn't ask him what I looked like. He would ask me, and I'd be honest, but I was always too nervous to inquire about my appearance.

So, I asked the girl for answers. One day within the showers, the girl and I sat cross-legged across from one another as the water beat down on our dirt-covered bodies, and we told each other how we looked.

She went first.

Her voice was as quiet as the wind that blows through the jail, and she said. "You have a small nose that is round at the tip." Disapproval brimmed her features when she explained. "But there's a lot of hair above your eyes. Mainly in between them."

I anxiously touched the skin she described as hairy but felt smoothness. "I don't feel it," I mentioned.

"Trust me," my shower-mate said. "It's there, and it's gross. Also, there are little red bumps everywhere. Like, everywhere. The bumps are on your sunken cheeks, the tip of your pointed chin, and your large forehead."

Each malformed part of myself she criticized, I touched with an onslaught of insecurities I'd never felt before that day.

My expression must've held sadness because she muttered. "You're kind of pretty, though."

Even with dirt caked upon her arms and legs, my shower-mate was like a stream of sunlight in the darkest corner. Her bones protruded out of her shoulders, but I was in awe of her radiance with a competitive buildup of jealousy. Death and fatigue circulate around the deep bags underneath her doe-shaped eyes, but she was the most beautiful human I'd ever seen.

The girl's skin was much darker than mine; while I'm the stars in the sky, she's the beauty of the night. Her irises are brown, but lighter than her skin, while her lips are plump and pink. Her skin does not have the same red bumps as mine, except a single one on her cheek. She has the beauty that all dream to possess, but when she asked me how she looked, I lied.

"You are only kind of pretty, too." I told her.

After the day in the shower, curiosity about my appearance dissipated, and we stopped talking during our trips to the showers.

Now, as I stand to prepare for the arena, I wait to see my reflection and think of that upsetting day.

Before the arena, Lady Hecate uses her magic and provides minor transforms to every human. She molds us into an appealing version of themselves. The usual muck and malnourishment that decorates our skin is replaced with the false lie that we're treated humanely in the prisons. She does not alter our natural appearances, but she removes the trauma and neglect our bodies have withstood for eighteen years. Lady Hecate gives us a glimpse of what we would've looked like if we were free and not enslaved. To me, it's her greatest torture.

I am last in line, and while seven girls before me are in pleasant disbelief of their appearance, I refuse to look when it is my turn.

Lady Hecate's green smoke slithers around my thin, deprived body, and pain overtakes every sense. A scream threatens to break through the surface, but the agony is so overwhelming that my throat can't produce the sound to accurately explain the torture.

As smoke dissipates and I stand in front of Lady Hecate; for the first time, Lady Hecate's jaw slacks in an unfamiliar expression.

Shock, maybe?

She opens her red painted lips but closes them a second later.

"For the love of Olympus," Lord Phobos swears, his face mirroring Lady Hecate's shocked expression. "She looks just like-"

Before he can finish his sentence, Lord Deimos elbows his brother in the stomach and says. "Quiet. Don't say it."

I look at Lord Phobos, and while humans are forbidden from directly speaking to an immortal, I ask. "Who do I look like?"

Lord Phobos opens his mouth to answer me, but green magic pulls his lips shut. I turn to face the source of the magic, and Lady Hecate is glancing down at me. Her shocked expression is gone, but she takes in my appearance with a peculiar gleam in her eyes.

"Beneath the dirt and displeasing personality, I almost forgot you were attractive." Lady Hecate muses, then holds up an item and orders. "Take the mirror and see what you look like. It may be the only chance you get."

A mirror, she called it, is offered to me. I reach out my hand but hesitate before I can hold on to the handle. My shower mate's negative words about my appearance reiterate in my head. Each movement is slow and stemmed from fright, but I guide the mirror towards my face until I'm met with brown eyes that swell with unabashed surprise.

Regardless of Hecate's magic or the gods' reactions to my appearance, I hear the insults from my past and expect inadequacy, but that is not what the mirror shows me.

The hair above my eyes is thin and arched, further highlighting my prominent physical features. My lips are not as big as my shower mate's, yet they're well defined like hers. High-risen and plump cheeks best define my face. Brown hair reaches my chest, and I run my fingers through my once-long, matted locks with newfound appreciation.

Once skeletal and on the brink of death, my body experiences the most prominent changes. My thighs have grown three times their original size, and my stomach becomes full enough to create a pouch at the bottom. The top portion of my body isn't as thin as it once was, but it is smaller than the extrusive curve of my bottom half.

Gone is my thin physique, and it's now replaced by a voluptuous figure. The other girls around me vary in weight after their transformation, and while many other girls remain thin, I am far from that. The thought makes my smile grow wider because I look more than healthy for the first time in my entire life.

I look full.

For eighteen years, I've been naked. My starving body has been without a scrap of clothing, and I always gravitate my gaze towards Lady Hecate's gowns with an overwhelming desire for one of my own. While my greatest wish is to be a freed woman, my miniscule desire for a dress has come true.

While many girls who remained thin are in gowns which barely conceal their new healthy builds, my dress is modest. The gown is white, and it wraps around my neck and glides down to my ankles, where gold shoes are on my cleaned feet. Gold objects are around my wrists, but they are not handcuffs; these are something beautifully different.

As soon as I see the allure of my smile, I know the girl lied when she said I was only kind of pretty. I stare at myself in this mirror with a radiance I did not think a human could possess. I look around the room, and the other humans in this room are staring at their own reflection in the mirror with the same wonderment as I am. They are touching their cheeks in disbelief, and a few girls like my shower-mate are sobbing with elation over the sight of their attractiveness. Yet, I still feel different from them, as if my transformation surpasses theirs.

Only one person stands far away from the mirror with a solemn expression on their face. I walk towards my best friend from my cell, who I have watched grow from a boy into a man within these past eighteen years, and this is the first time I barely recognize him.

His once shoulder-length brown hair, which he often complained about, is cropped short into a similar fashion to Lord Phobos and Lord Deimos's. His hair is so short that when my hand runs through it, it is spiky and pokes at my skin. I haven't seen him without facial hair for years, and the smoothness of his face makes him look young again.

Too young to die today.

"I don't want to leave you," he says the words we were both too afraid to say earlier.

Tears accumulate as I look at the face of my closest friend. I let my words of optimism spill from my lips at the same time as the tears. "Maybe we will be lucky enough to meet again in the Underworld."

"What if the Underworld is as depressing as the prison?" His voice's dejected, lacking the reverie which once swelled in my best friend's chest.

"No, it has to be better than this."

"Because your dreams say so?" He asks and I nod my head, believing every word from my storyteller within my dreams, but a deep frown creases my friend's lips. "I have never had a single dream before. Once I fall asleep, darkness is all I'm allowed to see. I thought I was crazy when you told me you can dream while I see nothing, but when I asked my shower-mate and the people in our cells if they see anything when they fall asleep, they said no. You're the only one."

My breathing comes to a full halt. In this dark and desolate world, my best friend whispers these words in fear of my safety if anybody eavesdrops. He looks around the room with a line of suspicion, and he is careful to ensure nobody is listening to our conversation.

I wouldn't have survived this abysmal prism without my dreams at night. If I didn't have my storyteller when I slumbered, then insanity would've infested my mind. The tales he spins each night are my lifeline in the treacherous ordinance that submerges me. He is the escape from Lady Hecate, Lord Phobos, Lord Deimos, and the looming doom of the arena.

Every tale about the gods and goddesses that my storyteller taught me in the jail cells is my lifelines. Because of him, I hear about fantastical lands I hope to one day see in the waking world. He fills my night with his ethereal voice speaking about demi-gods slaying monsters, Lord Heracles's twelve labors, and the most wicked Olympians.

I wish I could always live within my dreamworld, where the veil which separates my Storyteller and me is severed, and I am there with him forever.

"I'm not crazy," my voice trembles as I whisper. "I know what I see at night."

"You're not crazy," he confesses these words so quiet that I have to strain to hear him. "I believe you see the shadowed man in your dreams. I believe everything you've ever told me about the gods and goddesses."

"Then what are you saying?" I ask.

There is a prolonged period of silence between my question and his answer, but when he gains the courage to speak again, he shuffles closer to me. He wraps his arms around me in a tight-gripped hug, and his lips graze my ear.

In this close embrace, beneath the heavy thumping of our hearts, my best friend murmurs. "I'm saying you can't tell anybody about what you see when the rest of the world does not. Even when you get your master and you think you can trust them, don't say a word about what you see. No other humans have dreams."

"But I'm normal."

My friend hugs my body tighter, and he speaks his truth in a quieted, frightened cadence. "No, I don't think you are." His hands tangle themselves in the soft curls of my hair and sincerity leaks through his voice. "I wish I could save you forever, to shield you from whatever is to come, but I don't think we will be lucky enough to see each other after today. "

"I don't understand," I admit.

He pulls away from the hug, and just as our arms slip from each other's hold, green smoke surrounds our bodies. The smog invades my vision, leaving me blinded and unable to see anything but Lady Hecate's powers. I try to reach for my best friend, to feel his arms around my body in comfort once again, but I'm alone.

As soon as the green smoke dissipates, I am pulled down towards a merciless ground with no preparation to stop my fall. My bottom hits the ground, and as I groan, a hand is extended forward.

My closest friend hoists me up to my feet. Then, I look at him, and I see his fear as if it were a beast that holds onto his throat, slowly squeezing out every breath of strength from his lungs.

He feigns his former gallantry and asks me. "Are you okay?"

"I'm okay," I say.

But I'm not.

Because I'm in the arena, standing beneath the stares of a hundred Immortals, who wait to feast upon my fear and serfdom as if it were a delicacy.

THE THIRD CHAPTER

Turning my body away from my friend's, I stare at the infamous arena I have dreaded since I knew of its existence. Upon this ground, which is perpetually stained with spilled blood and servitude, I will become a slave to an immortal. This is the land where the quickest god with a blade will become my master, and fear slams into my chest as if I were struck by one of King Zeus's lightning bolts.

I promised myself I would remain strong. I vowed not to let the intensity of this day befall me, but now I am here, and my entire body is quaking in petrification. My friend beside me shakes too. I can feel it in our intertwined hands, but I can provide no comfort. I am paralyzed at the spot, staring at the many faces of malignant gods and goddesses who look down upon us as entertainment.

An overarching display of decadence threatens to swallow me whole. My storyteller told me about the arenas, but he couldn't prepare me for the magnitude of the colosseum, which stands over three hundred feet high and twice that in width. The marble seats surround the circular perimeter, with four rows that start ten feet above the arena ground and end at least a two hundred feet above us. The gods and goddesses who sit in the highest seats are blurred faces because of their distance.

The light-colored walls nearest the arena ground are splattered in dried blood. Godly magic could've absolved the secretion, but I know the blood is left on the walls as a reminder. It reminds every human that our premature death is a god's best kept promise. While many of us will not die in the arena grounds in front of a crowd of raucous gods, our blood will inevitably decorate somebody's walls.

Over one hundred immortals take the pews. They are laughing, socializing amongst themselves with glasses of nectar in their hands. Immortals see today as the social event of the month. To them, it may be enjoyable, but to us it is the soul-crushing moment that all of us are sold to slavery and might be killed before the sun sets.

Every god and goddess is just as otherworldly gorgeous as Lady Hecate, Lord Phobos, and Lord Deimos, who now sits relaxed in the crowd. Because of the gods, I do not correlate beauty with kindness. I stare into the crowd of immortals, who look at us with a lethal desire to purchase us for their own sick desires, and I loathe their attractiveness that masks their internal hideousness. These gods are monsters who sit in the arena pews on the worst day of our lives with the prettiest of smiles and ugliest of souls.

A myriad of immortals examine every inch of our bodies to see if we are worth their time. Their perusal is excruciating for the soul, and I squeeze my friend's hand tighter. Yet, no matter how tight my grip on his hand becomes, nothing can stop my overwhelming emotions.

All the surrounding humans are just as frightened as I am. My shower-mate is dazzling a green dress, which brings out the smooth darkness of her skin, but she is sobbing on the floor. Others are trying to hide themselves with their hands over their faces, as if this turns them invisible.

I turn away from the others in time to see the first god flying towards the arena ground on a pair of winged sandals.

Lord Hermes lands on the floor with grace, and he stands across from me with his *caduceus* in hand. I know the man in front of me is a god, but he stands in the middle of the arena looking like an ordinary boy. Lord Hermes is the messenger of the gods and the god of thievery, but he looks no older than me with a lopsided, adolescent smile on his face that contrasts his immortality.

The messenger god looks to me, and I'm swallowed whole by his gaze. Green eyes, deep like a forest my storyteller once showed me, stare at me with so many emotions I can't decipher fast enough. I'm stunted by him, a male who looks more human than god, and for a second I believe I have him enraptured, too.

But then, his attention turns to the gods sitting upon the pews. His back is to me, and he is looking at his allies in torment and immortality once again.

With enough strength to shake the pews, he yells to the crowd. "The rules are the same as each arena event. If you want to fight for a human, then you come down and challenge anybody for the one of your choosing. Then, whoever else wishes to duel for the human may do so. You fight until your blood is spilled, and the last god or goddess unscathed in the arena will win their possession."

Possession.

I hate that word because it's true.

We are property, spoken about as if we were not here. The gods, who Lord Hermes speaks to, are excited by his words. Their clamors of excitement are loud enough to crumble the arena.

"You are limited to a maximum of two humans per arena." Lord Hermes continues, his voice loud enough to be heard for miles. "Once you win either one or two humans, then you must leave the arena with your new belonging to begin their renewed life and journey. You may start the battles once my feet leave the ground."

Lord Hermes looks back at me once more, but he doesn't glance away a second later. His gaze lingers as the crowd of gods and goddesses continues to shake the arena. He is taller than any being I've ever seen, towering over my friend and me. The god's visual inspection wanders down to my hand, which is wrapped around my friend's, and looks back at me.

As the bellows from the immortals cease, Lord Hermes prepares flight. Yet, before he flies off and the fights begin, he winks at me. Then, as quickly as he appears, he is out of the arena and sits in one of the farthest pews.

My friend and I are the only two standing up on our feet, and that garners too much attention. A bark of laughter begins the arena's fights, and I gravitate my scrutiny towards the noise. The god stands in the middle of the second row of pews with a spear materializing in his hand. His fixation is on the two of us, and my friend pulls me behind him.

My friend's chivalry intrigues this god.

He is in armor similar to what Lord Phobos and Lord Deimos wear, except he has an intricate boar's head upon the bronzed chest plate. While those two lower-level gods were clean shaven, a thin beard covers the lower half of this brawny god's face.

I look up at the most handsome immortal, and my body becomes electrified. Tiny pricks, which feel like miniature lightning bolts, dance across my skin. The sight of him churns the pit of my stomach with an unknown, unexplainable new feeling.

With a newfound burning against my cheeks, I try to steer my attention away to no avail.

"Do I see a fighter on my hands?" The god implores with undeniable excitement lacing his words.

A shield materializes in his other hand, and once he is ready for battle, he leaps into the air. The god soars in the sky and jumps over the immortals who are in the pew in front of him. His feet slam against the arena ground, and the floor splinters in half upon his weight.

I stumble back when the ground shifts, but my friend keeps me steady with his grip on my hand. The god's lips curl with a snarl when he notices our linked embrace, and he takes an advancing step towards us. The closer he nears, the tighter my friend's grip on my hand becomes.

The god is several inches taller than my naturally short friend, and he doubles him in muscles alone, but my cellmate stands against the immortal. He is terrified while facing off with an Olympian, but he never wavers. The spear within the god's grasp lifts to the bottom of my friend's chin, tempting him to cower like the rest of the humans. But his submission would leave me alone with the god of war.

So, my friend doesn't look away.

There is a cruel expression growing on the god's face, and he applies pressure to the spearhead against my friend's chin. My friend flinches when the god cuts skin, and a trickle of red blood slides down the spearhead.

"Lord Ares, stop!"

A voice rings out and silences the erratic thumping in my chest, as well as Lord Ares's assault against my friend. The sound of those three words muted the arena, and they focus on the source of that voice, and the command which spilled from undeserving lips. I spoke the name of an immortal I am not supposed to know, and every god, goddess, and human in the room stares at me with confusion contorting their faces.

"You should've stayed silent, my queen," my storyteller coos inside of my head.

Effortlessly, Lord Ares pushes the barrier between him and me out of the way, and my friend flies halfway across the arena floor. I gasp, watching as he smacks against the wall and crumbles onto the ground without a stir of consciousness moving him, but then Lord Ares's blood dripped spear is on the tip of my chin.

His nearness leaves me breathless, and while a foreign emotion bubbles by our proximity, fear is paramount. Pain is this god's weapon, and with his nearness, I want to scream in agony. His stare pierces into me, delving into my soul for my deepest, darkest secrets.

Then, he growls. "Do I know you, human?"

THE FOURTH CHAPTER

Death has been on the precipice of my mind since I was a child and watched horror unfurl without an escape, but now that the thought becomes a genuine possibility, I realize how desperate I am to live.

The spearhead presses against the skin beneath my chin, and the danger in Lord Ares's stance is like standing on the edge of a cliff. Immortals, from their protected seats several feet away, watch the desire for murder lay unspoken on his face. Lord Ares stares down at me and sees a frightened human, who he deems weak in front of the mighty, but a fire burns through me that vows survival in the depths of dread.

I spill out a lie. "Lord Phobos and Lord Deimos spoke about their powerful parents all the time, your majesty." When Lord Ares lessens his grip on the spear, my ability to breathe is restored, and I am quick to add. "I made a guess you were the great Lord Ares they spoke so highly about when I saw your matching armor."

There are two seconds between my lie and his answer. The entire time, our eyes are locked. Navy blue clash against deep brown, and my fear lays visible for him and the onslaught of gods watching from the pews. However, I am the only one who sees the hesitance within his own gaze. The god of war and bloodshed does not know how to trust anybody's words or actions, and I wait for him to denounce my words and execute me.

Instead, the spearhead descends, its tip pointing at the ground. He does not fully believe me, I can tell, but Lord Ares doesn't question me further. Lord Ares turns away from me, and he strides towards the middle of the arena.

His muscular arms are opened wide, and his voice is thunderous as he announces. "I bid on both the girl and the boy. Who dares to fight me for them?"

The relief I possessed evaporates upon his declaration. While Lord Phobos and Lord Deimos did not speak about their father, my storyteller did. He told me about every god, both extraordinary and subsidiary, which sits upon the coliseum pews. I drink in the sight of hundreds of gods and goddesses, and the storyteller ensured I recognize every single one of them for this day.

Because of my storyteller, there is not a single immortal within my line of vision whose name is unfamiliar to me.

His velvety voice spoke of each gods' powers, their origin stories, and their standing as a master. There was caution within his cadence whenever he spoke about particular immortals and their treatment of their slaves; Lord Ares was one of them.

Betwixt in darkness within the dreamworld he has concocted, my storyteller is only a tall, lean figure of shadowy wisps and obsidian ascendance. He sits on a black object, which he calls a throne, where the shadows of his body slither around the arms and legs. Nothing of his face is visible, but a silver crown lays haphazardly on the outline of his head.

He is a daunting sight, who has graced my dreams since I was sixteen years old, and he should've frightened me the first time I saw him. I should've seen my Storyteller and screamed until consciousness freed me, but I did not. I could not see a face, only a frightening man coiled in shadows and disparity, but I felt safest within his company.

Within a space in my dream that he said was his future throne room, he told me about each god and goddess who ransacked my world. I had no face to gauge for emotions. Only his voice, and a deep ache of austerity, changed his cadence when he spoke about Lord Ares, the god of war.

"Ares is one of the greatest warriors this world will witness. He is a living weapon, my sweet queen, but he only realizes the strength in men rather than women. Athena is his sole exception to that rule. Therefore, he only takes male humans as soldiers. Rarely ever will he fight for a woman, but if he does..."

Hesitation lined my storyteller's voice as he spoke about Lord Ares. When he halts and the silence encases the room, fear always creeps inside.

"If he does, then what?" I probed.

"It will be because his lover, Aphrodite, and him are no longer together," he ground out the words with anger intertwined with heedfulness. "If he fights for you and wins, then every inch of anger he has towards his recent separation with her will unload on you. You can't control the victors of the game but avoid this god as much as you can."

I try to tether myself to bravery, but upon Lord Ares's words, there is a crack in my resolve. I stumble backwards, trying to distance myself from the god who never allows women to live past a single night. My back hits a chest, and I jump to the side in terrible anticipation that another god has come up from behind me to fight against Lord Ares.

But it isn't.

My best friend takes a step towards me, with a new slight limp in his step, and he grabs my arms. He wraps my body in his embrace for what will undoubtedly be the last time if Lord Ares wins me. While my friend cannot dream like I do, he believes each story I've told him and squeezes me harder.

There isn't anything motivational from my friend because that is not our world. Instead, he presses a kiss on the top of the back of my head, and together we stare up at the pews to see the story of our lives dictated by vindictive immortals.

Centered in the middle of the arena, at the very top, are three balconies. On the left, King Hades and Queen Persephone sit on thrones. Their loyal dog, Cerberus, is seated in between the mighty rulers of the Underworld. On the right, King Poseidon and Queen Amphitrite are on their thrones. King Poseidon has a goblet filled with nectar in one hand, while the other holds his mighty trident.

Last, in the middle, the king and queen of all the gods and goddesses sit upon their thrones made of humanity's suffering.

The king's appearance gives off the false pretense that he is the oldest out of his five siblings. He is the only one with once-black hair now peppered with both white and gray locks. While small snippets of his hair have black creeping through the surface, his beard is completely white and gray.

No other God displays a physical feature that would age them, but King Zeus proudly displays himself with streaks of white hair. For a second, I meet with the king's electric blue ones, and the world halts. Hatred forms within me upon the sight of the god responsible for a world, which was once free, that is now shackled in chains and subjugation.

When the Olympian king sees me enclosed in an arena as Lord Ares's centralized fixation, shock overtakes his features. His mouth drops, and his head tilts to the left, the way mine does when I am confused. My presence in the arena surprises King Zeus, and he tears away from my sight to look down at Lord Ares.

A hundred eager souls wait for King Zeus's decisive words regarding the first fight.

"You already cut the boy," King Zeus's declaration is absolute, and he bellows the statement across the arena with the strength of a thousand screams. "You will fight for him first. The girl will go second."

The king of the gods raises his hands into the air, and the ground beneath me quakes under his might. Lightning bolts materialize in both of his hands; as they strike upon the ground, I am flung across the arena.

My body soars through the air as if I've grown wings, but with no control of my movements. I reach out my arms, trying to keep my best friend within my reach, but I fly thirty or more feet away from him until my back claps against the wall. It momentarily takes my breath from me, but I don't care. I fight the pain the way a warrior duels with a sword, and I am quick to rise to my feet once again.

"Stay down," an angry voice snaps. "You're begging for death by standing."

It's my shower-mate who spoke, and she cowers against the wall. Dirt covers parts of her new green gown and silver streaks slide down her cheeks. I once envied her beauty, but fear misshapes her. We're in a world where all we can control are our reactions to the strife, but my shower-mate submerges herself in submissive fright.

"Why is death seen as a thing to fear?" I respond. "It sounds like a welcomed gift compared to all of this."

I rise to my full height but cannot rip my back from the wall King Zeus pushed me against. I try to reach out a hand, to move enough to escape the hold the king of the Olympians has on my body, but my sentiment is futile. Helplessness clings to me like a foul odor, which grows worse by the second, and I look at my best friend with visible dejection.

While everybody else is against the wall, unable to move, my friend and Lord Ares stand in the middle of the arena. My friend looks back at where I am, and this time he does not try to shield me from the sight of his fear. His trepidation lies in his agape mouth, his widened eyes, and his hands that continue to open and close into fists.

I mouth three words to him. *We will survive.*

There is no certainty in my words, but the smallest smile grows over his lips, regardless.

Winged sandals once again flutter onto the battle grounds. Lord Hermes lands delicately upon the arena, but his *caduceus* glows within his hand, and the taunt in his raised eyebrow contradicts his ginger landing. Just like Lord Ares, Lord Hermes is ready for bloodshed.

Golden wings whoosh onto the battlefield. A goddess stands in front of Lord Ares with two majestic wings, which overtake a quarter length of the arena when outstretched. She is slim and pale, with blonde hair pulled back into a tight, high-risen braid. The goddess appears docile with a button-nose and a dimpled chin until two knives materialize in her hands and a deep scowl matures her face.

Lady Nike, goddess of victory, readies herself to fight for my best friend.

Then, one of the mightiest gods crashes upon the ground. A lion's sheath covers his otherwise naked, muscular torso. The mouth of the slain lion lays as a crown upon the God's auburn, cut hair, to remind the world he is the god of heroes and the slayer of the Nemean Lion. A metal club decorated in sharp spikes is swung around in both of Lord Heracles's burly fists.

Seconds pass as the arena waits for any other prospects. When it is clear that no other gods will emerge from their seats, Lord Ares's spear and shield re-materialize. A blood red helmet, which matches his shield, forms over his head and obscures most of his face from view.

"Shouldn't you be sitting up there, Nike? I'll be needing a victory wreath soon." He lets out a condescending laugh, which is devoid of any humor. "We both know you are not a fighter."

Oh, how wrong he is.

"Dear brother," Lord Hermes's playful cadence cuts through the air. "Could you not be a sexist, arrogant, mess of a god for just one day?"

Lord Heracles snorts, and Lady Nike gives the tiniest nod of appreciation to Lord Hermes, but Lord Ares frowns in disapproval. All four gods are skilled warriors, and they impatiently squirm for their chance to fight one another. Yet, the arena waits for King Zeus's permission.

In order for a battle to begin, the fighters need King Zeus's allowance. The arena ground is quieted in anticipation, and I silently pray to the merciless king to show a sliver of benevolence. I stare at the podium, where King Zeus stands, and I mutely beg for my friend's safety.

Per usual, my prayers remain unanswered as King Zeus outcries a single command.

"Begin."

THE FIFTH CHAPTER

The four gods are hungry, and my friend is their treat.

They circle around one another, weapons raised and confidence high, as the ground below me trembles in fright. None of them wish to attack first, and their feet shuffle side-by-side in anticipation for the battle to start.

Lord Heracles spins his cudgel, while a bow and arrow are slung across his burly shoulders in case of emergency. My storyteller told me Lord Heracles's arrows are dipped in the blood of the Hydra, making them nearly indestructible. I pray to whoever listens that my friend will never have to find out the blood's grody powers.

Lady Nike is a goddess of regal beauty, whose petite frame dwarfs people's expectations. Her wings are golden, glittering upon the parlous arena ground like they are a part of the sun's rays. Her knives stay tight in her grip until her knuckles whiten and her golden veins threaten to break through her forearms.

Lord Hermes is the only one lacking battle armor. He's out of place in an arena filled with warriors, with only his *caduceus* and a blade the size of my hand twirling on the tops of his fingers. Yet, while the rest of the battlefield has strength, Lord Hermes has intelligence that is paramount against his opponents. His sandals' wings flutter with excitement, and his adrenaline spikes at the thought of making my friend his property.

The god I fear becoming victorious is Lord Ares, who smirks as if he has already won the battle.

I try to fight the urge to look in Lord Ares's direction, but he continues to garner my attention. His armor is the most impressive, and terrifying, out of the four gods who circle each other. From his helmet down to his shin guards, he is emblazoned in bronze armor. Red and white outlines accentuate the material, highlighting the details of his chest plate and helmet.

In one hand, Lord Ares holds his spear, which is already tainted with droplets of my friend's blood. His other hand has a white-knuckle grip around the handle of a magnanimous sword that demands carnage. The silvery blade glistens in the arena, custom made for battles against immortals.

The gods continue to circle around one another, but Lord Ares risks himself and looks at me. Dark, navy-blue eyes glow as bright as the sky underneath the shadows of his helmet. I watch the way battle enlivens him, completely transforming his appearance, and electrical currents rush across my arms at the sight of him.

As soon as Lord Ares looks back at his opponents, he strikes.

Lord Ares runs towards Lady Nike, but she's quick to react. She flies into the air, and as she soars upwards, one of her knives spirals out of her hand towards its intended target. Just as the tip of the blade nears his nose, Lord Ares flips into the air and kicks the knife back in her direction. The goddess catches her thrown knife by the handle with ease, but her lips are narrowed in displeasure.

"Is that all you got, gorgeous?" He outcries with a widespread grin.

Lady Nike's face contorts in anger, and she lets out a vengeful cry as she soars down to the battlegrounds. Lord Heracles runs towards Lord Ares, ready to eliminate him while he is distracted, but Lord Heracles forgot about Lord Hermes's presence. The god of mischief—Lord Hermes—is quiet and quick, and he hits the back of Lord Heracles's knees with his *caduceus*. When Lord Heracles collapses onto the ground, the floor splinters against his mighty weight.

Lord Ares hurdles his spear through the air towards Lady Nike's face, while Lord Heracles lets out a terrible scream. Lord Heracles swings his spiked cudgel backwards towards Lord Hermes, who already flew up into the air and out of reach. Lady Nike turns her wings, narrowly avoiding the spear's wicked touch, and Lord Hermes throws his miniature dagger towards Lord Heracles. Lord Heracles turns around just as the dagger is about to pierce the back of his neck, and he catches the weapon with just two fingers.

There is a cruel expression on Lord Heracles's face as he rises to his full height again. He flips the dagger in his hand once before throwing the weapon back towards Lord Hermes. Lord Heracles doesn't aim for Lord Hermes's face like the latter god expected. The dagger spirals, and faster than Lord Hermes can anticipate, it slices through the wing of his left sandal.

As Lady Nike lets out another battle cry and soars down towards Lord Ares, Lord Hermes loses his balance and tilts in the sky. Lord Heracles dematerializes his cudgel and unsheathes his bow and arrow. Arrow after arrow is slung in Lord Hermes's direction, and while the quick god evades each arrowhead from nicking his skin, Lord Hermes materializes a dagger.

Their battle for possession becomes slowed. While Lord Ares and Lady Nike are lightning, striking through the air with lethal accuracy, the moment Lord Hermes throws his dagger, life goes into slow-motion. One of Lord Heracles's arrows flies past the dagger, both of them intended for different targets, and neither god has time to evade the weapon that promises their defeat.

The arrow drives itself deep into Lord Hermes's thigh, causing ichor to spill from the wound. He spirals downwards, no longer lifted by the remnants of his winged sandals, and crashes upon the arena ground in decimation. The tiny dagger slays Lord Heracles, just as the arrow marked its target. Ichor bubbles to Lord Heracles's chest, the golden blood staining his armor, and he collapses onto the ground beside his fallen half-brother, Lord Hermes.

I should draw my attention towards Lord Ares and Lady Nike to see who the victor for my friend is, but I can't tear away from the rich color of the two gods' blood.

Gold liquid, shimmering in the sunlight as if it stole some of its excellence, lasts only a few seconds on the gods' skin, but I am infused on the sight. My storyteller always told me ichor was beautiful, a sight only a few humans are fortunate to ogle upon, but I did not expect the three seconds where golden blood spilled before the wounds healed to steal the breath from my lungs.

Yet, when the ichor dissolves from Lord Hermes's thigh and Lord Heracles's chest, I'm quick to look back at the two remaining warriors.

Lord Ares thrust his sword forward. A mere centimeter separates the tip of his blade and Lady Nike's flat stomach before she soars rearward, kicking the blade from her feet on her backward ascension towards the sky. Her mighty wings slice through the air with the vengeful force of a woman scorned, narrowly missing Lord Ares's jaw as she soars upwards.

The god of war stumbles with anger etched on his face, but Lady Nike sees a weakness and swoops in for the victory. She flies downwards towards where Lord Ares stands, and she uses her wing to slap him with magnifying efficacy. Ares sails across the battleground like a single feather against a gust of wind.

Humans scream, rushing away right before Lord Ares's body smacks against the wall they once cowered upon. The entire arena wall fractures, a crack forming where his body fell, and his head blasted against the unrelenting stone. The god of war, who once brimmed with confidence, collapses in defeat.

Leaving Lady Nike as the victor of the arena.

My best friend now stands next to the majestic Lady Nike, his life claimed by the goddess of victory. The petite, regal goddess looks up at my friend and shows pride in her prize. My attention swivels towards my friend, who is relaxed, standing next to his master. There isn't fear on his face, contrasting against the affrighted expressions of the other humans within the arena.

"This is ridiculous." Lord Ares stands to his feet. While the god is awakened and healed, he seethes with anger over a lost battle. "You can't defeat me."

Gold, feather-like handcuffs cinch my friend's wrists, his enslavement to Lady Nike official with a prominent clink of his chains. She looks back at her defeated opponent with a swish of her blonde braid.

"Maybe during next season's arena, you can redeem yourself," she snaps her fingers, and she places a victory wreath on the top of her head like a crown. "Or you can lose against me again. I'm appeased with either alternative."

Lady Nike grabs onto the chains in between my friend's cuffs, and as her wings extend, he looks back towards where I stand for the final time. This is goodbye. We both know it whilst standing across the arena from one another. There is a possibility we will see each other again, but an instinctual part of me knows that this is our last encounter.

Before she flies him into the sky to disappear from my life, he mouths three words.

I'll miss you.

I do not have the chance to mouth back any words. To tell him I cherish our friendship. The familiarity of his angular, newly shaven face is gone and is replaced with an empty spot where he once stood.

I knew this day would come, where I'd lose my best friend forever. It was etched into destiny since we were old enough to know what destiny was, but I still had a stupid sliver of optimism. A far-fetched hope we'd live in the same benevolent house, free from the looming promise of a premature death.

When he leaves, I realize my sanguineness is futile. This world is not fair, and only the idiotic dream of another alternative. It is a nightmarish universe overrun with immortals who are drinking and celebrating our imprisonment and inevitable death. I live in a place infested with desolation and solitude, where hope goes to die.

"The world won't be like this forever," my storyteller promises within my head.

For the first time, I'm not sure I believe him.

Rage brews in Lord Ares as he stampedes towards me. Two mighty swords, stained with human red blood, materialize in his hands. The danger in his stance speaks a hidden story I do not wish to unravel. He drawls his manic attention towards the pews, where hundreds of gods and goddesses sip nectar and socialize amongst themselves in apathetic bliss.

Lord Ares points both of his swords towards his potential opponents and a scream of vengeance spews. "Now onto her. Who dares to take her from me?"

I am the spectacle of many gods' attention. A plethora of them stop their fruitless conversations, and their gaze is on me.

Upon the sovereignty of their attention, and of the power which courses through their godly veins, they stare down at me with a question in their mind. The same question I wonder as I stand beside Lord Ares.

Am I worth fighting for?

THE SIXTH CHAPTER

There is a distilled silence in a crowd of previously gossiping and sloshing drinks.

They no longer stare at me the way I would look upon the jail cell walls, with callous disinterest. No, they look down at where I cower beside Lord Ares with intense probing. Gods and goddesses assess the prominent curves of my hips, the curls of my brown tresses, and the nervous quiver of my bottom lip with the same question.

Am I worth facing Lord Ares?

At least one other immortal seems to think I am worth the battle, and she rises from her seat. Lady Hecate, the goddess who has tormented me since I was old enough to remember, snaps her fingers and encases herself in her green smoke.

When the thick mist diminishes, she's upon the battleground with two daggers in each of her hands. Her power thrives within her bulbous gaze and slithers down her thin biceps. Green magic whorls around her arms, scattering down to her hands, and coiling around each individual finger.

Fear is wrapping around my throat, tightening its grip until I cease to exist. My friend is gone in the sky with a benevolent goddess, and the time to cower behind his frame has passed. I must face the witch deity's fire as a psychotic smirk lifts a corner of her blood-red painted lips. I stare at the malicious goddess and can hear every taunting promise she's given me throughout the years to make my death the most ruthless one she's ever inflicted.

As if she can hear her own words within my head, that cruel smirk grows.

"That's it?" Lord Ares purrs, confidence changing his once manic cadence. "Just you and I are fighting for the girl?"

"No."

The male's voice sends a shiver down my spine. Death has emerged from his obsidian cage, and my heart stops beating. My body reacts to his presence as if it has begun its descension towards oblivion. The beginning stages of decomposition stain the air because the personification of death has come for me.

Lord Thanatos has a black robe draped over his tall and imposing build, which conceals every inch of his body. A midnight hood places a shadow over his features, but I still see a small snippet of his face, which is not concealed by darkness or his thick beard. A plush mouth rests in a state of indifference, never raising or lowering, but remaining unfazed.

Lord Ares's confidence depletes upon the sight of him, and the three friends whose stride beside Lord Thanatos.

A god stands beside Lord Thanatos in a robe with a hood of the same design but contrasting color. His robe's dark gray hue overtakes this god's similarly brawny, imposing physique. He is identical to Lord Thanatos in appearance, except he has a clean-shaven face and a frown marred with silver and gold scars.

It's Lord Hypnos, personification of sleep.

A woman is beside the twin primordial beings, her arm intertwined with a god wearing a blackened crown. Her eyes are brown, with a purple tint to them which sets her apart from any other goddess, and they brim with power. She is the goddess of the spring, the clear queen of the Underworld who walks arm-and-arm with the king himself.

King Hades.

The king of the Underworld has irises as blue as his brother King Zeus, but while the latter holds power and electricity, King Hades does not. There is kindness within him and compassion as he stares at me beneath a fan of black bangs, which cover the entirety of his pale forehead.

There is something familiar about him as he and Queen Persephone stride towards the battle front. He only looks at me for one second, but I stare at the man with skin as pale as the moon with both confusion and curiosity. There are a few questions my storyteller could not answer for me, and I stare at King Hades as if he holds the rest of them.

Neither King Hades nor Queen Persephone have weapons in their hands, but the four imposing deities stand in front of Lord Ares and Lady Hecate with power in their presence. Lord Hypnos and Lord Thanatos extend their wings, both magnificent in an ashy gray and onyx black. The mighty feathers encompass where their king and queen stand, and I swear Lord Ares flinches at the sight.

Lady Hecate migrates closer to Queen Persephone, who she follows dutifully in the Underworld, but the queen glances up at Lady Hecate and orders. "This is Hades and my girl to take. Go back to the pews."

The green fire within Lady Hecate's eyes diminishes, returning to their tame blue, and she succumbs to her ruler's orders. Lady Hecate snaps her fingers, and she disappears out of the arena grounds and back to her seat. She glowers at me from where she sits, hatred manifesting in her scowl, while the roars of her promises to kill me turn into a dimmed resonance.

I stick my tongue out at her and turn back towards the other gods, where another goddess has emerged.

A spear sits in the woman's hand, while armor of magnificent silver and gray covers her lithe, muscular build. Her hair is blonde, lighter than any other immortals, and pulled back so barely any of it can be seen underneath her helmet. Behind the helmet, I can see the deadly stoic frown that stares back, assessing me as if I am an experiment.

Lady Athena, the goddess of wisdom, has entered the battleground.

"She is Zeus's favorite daughter," my storyteller told me one night. "The first and only daughter between Zeus and Metis, one of the most powerful titanesses to exist. Metis was so powerful that a prophecy spoke of her second child with Zeus. The prophecy foretold their second born becoming powerful enough to overthrow him. He was so frightened that he tricked her into turning into a fly and ate her while she was pregnant with Athena."

"He ate his wife?" I asked with disgust lining my voice.

"One of thousands of Zeus's terrible acts against the world." My storyteller lets the rage in his voice carry like an echo in the shadowy halls. "Athena sprouted out of Zeus's head a few months later, and she was sheathed in battle armor. She is more powerful than any other child of Zeus, and if you become her slave, then she will turn you into a wise warrior. Be careful of her rage, though, for she does not tolerate insolence. Especially from humans."

Lady Athena looks at her brother, Lord Ares. "I'll help you fight and defeat them if you and I duel for the girl separately at the end." Her words are strategic, each word over enunciated. "You and I both know who her appearance mirrors, and I'm curious. Curious enough to want her."

Lord Ares nods at the other war deity, then moves his attention towards the marble benches. Every god and goddess in the audience is silenced, their bodies frozen in disbelief. Nobody speaks a single word, but they stare down at the battleground, where some of the fiercest immortals in history vie to claim me.

Lord Phobos and Lord Deimos, Lord Ares's loyal servants and twin sons, jump out of their seats and crack the arena ground under the weight of their presence. Spears materialize in each of their hands, just as weapons emerge in King Hades's and Queen Persephone's. Eight immortals, all impressive in their own right, stand in the middle of the battleground.

Nobody talks or breathes too loud in undeniable befuddlement. The gods stop drinking and laughing, and they look at the fight of the year. Perhaps the century. I can see Lord Hermes from his place in the pews, and his knee is shaking with nervousness. He almost stands to join the battle, half-standing before lowering himself and remaining a spectator.

I finally believe my best friend's words.

I'm not normal.

"Let the fight begin," King Zeus outcries, and the first page of the story of my life is about to be written.

THE SEVENTH CHAPTER

The ground splinters in between the eight furious immortals. The arena floor tries to run from the power of these deities, and I stumble backwards as the fissure splits between my feet. Queen Persephone looks back at where I fall before she fixates back on the fight at hand.

A decomposing hand emerges from the cracked ground. Clumps of decayed skin linger on the skeletal hand, dried brown blood coated on the white bones, and the stench of decomposition I wish I did not recognize creeps to the surface with this creature of death. Inch by inch, it enters the domain, and the warriors gape with disbelief.

The skeletal hand outreaches its black nails, testing the unfamiliar air, before piercing the ground. A hand from the pits of the Underworld is pulling itself out of the trenches to come alive once more for a battle. The king and queen of the Underworld wear a smug expression, while Lord Phobos and Lord Deimos stare back with mounting fear.

Lord Deimos rushes to the skeletal hand, his foot stomping down until the bones disintegrate under the weight, but the creature's other hand derives from the pits of the Underworld and wraps its tendons around the god's ankle. Lord Deimos, the god of terror, lets out his own frightened squeal and desperately tries to free himself from the skeletal creature's viper grip.

The corpse's black nails are merciless, and they dig into Lord Deimos's skin until rich ichor spills out of his ankle. This skeletal being uses his grip on Lord Deimos's ankle to rise out of the crack, and an abominable creature of death emerges into the sunlight. Holes, where the skeleton's eyes once sat, turn to Lord Deimos, and the defeated god falls unconscious with complete petrification.

A dozen more undead mutations crawl themselves out of the fractured ground. Clumps of dead skin, remnants of dried blood, and razor-sharp teeth gnash in the warmth. King Hades snaps his fingers, manifesting Stygian black weapons for the skeletons that thirst for carnage.

They stand at the back of the battleground, swords raised behind Lord Hypnos and Lord Thanatos. Lord Ares glares down at his already-defeated son, then deviates his fury on King Hades. Lord Phobos is frightened. It is clear in his trembling hands, but Lady Athena is calm.

She looks at King Hades and asks. "Was that necessary, Uncle?"

"What can I say?" King Hades says with a shrug of his shoulders. "Achilles and Atalanta were just *itching* for another fight. I didn't want to disappoint them."

The first skeleton, now only with one hand, looks to the only one with long brown hair, and I swear it winks. Both Achilles and Atalanta, who are silent in death, serve as co-generals for the army of the dead.

"Seems like a bit of overkill for one girl," Lady Athena hums, and she glances to where I sit on the ground. "What are you hiding?"

"Nothing," I whisper.

"I'll be the judge of that," Lady Athena muses, then looks back at King Hades and Queen Persephone. "Any more parlor tricks?"

"I guess you'll have to wait and find out," Queen Persephone says.

Lady Athena spins her blade and coos. "I guess so."

The fight between death and war begins, where more bloodshed is irrefutable. The skeletons run towards Lord Phobos, and he readies himself with a spear in one hand whilst spinning a sword in the other. Moans are all the skeletons can utter as they rush towards Lord Phobos, and the immortal returns their hatred for him with the bloodthirsty kiss of his blade. Bones fly across the battlefield, a rib narrowly avoiding one human girl's throat.

Lord Thanatos flies up into the air just as Lady Athena's sword is about to slice across his legs. Wind greets Lady Athena's blade, but she does not dwell long. In the same breath, she swings her blade towards Lord Hypnos, who is not as quick to avoid her unrelenting weapon.

One long, jagged gash breaks through the armor underneath Lord Hypnos's gray robe, and he crumbles onto the ground. Bubbles of golden blood emerge from his robe, and defeat speckles his face. I can't see the top of his face beneath the hood of the robe, but I swear the deity turns to me with pity marring his scarred mouth.

As if he was about to apologize.

Lord Ares fights the king and queen simultaneously. Sweat streams down his forehead as the rulers of the Underworld block him in. He is constantly evading the next attack. The god of bloodshed is in continual defense. The battle moves towards the side of the Underworld.

I almost dare to hope.

Lord Thanatos is high in the sky, his black wings contrasting with the light of the sun, and he throws his scythe through the air. His scythe goes straight towards Lady Athena's head, following the harsh wind's direction. She is quick to duck, avoiding the blade's antagonistic caress, and she is back on her feet with the handle of the scythe in her powerful clutches.

I can only watch, unable to make a noise to stop the imminent circumstances. Lady Athena throws Lord Thanatos's own weapon back at him, and he doesn't have time to block himself. His blade plunges into his chest. The sound of his weapon splintering bone echoes throughout the arena, declaring his defeat.

He spirals downwards, away from the chance at victory. When he collapses onto the ground, he is beside his brother's fallen form, and his head turns towards where I sit. Just as Lord Hypnos had, he stares with a sadness I cannot see beneath the hood but can feel within my chest.

"Look at them," my storyteller says in my mind. *"Look how the Gods stare at you; adore you the way they would never would an ordinary human. Look how they gawk at you and see what I've always known."*

I drift my attention towards the seats. As Lady Athena strides towards Queen Persephone, leaving King Hades to duel against Lord Ares in an individual battle, I look at the other gods who are in the audience. They all gape on with bated breaths, enjoyment paralyzing their movements.

From what my storyteller has said, it is common that the gods use the arenas as a social event. Except for rare occasions, most immortals do not interact in the duels that take place. They come to a human's worst day in existence and gallivant around. Today, as well as every seasonal solstice of the year, is a human's awakened nightmare, but it's the gods' party. They will socialize, fornicate, and drink until they are incapacitated.

The female goddesses and Lord Dionysus use this time to flaunt their newest outfits. Most of the fights in the arena garner little attention, but they will gossip about the outfits for weeks. On a typical seasonal solstice, two-to-four immortals of varying prowess will duel one another for a human. During a typical arena day, the duels are war immortals bitter from a previous defeat. Only on a rare occasion will other gods partake in the arena.

It is rare that five deities will fight for a human, but the reason behind their actions is obvious. The humans coveted and fought for by more than one god are the most beautiful or they're sinewy men. They stand out amongst the crowd of sobbing, demure contenders.

The gods' fixate on each other rather than the enslaved human race, but today is different. Eight notorious warriors stand upon the battleground, and they incite a story that leaves the most prattling extraverts silent with concentration. The burn of garnering the spotlight for the immortals' rapt engrossment scorches my pale skin.

Even King Zeus, who sits high in the balcony seats, has his electric gaze centralized on every movement the gods make. Every few seconds, he seeks my whereabouts, and he stares with a crinkle of confusion. His hands are curled against the arms of his throne, and Queen Hera stares more at me than the battle with a purse of her red-painted lips.

Every human accompanying me on the worst day of our lives is staring at the arena, and then me, with awe and befuddlement. The humans I've spent my entire life besides, struggling to survive in the cells with, stare at the scene unfurling. They forget they will be the next fought and sought after, and they distract themselves with the battle at hand. I look at my shower-mate, who is staring back at me like I'm a stranger. Different from her in a thousand ways.

Everybody in the arena is watching with entrancement as they are observing every swipe Lady Athena makes with her swords, and each deflect Queen Persephone makes to keep herself from the tip of the blade. They obsess over the sight of King Hades and Lord Ares, two powerful deities, matching blade-to-blade in a brutal dance for possession. Skeletons surround Lord Phobos, whose feet stomp on the discarded bones of the defeated and discarded.

Not a single human, or god, can steer their attention away from either me or the battle.

Every time one of Lord Phobos's spears breaks, he throws the now useless weapon upon the floor to join dozens of bones, and another materializes in his callused palms. Only Achilles and Atalanta remain intact, and they're working side-by-side to ensure Lord Phobos does not emerge as the victor.

Each movement of the gods is lightning-fast, where no fault can be witnessed. Their pride is on the line, the battle for victory paid with their egos, and none can afford to make an error. One miscalculated move will end in their demise.

Lady Athena swings her sword, a battle cry escaping her lips as the weapon slices through the air. She believes she is about to decimate Queen Persephone, but she makes an error. Lady Athena knows of the sword in Queen Persephone's hand, but she does not see the dagger Queen Persephone unsheathes from its hiding spot.

While the queen's sword deflects Lady Athena's, the small dagger within Queen Persephone's other hand plunges into her opponent's rib cage. It is the one part of Lady Athena's armor left open, and the skillful goddess of wisdom crumbles onto the floor. She is clutching the dagger embedded in her abdomen, and the audience gasps in disbelief.

Lord Phobos makes the next mistake. He hears the gasps from the audience and momentarily turns his attention away from his opponents. He looks at his father to make sure he is unscathed and then finds Lady Athena's defeated form. For only a second, Lord Phobos forgets about his skeletal enemies, but the two decomposed warriors do not make the same mistake.

Achilles and Atalanta simultaneously slide a blade into Lord Phobos's back, and a scream bellows out of the god as he crumbles to his knees in defeat. The skeletal heroes pull their swords from Lord Phobos's body, and they turn to face the rest of the battle at hand with ignorance.

They do not know that it has already ended.

A battle isn't about how fast you are, but it is about deciphering your opponents' weaknesses. Queen Persephone rises from the ground, her face splattered in Lady Athena's ichor, and pride makes her unaware of the spear Lord Ares throws. The weapon spirals towards her stomach, but she is heedless until it embeds deep within her thin body.

The effervescent goddess of spring collapses onto the ground, and her trembling fingers move towards the spear deep within her stomach. A cry of agony rumbles out of her lips when her fingertips touch her golden blood. She screams with an absence of pain but a surplus of guilt, and she turns to me. Ichor trickles out of her, sliding across pale flesh like a stream of gilded water, but Queen Persephone gawks at where I stand with tears streaming down her cheeks.

Then, the ultimate mistake of the battle is made.

King Hades is a skilled fighter, but his love triumphs his rationality. He turns his attention towards his wife, who is crumbled upon the floor and staring at me as if she has disappointed me. The king of the Underworld's face slackens with sympathy, but when he turns to face Lord Ares again, it's too late.

Lord Ares uses his last remaining opponent's distraction to his advantage, and he swings his dagger.

A thin slice cuts across the king of the Underworld's throat and the blood of defeat trickles out. King Hades collapses onto his knees and crawls towards where his wife lays upon the floor, a spear holding her to the ground. Blood cascades down his neck and underneath his black armor, but he collapses on top of his wife with worry clear on his pale face. Both king and queen of the Underworld look to me, their sadness paramount.

King Hades repeats. "I'm sorry. I'm so sorry."

Atalanta and Achilles, unable to fight without their king, disappear in a puff of Lady Hecate's green smoke. Lord Ares is declared the victor. The winner of my body and life. Lord Ares strides towards me with dominion seeping from his smirked lips.

He steps across the discarded bones and fallen warriors, and each step he takes sends a shiver throughout my body. I want to fight him, to slam my fists against his chest and challenge him myself. I want to choose the decisions in my own life, but that is not the world I am a servant to.

My life is not my own.

It's Lord Ares's.

The god of war's hand convolves around my bicep, and I do not have a choice but to obey his silent command to stand up. I do not have a choice in any of this. My fate was decided long before I was born, forever a piece of materialistic possession for the gods to play a game with rather than care for. They made me a toy of their wicked devices.

I do not get to decide who pulls the strings of my life, and I do not have the power to slap away Lord Ares's touch. I am treated as if I do not have a mind that screams and begs for freedom. In their clouded perception, I am devoid of emotions. Of dreams and aspirations surpassing blind obedience. Of dying upon their everlasting whim.

To these gods, I am just property, and property gets discarded if it tries to fight back. I can't deny Lord Ares from the prize he just won because that is all I am. Just a prize. A materialistic object. A human.

Lord Ares sends a mocking glare down towards King Hades and Queen Persephone, who are still upon the ground with defeat brandishing their cheeks with tears. They wanted to win me, to covet me, and a part of me wonders what makes me so important. Why is she crying over the possibility of losing me, a measly prize amongst a crowd of a dozen mortals? Why mourn my loss?

"Because you are a grand prize," my storyteller purrs inside of my head. "You are everything magnificent in this world. The ignorant don't know any better."

A victory wreath materializes around Lord Ares's neck, and he stares down at me with deviant desires. "Are you ready to go to your new home?

"Save me," I beg to my storyteller, who always watches over me within my mind.

A blood red chariot metamorphoses upon the battleground. Lord Ares hoists me up, and when my feet land upon the chariot, ankle cuffs wrap around my skin. A whimpered noise leaves my lips, too quiet for even Lord Ares to hear, and I look up to the sky and the beating sun.

"Save me, Storyteller," I plead once more within my own frightened mind.

Lord Ares is upon the chariot now, and as it whisks away us from the arena, the Storyteller responds.

"I will free you. Stand strong when the time comes, knowing that you'll eventually be with me, my queen"

THE EIGHTH CHAPTER

The only home I've ever known was the ten-by-ten cell I inhabited with at least four other humans.

My former home was foul in both stench and appearance. Two buckets sat in the far corner of the cell, one accredited for feces and the other for urine. It was common that vomit sprayed the floors of the prison, which resulted from uneasy stomachs or physical abuse by Lady Hecate and the twins, and it was never cleaned up. The vomit would always linger, staining the ground already blackened with soot. The three pungent smells would permeate, along with salty, desolate tears.

Until today, that prison was my only correlation with home.

Lord Ares helps me off of his chariot, his fingers burning through the thin material of my gown. He electrifies my pale skin, no matter how valiant I am to dismiss the sensation. He turns my body, so the first thing I see is his mansion. I follow the sight, but I know better than to correlate this enormous expanse of land as comforting or homely.

All of my homes are torture devices.

Lord Ares's abode is the derivation of one's worst distress. Two statues of Lord Ares's sigil animal—the boar—are on either side of the large front door. Crimson blood spills on the top of their heads as if humans rained down on the inanimate objects moments before their inevitable demise.

This home of carnage is the same imposing size as the prison. Similarly to the prison I lived in, terror flocks to Lord Ares's house. His hand stays on the small of my back, leading me away from the chariot that disappears in a blaze of ash, and guides me towards his land of torment.

The god of bloodshed could transport us inside, but he doesn't. Lord Ares strolls through the front yard at a leisurely pace, so I see each traumatizing detail. He is luminous with eerie exhilaration, and he watches me as I let my concentration wander across the acres of land.

From the beginning of his estate, which is a quarter of a mile from the front doors, there is a cobblestone pavement. Each step mirrors a face, one of consuming dread, as if the muse for the rock died with their head smashed against it. Lord Ares stops walking beside a bare faced piece of cobblestone.

"I think your face would look radiant here," he muses.

I say nothing at all, and when he realizes I have no plans to humor him, he continues our journey.

Along the sides of the cobblestone pavement, spikes lead the way. On each spike, there is a decapitated human head. The heads vary in the decaying process. Some spiked heads are fresh, but others are peeling flesh and empty eye sockets.

His attention never wavers away from my face. Several times, I want to vomit and scream, but with my storyteller's former words of warning playing in my head, I let the bile of disgust slide back down my throat. My expression is apathetic to the two dozen decapitated heads, which lead the way towards the blood-painted boar statues.

Lord Ares stands close to me. So close, in fact, that I feel the ghostly remnants of words he never says aloud. His fingers slide up and down the small of my back, and he leans forward so his lips graze the shell of my ear.

"You are the first in many decades not to vomit upon the sight of my home."

If I did not know any better, then I'd assume I impressed Lord Ares.

"I can't control much in my life, Lord Ares," I whisper the truth in the quieted air, all the while ignoring the stench of decomposing flesh. "But I can decide what I fear, and I forbid you from taking that, too."

He wants me to turn to face him, but I do not give him the satisfaction. I walk across the cobblestone pavement painted with humans' last expressions before death, and I ignore the pungent stench of rotting flesh as we pass the spiked heads of his former slaves.

His mansion's first floor has floor length glass windows, and two slaves are posted at each window. Their armor's color is duller than Lord Ares's, and it appears rusted from aged overuse. They are as still as a statue, with hands holding up a shield with a boar's head and a six-foot tall spear. Around twenty men stand across the perimeter of the house, but I do not see their mouths moving or a human expression on their faces.

The second floor has two balconies which face the front yard. Vines coil the marble banisters, and the sight might've been beautiful if there weren't guards stationed. Two guards are posted on each balcony, and they hold the same shield, spear, and stoicism as the men on the first floor.

I refuse to look at Lord Ares's face, which is only an inch from mine, but I stare at the guards' appearances. I can't hide my mortification when I look at them because their faces are mutilated by their specific scarification mark. While their vision is intact, the human men were made grotesque by the brutality of their scarification mark. Lord Ares wants anybody who sees his house to look at his guards and fear them, and so he made them more beastly than man.

For a terrible second, I imagine my face like theirs, and I want to die before I enter the house.

A boar-shaped knocker sits in the middle of the door. Just like the boar statues on either side of the door, the knob is stained with human blood. Lord Ares's hand wraps around the bloodied object, and he knocks on his front door three times. He pulls his hand away from the knob, and his palm comes back bloodied.

Before the door opens, Lord Ares turns to look at me. The same hand that is coated with blood grips my face and forces me to look at him. A vicious grin seizes him, while his manic fascination centralizes on the red blood streaking my ivory cheeks.

I can see it now, the excitement that seeing red blood coating my skin gives him. The front door opens, but I continue to stare at my captor with ire rather than fear. I stare at him, and I imagine golden blood across his cheeks the same way he looks at me with red on mine.

As if he can hear the murderous thoughts swimming through my brain, his voice holds a gentleness as he says. "You are magnificent." His thumb is still coated with red blood, and he slides the digit across my bottom lip. His rapt attention travels with the movement as he murmurs in a husky cadence. "I can't wait until I wipe that defiance off of your beautiful face."

"The only way that'll happen is when my heart stops beating," I sneer at the promise with lethality.

"Don't tempt me with such an inviting thought." Lord Ares

is the first to pull away. He takes two steps back, and he looks at the slave who stands in the opened doorway. "I want her cleaned from the arena and brought to my room in two hours."

He does not spare the male slave or me another glance before walking into his own house, his head held high with arrogant power.

Only once he is out of sight, I inspect the human male in front of me.

He is older than me by a few years and is clad in armor similar to the other soldiers standing at their post. He is the first human I've seen with a scarification mark close up. The man wears a symbol of our enslavement and our name, but the sight makes my stomach churn.

The slave was attractive before his scarification. This man has a strong, clean-shaven jaw, and a sharp, narrow nose that could cut through bone with the same brutality as a sword. Golden blonde hair counteracts his tan, slightly burned skin. His eyes are like a storm, mixed with both blue and dark gray, and they stare down at me with unbridled kindness.

Even his smile, lopsided with full lips and a front tooth longer than the other, is gorgeous. He was beautiful before an immortal's sinister blade vitiated him.

Most humans, after being claimed by a god in the arena, are given scarification marks. These marks give a name to the once nameless. If an immortal wants their human to be beautiful, then the scarification mark will be small and in an easily hidden spot; however, gods like Lord Ares use the scarification process to further minimize humans' worth. The man in front of me is proof of the vileness of the Olympian.

The man's scarification mark starts on his left temple. A deep, black scar zigzags down the entire left side of his face. He has a cruel mark that curls around his chin, cutting right in the middle of his plush lips. While the right side of his face remains flawless, highlighting the beauty he once possessed before becoming Lord Ares's slave, the left is brutalized.

The slave sparkles like a star when he takes in my appearance. Redness blooms over his high-risen cheeks, and he bows in front of me as if I were royalty.

While still bowing, he says. "Forgive me, milady, but you're the first human girl I've been in the company of for eight years, and none as gorgeous as…"

He stops talking, never finishing his compliment.

As he rises from his bow, he extends his hand towards me. "My name is Zig. It's a pleasure to meet you, milady."

I stare at the hand he hangs in the air with confusion.

A joyful laugh in a land as dark as Lord Ares's home lights up the room. "This is a handshake. It is customary for you to close your hand around mine and shake it." He expels with happiness as he adds. "Otherwise, this is a tad awkward."

His hand is warm as I place mine on top. His fingers curl around the top of my hand, and I almost dare to smile in this miserable place. Zig teaches me how to shake his hand, yet, too fast, he removes his hold. Yet, his smile remains.

I ask. "How are you so happy?"

He shrugs. "It's the only thing Lord Ares hasn't been able to steal. He tries, but he'll never take my happiness from me."

I shouldn't, not when Lord Ares's bloody promise for my wellbeing sticks to my cheeks, but I let myself find a friend in Zig. I let his infectious personality worm its way into my mind, which was murky with fear and anger. For two seconds, I allow myself to see the world the way Zig does, but a loud crash has me moving towards the deadly truth.

One guard, a man as thin as I once was in the prison, collapses.

No guard moves from their post. They do not glance at their comrade, who lays unmoving on the ground.

"Is he…" I turn to look back at Zig, whose happiness falters upon the sight.

"Yes," Zig's words are grave as he explains. "Our post does not end until the first person collapses dead, and then their replacements take over."

I twist my body towards the guards who are still standing. A white towel is placed under their boot clad feet. The white material is destroyed with the soldiers' urine.

"Come on, milady, let's get you away from all of this." He pauses for a second, then adds. "And clean the blood off of you."

Zig leads me up a staircase just as a fresh round of guards runs downstairs, a clean white towel under their arm.

THE NINTH CHAPTER

Zig informs me almost two hundred male humans live here, but even in a mansion as vast as Lord Ares's, there are only four bedrooms designated for the slaves. The rooms separate the men by their shifts. Fifty humans, their faces all mutilated with scarification marks, are guarding Lord Ares's home at a time, while the remaining one hundred and fifty eat, train, and attempt to sleep away their existence.

The door with the carved X in the middle is Zig's, and he looks at me with an unspoken apology in his eyes before opening it.

The room is larger than my prison cell, but there is no comfortability inside. They cover every inch of their bedroom in blankets. Mangled men lay beneath the blanket, sleeping on the floor with dirt still upon their faces.

There is one window in the room, which is no larger than my hand. This tiny opening allows a stream of light where the men slumber in a dreamless state, but Lord Ares keeps bars on their only escape. We're on the third floor, and if the bars were removed, and the dread was too much, then one terrorized human could fling themselves from this window and escape the world of the living.

So, bars lay inch-by-inch across the window.

"There might be some girl clothes in here," Zig mumbles, more to himself than me, and he ventures further into his bedroom.

We make it two steps before a man blocks our path, anger thriving in his pitch-black eyes.

Similar to Zig, there was once beauty where there are now only scars and affliction. His skin is umber brown, and I know the gorgeous complexion once stressed a powerful jaw and plump pink lips. While most of the men in the room are sleeping and their bodies are concealed by their blankets, this man appears the largest in both height and muscles.

His scarification begins in the middle of his forehead, and it creates a diamond shape around the perimeter of his face. All the lines are jagged and hateful, and if I did not know any better, then I'd guess Lord Ares was trying to peel off the center of the man's face.

The left and right edges of the diamond end on his sharpened cheekbones, but the bottom of the jagged shape is on the tip of his pointed chin, where the smallest accumulation of black stubble forms.

While Zig sees a sliver of allurement in his world of torment, this man does not. Acrimony lives in his dark gaze, but the worst aspect of this man is the absence of life across his face. He has a perpetually carved frown, which mars his face worse than the scarification.

"What is a girl doing here?" His voice is as rough as a rusted blade, and I flinch.

"She's a girl?" Zig looks down at me as he feigns surprise. "I did not notice."

I try to smile at the man, but he growls in response.

"Quit trying to scare her, Diam," Zig says to the man staring down at us, and he sighs. "I'm just trying to find her something to wear for tonight."

"What's the point of dressing her up?" Diam's words are harsh, like sharpened canines. "We all know she will be in the Underworld by morning."

"Diam," Zig grits, but his hand flinches on the small of my back with his own brand of fear.

Diam's hatefulness slashes towards Zig. "Unlike you, I'm being honest with the girl. When you look like her in this house, death waits around the corner," without looking at me, he sneers. "Hopefully, I'll be joining you soon."

He turns away from us and saunters towards the far left corner of the overcrowded bedroom. Once in his designated spot, he curls up into a ball and covers his bulky build in a blanket half his size, but he doesn't sleep like the rest. He stares at the barred window with a forlorn dimness.

"Stay put." Zig retreats near the staircase. "I'll find you something to wear in our closet."

He is gone only for a minute or two, but his absence seems boundless. Every man's face is etched in terror as they lay on the floor, suffering travesties even in a dreamless unconscious. Almost fifty men are compacted together in this room, the pungent scent of their body odor mingling together to produce a stench so vile that bile rises in my throat.

When Zig's hand finds my wrist, I almost scream as I jump.

Sympathy is clear on his face, and Zig says. "Let's get you away from them, milady."

I do not object, and neither of us speaks as we leave the room of despondency. We are walking down the hallway, where all the slaves' bedrooms are located, when Zig breaks our silence.

"I'm sorry about Diam. He's the longest living soldier in Lord Ares's mansion. He can be senile sometimes." I do not ask, but curiosity must be clear on my face because Zig elaborates. "This fall will make him the first in Lord Ares's home to live ten years. Some of the other soldiers think Lord Thanatos is tormenting Diam by forcing him to live here longer than anybody else."

Zig stops in front of a door and turns to face me. "Here, I got you the biggest shirt I could find."

He extends a white shirt, simple in design and humongous. My hands tremble, and the garment slips from my grasp. Before the material can fall, Zig is quick to catch it and extends the shirt towards me once again.

I reach out for the shirt, but before my fingers graze the material, I find Zig staring back and falter. "Milady," he says, the humor in his cadence gone. "I swear on my life I will make sure you live for as long as I do. You will not die tonight, not if I can do anything about it."

I listen to his lie for his sake rather than my own, and I take the shirt from him as he opens a light brown painted door.

"It's called a bathroom." Zig points towards the one familiar thing in this room, which is a shower, and he says. "Lord Ares will want you to use it. Change into the shirt when you're done. If you need any help, then I'll be right outside this door."

"Okay," is the only word I can muster.

I am given my first glimpse of privacy throughout my life as Zig closes the bathroom door. I strip out of the dress I once adored, which is now covered in golden blood and dirt, and I walk into the shower. The knobs differ from the ones in the jail cell, but after a few tries, warm water sprays downward.

My skin is cold, numb like the corpse upon Lord Ares's mansion floor. I do not process the warm water, nor do I react to the steam that emanates from my pale flesh. My mind ceases its ability to think, to plan its next step as I scrub my body with sweet-scented soap. I can't formulate tears of sympathy for my own circumstances as I bunch my hair into my hands, washing the shampoo from each tendril.

The roaring nothingness drowns my storyteller, who is a constant voice of positivism within my mind.

I do not remember stepping out of the shower or pulling the shirt on. When I leave the bathroom, there isn't a fragment of awareness. My mind is an unfamiliar haze, which only ebbs towards clarity when Zig is knocking on a crimson door. Each time he hits his fist against the door, he looks down at me with clear nervousness.

No, not nervousness.

Unadulterated fear.

I look away, and I fixate back on the crimson door, which swings open and welcomes me to my heinous demise.

THE TENTH CHAPTER

There is something frighteningly beautiful about Lord Ares.

A vibrant aura of various shades of red encompasses Lord Ares, wrapping around him like daemons who both protect him and elicit fear from whomever dares to get close enough. He is a noxious combination of beauty and danger. He is a death wish laced in captivating navy blue eyes and a half cocked smile.

I can't deny the way my body is electrified in his company; this god of both beauty and irrevocable insanity sparks a foreign sensation in my body that I do not understand. He is both divine handsomeness and the core result of every nightmare his male slaves have ever had. Lord Ares is terrifying, but he stands a few feet away from me with a dimpled, devious grin, and I wonder if my haggard breathing results from my fear or something far less rational.

A few feet behind me, the sound of the door shutting behind Zig serves as a calamitous echo in an otherwise muted room. Zig, with no freedom of his own, leaves me with a god derived from carnage. Lord Ares, who orchestrates the cataclysmic torture of every male human who has walked into this mansion, looks at me with malice delight.

Zig, whose face is an unforgiveable result of Lord Ares's mistreatment, locks the door from the outside.

The final *click* to the end of my life.

Tonight, I will die because of the monster's hand, and I stand at the threshold of my execution block with my chin risen high.

This room is not a bedroom because the expanse is bare of a bed, but this does not ebb away my anxiety. As long as I am near Lord Ares and a room of blades, then I'll always find fear breathing down my neck. The walls are a deep gray like clouds moments before a ruinous storm and are decorated with his grisly accolades. The god of war watches me as I observe the room centered in his pride.

In the far left corner of this large room that's fit for a bloodthirsty monster like Lord Ares, there is a black shelf that reaches the ceiling in height. Eight rows decorate the shelves, and each row has a myriad of red and gold splattered, heavily dented helmets. Some, due to age, are rusting around the corners. Others are in glass cases and preserved better than the rest.

Another shelving unit, identical in size and color to the primary one, is in the far right corner. This eight-tiered shelf does not have helmets; instead, broken and bloodied weapons are displayed. Spears are splintered in half, knives' blades shattered, and shields unrecognizable with dents.

He's proud of everything in this room, a piece of the world dedicated to his moments on the battlegrounds. My storyteller told me everything I needed to know about Lord Ares. Before today, I was informed about his thirst for bloodshed, his inclination towards maiming his slaves, his animal sigils, but I was never informed about the pride that coincides with the battles he's fought. He has decorated this room as if war is his only proud moment in life; the only memorable fact about him.

There is a roaring fire in between the two shelves, a unit I think is called a fireplace. I fixate my attention on what sits above the flames. A woman's head, covered in dozens of limp snakes, is on a mantle plastered to the gray wall. I'm at least ten feet away from the woman's head, but I can feel the iciness behind her gaze, which is covered with a white piece of cloth.

I take a single step closer to the woman's head, who rests above the fireplace as Lord Ares's greatest prize. She was beautiful, from what I can see, before she was killed. Her dark skin is smooth, her cheekbones defined and high risen. While it is set in a firm line, her lips are full. She was gorgeous, and now hangs on a monster's wall as a prized property.

I feel, rather than see, his proximity.

My back sizzles with electricity, one more powerful than King Zeus's lightning bolts, as his chest dares to touch my skin. There is only a breaths-width separating Lord Ares and me, and neither of us takes the last step to break the threshold. I stay focused on the woman's decapitated head, but he watches me ogle at her with searing sharpness.

"Her name was Medusa," as Lord Ares talks, his warm breath fans across the side of my cheek. "And her eyes could turn any person, mortal or not, into stone."

My storyteller never told me about her; why?

"How?" I ask.

My voice shows my trepidation, but I am unsure if its origins are from his proximity to me or the woman's death staring me in the face; regardless, he does not acknowledge the tremor. Lord Ares is silent for several seconds, intensity like a growing hearth as he scans every inch of my face. I refuse to look in his direction, but I remain infused on the woman's head upon a mantle.

"The Ancient Greeks adored her story enough to make over twenty deviations to it. To the world, she is the snake haired beauty with the power to turn men into stone, but the Gods know the truth no human has ever heard before."

I am quiet, too cautious of our current tenuous situation to make a single noise, and I wait for Lord Ares's next words. In the dawn of my slumbers, I've never heard the story of Medusa. I thought my storyteller told me everything, but I stare at the woman with snake-filled hair and sadness on her face, and I realize I don't know everything.

"Long ago, when humans were first created by a titan named Prometheus, Zeus wanted to curse them. He created soulmates, the other half to another's heart, and made humans search their entire lives for this one person who would make them feel whole. Humans thought their bodies were originally one with their soulmates, but humans so often get the stories wrong."

"What's the actual story, then?"

I dare, despite the erratic thumping against my chest, to look back at Lord Ares. He is already staring, peering into the depths of me with an intensity I've never known before. Neither one of us breaks the threshold to touch one another, but our nearing proximity dares to burn us whole.

"Zeus wanted to ensure the humans suffered with not one, but three great loves. Despite their lack of compatibility, the first love is one of raw passion. The first love will always end in a fiery rage, and it's the one love most often mistaken for soulmates. The second love is more a friendship than a relationship. It is with them you feel safest. The second love ends because there is a lack of passion, not like what you had with your first love."

Lord Ares drifts into silence, but not once does he look away from where I stand. He lets the words settle, and he waits in the quiet. The god looks away from the carnage of this room and stares down at me with both softness and electricity. I should run from him and the abysmal fate that awaits me in his company, but I don't. I can't move from him because I don't know if I want to.

"And the third?" I inquire.

Beneath the thin layer of facial hair, I notice his dimples, which grow when he gifts me with a barely there smile.

"The third love is your soulmate, the other half Zeus pulled you apart from. He made the third love the soulmate because after two heartbreaks, you won't trust the person your destiny is intertwined with. Zeus tormented humans with heartbreaks because he doesn't want anybody to be happy, not as long as he's in an unaffectionate marriage."

Lord Ares is the first to look away, and his gaze flutters up towards the mantle. He stares at the woman, with limp snakes hanging from her scalp, and grimaces. Lord Ares, who forces the men downstairs to be soldiers, blanches at the sight of a long-since dead woman he plastered upon his mantle. A god, who I believed to be fearless, shows a sliver of humanity in this moment.

"Zeus didn't realize he cursed everybody with this fate, not just the humans. Titans, gods, monsters. All of us." He points towards the mantle, and my attention moves towards the woman's head upon his silent command. "Medusa was Poseidon's mate. Did my sons tell you who Poseidon was while you were imprisoned?"

King Poseidon, the god of the seas. One of the Olympians, who reigns over all the water in the world. He is King Zeus and King Hades's other brother, who is married to Queen Amphitrite. Together, they rule the seas and everything that lives within it.

Lying to Lord Ares, I nod my head. I know who King Poseidon is, but his sons are not the source of my knowledge. I can almost feel the pride on my storyteller's face as I lie to the god who stands behind me.

"There are many stories about Medusa and Poseidon and their relationship," Ares persists. "Most stories that the humans concocted say Poseidon was her rapist, forcibly having her in Athena's temple. Others say they were lovers, who hated Athena and fornicated in the virgin goddess's temple out of spite. A rare few even believe Medusa was born a gorgon rather than a human woman. According to Athena and Poseidon, none of those stories are true."

"Then what is true?" I ask.

Lord Ares answers. "Poseidon was already married to one of his great loves, Amphitrite, when he met Medusa. After a heartbreak, Medusa swore off men and became a priestess in Athena's regime. Poseidon and Medusa met and knew with certainty what they were to one another, but it doomed them from the beginning."

I stare at the beauty upon the wall, a gorgeous vision even while partially covered with a piece of cloth, and I swear I can feel her agony as he retells her story. She is dead, gone from this world, but the smell of salty tears permeates from the room, the sound of a heart cracking like a bone shattering into a hundred pieces.

"They tried to stop their attraction, but they were a part of one another. Destined forever," Lord Ares whispers the story now, his breath warm against my skin as he finds the side of my face again, but I keep myself riveted on Medusa as he speaks of her cursed tale. "One night, Poseidon consummated his love with Medusa in Athena's temple. My virgin sister, who already hated Poseidon because of a city called Athens, caught them in the act."

I know the story of Lady Athena and King Poseidon's hatred. A rivalry, which involves sea water, an olive tree, and the city of Athens. The hatred Lady Athena and Lord Poseidon have for one another, starting with the city of Athens and growing because of their opposing views during the Trojan War. Acrimony multiplied when Lord Poseidon tried to have Lady Athena's prized hero, Odysseus, die on countless occasions throughout his journey home from the before-mentioned war.

Yet, I stay silent.

"When Athena found out about the couple, she turned Medusa and her two sisters into monsters. Where silky black hair once was, snakes formed in their place. Her once brown eyes turned white like stone, which was the only warning to anybody who dared to stare at her. The woman was Poseidon's other half and became a monster who could turn him to stone with just one glance. She fled from Poseidon, blaming him for her ghastly transformation, and vowed to kill anybody who dared to look upon her again. Her heart shattered without repair that fatal night, and she became something uglier on the inside than her dastardly outward appearance."

"How did she die?" I ask in a hushed whisper.

"Eventually," Ares drawls out. "A demi-god named Perseus killed Medusa, cutting her head off with a mirror for help. He heard the ghastly stories about Medusa rather than the truth of soulmates, and he was praised until his death for killing the wicked monster."

I do not utter a single word, but I stare at the woman with a new perspective. The cut across her neck, severing her from her body, is jagged and vicious. An undeserving end for an unfortunate woman. A woman, not a monster, sits on this mantle above a roaring fireplace.

"When Perseus died, several of us fought for possession of Medusa's head. Unsurprisingly, one of the few who did not fight for her head was Poseidon. When I won, many jeered that I wanted the head to kill my enemies, to make statues of my fallen victims."

"But you didn't," I do not have to look back at Lord Ares to know I am correct. "Then why did you take her head and keep it like some prize?"

There is no harshness in my cadence, despite my question. Only naked curiosity. A rapt fascination in Lord Ares, which I know I should not have.

"I have a lover," he said with a tinge of despair in his voice. "Named Aphrodite."

The goddess of love is married to Lord Hephaestus, who is the god of blacksmithing. On a regular basis, Lady Aphrodite cheats on her husband with gods and humans of superior beauty. Also, she's Lord Phobos and Lord Deimos's mom. Her most infamous affair away from her marital bed is with Lord Ares, and an unfamiliar pit in my stomach forms when I remember this detail.

"She's not my soulmate, or even one of my great loves, but she taught me something throughout our eons-long affair. Love is dangerous, a death sentence more violent than anything a blade could inflict."

Lord Ares takes the ultimate step. His chest is warm against my back, and his hand is a comfort as it rests on my left hip. Instinct guides my hand on top of his, but my body halts in terror when my fingers graze upon more than just skin.

A knife is within his grasp.

"It's possible that Poseidon might've lied about his tale with Medusa, which is one of love and heartache, which almost shattered his marriage into a thousand irreparable pieces. He might've raped her like the humans said, or she might've always been a gorgon and spent some nights with Poseidon. Only Medusa and Poseidon will know the actual truth, but I believe Poseidon when he talks about his lost love with a broken ripple in his voice. I believe that my uncle, who was once compassionate, was ruined by the grotesque transformation and eventual death of his true love and is now the drunken remains of his former self."

There is a defeated sigh from his lips, which tickles the side of my neck.

"I fought for Medusa's head, so it may be a daily reminder to never fall in love. I so rarely fight for women in the arena, but when I do, it is to spare myself."

When I feel the blade turn in his grasp, I drop my hand. There is nothing sensual in his touch as he lifts the shirt that covers my body, the blade cold against my bare hip. I do not dare to look back at him, as his knife clad hand slides up my stomach, threatening to cut flesh.

I stare at Medusa, silently begging for the cloth to fall to the floor.

"You are the most beautiful woman I've ever seen. Your beauty beats Helen of Troy's, and I watched her face sail a thousand ships into battle. The human male in the arena with you was ready to die for you, and if I let you live another day," his voice is breathless against my skin as he corrects himself. "Another hour, even, then what could you do to a god's heart? Your beauty could crumble poleis, *worlds even*."

His blade has reached my heart. His hand rests in between my breasts, and he angles the knife, so the tip is resting against my flesh. He wraps two hands around the handle and flushes our bodies together.

"I've never professed this aloud, but everything I've done in the five hundred years since we were ejected from Mt. Olympus is live in fear. My front yard is a ruse, a tactic to scare any titans away. My soldiers amplify the terror of this place just enough, so nobody comes to throw me into Tartarus. I was once a man who feared nothing and thrived on a battlefield, but now I fear everything. Even the possibility that I could find one of my three great loves and allow myself to love them just enough to be ruined by them."

To anybody who would walk in now, without being able to see the blade, would think this moment was intimate between the two of us. He wraps his arms around my body, his hands underneath my shirt, and his thumb makes gentle sweeps across my hip. However, the tears that stream down my cheeks, and the death that creeps to the surface contradicts any morsel of sensual tension.

"Save me," I beseech to my storyteller, and I wait to hear his response.

Yet, there is only silence.

"The Underworld will be sweeter to you than this world would ever be." His lips are a ghost of a kiss against my cheek. "Anywhere is better than with me. If I let you live, then I fear I'd destroy you worse than sliding this blade into your heart. And in return, I know you'd be my ruination."

"Can I ask one question before you do this?" My voice is weak, and I let my tears slide down my neck and onto his hand.

"One question," his voice is fragmented when he responds as if he, too, is crying in mournful sorrow for my death.

"How many women have you killed before me?"

While this question holds no factor over my limited life, I ask in a veiled attempt to stall my demise. I let him feel the tears he has caused, and I wait for him to show a side of himself I could never forgive. Lord Ares is a murderer, who I presume has killed hundreds, thousands of innocent human women before me because of his own fear of love.

"Just one other," his voice cracks as he admits this truth. "But when I looked at her, it was only a tenth of how I feel when I stare at you. You would ruin me. I know it with no doubt in my mind."

The blade is merciful as it slides into my flesh. The very tip of the knife pierces my flesh before it stills in his hands. A gasp leaves my lips, pain encompassing my body at the foreign feeling of my skin tearing apart.

Before he can deliver the death he promised, Lord Ares pulls the blade out of my chest and stumbles backwards. I turn around, facing the god. Those navy blue eyes widen in disbelief, but they are not looking at my face.

He is staring at where he stabbed me.

My blood seeps through my white shirt. Lord Ares and I latch onto the possibility of my reality. Disbelief squanders our voices, leaving us muted. My blood's hue is red, dark as the maroon splatters on Lord Ares's prized helmets, but the other color upon my white shirt is our nihilism.

It's gold.

It's ichor.

THE ELEVENTH CHAPTER

Downstairs, thunder crackles and screams erupt, but Lord Ares and I hold an unwavering state with one another. The wound, which should still bleed, is healed. I do not have to peek underneath my shirt to know the puncture wound is gone, with not even a scar in its wake.

When my friend from the cells vocalized my differences, I claimed I was normal, but now his words are roaring through my brain.

No, I don't think you are.

The commotion downstairs grows louder, but nothing is as cacophonous as the pounding of my chest; nothing is as lethal nor silent as Lord Ares's glare. His look of mortification forms a wound within me larger than his bloodied blade. While he stares at my shirt, stained with the truth, I look at the blade within his white-knuckled grasp.

Red blood coats the tip of the blade, but gold speckles are visible, too. Only the immortals have gold ichor spilling from their veins, but my mundane blood is somehow tainted with the godly touch.

I'm not normal.

I'm not human.

One second, Lord Ares stares from afar at the impossibility of my blood, but with unparalleled quickness, he has his free hand wrapped around the back of my neck. Lord Ares pulls me close. Our noses press into one another and our lips are centimeters apart. I can kiss his heavy breath upon my mouth, but there is nothing passionate in the embrace.

His words are ragged as he stammers. "It's not possible. You're not possible."

Irately, he stares at me and deciphers every square inch of my appearance with scrutiny. Only a minute ago, he cited me as the most beautiful human he has ever seen, but now I am a monstrosity that he must eliminate. The blade, still bloodied with my truth, is pressed against my throat.

"What are you?" Lord Ares's hand tightens around the back of my neck, but his question is formed through gasped breaths. Fear is manifesting in a god who has fought every victorious battle in human history.

The blade against my neck shakes, his hand quivering as he stares at me the way I see myself: an abomination that does not belong. I am neither human nor godly, but a damnable creature. I am the definition of the dirt upon the ground.

The noise from downstairs grows louder.

Swords clash and screams ricochet from the lower floor, but Lord Ares does not care. He is gazing at me, the atrocity, as the blade threatens to break skin once again. The only reason I am alive right now is because, just like me, Lord Ares is frightened by what should not exist within my veins.

"Which god created you?" He asks, but he appears too frightened to hear the response.

"I…" I gasp, my chest hammering a thousand miles a minute. "I don't know."

He presses his blade closer to my throat, the skin threatening to spill, and with a hatred that burns like a thousand suns, he sneers. "You should not exist."

I expect the darkness before death to encompass me, but a shadowy man is waiting for me.

My storyteller is waiting behind my closed lids.

He stands on the brink of the abyss, and he embraces the blackness as if he belongs in the disparity. The darkness shields his face from my prying inquisitiveness, but he is home when the world becomes too violent and frightening. He has always been faceless, unable to see, but his power is felt in the dreamworld air as if it were a sweltering change in the weather.

The shadowy figure that shields my storyteller's appearance is tall, as mighty as the walls within this world, and he must crouch down in order to reach me at eye level. For two years, I have been surrounded by the storyteller and the dreams we share, and I've only ever seen his hands, which are littered in black ink.

Stories of his worst fears, he once told me, decorate his pale flesh. On the top of his right hand shows a bird he calls a crow. With that hand, he delicately captures my chin. I can't see his face, but he is there like the wind; I may not see him, but I feel him everywhere.

"Why are you letting him hurt you?" His voice is beautiful, a serene melody gracing my ears amid the chaos. "There are weapons all around you, and yet you are the most powerful one in the room. Show him the power living within your veins until he fears the thought of ever touching you again."

Without leaving the comfort of the twilight, I show Lord Ares the very power he feared upon the first sight of my blood.

The shrill sound of Lord Ares's screams jolts me back to reality, and I witness the first sliver of power the storyteller always told me was within me. One spearhead from his shelf of memorabilia—the only one made from a hard, white material—flies out of the glass case upon my command and lodges itself in Lord Ares's neck. The god of bloodshed stumbles backwards, golden blood spilling down his shoulder.

I stumble backwards, while candor stares back at me with aching clarity. I'm not human, I can't be. The dreams, the words of doubt from my friend, the discolored blood, and the comments about my appearance spin through my mind. I can't ignore the obvious any longer: I'm not human.

"No, you are not human, my queen." My storyteller confirms. "You're unadulterated power; now use it against your enemy."

Lord Ares rips the spearhead out of his neck, and he is inflamed with rage. He strides towards me with the knife raised and murder on his mind. Before, Lord Ares had fear intermingled with curiosity. He saw me as an abomination, but I was going to live until he discovered who created me, but now that I drew his blood, death awaits me.

The screams from downstairs are now silent, and the only sound in the house is Lord Ares's ominous footsteps, which pound against the ground with brutal promises.

With no other option, I lift my hands in the air and wait for some magnificent magic to manifest. I am weaponless, weak compared to a god, but my hands raise with a futile hope the magic that moved the spearhead will obliterate my enemy before he can destroy me. I wait for the sensation of power to bubble through my skin and to erupt from my hands, but nothing happens.

He swats my hands away, and I'm his victim once more; his knife returns to its place against my throat. "Did he send you?" Lord Ares asks this question with every bit of hatred seeping from his words, but I do not mistake the fear that also ebbs to the surface. "Did my-"

He doesn't get the chance to finish the sentence.

Before the question can leave his lips, the locked door is kicked down. The home previously exploding with pandemonium is silent. The room is stifled with tension, swimming in the rigidity, until three figures step through the threshold.

Lord Ares barks out a laugh. "You shifty little-"

Light blue smoke spills into the room, silencing Lord Ares mid-sentence. The three figures at the doorway do not move, but they watch as the blue smoke imprisons the room and all of its inhabitants. The smog slithers through the air until it finds its target—Lord Ares's nostrils.

Confidence transforms into confusion, and Lord Ares stumbles and drops his weapon. He drowsily points at the male figure on the far left, accusing him without words for the colorful mist. He coughs up the unfamiliar powder, but after a few seconds of trying to fight the magic that enters his system, Lord Ares collapses onto the ground. He twitches once, then does not move again.

Once Lord Ares is snoring on the floor, the three figures step out of the shadows and into the room. I am trembling where I stand, but I keep my eyes on the doorway. The blue mist is still in the air, but the trio walks through the fog, steps into the light, and reveals their identities.

Lord Thanatos is drenched in black, just as he had been a few hours earlier in the arena, and he is gliding into the room as if he is floating above the ground. Meanwhile, Lord Hypnos, who is in a light shade of gray, flicks more blue powder on top of Lord Ares's head for good measures. The personification of sleep smirks with his scar ridden lips, proud of his handiwork, but Lord Thanatos rolls his eyes at his twin brother.

"You're just jealous I have a cooler power than you, little brother," Lord Hypnos quips.

Lord Thanatos's frown deepens. "We're twins, we're the same age."

"Semantics," Lord Hypnos says, and he waves Lord Thanatos off with a sudden annoyance at the conversation.

My focus shifts to the immortal in the middle, who orchestrated this break-in, and he ogles at me as if he has won the greatest prize. While I cower where I stand, he strides forward with a boyish confidence that is polarizing from my connotation of the gods.

"It looks like we showed up right on time," there is humor dancing in his voice, but when he takes an extra step towards me, I flinch. His amusement dissipates. "You do not need to fear me. I'm here to help, my name is-"

"Lord Hermes," I cut him off, surprising both him and me with the courage to speak. "You're the god of thieves and tricksters."

I shouldn't know who he is because the gods reigning over the prisons do not teach us. My knowledge should be hidden, but I accidentally announce it and I wait for his fear to set in. He must know I am different. A malfunction to the gods' world. While I can try to excuse the blood on my shirt for Lord Ares's, I do not think I can trick the god of tricksters if he questions me.

He doesn't comment on my education of the gods; instead, he says. "Then you know what I'm about to do next."

The same blue smoke that has Lord Ares snoring on the floor is blown into my face. It's material slithers into my nostrils, and the world twirls and tilts upon the magic's command. I look at the three deities standing over me with visible fear, but my gaze levels with Lord Hermes's, who stands closest to me.

"Don't worry," Lord Hermes says, his tone softer than before. "When you wake up, you'll be safe."

While Lord Ares tried to fight the sleeping magic, I welcome the darkness because anything is better than this world. I close my eyes and yearn to disappear for a few hours from a world I no longer recognize.

THE TWELFTH CHAPTER

Smoke, in varying shades of black and gray, swirl through my vision. Darkness encompasses my soul, and I invite the pernicious cold with inviting arms. I let the thickened mist, and its swirls of deleterious sorrow, coil around my biceps, graze my bare neck, and lead me away from the emptiness of unconsciousness.

The obscurity pulls me towards the world where my storyteller dwells. I glide away from the vacant land where humans commonly slumber, and the smoke leads me towards a new realm of shadowed secrets and veiled electricity. I let a smile lift over the curvatures of my lips as the familiarity of my storyteller's throne room comes into my view.

The room is draped in onyx sophistication. Obsidian curtains drape over an arched window behind a throne meant only for a king. The curtains are made from the feathers of a crow, his sigil. They decorate the curtains, darkening the room of smoke and enigma from any glimpse of the sun. The only sliver of color comes from the walls, which are painted in the darkest shade of purple.

Upon the gargantuan throne of varying jewels and blackened mist, sits my storyteller.

His appearance is enshrouded. Every night he and I spend with-

in this dream world, the shadows and smoke he controls conceal his face. The only aspect of his body unobscured are his tattooed hands.

On the top of his right hand, a crow is painted with brutal, black swipes. It's an irate creature, with squinted, dark eyes and a mouth open in a furious scream. The wings are widespread, as if the bird will take flight off his pale flesh and soar through the sky.

A monster rests on top of his left hand. The design is devoid of color, and instead of eyes, the creature has my storyteller's smoke seeping out of the sockets like a disease ransacking its body. The monster is frozen in complete petrification, and it lays in permanent sorrow upon his skin.

His tattoos are the first piece of artwork I see on his hands, but I always drift towards the many rings that decorate his fingers. All the rings have silver bands, but the gems are different on each digit. There are rubies, emeralds, topazes, onyxes, sapphires, and tanzanite. My favorite jewelry is on his pinkies, which are black sapphires. His rings dance along his fingers as he caresses the shadowy elements he controls.

When he speaks, the air stills in anticipation of his magnifying words. "Are you ready for another story, my queen?"

My storyteller has taught me everything I know. He is the reason I recognize the gems on his fingers and the gods infesting my world. While I can't see his appearance, he can see the widespread grin that encompasses my face upon his words.

"Yes," *I say.*

"Good," *he purrs with satisfaction. Then he begins.* "There was once a time when the Olympians reigned over Mt. Olympus, the land within the clouds. When Zeus was upon the throne of glittering gold, he stared down at humanity with only two emotions. There was ire in him as he looked at a species that Prometheus created without permission. Then, there was lust."

My storyteller sighs in disappointment, and if the smoke dissipated for a moment, then I'd know I'd find hatred within his expression.

Still, my storyteller continues. "Zeus does not care about the gender of the person who gives him pleasure. Men, women, and even the occasional woman turned into a cow. He preyed upon people, and he'd swoop down from Mt. Olympus to pluck apart the sanity of whomever caught his eagerness that day."

For two years, I've drifted towards the throne room, and each time I've met with my storyteller. The first time I met him, there was an initial prickle of curiosity to see his face. Now, I stand only five feet away from the precipice of my fascination, and the urge to break through the smoke and see what lies beneath possesses me. Each time his voice vibrates through my body, I want to lift the veil of shadows to see what remains beneath the secrets.

His words seep into my bloodstream, becoming a part of me, without ever witnessing the undoubted beautifulness of his appearance.

"Mt. Olympus was Zeus's coveted home, one created after he defeated his father in the Titanomachy War, but Earth was his favorite playground. Zeus and all of his malicious kin would land on Earth's ground and take whatever they wished. Humans were not slaves to the Olympians when they lived upon Mt. Olympus, but they were toys."

Hatred makes his cadence tremble, his stance rigid upon his throne of blackened jewels. His hands curl around the armchair with vicious intent. As his nails dig into the wood, I wonder if he is imagining the chair as King Zeus's throat.

"Gods have always seen the humans as tools to fornicate with, banish if they provided them with another bastard child, and kill whenever they please. The Olympians were always monstrous when *their feet landed upon Earth, but the humans still worshipped the gods. The humans would ignore the death and bloodshed of their loved ones by immortal hands because praying to the gods when they were frightened was a better alternative than accepting an empty afterlife. Fear has always been the gods' greatest asset towards possessing humans."*

My storyteller, with his nails embedded in his throne's armchair, rises to his full and imposing height. He stands before me, and his smoke drapes itself around his body. An obsidian spiked crown lays upon his head, and I stare with magnifying curiosity to see the face that wears the sigil of a king.

There are three steps in between him and me, which always separate us, but today he breaks the barrier between us. Each step he makes to eliminate the space sends vibrations through the ground, which shutters under his might. When he stands a heartbeat away from me for the first time, the same electrical current I felt in Lord Ares's company surges through my veins. I look up at my storyteller, who is within arm's reach, and my body craves him.

The warmth radiating from his skin is a fireplace that's too close, both burning my skin and delighting me in its hickory scent. His chest is a breaths' width away from mine, so close that I can feel each erratic palpitation. He's nervous, an emotion that I never thought would correlate with my mysterious storyteller, but my curiosity behind the fear's origins is short-lived.

The smoke listens to my storyteller's silent behest and it no longer hides his appearance. Blackened mist coils around both of us, and it draws me flush against his chest. Our bodies make contact for the first time, and the all-consuming warmth he elicits is how I'd imagine ambrosia to taste like. Pure utopia.

The smoke, which he controls, leaves his pale, moonlight flesh and enraptures both of us in a web of his creation. I drift towards the face I've imagined and prayed to see each night for the past two years, and a veracious gasp seeps from my lips upon the sight.

Zig and Diam's scars are unappealing because they were delivered with brute ferocity and were catastrophic to once gorgeous faces. I regret to admit it, but I could not stare at the two of them for long because I was repelled by the sight of what Lord Ares destroyed. But my Storyteller has more scars than them both. Queasiness racked my stomach when I met Zig and Diam, but I do not feel disgust when I see my storyteller. I look upon my storyteller's face, which rests on a multitude of scars, and I see beauty.

My gasp is one of amazement, and I am cautious as I raise my hand towards the largest scar. His milky flesh, devoid of any sunlight, is slashed with hundreds of scars. They vary in size and discoloration, but there is one upon his neck that garners my fascination above all others.

He tried to hide this scar with a tattoo of a sword, but I can see the scar as if there was no tattoo. The wound starts on the bottom curvature of his chin and continues down his shirt, which conceals its size. The tip of the sword is on his chin, and my finger glides across the risen skin with enthrallment.

Smaller, less noticeable scars decorate his high risen cheekbones and thick black eyebrows. A more prominent one cuts the left corner of his lip. It is undeniable that this scar is meant to demoralize him, but there has never been a pair of lips I've wanted to kiss more than his. Whoever mutilated him wanted to persecute him both mentally and physically, to ensure that nobody would look upon him without recoiling with disgust, but his tormentor did not achieve their goal.

He's radiant.

Curly, black locks accentuate his angular, clean-shaven face. The thick coils rest below his ears, concealing the sides of his neck from my inspection. Each tendril of his hair is crafted to perfection, and when I run my fingers through them, it's the softest material. My smile continues to grow until it threatens to devour my face whole.

"You're," *I whisper out.* "So beautiful."

His hands are on my waist, holding me steady as I draw my gaze towards his exotically gorgeous eyes. Twinkling like an unblemished blade underneath the sun's rays, my storyteller's eyes are a magnificent shade of silver. I'm blinded by his beauty, for I have never seen a man as magnificent as him.

My storyteller's expression slackens in disbelief. "You're not lying to me," *he concludes, but he continues to assess my face for a hint of a lie.*

I shake my head. "I don't think I know how to lie to you."

"How?" *He asks in bewilderment, his voice devoid of its powerful cadence; instead, a quieted sound seeps through the air.* "How can you see beauty in this? In what the Olympians created to ruin me?"

There is an unmistakable self-deprecating bite in his words, but just as I always have, I gift him with my honesty. "It would take me eons to describe all the ways I find you beautiful. I thought scars make a person grotesque, but I was wrong. Scars are a story told upon the skin, and you're more gorgeous because of the stories you tell."

His thumbs stroke my waist, but he lingers on my face in ready anticipation to find lies. When seconds, then minutes pass without a flicker of disbelief misshaping my face, his intensity moves towards my unblemished lips.

"Today is the beginning of many things, my queen." *His words are still in a breathy and unraveled cadence.* "You learned the truth about yourself and the blood that runs through your veins. Beneath the smoke, you saw my scarred face I've hated until today. Until you. Now, you will discover my name and the fight towards eliminating the Olympians."

"Wait," I say. "Did you know before today about my blood?" The smile I once had disappears and worry overtakes every inch of my once barely collected sanity.

He ignores my question.

"Today, I'll tell you the one story that I've wanted to tell you since I found you two years ago, but I'll start with my name," one of his hands drifts upwards and cups around my round cheek, while he lures me nearer. *"While I enjoy your adorable nickname for me, I've wanted to hear my name on your lips for too long."*

Standing in his embrace, both frozen and electrified, one word that I've waited to hear enters the air and slithers into my ear.

"I am Epiales, the personification of nightmares, and together we will help the true king of the skies finally kill the gods that enslaved you and millions of other humans."

"I don't understand."

His thumb brushes my cheek, and he fixates on the movement. "I wish we had more time tonight to speak, for me to tell you everything, but it will have to wait." His lips pour out one last sentence before I am pulled from our dreamworld. *"Once we kill those heinous gods, then we will take the Underworld as its rightful king and queen."*

I bolt upwards in a start, my hand pressed against my chest, but I am not given a second of reprieve from my discombobulated mind. I do not have time to think about the name tingling upon my lips, or the promises spoken from a man derived from scars and nightmares, because Lord Hermes is sitting at the foot of the bed I lay in. There is a tray of food on his lap and a lopsided grin on his boyish face.

"You hungry?"

THE THIRTEENTH CHAPTER

"You kidnapped me."

There are a multitude of sentences I could've strewn together when I first see Lord Hermes. Appreciation for saving my life should've been at the tip of my tongue. A molecule of gratitude should've been found in my words, or at least asking for a reason behind his heroic act. After all, gods aren't supposed to be saviors of the humans.

They're the demise.

The god of mischief and thievery dwarfs the bed I lay on, his thin but tall physique twice the size. Even the plate of food on his lap is small compared to the large hands that grip the sides.

He doesn't flinch at my accusatory words or the hostility in my voice. As the three words register, there isn't anger. Amusement, maybe, but not anger.

"Astute observation," he says with amusement. "Now that we have the obvious out of the way, do you want breakfast?"

"Why?"

A raised eyebrow hides itself in the thicket of his mousy brown locks. "Because breakfast is the most important meal of the day?" He answers with skepticism, as if he believes I was asking about breakfast rather than saving my life from his half-brother, Lord Ares.

Silence drifts through the room, a third member to the conversation of veiled secrets and unspoken answers. It nestles in between us, dividing the enslaved from the captor and reminding me that pleasant banter does not deviate from fact; I am the prey, and he is the victorious predator.

With the tray of food in his hands, he breaks through the wall that silence had created and places breakfast upon my lap. An unfamiliar smell, one that tickles the hairs in my nose, deviates my attention away from the tension in the room and towards the pile of food.

As I'm salivating, I ask. "You will not tell me why you kidnapped me, will you?"

"No, but I will answer the next question that you have for me," he points towards the food and says. "Yes, the food is absolutely delicious."

The realization that I haven't eaten in over a day sends an irritated grumble through the pit of my stomach. Eager hands move towards the round, red objects on top of the brown circles. I look up at him, silently asking him a question with a raise of the food.

"That is a strawberry," he answers.

As soon as I bite into the strawberry, a surge of taste buds invades my mouth. I let drool slip from the corner of my mouth, the saliva dripping down my chin, but I could not care less. I lean forward with eagerness and pluck two more strawberries from the top of the stacked brown circles, and I eat them in the same rushed fashion as the first one.

There are five left on the plate, and although my fingers become coated with the sticky substance lathered on the brown, circular foods, I hurry and shove the strawberries into my mouth. I fill my mouth with the sweet red substance, and my cheeks are twice their normal size when I look back at Lord Hermes.

He glances down at my plate, now strawberry-less, and slides off of the bed with a crinkle between his brows. "I'll be right back."

He is at the entryway, the door now opened, when I ask. "Did I do something wrong? Are you leaving because I'm going to be punished?"

I mumble because of my full mouth, but he can hear my words because he is quick to answer. "No, you didn't do a single thing wrong. A good thing, actually."

He smiles at me before disappearing; the door closing behind him.

The sound of his feet retreating from the room brings my fascination towards the plate. Without strawberries, only the circular brown food and the sticky stuff on top of it are left, and a frown peppers my face.

There are silver instruments sitting next to the pancakes. One is weird, with three sticks pointing upwards, like King Poseidon's trident. Then, there is one that reminds me of a miniature dagger, but the tip is not sharp enough to inflict damage. A self-destructive part of me wants to grab the tiny, less powerful dagger from the plate, but I think of the Epiales's face, and I change my mind.

The miniature dagger remains untouched beside the plate.

I pick up the first brown circle with my hands, but as soon as it is within my grasp, my fingers become sticky with the dark substance lathered on top. I grimace, but otherwise ignore the adhesion, and I take a vigorous bite. It's too sweet, I realize, as the sticky substance slides down my cheek.

My stomach growls, demanding another bite, and I obey. I continue to eat the round object with a clear frown on my lips. Glaring down at the food, which only stains my face and fingers, I eat in frightful anticipation that this could be my last meal in this short world.

"Do you not like pancakes?"

Lord Hermes leans against the doorway as I snap my head upwards. I drop the brown circle—the pancake—onto the plate, and I look and see a bowl in Lord Hermes's hands. Inside, there is an entire container of strawberries.

As soon as Lord Hermes places the bowl of strawberries on my lap, the plate with the unpleasant pancakes is thrust in his direction. He huffs a laugh as he takes the plate of pancakes while I shove five strawberries into my mouth.

I swell my cheeks with strawberries when I try to speak to him. "Mdomtlimethemsmickmysmuff."

He takes his place at the foot of the bed again, the plate with the pancakes, mini trident and dagger gone because of his magic. There is amusement dancing on Lord Hermes's face.

He remarks. "I didn't understand a single word you just said."

When I have finished the strawberries in my mouth, I repeat. "I don't like the sticky stuff."

"That's called syrup, and a good shower with some soap will get all of that off." He turns his body towards a second door in this room, one white, and Lord Hermes points to it. "After you're full, there's a shower and a warm towel waiting for you."

"I get to shower?" The question, laced with suspicion, slips from my lips before I shut myself up with more strawberries.

He doesn't seem perturbed by the question; instead, he answers. "Yes, you get a shower. It's your personal one in my home.

This will be your bedroom, and we can add anything you'd want to these chambers. All you have to do is say the word."

I should talk and ask a myriad of questions. Gods are evil. They bear beautiful faces but are injurious to humanity. The Olympians are the source of humans' waking nightmares, and they're the reason behind our screams of anguish and defeat. They're the monsters in our story.

All of them have to be.

The strawberries turn dry upon my tongue, and as they slide down my throat, they're daggers slitting the skin.

"Why are you being nice to me?" I ask.

There's not just anger in my cadence, but hatred. I look at the young God, who saved me from Lord Ares and gifted me with strawberries, but I do not see him behind my fury.

I look at Lord Hermes, and I see the malign smile on Lady Hecate's blood painted lips. The phantom touch of Lord Ares's blade returns against the skin of my neck. Lord Phobos and Lord Deimos are here with knuckles red with human torment. Worse than all the rest, I see Lord Hermes and I hear the hatred seeping from my storyteller's scarred lips.

My voice is impersonal, far more distant than it had been a mere minute before, and it thickens the distance between Lord Hermes and me. For a moment, he does not know how to respond to the shift in tension. He slides off of the foot of the bed, moving to his full height without an ounce of intimidation in the movement.

To solidify the hatred I should have for him, I wait for a threat to spill from his lips. For his face to elicit searing white rage, just like the other gods I've become familiarized with. I wait for the god that saved me to become my greatest tormentor, a creature more inwardly grotesque than Lord Ares and Lady Hecate.

After a long pause, he responds. "You may not believe me right now, but I'm not like Ares, or many of my other family members. I do not enjoy antagonizing humans or causing them harm. My words trick, so I plan to show you with my actions how different I am from the unfortunate gods you've come across before today."

He takes a step towards me, but I flinch with the same fright as I hold all the other gods. The sentimental moment between us and the bowl of strawberries, as fickle as it was, is gone with the wind from the ajar bedroom window. Lord Hermes does not near me again, his bare feet planted firmly on the floor, but he stays focused on where I sit with an intensity that makes the hairs on my arms fly to attention.

"I won't hurt you. Not today, or tomorrow, or a decade from now. You have my solemn promise."

He nods his head in my direction just once as an unspoken goodbye, and he walks towards the bedroom's exit. He opens the door, but before he leaves, he turns to face me one more time.

"This will be your bedroom for the duration of your stay in my home, and there are dresses tailor designed for you in the closet to your immediate left whenever you want them." He clears his throat before he adds. "I'll be back in here when the sun sets to give you your scarification mark."

He takes one step out of the bedroom when I let the question gnawing at me burst from my lips. "Why am I here, Lord Hermes?"

He doesn't look back at me, but he responds without hesitation. "I like the company of pretty girls with a newfound obsession for strawberries."

The door slams closed with his exit.

THE FOURTEENTH CHAPTER

This bed, plump with pillows and blankets unscathed from hungry mice's teeth, was once an unachievable goal. I knew what a bed was. Epiales promised I'd one day slumber in one when he freed me, but I did not understand the gravity of his oath until Lord Hermes leaves the bedroom and the bed is my sole company.

It's comfortable, but too much so.

I accustomed my body to the cold, rough caress of a bloodstained floor. The leftover, pungent stench of copper tickled my nose. Varying level of uproarious snores would fill the stilled air, a lullaby that reminded me that every member of my cell survived another melancholy day.

This room is warm, a mighty fireplace roaring next to the door that leads to my personal bathroom. There is not a coppery scent in here; instead, a sweet aroma differing from the strawberries or anything that I've smelled before wafts through the wind. There is the hum of burned wood permeating, but there is an additional smell that does not remind me of the deadly stench of the jail cell.

Neither snores nor additional voices grace my ears. I have never been without another person within a five-feet vicinity.

Even as I showered, I had my shower-mate as company. My consciousness was occupied with the other humans from my cells, and Epiales inhabited the world, which lived beneath the veil of actuality. Now, it is only the noises of crackling wood and the occasional creak from the bed as I shift from side-to-side.

I flinch when the silence ruptures by an unfamiliar voice, which is shrill and eccentric, on the other side of the bedroom door. "Are you awake?" She asks. I open my mouth, a response ready on my tongue, but the girl does not wait. She thrusts open the door, and a smile larger than the arena spreads across her young, freckled cheeks. "Good, you're awake."

The first noticeable features are her freckles. From the tip of her forehead, down to her sandaled feet, deep orange spots pepper her pale complexion. She is a fire, blazing in deviating shades of oranges and reds, and the sight is radiant.

While her skin is sprinkled with orange spots, her hair is the hearth of the flame. Deep red pin straight locks slide down a thin neck and rests on her shoulder blades. Shorter hair conceals the left side of her forehead, hiding her dark red brow and dusting across the top of her lashes.

Her eyes are round like mine, but it's the only similarity the two of us have. I look at her and see the brightest shade of green eyes. A ring of gold rests in the middle of them, but a majority of her irises are that blinding green.

A gasp escapes my lips when I look at her, but the shock that passes through the air is not because of the vibrant green eyes or the freckles that stipple across every square inch of her skin. I look at this girl, who is thin and tiny in stature, with incredulity because her face is unscathed.

No scarification mark destroys her appearance.

She looks *fine*.

Better than fine. With a crooked yet genuine smile, she appears happy. Her clothes aren't covered in dirt, and her hair is clean. She stands in front of me with ordinary, mundane features, but she looks too healthy to be a human.

"Where is it?" My voice cracks, personifying my disbelief with the words that pour out of my lips.

The cheerful woman, who glides into the room and shuts the door behind her, does not ask for clarification to my question. She is wearing a floor length green gown, which covers her arms, until she rolls up the right sleeve. I wait to see a mutilated atrocity upon her pale flesh. I wait to find the reason that Lord Hermes is just like every other egregious Immortal, but when her sleeve is over her elbow and she is presenting her scarification to me, it isn't unseemly. She does not fear the mark Lord Hermes gave her, claiming her as his slave until her dying breath. She looks down at her scarification mark when I do, and she gleams with pride.

On the smooth flesh of her forearm, there is a creature sitting there. Green leaves surround the creature's face, with red fur like her hair and white ears as pale as her skin. I expected a fearsome sight, but the beady gazed beast upon her white flesh is adorable.

"It's a red panda," her crooked tooth smile returns as she explains. "Lord Hermes gave me the name Panda because my hair reminds him of this little guy. I adored my scarification mark so much that Lord Hermes bought me a red panda a few weeks later. I named him Roscoe. If you ever visit my room, then you can meet him."

I've always been told to fear the moment I will be branded as a god's property. In the prisons, Lady Hecate always said scarifications are the greatest tool used to destroy a human's soul.

ICHOR

My mind burns with memories of Zig's and Diam's, and the fright I'd been taught solidified with the sight of their mutilated appearances.

Panda doesn't seem destroyed, though. She's happy and walking towards me with her scarification arm outstretched.

"Do you want to touch it?" She asks, but I flinch at her question. "I've been here for almost four years, so it does not hurt anymore, I promise."

My finger outlines the ridge of the panda's nose, then the ears that stick out of its head. I admire the wisps of hair that poke through its pointy ears, as well as the creature's round cheeks covered in both red and white fur.

"It's beautiful," I murmur, more to myself than Panda.

Still, Panda replies. "Thank you." She is no longer staring at her scarification mark, or my fingers that gingerly trace the outline. She's gauging my reaction to her words as she breaks the silence. "Tonight will be the night you get your own scarification mark. Lord Hermes will make sure that it is beautiful, like mine. He always makes sure that you're happy with the outcome."

I drop my hand from her scar and scoot back in the bed, distancing myself from the woman, who is happy as a slave. My back hits the wall, but she is still too close to me. I do not look at the fiery-haired woman, or her scarification mark that is neither appalling nor mutilating, but I stare at my unblemished skin.

The blue veins on my pale flesh have a dangerous secret. A gilded tint lives beneath the surface, and it will condemn me to an early, unmarked grave.

"Doesn't it hurt?" I ask, but the pain is the least concerning question on the tip of my tongue.

"The gods who ruled the cell made it seem a lot worse than it is," Panda says. "Just think of it as a small little pinch that happens over and over again."

Still, I won't look at her. I remain engrossed in a large vein that begins at the base of my palm and glides up to the underbelly of my elbow. The line, varying in thickness as it progresses up my skin, is a shade of blue that's deeper than the sky. Yet, the longer that I stare, I can make out gold horizontal lines glistening with the otherwise mundane blood flow.

Panda is oblivious to the magnitude of my fear, and she saunters towards the door that hides the clothes Lord Hermes said were custom made for me. She throws open the doors with theatrical exuberance, and she begins a pilgrimage of the gowns.

"In honor of your first night here, I volunteered to show you how to dress and pamper yourself," she peeks her head out of the room with the clothes, and her severely crooked front teeth gleam in the light as she quips. "It might take you a few tries to understand a life that's outside of the prison, but I will always be here to help you."

My confession of gratitude dies on frightened lips.

The once quiet room has erupted with Panda's voice and my endless thoughts roaring at me to run and escape before my blood is spilled. She is complimenting me, then telling me the step-by-step process Lord Hermes takes during the scarification night. A part of me is listening to her, but my anxiousness is growing and festering until my mind is a barrage of thoughts.

"Storyteller, where are you?" I ask and search for the gorgeous man in my head, who holds a million stories within the dozens of scars on his flesh. *"Epiales,"* I outcry into the dark void in my head. *"Come save me."*

There is no answer.

I stare into a room too large to belong to me. Panda never ceases her conversation to a dazed audience, while I look at a purple, dainty object enraptured in a clear cylinder case nearest to the bathroom door.

"Are you listening?"

Panda's voice crashes through my discombobulated thoughts, and she stands a few feet across from me rather than over by the dresses. A gown is folded in her arm, the hue a faint blue. Panda blocks the purple tipped item with her thin frame.

"This is important," she says.

"Sorry," I mutter unapologetically, while my finger rises towards what stands behind her. "What is that?"

She turns, responding a second later. "It's a flower in a glass vase," she walks towards the table where they sit, and she lifts the thin, green part of the flower from the vase. Panda stares at the delicate purple strands, which rests at the top, and the plums of yellow and red that seep out in the middle. "But I don't recognize this kind of flower. Looks a little like a lily, but it isn't. It's not in the garden, either. How strange."

The flower only garners Panda's interest for a few seconds. She is quick to put the flower back into its vase and then veers all of her attention back to me.

"If you like the flowers, then I'm sure Lord Hermes would let you build a garden in the backyard." She traipses towards me, and when her hand wraps around one of my wrists, she pulls me off of the bed. "Let me help you start a bath," the tip of her tiny nose crinkles as she adds. "We'll get you some flowery body wash."

"A bath?" I ask.

"It's like a shower, except the water is in a round container called a bathtub," Panda explains as she moves me towards the bathroom, but her answer amplifies my confusion.

"But," I remark, making a full stop at the same time Panda uses her free hand to open the bathroom door. "I already showered twice this month."

That crooked, front-tooth grin returns.

"What I am about to say," she begins. "Is going to amaze you."

THE FIFTEENTH CHAPTER

According to Panda, I am supposed to bathe multiple times a week. Panda also showed me a toothbrush, which she advises I use daily instead of once a week. I sit on a chair facing a mirror when she places a little blue box in the palms of my hands.

"Try to put the thin, white string in between your teeth either every day or every other day. It's called floss," through the mirror's reflection, Panda shows me the object in her hand and explains. "And this is a brush you'll use on your hair every day. Lean your head back and I'll show you how to use it. I'll even teach you how to braid your hair, if you'd like."

I do as she commands. Strips of wet, brown locks trail behind the back of the chair, and then Panda runs the brush through them. She's gentle, pulling the brush through my hair as if I could break upon contact.

As if she cares about me.

A complete stranger.

"Do you have questions for me?" Panda lets out a huff of a laugh and adds. "I had so many for another slave, China, that I didn't stop talking for three days straight."

I'm not surprised about that.

"What is your job?" I ask.

"I am his interior designer," she answers my question with elation, her happiness never-ending. "He gives me final say to any furniture, artwork, and style of the house. Funnily enough, the only room in this house that I've never designed was this one."

She brushes my hair, twirling chunks into a fashion that she calls a braid, and blathers on about her job. Panda tells me about the newest artwork she asked Lord Hermes to purchase, which sits in the dining room on the far left wall. She becomes often distracted throughout our conversation. One second, she will talk about the vase that she bought for the living room, and the next second, I will have a thing called a hat on top of my head to see if I look good with them on.

According to Panda, hats are not for me.

At some point, I am pulled away from the mirror and forced to look at her while she applies an assortment of colorful pastes to my face. "What is this stuff you're putting on my face?" I ask with a grimace.

"Makeup," Panda replies.

Quickly, I realize I hate makeup.

I listen to her explain her job, but I wait to hear the occupation Lord Hermes compels her to complete behind closed doors. I listen to her ramble about the paintings on the walls and the new beige carpet on the floor, but I never hear a complaint. Lady Hecate told me all gods hurt their human women at nighttime, and I would never be strong enough to refuse them. However, Panda doesn't shiver with fright when she talks about Lord Hermes.

Finally, I let the curiosity become known, and I ask. "What about at night? Does Lord Hermes-"

Panda never gives me the opportunity to finish my sentence, and she asks. "Were Lady Nemesis, Lady Achlys, and Lord Enyalios in charge of your prison, too?"

The disparity in Panda's words gives me a glimpse of the trauma she experienced within her prison cell. One I wouldn't have assumed because of the widespread smile she wears almost constantly.

"I had Lady Hecate, Lord Phobos, and Lord Deimos."

"Then it seems the gods tell similar tales." Panda's finger is against my bottom lip, applying a light brown material to the sensitive skin, but her absorption is on her words as she adds. "But that's what their words were, beautifully spun tales designed to cement fear in us."

"The tales must come from somewhere."

"Rub your lips together," Panda commands in a faint murmur, and while I oblige, she responds. "There is viciousness with the gods, but there's only kindness within this house. Lord Hermes isn't the source of those tales. In fact, I think if more kids in those cells realized most immortals treat their slaves how Lord Hermes does, then there wouldn't be as much fear."

"His kindness doesn't change the fact that he's part of the problem. We're his slaves, even if our cage is prettier than others."

"He breaks the rules for us, too," Panda counteracts. "There are three other humans in this house, and one of them is my boyfriend."

"What?"

Except for Laborers, the immortals forbid humans from being in a relationship with one another. We are not creatures deigned worthy of infatuation. Toys are forbidden from feeling affection, especially with one another. We are only creatures of convenience for the gods, our life equivalence no greater than the furniture in this room.

For humans to be gifted with love is a punishment with only one outcome: death.

Yet here, Panda stands unscathed and in a relationship with another human being. She does not look over her shoulder, frightened to admit the illegal truth in a house with an immortal. Her words aren't hushed. There's pride in her green gaze as she professes her illegal relationship.

"How?" I gasp.

"Because it's like I told you. The stories you heard in the prisons may be true in some households, but not Lord Hermes's. He's given me the closest thing to freedom I'll ever have, and he'll do the same for you, too."

We spend the rest of our time together in silence. She adorns my body in pearls, which decorate my neck and two of my fingers. A gold band compliments the pearls around my fingers, while a thin gold chain rests around my neck with a single pearl.

Panda helps me slide into my pale blue gown. Two thin straps hold the dress up and are decorated in a silver and gold mixture of stars and flowers. The entire dress is spattered with them. From the partially see through bodice, with a built-in material that Panda called a corset, to the bottom of this ankle-length gown. Stars and flowers, the epitome of night and innocence, decorate my body.

Next, she assists me with the shoes. They are white, with the same flowery design as the dress. Panda slips the material on my feet, careful to place the part of the shoe that wraps around my largest toe. Once both shoes are on, Panda stands beside me as we both stare at my reflection in the mirror.

"It's time," her freckled face meets mine in the mirror's reflection. "You're ready for your scarification mark."

THE SIXTEENTH CHAPTER

There are two wings in this mansion.

Panda explains that the left wing is where the slaves typically slumber. Their rooms are in the same hall as one another. There are four vacant bedrooms in the left wing, but I am on the opposite side of the mansion from the rest of the slaves. My bedroom is in the right wing of the mansion. With only an adjoining bathroom in between us, my room is next to Lord Hermes's.

I've noticed that Panda tries to fill every silence with conversation. If there's a pregnant pause, then it's promptly diffused with her voice. There is a short walk from my bedroom to Lord Hermes's, but Panda surprises me and doesn't fill the space with incessant rambles. She's silent, and the only sound between us is her shuffling feet and my hammering heartbeat.

We stand in front of the door, but neither one of us makes the move to knock; instead, Panda whispers. "It'll hurt, but then you can come to Pyro and my room afterwards." Her smile is fabricated and scanty. "We can share a bottle of wine until the pain subsides."

I won't survive past my scarification when he sees the colors in my blood. Panda doesn't realize that I am an abnormality. I stare at this door, unblemished with our knuckles clacking against it, and I see my death.

As if it were occurring right now, I can feel my throat being slid open with one of Lord Hermes's knives. Lord Hermes sees the peculiarity within my veins, and I can hear the smirk in his tone. I can smell the coppery tang of my blood as it spills upon Lord Hermes's bedroom floor, forever staining my white flesh.

"I'll see you after," I lie.

She squeezes my shoulder. "See you then."

Panda leaves with a skip in her step and obliviousness clearing her conscious. I watch her, the gentle bob of her fiery locks as they sway to her jubilant jaunt. As she caroms down the staircase, leaving my line of vision forever, I say a silent farewell to the boisterous woman that foolishly believes I will survive to see the next morning.

"Are you ready?" A male voice asks, and my hammering heartbeat stills.

I whip my head around, abandoning the shadow where Panda once stood, and I face my executioner. Lord Hermes is taller than his doorframe, but he still attempts to lean against the frame. His back is bent at an awkward angle, and he crosses his lanky arms over one another upon his chest, but his face is solemn and rigid.

Am I ready to die?

Without responding to the god of thievery, I take a step towards the opened door. He nods once, understanding my silence, and walks into his bedroom with me. I saunter a few steps behind him, still too nervous to get too close.

His room is just as large as the one that I woke up in, but while they decorated mine in pale colors and purple flowers, his is paradoxical. A deep shade of brown decorates white walls, from the frame that holds his bed up to the rim around his bedroom window. A mighty rectangular object is sitting against the wall to the right of his window, covered in smaller items with strange symbols across them.

I'm going to die tonight in this bedroom.

My gold and red blood will stain the brown rug, splatter upon these strange symbols, and fill this room with the malodor of my decaying corpse. I shouldn't look around my death site, but I remain imbued with the symbols and the large, rectangular object that holds them.

The words tumble out of my lips before I have the common sense to stay silent. "What is this?"

His voice is coming from behind me, several feet away. "This is my bookshelf with my favorite books on them."

"Books?"

I turn around and I face the source of my curiosity. Lord Hermes is sitting on the corner of his bed with an oddly shaped object in his hand, and his brows in a slight furrow. His fascination is on the books behind me, and they roam around the plethora of them.

"They are filled with words, and these books tell a story. Sometimes, the stories exist in the real world, but sometimes they are make believe," Lord Hermes says. "I teach all of my slaves how to read. I'll make sure that you get to read every book on that bookshelf by the end of this year."

"Don't make promises you can't keep, Lord Hermes."

"I've kept this promise to all of my slaves; why would I make a dreadful exception for you?" He inquires.

I meander my focal point away from him and towards one prominent vein, and the subtle strips of gold that exist within them. I look at the atrocious truth, which caused Lord Ares to recoil with fear, and I silently answer his question.

Because I'm not human.

"Come sit down," Lord Hermes's voice pulls me from my thoughts, and as tears bloom in my vision, I obey.

I take my spot on the edge of the bed beside him, and we instantly migrate towards one another. He has never been this close to me, but with a faint sizzle filling in the limited space between us, neither of us pulls away.

His hands are dangerously close to my skin, but he never touches me. He opens his mouth to speak, but instead of words spewing out, there is only the faint scent of mint leaving his lips. Lord Hermes is quick to shut his mouth, and he rummages his hand through his dark brown locks. If I didn't know any better, then I'd think Lord Hermes is just as nervous as I am about this scarification mark.

He has scarified many slaves, Panda and the others are proof of this, but he sighs as if this terrifies him. I wait for him to break the silence and begin the scarification process, but he is speechless. He tries to speak a few times, but each attempt is futile.

My fate is death. The moment Lord Hermes sees the oddity of my blood, he will know that I am an abomination, and his nervousness will transform into unspeakable rage. Lord Hermes, who is currently terrified of breaking my skin and causing me harm, will show me the monstrous side of him once my blood becomes visible.

So, I hold out my arm where Panda has her scarification and I start his transition from a kind god to a ruthless one. My arm is shaking frenziedly, my fear paramount, but Lord Hermes does not start the process. I keep my attention on that one long vein on my forearm; the tears blurring my vision, but Lord Hermes changes my expectations when his large hand wraps around my forearm.

Electricity, small and subtle, tickles my skin where he touches me. I jolt my eyes back up to him, but his attention is on his hand as he drags my arm back down to my side. I look at him with unspoken questions, but he shakes his head.

"Turn around," he says in a soft cadence. "So that your back is facing me."

I am trembling, but I obey his command. Once my back, which is mostly bare because of the dress, is in front of him, then his hands rest on both sides of my waist. He pulls me backwards, his legs slide across the outside of mine, and his body cages me in.

My back is too close to his chest, and my backside is pressed against his inner thigh. His hands ascend from their place on my waist, and I lose the ability to breathe. My heart goes to a full stop when one hand grazes the back of my neck.

He's going to kill me before he ever draws blood, I realize as tears slip down my round cheeks.

His breath, warm and saccharine scented, brush against the back of my neck, and I expect his hand to move to the front of my throat. I wait for him to curl his long fingers around my windpipe, slowly but auspiciously draining each breath from my lungs. I remain in dreadful anticipation of my murder, but he moves my braid off of my back and over one of my shoulders.

A few seconds later, and the tip of an instrument presses against the middle of my spine.

"About two hundred years ago, there was a girl who escaped her enslavement. An immortal, who was infatuated with her, aided her escape. She vanished from thin air. No matter how severely Zeus punished the guilty immortal's friends and family, who may or may not have helped them escape, we never found her or the immortal again. After her, the girl with hair as white as snow; my brother Hephaestus had to make amendments to the ink used during the scarification process."

There is a pause of silence between his story and the reasoning behind it, and in the quietness, I hear my life ticking away.

For a majority of my life, I have yearned for death and freedom from this world. I've wanted to live in the Underworld since I learned about the land of the dead, but then I see Panda's youthful, exuberant face. I hear the hope dripping from Zig's face despite his horrendous situation. After learning the name of my storyteller, I no longer want to die.

I'm not ready to die.

"The ink makes anybody, human or immortal, traceable. Hephaestus can track down anybody with this ink in their skin, but this power came with a price," his breath fans against the back of my neck as he speaks. "The blade we used to scarify humans never breaks flesh but fuses with the skin. This blade is meant to not only puncture human flesh, but the ink exists can fuse with gods' flesh as well. This will be more painful than it once was, I'm afraid."

His words give me a morsel of hope.

"But it doesn't break my skin? I won't bleed?" I ask.

"You won't bleed," he confirms.

I can hear my sigh of relief for miles.

"Are you ready?" Compassion laces his voice as he asks.

I nod my head.

A sharp pinch marks the beginning of the pain. Once the discomfort of the pinch subsides, an intense sensation of fire enlivening in my flesh begins. I clamp my eyes shut, and I try to imagine I'm somewhere else. However, nothing can deter me away from the agony.

The repetitive pinch into my flesh isn't the perturbing factor, but the burning sensation is unbearable. Tears form again.

No matter how valiantly I try to keep them at bay, now that my life is not on the cusp of death, they stream in mighty waves.

I use one of my hands to wipe away the sight of my weakness, but the second tears glisten my fingers, the pain abruptly ends. I turn around, expecting him to be finished, but he is staring back at me with pain in his expression, as if he is the one being branded.

"Are you okay?" He holds the pen an inch above my skin. "I'll stop for a bit until you're ready to begin again."

"Don't many humans cry during the scarification process?" I ask.

He sighs. "Every time."

"Do you stop for all of them, too?" When he moves his head no, I turn around so that my back faces him once more and I remark. "Then please continue, Lord Hermes."

I expect resurgence and after a few seconds of empty readiness, the pain makes its reappearance. I suffer, let a few more tears fall, and bite back screams for at least thirty more minutes until the pen is finally removed from my skin and I can take a breath of relief.

"It's official." Lord Hermes breaks the silence, his breath sliding across my bare skin. "You're a slave in my house. Ares won't be able to take you back now."

"Can I see it?"

He holds up a mirror at an angle where I can see both the reflection and my scarification mark, and once I meet with the inked flesh, a gasp escapes from my lips. While Panda's mark takes up a majority of her forearm, mine is smaller. The scar starts in the middle of my back, just a few inches above the start of my dress, and is a radiant bright shade of purple.

The stem is long and thin, and at the top sits two flowers. One flower has bloomed, displaying oval shaped petals, while the other one has not yet transformed into its beauteous form. At the top of the blooming flower, there are wisps of red and yellow strands that peek out.

They're identical to the flowers in the vase in the bedroom.

I glance back at Lord Hermes as he places the pen in a wooden container, and I declare. "It's beautiful."

He closes the top of the box, which holds the instrument that marred my skin, and he glows with appreciation. Then, he asks. "Do you know what flower this is?"

"No, but I've seen it in the room that I woke up in," I answer.

"This is the saffron flower, and it is my personal favorite."

"Why?" I ask.

An expression I recognize too well encompasses him. Sadness strips away the happiness that once possessed Lord Hermes, and a raw stab of mournfulness takes siege. As he sits in front of me, a man destroyed by death or abandonment, I can finally see the immortal age in his boyish features.

"Many eons ago," he says solemnly. "I had finally met a human that did not care that I was a god. He and I became quick friends, and for the first time in my Immortal life, I wasn't just a messenger for the gods. I wasn't just an immortal with a responsibility of traveling deceased souls to the Underworld. I was just a friend to a human man named Crocus."

"What happened to him?" I ask, but I know where this story leads without ever hearing it from my storyteller. I know because of the sadness encompassing his face and darkening his green eyes.

"One day, we were playing a game called discus. Crocus was my first human friend, and I didn't realize my power compared to him. Or, worse, how fragile he was. I threw the discus and killed the only human friend I had because of my idiocy." His gaze wanders from my face down towards the flower that sits on the middle of my spine, and he continues. "I transformed him into the saffron flower with the promise that if anybody owned that flower, then I would protect them for the rest of their mortal life."

"My name is Saffron," I say my name for the first time in eighteen years, and while the origins are abysmal, I smile from ear-to-ear.

As soon as the name leaves my lips, Lord Hermes's sorrow falters, and an impish smile grows over his pink lips. "Yes, you're Saffron."

I laugh, my cheeks burning with pride as I affirm what I always feared I'd never get to achieve. "I have a name."

He rises from the bed, the scarification pen's wooden box under his armpit, and he nods his head. "A beautiful name fitting for a beautiful woman."

I cock my head to the side, confused. "Wait, did you just call me beautiful?"

His laugh bounces off of the walls and warms up a room once chilled with frightened tension. "I have to go to work. I'll see you tomorrow, Saffron."

My back still stings, and my cheeks now burn with a foreign feeling of giddiness. I almost forget the next step of the scarification night until Lord Hermes is one step out of the bedroom, his winged sandals ready to take flight.

"Wait."

Because of my words, Lord Hermes stills to a stop and turns to face me. "Yes?" He inquires.

"What about my job in the house?" I ask. "Aren't we going to talk about that?"

Mischief overtakes his features, as he says. "I'll see you tomorrow, Saffron. Have fun drinking wine with Panda and Pyro."

And he's gone.

THE SEVENTEENTH CHAPTER

When the room twirls and tilts, Panda informs me it's called intoxication. It's a fun, bubbly sensation that happens when a human drinks too much wine too fast, and while I stumble back to my bedroom from Panda and Pyro's, Panda giggles as she guides me towards the bed that awaits my rapt embrace.

"Goodnight, *Saffron*," she enunciates my new name as she lowers me onto the mattress and slides the blanket over my clothed body. "I'll be upstairs tomorrow with a glass of water. Sleep tight."

My heavy lids fall, and my unconscious is whisked away from the mansion and towards the obscurity I know too well.

The drunkenness enveloping my body is gone, and a room shrouded in darkness greets me like an old friend. Onyx hued feathers drape across the windows, the caliginous curtain concealing our dream world from everything else.

My storyteller sits on the throne of obsidian elegance. Epiales sits with pride in his chair with a face that no longer shields itself from my curiousness. Scars decorate his milky flesh, but his plush lips curve upwards into the smallest smile because he sees no fear as I look upon his face littered with stories of survival.

Ring clad fingers curl around the arms of his throne and he hoists himself to his full, magnificent height. His eyes, as silver as the stars in the night sky, stare upon me with hypnotic enamor. If I could see my reflection, then I am certain that I am gawking at him with the same fascination.

Epiales is the moon the rest of the world stares at in rapt reverence. His presence is a beacon that only the foolish would look away from. He walks down his throne's stairs, and he advances towards me. Each stomp of his feet on the ground sends a thunderous hum through my veins. He is the manifestation of darkness, from the top of his curly locks down to the shadows that nip at his shoes, and I am hypnotized by it.

My storyteller is in front of me, staring at me for the second night in a row, and there's no denying the fascination laying across his handsome face. His fingers are on my chin, and the cold caress of his rings tickles my skin. Epiales moves my head upwards and guides me to his silvery irises. Immediate warmth enraptures me.

His scar riddled smile is mesmerizing, but his voice is like nectar, a tendril of sin and decadence. "I've missed you, my queen," his thumb that holds my chin gravitates higher, just barely brushing the curve of my bottom lip.

"I've missed you too," is my whispered response.

His thumb halts on my bottom lip. "I have a present for you," he announces.

Epiales turns his head back to where his throne rests upon a black pedestal. Upon his command, his shadows move to the space to the right of his throne. The gray and black mist intertwines together in a tornado, creating something from nothing. When the shadows depart, a throne of black, gold, and red sits in their wake.

The shadows, once completed with their masterpiece, slide back to the ankles of their master, while I stare upon the throne of daz-

zling jewels with my jaw ready to drop to the floor. While Epiales's royal chair is black and silver, the beautiful onyx gem glimmering under the dimmed lights, the other throne tells a story with the intermingling of red and gold.

Epiales has shown me every jewel, familiarized me with the beautiful gifts that the world offers, and this blackened gift is veiled in glimmering gold and gleaming rubies. A story of my blood plays in the spirals of multi-colored excellence.

I turn to look at my storyteller once again, whose hand has dropped from my chin, and I ask. "Is that meant for me?"

"When the time comes and I'm allowed to," Epiales's voice is gravelly but deepened in sincerity as he looks down at me and vows. "Then the throne, the crown, and the title of the world's queen will be yours."

He takes an additional step towards me, and that is all he needs for our bodies to collide. Electricity, more potent than any strike of lightning that King Zeus could throw, scours through my skin upon his touch. One hand lies on the plump curvature of my hip, while the other one cups my cheek. Blazing silver irises stare down at me, admiring me with mutual enthrallment.

"I've spent almost every night in this dream world with you for the past two years, and soon enough, we will spend every moment together. Not just in a world that does not fully exist, but in a realm that we will jointly rule. Once he has everything else in place, then we can be together as equals. There will be no gods to-"

"Wait," I interrupt. "He, who? I thought it was just the two of us."

His soft curls bounce as he divulges. "If I could achieve this on my own, then I would've, but I'm not strong enough."

He pauses, the past reliving itself in his mind. Epiales had an impish smile upon his scarred lips, but there's now an outstanding frown. He grimaces in solemn remembrance of the atrocities he's endured. The sadness is painted on his face like a ruined piece of artwork; perfect to all but the artist who created the melancholy painting.

"Sometimes," Epiales murmurs. *"We have to work with evil in order to defeat evil."*

I am shaking my head, a flood of thoughts rushing through my mind. "You're scaring me, Epiales."

"Am I scaring you in the same way that Ares scared you with a blade to your chest? The same way I am scared each night, when I am forbidden from saving you from a god who could kill you without a second thought? Or am I scaring you in the same way that Hecate would each day in the cells with stories of the morbid truth?"

My body deflates, my thoughts switching from confusion to compassion, and I let my hands speak my words. Epiales is much taller than me, but I move on the tip of my toes to wrap my hands around the back of his neck. I thrust him down to my level, and when the warmth of his breath nuzzles my cheek, I propel him forward into a hug filled with electricity and tenderness.

His arms move to my waist, uniting our bodies with a yearning for comfort in a world that provides none. His lips skim my cheek in a fond kiss, the closest I've ever come to embracing a man. Epiales does not tilt my head towards his, for our lips to join, but he holds me with the same earnest desire as I do with him.

Time is infinite in each other's grasps, but I pull my hands from around his neck and grab both sides of his face. Underneath my fingertips, I can feel the jagged barbarism of his scars, but when I am at his focal point, I only see his handsomeness. The beauty with the scars, not despite them.

"All I need are our dreams together, Epiales. I'm content knowing that when I am asleep, you will be there, and the world is a little better."

His hands clamp on top of mine. He draws one hand close to his lips, pressing a kiss on the center of my palm, before focusing on my face once more. The sadness which sharpens his features is pulled to the surface.

"That's the thing, my queen. I do not just want you in the dreamworld I've created for us. Every morning, I want to awaken with you in my arms. To talk with you over a blistering evening and hold you in my arms when night has come. I'm not sedated with just the dreams in which I only get a glimpse of what I want, and my power drains with each passing day. The power to go into nightmares, to control humans' unconsciousness, grows more difficult by the day as I wither away into nothingness."

"Wither away?" I whisper as an agonizing sense of abandonment infiltrates every fiber of me. "What do you mean?"

His fingers curl around mine in our embrace, and he hums. "I have none that pray to me, and I'm disappearing slowly and painfully from existence. It's why we must work with him."

"You're not making much sense. Who is he, Epiales?"

He evades the question as he explains. "I am desperate, my queen, but so is humanity. We're all desperate for the same thing: survival and freedom. We need him. He's our chance to destroy the gods and save ourselves." Epiales squeezes my hands and stares at me with fire burning him from the inside out. "He's how we get our revenge and our thrones."

I know the gods are monsters, but instinctual fear crawls into my chest upon Epiales's words. Freedom has been on the cusp of my greatest imaginations before I had dreams with Epiales, but death was never on the precipice of my mind. Escaping servitude is every human's dream, but I will not accept my independence with blood marring my skin.

Stumbling back from Epiales, my abhorrence for his words clear, and his hands drop from my cheeks. I only retreat two steps before my back collides against a warm body. Jumping backwards, I turn my body around and face the second figure in a dreamworld that used to just be Epiales and me.

First, I see the watches that decorate his tanned wrists. There are three of them on his left wrist, all ticking at different intervals. The Immortal proudly wears them over his white, long sleeve shirt that is taut against his muscular chest. I can see each ridge of his arms distinguishingly brawny underneath the thin material.

Then, I drift towards his face.

He has golden brown hair, styled to perfection on the top of his head. The gilded parts of his hair are only a few shades brighter than his tan skin, which appears kissed by the sun. His face, unlike Epiales's, is unscathed and demands dominance. From his strong, narrow nose, the subtle dimple on his left cheek, his sharp jawline, and round eyes, he appears too perfect. But long ago, I learned to distrust a face as pretty as his.

His irises are the color of a storm just as lightning crashes through the sky, identical to King Zeus's in every imaginable way.

Epiales is right behind me, the warmth of his skin tickling my back, as he concludes. "He's our chance at a real life, my queen."

This immortal, whose power ripples off of him in steady waves, cocks his head to the side the same way King Zeus does and coos. "I've been waiting centuries for you, little one."

Epiales has only told me stories about the gods who enslave humanity. He's briefly talked about monsters from the ancient world, but his stories have always originated in educating me about the gods who could become my masters in the arena. Epiales never talked about the titans. Other than informing me of their sovereignty after usurping King Zeus, I know nothing of the titans, but I know this male who stands in front of me and turns my blood to ice.

"You're Kronos, aren't you?"

I am yanked awake before I can get an answer.

THE EIGHTEENTH CHAPTER

An arm tight around my left shoulder propels me out of my dream, where revenge replaces rationality.

I jolt awake, and I expect to recognize the face of the person awakening me. I thought I'd see Panda with the glass of water she promised. Even Lord Hermes's presence with a tray of strawberries. It's neither of them, though. A stranger stands over my body with a displeased frown on her lips.

"Finally, you're awake," the woman grumbles as she pulls her hand away from me. "Get up, you have a visitor."

"What?"

The short female, who has enough rage in her to burn down Lord Hermes's mansion, is already opening the closet door and perusing through my clothing options. I peel the blankets off of my body, assessing her with a mixture of confusion and fatigue.

She has long, black hair that reminds me of the crow tattoo on Epiales's hand. When the sun hits her tresses, there is a slight blue hue, and I lift my plain brown locks with an envious frown on my lips.

"For the love of the gods, you're still in bed?" The short, fiery woman stands in front of my bed with a dress in her hands, and her frown more prominent than before. "You don't want to keep a guest waiting. Get up and brush your teeth. I can smell the wine from here."

Hesitantly, I bring my hand up to my mouth and blow into the open palm.

I nearly gag at the smell.

The woman in front of me grunts, while her slanted brown eyes squint in displeasure. "You have about five seconds to get up before I find a bucket of water to dump on you."

I jolt up from the bed before she can finish the sentence, but she's unhappy. Her lip twitches in anger, embellishing the little black dot above the right corner of her mouth.

I enter the bathroom, where the woman is only a few feet away. I pick up the toothbrush that Panda showed me yesterday, and then turn around to face the woman glowering at me from the other side of the opened door.

"Where's Panda? She said she'd-"

"She's hungover and called in a favor," she retorts before I can finish my sentence.

I open my mouth to ask another question, but the woman slams the bathroom door in my face before I get the chance.

Okay, then.

I think through the list of hygienic requirements Panda told me people complete each morning.

"Step one," I mumble to myself. "Put toothpaste on the toothbrush and brush for two minutes."

As two minutes come and go, I pick up the little blue box that holds floss and complete step two. I brush through my brown locks until each knot is gone, go to the bathroom in a bucket that Panda called a toilet, and quickly wash my face with water and a little purple box of soap.

I open the bathroom door, where the girl's back is facing me, and I can see her scarification mark beneath her thickets of ravenous locks. Unlike mine, hers is devoid of color. Intricate swirls and spherical designs twine around most of the back of her left shoulder, making this scarification mark the largest one I've ever seen.

In the middle of the detailed designs of circles sits an outline of an object Panda showed me in my closet yesterday.

"That's a hat," I announce, and the woman that was unaware that I left the bathroom whirls around to face me head on. "You're Hattie, right?"

"Well, aren't you the smartest girl in the world?" Hattie's tone is dry, lacking any enthusiasm.

I crinkle my nose in confusion. "I'm smart?"

"The smartest," she drawls with the same lack of enthusiasm as her previous comment.

Yet, I smile. "Thank you, Hattie. That's sweet of you."

"For the love of the gods," she groans. "Just sit down so I can help you get ready."

The room is bathed in silence, which gives me an opportunity to overthink the dream plaguing me. While Hattie braids the top portion of my hair and wraps it around the back of my head, I think about Epiales's words and the pain within his expression. I can hear his need for vengeance long after I left the dream with him.

While Hattie places glossy material on my lips, I can see the stormy blue of Kronos's eyes, which crave death more than life. Epiales sees him as a necessary friend with mutual goals, but he did not see the look on Kronos's face when we met. While Epiales sees me as his queen, Kronos sees me in a nefariously different light.

I was a prize he was a breaths width away from finally coveting.

Even when I stood on the arena ground, stared at by hundreds of gods and goddesses, they did not see me with as much sinister promise as Kronos did. Kronos looked at me in that dream world and I was everything that he's been waiting for. He looked at me and I saw the world's annihilation in his stormy eyes.

I've been waiting centuries for you, little one.

A chill runs down my spine as those words repeat in my head on an everlastingly torturous loop.

He's our chance at a real life, my queen.

But is Kronos our chance or something much worse?

A pinch on my arm jolts me from my thoughts, and a yelp leaves my lips as I turn to face Hattie. A deep scowl is on her face, and she snarls. "I said to get up. We need to get the dress on."

The gown is a pale shade of pink and smooth to the touch. The material is long, reaching my feet, but the top portion of the gown is low cut. As I slide the garb on my body, it is tight around my ribcage, and a breeze brushes against my bare chest. There is a deep cut in the back, leaving my scarification mark clear to anybody.

Next, Hattie passes me a necklace that has a gold chain with two jewels that matches the color of my dress. She helps me clasp the necklace in the back, and then grumbles. "Let's go. It's not polite to keep a goddess waiting."

"Wait, a goddess?"

"Who else did you think you'd have as a visitor? A human?"

"Well, yeah," I admit.

Hattie glares at me and leaves the bedroom with the clear expectation that I must follow. A new trickle of fear bubbles to the surface as one question thrums through my head.

Does this visiting goddess know about my dreams?

I rub my sweaty hands up and down my dress, but even though the only thing I want to do is go back to the bedroom and evade my overgrowing disarray, I follow Hattie. She walks three steps ahead of me, and each time I quicken my movement to catch up with her, she expedites at the same time. Hattie doesn't look back to check if I'm behind her as we walk into the kitchen, but once we enter, all that I can see is the goddess of love.

Lady Aphrodite.

There is no definitive way to describe Lady Aphrodite, who sits in a chair with one long leg crossed over another one. I stare at her from the kitchen doorway, looking at her ever-changing physical features, which are always marvelous but constantly accommodating to the world's version of excellence. I look upon her skin color, which changes at the same rapid rate. Her hair is never the same, either its style or color or length or volume shifts.

She sips on a glass of nectar with pink lips that change in plumpness each second. Her gown is tight enough that it is a second sheath of skin on her consistently transitional body shape, but when she rises to her full, impressionable height, she takes one form.

Whichever form she embodies, Lady Aphrodite is gargantuan. While Lady Hecate is taller by an inch or two, Lady Aphrodite has legs that are on a never-ending journey towards the sky.

The appearance that Lady Aphrodite chose has light brown skin, with hair a few shades darker than mine. Two curly tendrils hang from the sides, but the rest is in a loose bun that further stresses her sharp jaw and high, risen cheekbones. Lady Aphrodite always ensures she is the world's version of beauty, and this form is no exception.

Hattie lowers herself to a curtsy upon entering Lady Aphrodite's presence, but the Goddess's amber eyes concentrate on where I stand. She ignores Hattie, who is showing her respect by curtsying, but Lady Aphrodite assesses my physique with a mixture of curiosity and amusement.

"This is one of my three favorite forms," Lady Aphrodite explains to me, but as if she just remembered another person is in the kitchen, a frown creases her face. "You may leave us, maid."

Lady Aphrodite sends Hattie off with a dismissive wave of her hand, but she doesn't look at Hattie. She continues to stare at me, the source of her fascination, and my fear continues to fester. Hattie shoots Lady Aphrodite a glare more dangerous than a thousand daggers, but she obeys the goddess and storms out of the kitchen without a word.

Once the swinging door closes behind Hattie, I lower myself into a curtsy, but Lady Aphrodite stops me. With two fingers, she silently orders me to rise to my full height, and I obey with trembling legs. She's Lord Ares's lover, I remind myself as I stand in her presence. She could be here to take me back to him.

"I heard Hermie gave you your scarification mark last night." She does not poise this as a question, but I nod my head. "Well, are you going to show it to me or am I going to continue to think of you as nameless?"

The phantom touch of Lord Ares's blade in between my breasts burns the skin, and a fear-spawned question spills from my quivery lips. "Are you going to take me back to Lord Ares?"

The smallest smile, filled with unspoken knowledge, flourishes on Lady Aphrodite's face. "Show me your scarification mark, nameless girl."

I'm powerless, like a stray mouse in a room full of starving children, and I have no choice but to obey. My back faces the goddess. I wait for a blade to pierce my flesh, but it's Lady Aphrodite's fingers which touch my bare skin. Her caress is feathery as she traces the flower's stem and petal.

"Saffron," my name upon her lips brushes against my spine as she coos. "A name with an infinite amount of meanings for many gods. How intriguing he chose that name for you."

Her face may be beautiful, but her words are frigorific, and I flinch from her touch. I walk a few steps forward, putting distance between us, but I can't escape a goddess. I turn to face Lady Aphrodite once again, and her appearance has transformed.

Her skin is now as pale as the moon. Her hair is shoulder length and in golden wavy wisps. In her previous image, all of her facial features were sharp and angular, but she is gentler in this version. Her nose is upturned, her cheeks are rounder, and little brown dots decorate the thin bridge of her nose and curvature of her cheeks.

She still wears the same gown as before, and she is still modelesque in height, but everything else about her has been changed.

Lady Aphrodite takes a step towards me again, her eyes now the color of the ocean and they are observing every inch of my body. "There was once a time when I fashioned my body like yours, where my curves were voluptuous, and a small flap of fat rested beneath my chin. Sometimes, especially when I look at women like you, I wish that the world saw ample bodies with the same reverence they once had. Alas, the world will forever be riddled with errors."

"Are you taking me back to Lord Ares, Lady Aphrodite?" I ask again.

"No, I am not," she fixates on my face once more, and they dazzle with questions not yet spoken. "I came to see you because I am an inquiring soul, nothing more."

"What are you curious about?" I ask.

Lady Aphrodite's barely there smile, filled with knowledge, returns.

"I'm curious," she says before her attention deviates to the kitchen doorway behind me. "About whom captivated my Hermie so much that he took the time out of his hectic schedule to not only steal from Ares, the most paranoid god I've ever known, but covet her so dearly. For the first time in our five-hundred years on Earth, he took a break from the busy job he abhors to save a young girl's life and turn her into his first ever concubine. Then, for her name to have so many meanings in our world, has me enthralled. Hermie is best known for stealing, but I never forget the sneaky, selfish part of him that will do anything to achieve his goals."

"Concubine?" I stumble out the one word that renders me confused.

As I say this one word, another voice breaks through the kitchen and speaks at the same time.

"Aphrodite."

I turn around, and Lord Hermes stands in front of the still swinging door. He is glaring down at Lady Aphrodite from where he stands, but she is unperturbed. Amused, even. Lord Hermes does not look at me, even as I gawk at where he stands with one word reiterating in my head.

Concubine.

Concubine.

Concubine.

"Lady Aphrodite must be lying, right?" I ask, but when he doesn't speak, I repeat. "Right?"

Lady Aphrodite runs towards Lord Hermes, and once again, her appearance changes. Her hair is black and trimmed short to her scalp, while her skin is a rich brown. She is as lithe as she was in her previous two forms, and she wraps her long arms around Lord Hermes's neck with elation.

There is no warning, not even as my question remains unanswered when Lady Aphrodite crashes her lips against Lord Hermes's. He pushes her away immediately, and he peels her arms off of the back of his neck.

Without dismay over his rejection, Aphrodite coos. "Welcome home, Hermie."

His frown worsens upon the nickname, and he snarls. "What are you doing in my home? You weren't invited."

"Because," Lady Aphrodite sings as she turns to face where I stand with chaos in her onyx hued eyes. "I needed to meet your concubine, *Saffron*, but now that I have, I will take my leave. Toodles."

Where she once stood, only remnants of pink smoke and thickened tension remain.

THE NINETEENTH CHAPTER

Lady Aphrodite leaves with her words remaining on boundless rerun, and we haven't found the strength to speak. For five minutes, we've let the room drench in silence and unspoken secrets. The smoke she disappeared in is long gone, but the words she spoke linger like a foul odor.

"I think I'm going to need a drink," Lord Hermes announces, breaking apart the muteness.

He strolls through the kitchen, opening the little doors that contain food or plates until he finds two glass cups. He sets them down on the counter, and after a snap of his fingers, a bottle of brown liquid manifests in between the two cups. There are no words, but an uproar of internal thoughts deafening the room.

He fills the cups halfway and walks towards where I have remained, frozen in disbelief. Lord Hermes extends the cup full of brown liquid towards me, but I do not grab the glass; instead, I blurt out one word. "Concubine?"

Lord Hermes sighs. "Aphrodite shouldn't have revealed your status like that. I don't know how she figured out. I only told H-"

"Should I disrobe, Lord Hermes?"

My hands are on the straps of my pink gown, visibly trembling as I squeeze onto the flimsy material and stare up towards my master. Lord Hermes slowly lowers the two glasses onto the table next to me, where Lady Aphrodite once sat, and looks at me with a deep set frown.

He shakes his head and says with great dejection. "No, that's not why you're here."

There is silence for too long, and my fingers are still hesitating on the straps of my gown. He is as quiet as I am, but while my feet are unmoving and plastered to the ground, Lord Hermes walks to the back of the kitchen. He opens a white door and removes a rectangular object.

The only noise in the kitchen is his feet, which are tapping against the floor as he moves back to where I am. He sits on the chair beside the two abandoned glasses of brown liquid, and then he sets the white, rectangular object on the rounded table.

He picks up the glass once more, and sighs. "Do you want to learn how to play my favorite board game?"

I ask. "You don't want to…"

I let my words drift into the wind, the purpose of them redundant when both he and I know the rest of my question.

Lord Hermes assures me. "That's not why you are my concubine, Saffron."

"Then why am I?" I ask with an undistinguishable tremor in my voice.

"Do you want to take a seat? You've been standing for quite a while," Lord Hermes evades my question while gesturing towards the empty chair across from him.

When several seconds slip and I am still standing, Lord Hermes sighs but leans forward to grab both sides of the rectangular shape he's called a board game. There are two parts to the box, and he lifts the top portion. Curiosity draws my gaze towards this unfamiliar contraption, where a myriad of different colored shapes and sizes await me.

He opens a bluish green square from within and opens it up while explaining to me. "The board game is called Monopoly, and when we came crashing into a modernized world to re-establish our ancient tyrannical roots, I kept this game before the rest turned to dust under Zeus's fingertips."

He sets the multi-colored items in their designated sections, while I watch on with my hands on my waist instead of on the straps of my gown.

"I haven't gotten to play this game with anybody in a very long time." Lord Hermes sets a shoe-shaped item on a corner and asks. "Would it be alright with you if we play a round of Monopoly, drink a bit of whiskey, and pretend that we aren't two very different people forced into a terrible world?"

When I finally find the ability to speak again, it's scratchy and opaque. "Is this what you want from a concubine, Lord Hermes? Somebody who will play board games, drink, and pretend with you that the world is all right?"

"Is that such a terrible request?" He responds, one of his brows raised a quarter of an inch higher than the other.

I shake my head. "This isn't right."

"What isn't right?" He asks. There isn't a molecule of judgement in his tone, only mild curiosity.

"My entire life, I have been told about the jobs we may get once an immortal wins us in the arena. Before the gods taught us how to speak, they made sure that we knew our job options and the duties that came with these jobs."

"It's not like that here, Saffron," he says, but I shake away his words.

"There is the job of the Laborers." I push through his words that he is different, and I explain the facts I know about the gods. The gods who Epiales wants to destroy with Kronos and me by his side. "The Laborers are the unfortunate humans that no god or goddess wanted on the arena floor. These humans would be forever nameless, sent to one of Queen Hera's labor camps to produce more children for the vicious cycle of human enslavement. Laborers' lifespans are only as long as their fertility. Then, the nameless and unwanted are killed without ever holding their children in their arms."

Lord Hermes's face slackens with sympathy, and he wants to say anything, to apologize for his species' actions, but I do not give him the opportunity.

"Then, there is the job of the dispenser, which is the most frequent job amongst humans." I sneer my words with hatred bubbling in my chest because it was my job in Lord Ares's home. "Dispensers are nothing more than death's brutal gift. Dispensers are nameless, like the Laborers. Before their lives begin outside of the jail cell, they are killed. That is all they are, quick kills for the gods. They never survive to see the next sunrise after the arena."

Glaring down at Lord Hermes, I try to imagine him with the same inkling of hatred I have for the other gods who have tormented me. I look at his boyish features, and I think about Lady Hecate and the blood drenched lipstick she wore. When I see Lord Hermes, I imagine Lord Ares's navy blue irises that brewed with disgust when he saw my mixture of gold and red blood. Lord Hermes is in front of me, and the image of Lord Phobos and Lord Deimos return, their taunting laughter when they held my ration of food just out of arm's reach like nails screeching down glass.

I try to picture them when I look at Lord Hermes, but all I see is sadness on his face as I show my hatred for his kind.

But I don't stop spewing my abhorrence for his family.

"The second most popular profession is the toy. An immortal's toy is the equivalent of a pretty piece of décor on a god's shelf. The toys are always attractive, but their bodies are always defiled by whomever purchased them. Their life expectancy is longer than a dispenser, and they are given names, but their existence is strife personified. Whatever a god wants to do with their toy is acceptable." Hot, angry tears stream down my cheeks as I snarl. "Anything, no matter how perverse."

"I'm-" He tries to apologize for his family, but I do not give him the opportunity.

"Another job is a maid," I snap while crying for the thousands, if not millions, of lost lives. "The maids clean the immortal's home and complete all the chores, but they are more frequently toys and rarely last longer than dispensers. All it takes is one dust speckled shelf or a spill on the floor, and an immortal would kill the maid that was inconsequential to their eternal lives."

"Saffron," he speaks my name as if it were a plea, but I do not stop speaking the truth.

I act as if I never heard him and continue. "A human could become a cook who makes food for the immortals. They refill empty glasses with nectar, supply ambrosia, and feed the bare minimum to the other slaves. But their fate is as abysmal as the maids. If there is an overcooked meal, then their death is wickedly sealed. Again, a short life expectancy."

I expect Lord Hermes to interrupt me again, but he is silent and staring up at me with his own sadness clear in bloodshot eyes.

"Soldiers are tasked with guarding their immortal against the enemies that their master has garnered from eons of mistakes and acts of vengeance. That's the duty of every male unfortunate enough to be won by Lord Ares in the arena, and most of them die within the first two months of their servitude. They're sometimes killed by the immortal's enemies, but most frequently they die of dehydration or starvation because their lives are so unappreciated by the gods that they forget to feed them."

I do not fight the tears, and the anguish slamming into my chest with the severity of a knife. I let Lord Hermes see the reverberation of the gods' fear and destruction upon my distraught features. Tears slip from the god's eyes.

"We could be decorators, like Panda, who make sure that the house is prestigious, but their lives are just as fragile as the cooks. If the immortals dislike *one* slight change to their house, then the decorators are killed with such savage exaction that even Lord Thanatos is told to weep in disgust. Again, just like the chefs and the maids, they are frequently toys as well. Distorted to whatever image the god, who won them like a piece of property, wants them."

I wipe at the tears streaming down my cheeks, but they spill in an endless downpour.

"Then there are concubines," I snap.

Lord Hermes flinches as if my title in his home was a slap across the face.

"The concubines are the most beautiful men and women in the arenas and are always the most coveted, but beauty comes at a price when you're a human. Concubines are the equivalent of a naked, unmoving body. They are inanimate objects rather than a woman or man with hopes and feelings. If you're tied to the right God or Goddess, then it's possible to survive a few years before reaching the Underworld, but most concubines die within the first three months."

I laugh, but the sound is devoid of any humor.

"Saffron, that's not why I want you as my concubine," Hermes says in a soft cadence, but I ignore him again.

"Or concubines survive a few days if they're tied to an immortal with a jealous spouse.," I continue. "Everybody correlates concubines with one thing, and it isn't their dazzling personalities. These cursed jobs are what I've learned my entire life, along with the abysmal expectancies that are correlated with them. I've expected carnage and mutilation, I've expected my body to no longer belong to me, and I've waited for the moment that I spend eternity in the Underworld. But then..."

I let my words become one with the wind, but Lord Hermes stands up to his feet and moves towards me with his own tears streaming down his cheeks. He walks towards me until he is at arm's width away, and I know he wants to comfort me. I can see the twitch of his fingers and anxiousness in his teeth that nip at his bottom lip, but he doesn't break the distance between us with an embrace.

He leaves the choice to me as he asks. "But then what, Saffron?"

"But then you didn't follow the rules, not even in the slightest."

The last of my anger and tears slip, but I do not dismiss them. I let Lord Hermes rivet towards the stream of sadness, sliding down my round cheeks and dripping off of my chin.

"I don't like those rules," he finally confesses.

"When I was at Lord Ares's, I was a dispenser," I reveal aloud for the first time. "My job made sense because that is how I've been taught. I was going to die if you, Lord Hypnos, and Lord Thanatos didn't save me, but I wasn't confused there because I knew what my job was and what it entailed. Yet, here I stand in front of you as your concubine, and you do not want me for anything else than company. Here I stand, and you see me as a person rather than property." I shake my head in disbelief as the last bit of truth slips from my lips. "You're different from any other god," I admit as a stream of brown locks falls from my braid and brush across my face.

"You'll be surprised how many immortals differ from what you've been told in the prisons," Lord Hermes raises a hand, and he inches towards the tendril of fallen hair, but he curtails his instinctual desire before he touches me. He clears his throat and moves towards the round table, where the two glasses of whiskey and the Monopoly game patiently wait for our attention. "I would like to explain with words that I do not want you to be my concubine for anything else other than company, but actions are much more potent. If you would like to, then please sit and enjoy a round of Monopoly with me. I think you'd like the game."

"And if I do not wish to?" I dare to ask.

"Then you may go back to your bedroom," he says. "Or anywhere you'd like in this house. China and Panda have created a beautiful garden in the backyard that you might enjoy."

"I'll play one round, Lord Hermes," I decide.

When he looks up at me, the eons-old immortal looks no older than I am. "Please, just call me Hermes. I don't want you to see me as your master."

"What should I see you as, then?" I ask, my hesitance clear in my voice.

For several seconds, he ponders this question before finally giving me an answer.

"You want to be seen as a person with thoughts and feelings, and that is what I'd like as well. My hope is that you see me as a man who has never purchased a human with the purpose of killing them. I want you to see me as somebody who has never had a toy, harmed his maids, chefs, or decorators. A man who cares for humans and abhors the slavery system with a burning passion."

"Then why do you own slaves?" I ask without judgement, but an abundance of curiosity.

"I'm not a skilled fighter, no matter how often I train for the arenas. Zeus limits us to two fights per arena, but I jump into the arena each time to save humans from gods like Ares, who wants them for certain death." Lord Hermes fiddles with a Monopoly piece in the same shape as Hattie's scarification. "I do not have the power to end slavery, but I can make as many humans' lives easier by giving them a glimpse of freedom in my home. The only humans who have died before they reached their elder years while living with me were when Athena and Poseidon got into a terrible fight in my home. Their fight ended in all but one of my slaves becoming casualties, and they have been forever uninvited from my home because of their actions."

"Your slaves become elderly?" I ask with disbelief lacing my tongue.

He nods his head and divulges. "The first slave I won in the arena lived to be one hundred and one years old," he looks at where I stand, and something in my appearance makes his sadness lessen; he murmurs. "How you're looking at me right now, as a person with feelings, is how I always want you to look at me. A male who despises human enslavement and vows to always protect every person in this house with every inch of my power. Including you, Saffron. Especially you."

There is a long pause, where I process his words while he waits for my response with a tight grip on the hat shaped Monopoly toy. For nearly five minutes, we are in complete silence until I finally look at him, and I see somebody other than a god. I see a sweet man who promises human safety more than anything else.

"You've never killed a slave before?" I ask once more, my tone laced in abashment.

"Never," he says as he passes the miniature shoe towards me. "Hecate put a spell on my house that forbids any god or goddess who has killed a slave to enter my home. I think it's why Ares hasn't tried to steal you back. Anybody who has permission to enter my home will never harm you. I promise, Saffron."

"Even Lady Aphrodite?"

Hermes laughs with a lace of humor attached. "Even Aphrodite. She may annoy me, but she does not harm humans. Never has and never will."

I slide my thumb across the smooth, cold material of the miniature shoe in my hand. "Do you promise I can trust you?"

Epiales's words of how terrible each god and goddess is to humans play on repeat in my head. His vows that I can't trust them are on an endless loop inside of my mind. Even in a world away from my dreams, I can see Epiales's scars, and I wait for Hermes to show his malevolent truth and throw a knife towards my head.

But I'm unsurprised when he responds to my question without a hint of a lie on his tongue.

"You are my first concubine, but you are not here for whenever I desire intimacy. You will rule this house beside me as a friend for as long as you wish to be, and I will let nobody harm you. I will not harm you," he restates with sincerity. "You are my equal in this house, and I will do everything in my power to ensure you grow to have fond memories of this home," he spins the Monopoly piece in his hand as he remarks. "My only request is that you partake in the best game in the world."

My attention deviates to the miniature shoe that rests in the palm of my hand. "And this is the best game in the world, Hermes?"

A genuine smile curls over his lips when he realizes I dropped the formalities, which are mandatory whenever a human speaks to an immortal. I should be whipped, or worse, for such a crime, but Hermes smiles at my words as if it were a grand gift.

"Yes, of course it is, as long as we never play a round with Apollo," Hermes fake whispers with his hand around the side of his mouth. "He's the biggest cheater I've ever seen."

A laugh burst through my lips without warning.

"I have to reveal something," Hermes says as he picks up two tiny white cubes with black dots on top. "There is one thing you said about concubines that is true."

My heart stops completely. "What?"

"You said that concubines were the most beautiful women in the house," he drops the white cubes onto the board game and says with a golden hue growing on his cheeks. "It's the truest statement I've heard in a millennium."

I finally take a seat in the offered chair, my cheeks burning brightly as a newfound flutter resonates in my chest.

With a smile still on his lips, Hermes teaches me the game of Monopoly.

"There is this thing called money," Hermes explains. "That you must get through the game. In order to make more money than what you've already gained, you must buy little boxes and cards."

"I don't know how to count," I admit.

"I'll teach you," he promises.

Throughout the game, Hermes is true to his word. He helps me count out my money, which he told me is of no use in the real world. Near the end of the game, I steal a handful of pink dollars.

You know, just in case.

The game lasts around three hours, and once I am the crowned winner, I let myself care for the god who purposefully chose a game that would help me learn to count.

"Thank you," I say as we pack up the game.

He turns his attention back to me, deviating away from cleaning up the game of Monopoly. His shaggy brown locks flop to one side of his forehead as he tilts his head in confusion and asks. "For what, Saffron?"

"For being different from the others."

THE TWENTIETH CHAPTER

For the first time in my life, I avoid going to sleep. After my game with Hermes, fatigue tickles the back of my heavy lids, but I lay on my bed and stare unblinkingly at the ceiling. Epiales waits for me in my dreamworld, but who will join him there?

Will Kronos, a monstrous titan who sends caliginous fear down my throat, be accompanying him?

Sleep comes for me, forcing the conscious world to dissipate from my desperate grasp. My dreamworld was where I once correlated with safety, but now I fight the grip of sleep. Yet, with the same valiant effort as my experiences with trying to stay asleep, I lose the battle.

There are no sinister smirks, or the faint sound of three watches ticking at separate intervals. My body does not freeze with fright, and a voice created from melted gold does not slither through the dreamworld I once saw as my sanctuary.

Kronos is absent from sight, but Epiales is sitting on the steps leading towards our thrones with his hands burying his head.

His normally wind-spun, curly raven locks are manic, indicative of hands anxiously running through them. Pulling at them in hysteria. His back is hunched over, and the confidence I've always seen from Epiales is absent. The charm, which he wears like gem-encrusted jewelry, is gone. His shadows, just like him, sit limply on the steps towards a throne he always sits upon.

I take a step towards him, and Epiales jerks upwards. He centers on where I stand, with disbelief marring his appearance. He jolts up to a standing position, wiping away any debris from his knees, and moves closer to me.

"I thought you were avoiding me," he breaks the silence with vulnerability, which is such a foreign sound in his voice.

"Maybe I was," I concur with the same quieted cadence.

I take another step.

Then he does.

The thoughts of Kronos, of the fear that plummets into my chest when he is infiltrating my mind, are still there, but I cannot stay away from Epiales. My storyteller, my haven, and my friend. He, too, moves towards me with a magnetizing pull. Just as I can see him without the scars, he is the only male in the world who sees the somber, self-defeated side of me and still sees beauty.

His shadows yearn for my company with the same urgency as their master. The obsidian mist curls around my ankles, tickling my skin as they spiral around each leg and surround my body.

Epiales is only a few steps away from me now, and he outstretches his hand. "Do you care for a dance, my queen?"

I am in nothing but a long shirt, which stops a few inches above my knee, but when my hand lands upon Epiales's, I am transformed. The shadows encompass my body, removing the tie holding my hair together and disrobing me from the shirt. In a spiral of shadows and magic, I am manifested into a queen with a crown worthy of her excellence.

When the shadows dissipate, there is the familiar heaviness of lipstick on my mouth. My hair is falling down a little past my shoul-

ders in wavy ringlets. A weighted crown is on my head, while a gown of radiant red clings to my body.

The dress is floor length, leaving a slight trail in its wake. While the sleeves of this gown reach the top of my hands, they end in a triangle shape and loop around my middle fingers. The gasp, which leaves my painted lips, is not because of the gown's sleeves. My hand placed on top of Epiales's has an accessory on the fourth finger. A ring of brilliant red and gold garners my disbelief.

"One day, my queen." He raises my hand that holds his ring, and he presses his lips against the top of the jewel. "It will all become reality one day."

His kiss sends a current through my body. The pit of my stomach warms as he uses his grip upon my hand to bring my chest flush against his. His other hand captures my waist, while I guide my free hand towards the top of his shoulder.

I look up at him. "I do not know how to dance."

His smile is enough to still the heart of any woman, or man, in the world. "I'll take the lead. Just follow my steps and you'll be magnificent."

Epiales's movements are slow, his feet shuffling between the same two spots. The steps are simple, and when I take his lead with ease, he integrates an extra movement. Then another. Time is infinite when I am in Epiales's company, and as we tell a story with our rhythmic movement, his words filter through the air.

"May I tell you a story that I've told nobody, my queen?"

Without fear, I realize I am his prisoner. I am beguiled by him, enamored by each tilt of his head, each wayward glance that is dedicated to me, and each word that filters out of his scarred lips. I am a prisoner to his beauty because I can't bring myself to look away.

"It is a sad tale," he admits.

"What is it about?" I ask just as he lowers me back, dipping my body until my hair tickles the floor.

I am propelled upward again and brought so close to him that the tips of our noses graze one another. The smell of mint and smoke strokes my lips as his words breathe into me. "It's about how I ended up in Tartarus, the prison deep in the Underworld's belly, designed only for immortals."

He dances with me, his feet shuffling across the obsidian floor, but pain worse than a blade to the chest mars his soul. He spins me outwards, allowing me to feel the ginger brush of the wind, but when I am spun back into his embrace, his story begins.

"When the titans first usurped us from Mt. Olympus, the idea of enslaving humans was conceived. For many centuries, there has only been one way a god could die, and that is if we are forgotten. Zeus feared being dethroned from Mt. Olympus would cause the humans to forget him, and he'd disappear from the world. So, him and many other gods took Earth from the humans and forced them to become our slaves."

His movements slow down, and as seconds go by where there is only silence as I process his words, the dancing comes to a complete halt. Epiales still holds me, one hand intertwined with mine while the other holds my waist. I do not move, my fingers still cupping the back of his neck.

"Selfish fright blinded me," Epiales divulges, *his cadence weakened but dripped in honesty.* "And I followed my king along with many other gods, but one deity fought back. When he found his destined soulmate, his third love, screaming in her dreams for freedom and mercy, my nephew intervened. Morpheus was a benevolent god, and he no longer obeyed Zeus's orders to enslave the humans because of our own fear. He helped his soulmate escape, along with the other humans who lived with her, and nobody has seen them since the day they disappeared."

"How long ago was this?"

"Two hundred and fifteen years ago," he answers. "Humans do not have dreams anymore because of the clemency Morpheus gave his soulmate and the three other slaves who lived with her in Heracles's house. When he helped them escape and live freely, as all humans should, Zeus went mad with fear. The wicked king did not blame Heracles, who lost all of his slaves. He didn't blame Hypnos, either, who is Morpheus's father. Morpheus's brothers, Icelus and Phantasus, weren't to blame, either."

I already know the dreaded path this story is taking, and before he can say the terrible truth, I softly infer. "He blamed you, didn't he?"

He audibly gulps. "Morpheus and I were close. I have no children of my own, and he was the closest that I've had to a son."

Epiales's touch, which was once warm and elicited electricity throughout my body, has gone cold with grief. His thumb still strokes the waist he tenderly holds, but his silver eyes are a pool of sorrow where he and I drown without a way to break to the surface.

"Every scar marring my skin is a punishment from Zeus. I should've healed from every torture, but the Fates wanted me to become a mutilated version of myself. If my mangled appearance was the only punishment for my silence, then I wouldn't be working with Kronos. I wouldn't choose evil to fight against evil, but destroying my appearance wasn't enough for Zeus. I was stripped from every book that was ever written about me. Each statue in my honor destroyed, and any human who knew that I existed was murdered in front of me."

"He wanted you to be forgotten and disappear," I surmise with horror lacing my voice.

Tears form, but they never fall down his scarred cheeks. "After the last human who knew me was murdered, I tried to kill him, but I wasn't strong enough. I was thrown into Tartarus without a second thought. Zeus knew I knew where Morpheus took the humans, and since I wouldn't betray my nephew, I would disappear in a prison dedicated to the worst immortals and their unforgivable crimes."

One tear falls down his pale flesh. Another falls, then three and four join them in ominous unison. My hand, which rested against his shoulder, cups his angular face. He tries to brush away his sadness, and I help him. My thumb continues to swipe away silver streaks, but they continue to tumble down.

"That's where Kronos found me," Epiales reveals as he replaces the sadness with vengeful determination. "With my livelihood disappearing into the pit of Tartarus, where he was once imprisoned. He promised me a chance to destroy the ones who wronged me. He promised to free me from a prison of empty nothingness. If I did everything that he asked without question, then he would make me King of the Underworld, where I'd never disappear but thrive with a crown upon my head."

"Are you still there?" I dare to ask. "Are you still in Tartarus right now?"

His expression is sad, but his answer is harrowing. "It's why I couldn't save you from Ares when you called to me." More tears fall down his face, but this time, he doesn't hide his devastation and I stop wiping them away. With a mournful ache on his face, he tells me. "It's why I haven't taken you from Hermes yet. I'm still a prisoner, waiting to be freed by a titan I swore allegiance to."

"You're disappearing," I say with my heart breaking and my own tears building up.

"Our dreams will be less frequent after today, so that I can conserve my energy for when Kronos comes for me. For when he saves me, and you and I fight alongside him to destroy the gods who tried to kill us both."

"But…" I stop talking, my own thoughts no longer black and white but a blur of gray.

But do I want to destroy all the Gods?
Do I want to destroy Hermes?

"He is how I found you," Epiales murmurs as his hand gravitates away from my waist and moves towards the curve of my jaw. His touch sizzles my skin, electrifying me. "He found you in the prison cells, with blood that was neither human nor god, and told me to tell you stories about the gods. To tell you the truth of the monsters who exist in this world. I did not know you existed before two years ago, but he's been eager to meet you for many years."

Upon the mention of Kronos, of his eagerness to acquaint himself with me, Epiales's electrifying touch turns cold as ice. I stumble backwards, taking enough steps away that Epiales's hands fall from my body. As soon as our fingers no longer touch, the dress, the crown, the golden shoes, and the ring disappear, and I am back in the oversized shirt I slept in.

I stare at Epiales, who is only a few feet away but feels miles away, and I admit. "He scares me, Epiales. I can feel the hate in him, and it scares me."

Epiales does not move towards me, but he stares at me with a plea on the tip of his tongue. "He's our chance at survival, my queen."

"What am I, Epiales?" I do not dare to blink, much less breathe, as I look at my storyteller who promised to never tell me a lie and I implore to him. "Why was Kronos searching for me? Why is my blood two contrasting colors?"

He opens his mouth, ready to tell me the truth, but consciousness demands my arrival.

And I'm pulled towards the conscious world.

THE TWENTY-FIRST CHAPTER

A job I once correlated with grievance has awakened me to a god's kindness. When I was in the prison and only had Epiales's words as guidance, I loathed the immortals' existence and the deaths trailed in their wake. Yet, Hermes isn't like those stories. He contrasts them in every way.

Two days ago, I stared at Hermes, who sat all of his slaves at a rounded table in the library and taught us how to read in-between his duties to King Zeus, and I stopped seeing a villain.

I simply saw Hermes.

During our lesson, my first within his house, he explained that there are seven days of the week. I can't remember the names of all of them, but I know that he only has time to tutor us on a day called Thursday. He said that Thursdays are the closest he receives to a day off, but several times throughout the session, he left to complete his never-ending duties to the Olympians.

During those intervals of time when he was absent, the eldest slave named China took over teaching the group.

In the two days since my first glimpse of a book, which was a sea of jumbled whorls and designs, China offered to spend her mornings assisting me with my studies. China is a fair skinned woman, with wisps of black, gray, and white hairs perpetually pulled up into a messy bun on top of her head. When she smiles, which isn't often, her grayish blue eyes crinkle with a sight that I've never seen before.

Wrinkles, she calls them.

An impossibility for humans to achieve is what I call them.

For the past two mornings, China waits for me at the small, circular table in the kitchen, which Hermes and I played Monopoly on. Each morning, I sleepily tumble down the staircase, and she always has two glasses of steaming tea waiting for me. Along with the tea is a piece of paper with my newest assignment scribbled on the page. For the first two hours of the morning, while most of the house slumbers, she gives me an ink pen and watches me with patience as I trace the letters of the alphabet.

On the third morning since our studies began, I open my bedroom door with one hand while rubbing away the tiredness with the other one. I take one step forward, my mouth already watering in anticipation of China's steaming tea, but I halt.

Hattie has a single brow raised, judgement clearly visible in her pouted lips and she jeers. "It's important to look in front of you when you walk. I trust the cells taught you that much."

"Good morning to you, too, Hattie," I retort, my voice drowsy with fatigue, but I drop the hand that is covering my vision. I look at how she stands in front of me with a folded pile of clothes beneath a pair of shoes in her outstretched arms. "What is that?"

"Clothes," she jerks them forward, forcing me to catch them before they tumble onto the floor, and she remarks. "Get dressed and meet the rest of us in the basement."

"The basement?" I verbally ponder. "But in the morning, China and I-"

"You don't tutor with China on Saturday's," Hattie responds, and when she turns away from me, her ponytail smacks the tip of my nose. "On Saturdays, we get visitors."

Hattie is at the top of the staircase, ready to leave my line of sight with more questions than answers in her wake. Hurriedly, I ask. "Who are the visitors?"

She heard me. Her body shook as if in laughter at my question, but she does not answer. Hattie jogs down the stairs, leaving me standing numbly in the doorway of my bedroom with folded clothes and an abundance of questions.

⸺

Hattie never divulged the identity of our Saturday visitors, but when I hit the last step and look at the four women standing under swinging, flickering lights, I recognize them as neither immortals nor slaves.

I see four of Artemis's loyal huntresses.

Their clothing is identical to one another. Brown boots that reach their knees, sleeveless fur vests, and white shirts splattered and stained in the dried blood of their enemies.

I flinch, the movement caught by the slender-necked huntress on the far left, when Panda sneaks up and wraps her arm around mine. Panda's grin is widespread as she looks up at me, the gaps between her teeth more apparent than ever. Pyro stands a few feet behind her, his hands gripping an axe, and he glances at me in silent acknowledgement.

"This is my favorite day of the week," Panda coos, her grip on my arm tightening with excitement.

"Why are they here?" I ask, half of my attention on Panda's smiling form and the other on the slender-necked huntress who watches me with droopy, yet protruding, eyes.

"Hermes and Artemis made a deal," Panda says, and I do not mistake the lack of formalities on both immortals' names as Panda speaks. The friendliness in her tone as she talks about not one, but two gods, is enough cause for treason. "Each Saturday, Artemis will bring four of her huntresses here to help us train, and he will steal whatever she wants without question." Panda giggles as she adds. "Hermes said that he once stole an elephant for Artemis."

We're all here, the humans living in Hermes's mansion.

China is talking to the tallest huntress, who has a scarification mark of a large black bird, its wings outstretched across most of her chest. It's not a crow, I realize, but a grander onyx creature.

Hattie is picking up two bronzed swords, twirling the weapons as if they are hers to command. A tall, slender blonde huntress leans against the wall closest to Hattie, conversing with the normally rigid woman, and I watch with fascination as Hattie tilts her head back and roars in laughter. I don't think I've ever seen her smile before today.

The slender-necked woman, along with the portly huntress with untamed dark hair, starts advancing towards Panda and me. Panda is still talking, rambling about another item that Hermes stole for Lady Artemis, when the two huntresses stand in front of us. I am frozen, rigid to the spot as I intermittently flicker to the slender-necked huntress and that damning smirk on her large lips.

"Dýnami," the slender-necked woman says to the portly one beside her. "Train with Pyro and Panda today, please."

The slender-neck huntress looks at me, and the single brightest pair of brown eyes stare back at me. They are a few shades lighter than her complexion, with a gilded gleam to them, and they both droop and protrude from their sockets.

Everything about this woman is beautiful, yet odd. She has a long face with subdued features. Her chin is exorbitant but has a dimple in the middle that feminize the masculine feature. Plump lips that are twice the size of mine, but they're long, too. She has an enormous mouth that takes over her face.

And that large mouth curves into that knowing smirk again as she adds. "I'm training with the concubine."

Her hair is brown and voluminous, barely contained by the ribbon that's tied around the curls. As she slugs off her fur vest, her hair bounces in excitement at the fight that is about to take place. When the thick material drops to the floor, I can now see her scarification mark that rests on her left bicep.

There are antlers, two of them, sprouting around a thicket of green trees. The scarification mark is simplistic, yet gargantuan. The tip of the antlers starts at the top of her shoulders but does not end until it grazes the top of her elbow.

She answers my silent question. "Artemis named me after her most favored animal, the sika deer."

"Is your name Sika or Deer?"

"Sika," she answers, then walks away.

I do not need to ask; I trot behind her.

While China fights against the huntress with a magnificent bird scarification across her chest, and the blonde huntress laughs with Hattie as she swings two blades, I stand in front of a table that Sika leans against. She watches on with intrigue peppering her unique appearance while I look down at my inevitability.

There are five weapons that are set out on the table, and I have to choose one to fight against Sika with. The table, where weapons of destruction rest, is small. It allows the rest of the basement to remain open space, an ideal fighting ground.

Sika rests her hip against the edge of the table, her arms crossed over her chest, but although she is weaponless, I have little doubt in my mind she is a force on the battleground. Epiales told me all of Lady Artemis's slaves are freed upon exiting the arena with her. They are offered, not forced, to immortally tie themselves to her as a huntress of the wild. Sika looks only twenty years old, but she could be fifty or one hundred or even three hundred years old.

With the patience of an immortal, she is waiting for me to choose my weapon, but as my hands graze upon the sword, then the spear, I freeze. I know I am not human, but I want to pretend I am. Kronos and Epiales's words continue to play in my head, guiding me towards a war I want no part of, and it makes me pause in front of Sika and a row of weapons. While the rest of the room fights and trains, I want to hide.

"No, I will not allow you to be a coward." Sika's voice is tough, yet in a whisper, so that nobody else can eavesdrop. "You are more than your fears; now, choose your weapon before I decide to fight you without one."

"Why are we doing this?" I turn to face Sika, ignoring the five weapons that I could use to start a pathway to destruction. In confusion, I ask. "Why are we learning to fight?"

Sika is no longer leaning against the table with ease. No, the mighty huntress is now standing in front of me with only a breath of air in between us. She is taller than me, by at least two or three inches, and has to look down at me at this proximity.

The rest of the basement pays no attention to us, their own training paramount, but Sika still responds in a hushed voice. "Humans are always in danger, concubine. There are always monsters, gods, titans, and primordial deities stronger than us. We are nothing but ants beneath their mighty feet. At least with a blade in your hand, and skills to use it, then you have a chance. No matter how small the chance is, with training you still have one to slay those that dare to see you as easy prey."

Sika retreats, and she resumes her place against the edge of the table. She crosses her arms over her chest again, and if I weren't previously close enough to her to smell the eggs that she had this morning, then I might've doubted that she moved at all. The huntress lowers her focus onto the five weapons that I have to choose from and waits for my decision. Sika's patient and waits for me to no longer be a defenseless ant beneath mighty feet.

"What's an ant?" I turn to face her, the question slipping out before I have time to think it through.

"They're easy prey," she says. "Now, choose."

Five weapons mock me. They stare back at my cowardice with a laugh readied. "How will I know which one to pick?"

"Each god has a weapon that they are most skilled with, and it is sacred to them. Like Heracles with his club, Artemis with her bow and arrow, Poseidon with his trident, and Hermes with his *caduceus*. Their symbolic weapon strengthens them, and they become more confident with their skills upon the battleground," Sika says, while she latches onto the bow and arrow on the table. "I believe humans can have a signature weapon, too. There are few people better than I am with a bow and arrow, and it's because I chose that as my signature weapon. It's mine, and I'd dare any fool that tried to take it from me."

I look back down at the bow and arrow on the table, its size lesser than the four others around it.

"Look at these weapons and find what stands out to you," Sika orders as I stare down at the silvery objects below me. "Choose your symbolic weapon and fight me with it, concubine."

There are five weapons on this table, and each of them has a deer emblem. There is a sword, which has the symbol on the bottom hilt of the sword. Then, a spear, with the deer's head on the spearhead. A bow and arrow, which has the design across the quiver's handle, sits next to a scythe, its deer sign carved into the black handle. Last, two smaller axes sit side-by-side, with the marker across both sharp edges.

I do not have to ponder for long. Sika swore that the right weapon would stand out, and as if the sun had tilted towards it, my hands wrap around the handle. When I turn, the blade has become an extension of my arm. The tip of my sword points at Sika's head, mere inches away from the tip of her flattened nose.

Sika nods her head in approval. "One second, you feared touching any of the weapons, but now you-"

"I what?"

Sika declares. "You look like a warrior."

All of my life, I have been taught to hide beneath the shadows of the gods. I have been told that I am nothing but a human, an inconsequential and fragile blimp in the gods' fruitful endlessness. Lady Hecate raised me on the belief that I must always submit to the immortals' excellence, but as swords clank together and arrows swish through the air, I realize that there is another option.

The immortals side or Kronos's aren't the only two options. There are possibilities that do not involve serfdom or joining Kronos and the nefariousness that enshrouds him. Humans have not seen an alternative path like this in hundreds of years. All I have to do is fight for my version of freedom.

I look up towards Sika, a sword now raised in both of her hands, and I smirk. "Let's fight."

THE TWENTY-SECOND CHAPTER

We stand five feet apart, the tips of our blades towards the floor, as Sika announces. "We start on the count of three."

The background noise—the clashing of weapons between Panda and a huntress, the laughter from Pyro's lips, the exhausted grunts from China—they all dissipate into thin air. They're still existing, these noises within a capacious basement, but I can no longer hear them.

The endless repetition of Epiales's words, warning me of the danger of the gods and the need for vengeance, leaves as well. Even the wind silences in climactic anticipation of Sika's countdown. Neither one of us moves, but the slight curvature of Sika's lips tells me she's hiding a smile as excitement for battle races through her.

"One," she finally bites out, itching for her imminent victory.

Nobody in this basement is watching us, their own training garnering their fascination, but the hairs on my arms rise to attention. In my mind, I am on that arena ground, but not as a prisoner. I'm an Olympian, leaping off of the pews and slamming onto the dusted floor, readying to fight for a prize that I'd never thought achievable.

My freedom.

"Two," she says.

My fingers curl around the handle of the weapon, a resurgence of power sizzling my skin. I am not a slave within this basement, but I am Saffron. I am a warrior, a fighter, and a victor for my freedom. Epiales's words of destroying the gods vanish from my mind because whatever power I feel waking from a long slumber inside of my chest is all that I need to garner my emancipation.

"Three," is the last word Sika says before she charges towards me, a sword raised, and mayhem is the exuberant skip to her sprint.

She is speed and agility molded together into one person. Before I can raise my blade towards her, she is already swinging downward. A squeal threatens to break the surface as I duck my head, my hair nearly a victim to the might of her sword.

I stumble backwards a few steps, but Sika is approaching, her sword slicing through the air and towards where I stand. Steel smashes upon steel as I lift my weapon, stopping her from cleaving it into my neck. With all the strength that I can muster, I push her sword away with my own, and together, we take a step back.

An aberrant grin peels across her peculiar face, morphing it into one of pure terror. Then, she's running towards me again. She slashes, and I duck or block with my sword. It's a dance, I realize, similar to one Epiales and I had in my dream world. A shuffle of our feet, a precise movement of our hand, and then repeat.

Sweat dribbles down the side of my face as I circle around Sika for the third, perhaps fourth, time. The minutes and hours slip from my fingertips as I learn how to defend myself against those stronger and faster than I am. My body aches, an unfamiliar buckling of my thighs and strain of my biceps, but I welcome the sensation of pain intertwined with dedication as I look at Sika with a raised weapon.

Panda and Pyro have left already, I vaguely notice as their familiar laughter no longer fills the room, but China, Hattie, the huntresses, and I remain. I twirl the sword in my hand, looking at my opponent, as she teases me with a beckoning curl of her fingers.

"Let's see you on the offensive, concubine."

I attempt the same quickness as Sika, and I run towards her with my sword raised and my confidence inflated towards the roof. As I slash my sword, I can feel victory on my tongue. I expect my blade to nick flesh, which would declare a winner between us, but air kisses the sword, and an elbow greets my gut.

Her laughter and my dry coughs fill the air, while something within me *snaps*.

Humiliation burns my cheeks, while something otherworldly inhuman courses through my veins and demands retribution. Gold and red incinerate my vision, blinding me to rationality and mortal binds. I rise, but do not remember my actions. Beneath the golden fog, I swirl and twirl around the basement like it is my battleground.

My sword slashes through the air, but something else tugs against my chest. There are strings within Sika that I'm in control of, and when an ear piercing scream ricochets off of the walls, only then does the blindness ease and clarity come once more.

I am standing over Sika's writhing, fallen body. Her sword is on the floor, while both of her hands are gripping her left leg. I, too, stare, and nausea builds up at the sight. While she wears pants and long boots that cover her legs, the tight material does not hide what is obvious beneath.

A bone juts out of place, threatening to break through the skin and leave her body altogether. I've only seen a few bones, the sight always unpleasant whether in this basement or in the jail cells, but it's oddly placed. Almost as if it broke in half with fury.

She bellows and all the huntresses, plus China, rush towards her to help, while I stagger backwards in disbelief. My sword clatters to the ground, and I turn away from Sika's deformed leg as bile rises in my throat. It is then that I look at Hattie, who stands with her knuckles whitened as she clutches onto her weapon.

Mouth widening in fear.

She does not fear for the huntress's health, or the rest of their wrath because one of us harmed them. No, she looks at my cheek that burns in pain, and she fears me.

Especially when my cheek, split open by Sika's nails, spills two droplets of blood before healing altogether.

One red.

The other gold.

THE TWENTY-THIRD CHAPTER

Hermes flies down the staircase, his shoes' wings flapping furiously, a minute after Sika passes out from the pain. He is kneeling over her thin frame, quickly removing her boots, then cutting her leggings until the grotesque mutilation of her leg comes into view. I am trembling a few feet away, but all of us stare at the bone that threatened to break skin when Panda rushes down the stairs.

"Lunch is ready. Pyro tried something new and has made cucumber-" she stops talking as she stands on one of the middle steps of the staircase, her mouth ajar at the sight of Sika's leg. "Oh, dear Underworld, that's disgusting."

She runs back up the staircase, slamming the door behind her. A few seconds later, the far-off sounds of Panda vomiting creates noise in the quieted room.

"What happened?" Hermes looks to the huntresses inquisitively.

The tallest one, with the large black bird scarification on her chest, answers him. "We do not know. I was working with China," the huntress's eyes, nearly black in hue, look at me and squint incredulously. "Your concubine was training with her."

"Saffron," Hermes turns to me, hesitance lightening the green in his irises as he asks. "What happened?"

To admit the power that courses through my veins frightens me, I try to open my mouth. I raise my hand to my cheek and feel healed skin, while my gaze drifts to Sika's unconscious body on the ground.

There isn't a memory of touching her leg or slamming my foot against it. I remember nothing except the blinding power in my body that demanded retribution for her laughter at my expense. My mind was blinding gold, my body moving under something otherworldly inside of me I've always been too afraid to unleash.

"Sika fell on the butt of her sword after Saffron tripped her."

I turn around at the sound of the lie, and Hattie stares back. For only one second, Hattie looks to me and I no longer see the girl who has avoided and loathed me since I've arrived. I look at Hattie, and she looks at me, and we come to the mutual understanding that we are no longer on opposite sides.

Then, she looks at Hermes and elaborates. "I was training with Lamb, but I saw the whole thing. Sika did that to herself, and it was a simple mistake."

But the huntress with the blackbird on her chest frowns. "I've never once seen Sika trip, much less hit herself with her own sword."

Hattie responds without hesitation. "Then you must not be very observant, Raven. I suggest you take in your surroundings a bit more. It's an un-huntress like quality. Sika is very clumsy. It's those gangly legs of hers." She glances at the blonde huntress who she was training with, and Hattie asks. "Isn't that right, Lamb?"

Lamb, the blonde huntress, nods her head and daintily adds. "Sika's the clumsiest."

Hermes had heard enough. He slides his hands underneath Sika, who subtly stirs by the contact, and he lifts her up into his arms. Then, he looks at the woman with a black bird on her chest.

"Raven," he orders. "Grab Sika's belongings and join me in one of the guest rooms. She'll rest until Artemis comes to pick you all up." Hermes looks at the rest of us standing around the room and says. "The rest of you can enjoy the lunch that Pyro made," he dares a smirk and adds. "It seems like Sika and Panda won't be eating today, so there's plenty for everyone."

Raven, Sika, and Hermes leave while the rest of us clean up the basement. Not a single word is spoken, not as the questions live unanswered in our heads. We place the swords back into their rightful spots, along with the stray arrows, fallen quivers, and discarded spears.

Then we walk into the kitchen, where plates are ready for nine. I look at Hattie, but she purposely avoids me and glances at Lamb.

Hattie asks Lamb. "Do you think we should bring Sika and Raven their plates?"

A slight frown mars Lamb's lips. "I don't think Sika will be too hungry, but we can try."

The two women do not just take two plates. They grab four—two for the other huntresses and two of their own—before leaving the kitchen without a goodbye. I sit down, where a plate awaits me, while the sound of Panda dry heaving nearby can be heard.

My stomach is in knots, a coil of nausea and anxiety curbing any desires to eat, but the last remaining huntress—Dýnami—does not have the same lack of hunger as I do. Regardless of the sound of Panda vomiting in the distance, or that China, Pyro, and I won't touch our food, Dýnami digs in with ferocity. Dýnami doesn't just eat, but she annihilates her lunch as if it were a foe that she must thwart.

Pyro tries to pick up his food, but Panda vomits again, and he drops it and stands up. "I'm going to go check on her," and he leaves the kitchen altogether.

"His best dish," Dýnami grumbles through mouthfuls of food, but there is no response to her comment.

China looks back and forth between the closed bathroom door to the stairwell towards the guest bedroom and says nothing. She does not touch her food, or even ponder the thought of eating, much less starting a conversation to cease the thick silence encompassing the kitchen.

"I was there at the arena when you were fought for, concubine." Dýnami breaks through the quietness as she wipes her mouth with the back of her hand, and then says while displaying a row of crooked, yellowed teeth. "That was the best fight I've seen in nearly fifty years, not since my own."

She looks my age, but appearances can deceive in our world. Even an appearance as mundane as Dýnami's.

"I had five gods fighting for me," Dýnami says, then adds. "All of them were females. I set the record for the amount of gods fighting for one human in an arena before you had eight. Impressive, dude."

"Which goddesses?" I ask, breaking my fright induced silence.

"Artemis, Athena, Bia, Hygea, and Iris," Dýnami lists off the names without a single formality beforehand. She speaks their names as if they are acquaintances or equals in a world where humans are solely slaves. "They all wanted me as a soldier, except Hygea. She turns her humans into nurses for the Laborers, but I have about as much kindness and warmth as a corpse."

China and I don't laugh, but Dýnami barks out a laugh at her joke. She glances down at my untouched plate.

"Mind if I have your food?" She asks. "Fighting and talking of the past makes me hungry."

I slide the plate across the table to her, and with mouthfuls of food, she tells her story of becoming a huntress.

"They all stood there on the arena floor, weapons drawn and determination in their stance. I wanted to piss my pants," she bites into her sandwich and explains. "But I stood and watched each sweep of the sword, every trickle of blood, and all the mistakes the fallen goddesses made on the arena ground. I was fascinated, but more than that, I wanted to become like them. A tough chick with a weapon on my hip at all times."

She pauses from her story to take my glass of water, her own empty, and she chugs the entire content without a break. When she slams down the cup, she lets out a loud belch and bites into her sandwich once again.

Although she's muffled by the sandwich's bread, she explains. "Iris and Hygea were out within the first ten minutes, but the other three goddesses fought against each other for six hours. Their sweat was basically perfume in the arena near the end, but with three arrows on the same bow string, Artemis took out Athena and Bia. The first thing I asked Artie to do when I became her huntress, before she could even give me my scarification mark, was to teach me that trick with three arrows on the bowstring."

I centralize on the scarification mark on her collarbone, which is three arrows tied together with a string, and I conclude. "That's why your scarification mark is of three arrows."

"She said my question showed more strength than she's seen in a human in nearly twenty years," Dýnami takes the last bite out of my sandwich and mumbles. "My name is Greek for strength, and the arrows show why she saw strength in me."

"Oh, are we talking about our arena stories?" Panda asks, and when I turn around, her pet red panda sits on her shoulder, nibbling on the frayed ends of her orange hair. She's no longer nauseous from the sight of Sika's mutilated leg, and she sits on a seat where a plate awaits her. "Can I tell mine next?"

"Sure," Dýnami says, then looks to China's untouched plate. "Are you going to eat that?"

While Dýnami eats her third serving, Panda begins her story.

"I don't remember much about the jail cell that morning or receiving my makeover," Panda explains. "I was in such a fog of fear that I couldn't process the shift until I was standing in the middle of the arena."

Her hands tremble as she holds the unscathed sandwich in her hand. She looks to Pyro, who places his hand on top of her knee, squeezes once, and looks at her as if she holds his world in her grasp. He gives her courage to speak the truths of her past with the power of his love for her.

"I was the second to last human in the arena," she gulps as she adds. "I watched the two boys I shared a cell with leave, along with my shower-mate and every familiar face, and I was so scared. Priapus, a low-level god of fertility, came down upon the arena ground to take me. When I asked, Hermes told me later that Priapus made every human girl his toy, and because of his high fertility, his slaves are killed within six months of their servitude because they became pregnant with his children."

She flinches at her own words, but the fire from her hair transfers to her chest as ferocity possesses her petite frame.

"A demi-god," she growls the word with enough hatred to shake the floor. "It's a promised death to either birth one or be one, and Priapus plucks girls from the jail with certainty that they will become pregnant with his child and die for his own perverse desires."

"Panda, I'm so-" I start, but she shakes her head.

She doesn't let me apologize. Her words whip through the air and silence me mid-sentence. "Priapus went down with the thought that nobody else wanted me. I was the last girl in the arena, and I'm not as beautiful as most."

"That's a terrible lie," Pyro says, to which she responds by kissing him on the lips.

She continues her story. "He thought it'd be easy to take me from the arena with nobody else fighting for me, but then Hermes flew down to the arena and challenged Priapus."

There is anger in her cadence when she speaks about Priapus, but the moment Hermes's name leaves her mouth, the fury dissipates as if it never existed. Her lips relax, and the fire extinguishes.

"For a moment, as I shivered on the snowy arena ground, I thought my worst imaginations were going to become a reality. I looked at Priapus, at the way he stared at me with hunger rather than appreciation, and I saw my death with each tear that rolled down my face. I saw enslavement in each brutal detail the gods told me in the jail cells every night, but then Lord Hermes won on the arena ground."

She tears off a piece of her sandwich, but before taking a bite herself, she gives a fragment of bread to the red panda on her shoulder. The animal whines in appreciation, nibbling on the food, when she finally bites into her sandwich. Unlike Dýnami, she waits until she finishes her bite to speak.

"Hermes outwitted him in the arena, using his winged sandals to fly behind him when he wasn't looking. Priapus tripped on the arena ground and broke his nose. It was the quickest fight Hermes ever had, he said."

She actually laughs in amusement.

"I would be dead right now if Priapus won, but he didn't. Instead, Hermes did, and he let me choose my job in this house, gave me a name that I know I will keep for decades to come, and let me decide everything. With each passing morning, he defies the rules put into place, and he lets the humans living under this roof gain a glimpse of what being a free person would be like. Like how it was before the gods took over this land and enslaved us." Panda takes another bite of her sandwich, then looks at Pyro. With bread stuck between her two gaped front teeth, she says. "It's your turn, honey."

We each take a turn.

I think Dýnami told her story to break the basement's uncomfortable tension, but the origins of our conversation shifted into a chance to turn a terrifying day into a transformative moment. The stories all start with the fear of becoming property, less than human, but they always end with the gratefulness to be under Lady Artemis or Hermes's care.

Pyro explains how Lady Hecate and Lady Eris, who is the goddess of chaos and strife, were both fascinated by his red eyes that they wanted to win him in the arena. Yet, Hermes saw the oddity and knew that he would become less than a human, and she fought for him in the arena. Hermes gifted him with the name Pyro to show him the power of being individualized.

China's story is brief. Perhaps, because of her older age, she doesn't remember the day as vividly as the rest at this table, or hers was not as spectacularly significant as Dýnami and mine.

Regardless, China vaguely says. "Lord Momus jumped down first, and when it looked like nobody was going to fight him, Lord Hermes joined him and won. It was a quick fight, and he named me after a China doll."

"What's a China doll?" I ask.

China's eyes drift to the past, when she was a young slave in this house, but her words are brisk and unspecific. "Just some toy before the titans ejected the immortals from Mt. Olympus and overran Earth."

"Why did he name you after a toy?" Panda asks, but China shakes her head and does not answer.

By the time Dýnami has finished Pyro's plate of food, Lamb has come back to the kitchen with four empty plates.

"Aye, Lamb," Dýnami yells out, an effervescent smile blooming over her tawny complexion. "Tell us your arena story. Let's hear about how to second oldest huntress in our regime was won."

Lamb, the demurest huntress amongst the four, blushes a bright shade of red and responds in her quieted cadence. "Maybe another time," she looks at Pyro and asks. "Do you want me to clean the dishes?"

He responds. "I've got it, Lamb. Thank you, though."

Lamb walks over to the kitchen sink, and I follow her. I pick up everybody's finished plates, earning mumbled thank you's from all of them, and I walk towards Lamb. Everybody talks amongst themselves in the background, laughing and oblivious to the fear that coats my words as I stand in front of Lamb.

"Is Hattie coming back downstairs?" I ask.

Lamb sets the plates in the sink, then turns to face me. "Hermes said he wanted to speak with you. He said to meet him in his bedroom whenever you finished lunch."

My heart is hammering a thousand times at its normal speed, and while I try to find the ability to reiterate my question to Lamb, she steps around me and leaves without another word. Hattie covered for me in the basement, lying to Hermes when she did not have to, but my luck could slip from my grasp. The detested truth of my blood, and the power I hide within me, could come to light.

Each movement towards Hermes's room is slowed and sluggish. Previously, our time together sparks excitement and joy, but today I am anxious as I reach the steps. Every time my own feet hitting the floor reaches my ears, I think of Sika. I can hear her screams in my head, threatening to deafen me with the truth of who I am.

Demi-god, Panda had spit out the word with disgust. *It's a promised death to either birth one or be one.*

I stand in front of Hermes's closed bedroom door, and I flutter back towards that large vein on my forearm. The thin, almost non-existent, lines of gold within the blue mockingly stare back at me. They're laughing, this sliver of gilded proof that I am not equal to those conversing in the kitchen, but I'm less than the god who waits for me inside his bedroom.

Epiales once told me that demi-gods were the fearless creations of the gods throughout ancient history. Demi-gods had the greatest tales derived from their heroism and bravery. I swore his shadows were comforting me when he explained that demi-gods were killed in this new, repugnant world because the immortals feared the day that humans prayed to the halflings instead of them.

After all, my queen, Epiales, whispered that night. *Gods are nothing without the humans' prayers.*

The bedroom door opens, but not by my hands. Hermes towers over me, well over a foot taller than my smaller form, but he does not hold a weapon to prepare for my execution. He does not have anger in his forest irises or a malicious scowl on his lips.

Instead, he holds up our Monopoly pieces and asks. "Do you have time for a game or two?"

THE TWENTY-FOURTH CHAPTER

I've passed go twice when I garner the courage to ask. "How is Sika?"

He rolls the dice, watches it land on a two, and then answers while moving his piece to its new destination. "She will be fine. Artemis is taking her to Asclepius, so she should be good as new in a few days. He has medicine that'll expedite the healing process."

"Asclepius is the god of medicine, right?" I pick up the dice, but not before seeing the small smirk growing on Hermes's lips.

"Correct. Did China teach you that already?"

"Yeah," my lie is quiet, but he can still hear it. I move my shoe forward six boxes, humming each number as I go. When I land on the box with the blue top border, I ask. "What does this say?"

"Park Place," he answers. "And it's three hundred and fifty dollars."

"What color money do I need?"

He helps me count each dollar bill I place in the palm of my hand. I sometimes get confused if seven or eight go first on the count, but Hermes helps me with no semblance of judgement.

Regardless of today and its atrocities, I still smile when I count three hundred and fifty dollars, moving the small stack from my hand to his.

"You're getting better with the money," he says, and whether or not he's lying, my body warms with a newfound flutter in my chest. "What else has China taught you since I last saw you?"

"I know half the alphabet," I answer while he shuffles the dice in his hands. "Or at least, I'm pretty sure I do. I get a little tripped up near the end."

He stops shuffling the dice. My focus shifts from the dice to his face and it illuminates with joy. I stare at him as he looks at me with an expression on his face that bursts with pride for me. My achievement is minor, but I realize his happiness is my favorite sight in this world.

"Really?" A joyous laugh escapes from his lips. "That's incredible. Can I hear it?" He is quick to add. "If you mess up near the end, then I'm here to help."

"Are you sure?" I ask. "But we're playing Monopoly."

"I don't care about Monopoly, I care about you… learning the alphabet."

For a moment, I thought he was just going to say the first part of this sentence. That he only cares about me, a defect who should not exist in this world. I do not know why, but I wanted to hear that more than I've wanted to hear any other words in the world.

"Okay, I might go a little slow at first. We've only been working on it for two days now," I sheepishly admit, a newfound burning growing on my cheeks.

"I'm sure it's going to be the greatest version of the alphabet I'll ever hear," is his immediate, genuine response.

I take a deep breath, and the first letter slips from my lips. Then the one after that. I close my eyes near the middle, trying to imagine the letters China had me trace on the piece of paper. I fumble between H and I, but when I reach the letter M, I want to scream and cry and leap around the room with pride.

When I open them, Hermes is staring at me as if I were a victory wreath placed around his head like a crown. His smile is wild and authentic, while I stare at him with nervousness in my chest.

"Well?" I inquire with timidness. "I did it correct. Right?"

"Like I said, it was the best version of the alphabet that I've ever heard."

My smile soon matches his, while my cheeks burn bright. "That wasn't even the entire alphabet."

"When you learn that, my heart might cease beating," he jokes, but the humor slides off his face when he murmurs. "I was meaning to ask you about the basement. Are you okay? I'm sure her tripping and hurting herself was scary for you."

I can hear the cracking of her bones, the screams that left her lips and rattled the swinging ceiling lights. The fear in Hattie when she saw the multi-colored truth still eats away at my chest, while the paranoia that at any second, she could divulge the ghastly truth of my identity makes each second coveted and excruciating at the same time.

"I don't want to talk about what happened downstairs," I stare at my Monopoly piece, the lonely shoe on Park Place, and I ponder aloud. "Can I ask you a question?"

"Anything," he replies without hesitation.

I still stare at the lonely shoe as I inquire. "If I weren't what you expected, then will you kick me out of this mansion? I know that I'm scarified now and technically yours, but if I weren't what you wanted, then-"

"Saffron," he cuts me off and implores. "Can you please look up at me?"

His eyes are the depth of the forest, where thousands of trees thrive. They're endless, the pools of green, and if I stare for too long, then I could become lost in the thickets. He looks at me with the same rapt fascination, mesmerized by what he sees, yet frightened that at any moment he'll be stuck in the whorls forever.

"Have I ever told you what a pinky promise is?" He asks.

I shake my head.

"They're the most sacred of all promises, except for the River Styx. The River Styx is spawned from dangerous promises, but this," he motions to his now outstretched pinky, and elaborates. "This is the safest, yet truest, promise that anybody could make to one another." He uses his free hand to lift one of mine off of the table, opening my pinky with a curled fist and wrapping his around mine. Then he swears. "I pinky promise you I will always want you in any capacity that I can have you, from today until my last breath."

With our pinkies still intertwined, I add with a crack in my cadence. "Regardless of anything?"

I think of my golden blood, and the execution that would be inevitable if any gods discovered the truth, when he nods his head.

"You could sprout a lion's tail tomorrow, and I'd still want you here. Whatever version I receive, you will always be perfect. I promise."

For good measure, he squeezes our pinkies tight together.

He waits until I pull my pinky from his before he places his hand around the dice to our game. Only as he shakes the dice again, I admit. "I really like being your friend."

"I like being yours, too," he responds.

Our game of Monopoly is filled with more laughter, too. He tells me of the pranks he's pulled on his family members throughout the eons, and I read the letters of the alphabet I recognize on the Monopoly game each time I land on a new box.

Tonight, I realize the button of his nose crinkles when he yawns, and when I told him of my discovery, he said that I sometimes snort when I'm laughing too hard.

Then, he asks. "What is something I don't know about you, Saffron?"

The color of my blood comes to my mind, but I silence the roaring thoughts.

Instead, I confess. "I lost a friend once, too."

"Excuse me?" Hermes looks up, his confusion clear with a crinkle between his brows.

"The night of my scarification, you told me you named me after a friend who died during a game of discus," I explain. While he stares at me with curiosity, I keep my gaze on the board game. I can't bring myself to stare at him as I divulge one of the worst days of my life. "I lost a friend, too."

"The boy in the arena I tried to fight for?" Hermes asks, but I shake my head.

"I suppose, in a way, I've lost him too, but no. This was a friend I lost when we lived in the prisons together."

He is quiet for a while, then he asks. "How? Humans are protected in the prisons. Forbidden to die."

"Just because we're forbidden to die does not mean we are protected, Hermes. My friend did not die, but I still lost him that night. I may not know much about the world, but I know that a mind can die when a heart still beats."

"What happened to him?" Hermes asks.

Our game of Monopoly is paused, and he is staring at me with too much focus. I keep my gaze on the game, but my mind is elsewhere. It spirals back to a time when I was too young to understand the dark gravity of my world and the toll it has on a person's mind.

I begin my story. "When I was eight, there was a boy in my cell who helped raise me. He and a girl with blonde hair were the closest things to parents I've ever had. They were around the same age, too. Both two years shy of going into the arena, and each day they grew older, the boy became sadder. I didn't understand at the time why he was sad, but I quickly realized on one fateful night."

There is no other sound in the room but my voice. Panda's raucous laughter from downstairs has muted, and birds have quieted from outside Lord Hermes's bedroom window. We are doused in the silence so each word I speak is heard with perfection.

"The boy in my cell wanted to die, and one night he began smashing his head against the brick wall with aspirations of death. Rich, red blood splattered the floor, sprinkling across my toes as I laid two feet away. I should've run to him, to stop him, but the sight of seeing blood for the first time paralyzed me. Looking back now, I wish I had sprinted to him, but not to save a life desecrated in trauma. No, if I could change time, then I would've helped him end his anguish, but I didn't."

"What happened to him?" Hermes asks, his voice softer than usual.

I answer. "A mere second before he could end his suffering with the last assault, Lady Hecate materialized and snapped her fingers. Green smoke surrounded the boy, and when she and her magic disappeared a minute later, he was outwardly unscathed. While Lady Hecate healed all physical wounds, she destroyed him worse in the mental capacity. Because of her, he cried himself to sleep every night until they took him to the arenas."

Hermes is quiet for a while until he whispers. "I'm sorry about your friend."

"Thanks," is my weak response.

"I understand why you hate the gods," he admits. "But can I ask a favor of you? I have no right to ask, especially after that story, but I'm still going to ask."

"What's the favor?" I question, and I look up at his boyish face.

"No matter what, please don't add me to the list of gods you hate. I don't think my heart could handle it."

I mull over his words, then extend my pinky. "I promise," I say.

His pinky wraps around mine in an unwavering vow.

We eat dinner in his bedroom, along with a few glasses of red wine, and we laugh and talk the entire time. Night drifts in like a cool winter breeze and fatigue weighs heavier on me with each roll of the dice. The rest of the house quiets, sleep enrapturing the rest of the occupants, and my body obeys its wishes.

I move to a lying position, my head comfortable upon Hermes's feathery pillows, while we play the longest round of Monopoly. Then, at some point, my lids drift closed. He doesn't stop me, but I can hear the shuffling of his feet as he cleans up the game.

The last thing I feel before sleep claims me are his hands wrapping a blanket over my body and a pair of lips pressing a ginger kiss on the top of my head.

THE TWENTY-FIFTH CHAPTER

I am not in the Underworld, surrounded by wisps of shadows and two onyx thrones.

Clouds gingerly kiss the soles of my feet as I stand in the epicenter of excellence. White opulence, accentuated by golden trim and the beating sun, set this land of gilded piety apart from any creation on Earth's soil. I know, without uncertainties, that I am on Mt. Olympus, and the owner of this dream world is not my storyteller.

The ticking of three individual clocks, set on different intervals, warns me of the deity responsible for my arrival.

Glittering lights illuminate the land of the gods, where clouds are on the floor and magnificence exudes the expanse. My feet tread on preeminent glory, but then I see the titan, who freezes my blood to ice, leaning against an alabaster column. Kronos is drenched in the purity of a white tunic, but I see his truth. He is the dark stain on the rest of this land's beauty.

I was in a pair of leggings when I went to bed, and a shirt that was two sizes too large, but Kronos transforms me to his own preferences. A black gown stops at the middle of my thigh, and it clings to my skin. The material is thick and smooth to the touch, but the straps are cold and glimmering underneath the sun's rays.

My mind screams at me to run from the titan, who Epiales trusts for his own freedom. With instinctual foreboding, my body disobeys my mind's one request. My bare feet advance towards Kronos, who leans against the column with utmost certainty that I will come to his beckoning. I try to slam my heels against the clouds, to deter my movement towards him, but a magnitude of foreign power crashes into my chest and demands obedience.

The ticking of the clocks around his wrists grows louder with my nearing proximity, and I want to fight him. Fight this helplessness that claws at my throat and chains me to his forced company. My thoughts scream at me to find the same surge of power I had in the basement this morning and use to it to thwart Kronos, but it's futile in a land that does not exist.

When I'm at arm's length, our feet almost touching, Kronos holds up his hand and I am forced to come to a complete halt. "How am I here?" *I bite out the question to hide my fear and replace it with ire, but my words tremor with the truth.*

"Do you like the gown?" *He asks, and I hate how his attention moves from the waves he added to my hair to the tight gown that makes me feel as naked as I was in the jail cells.* "The diamonds on the straps are real."

"We're in a dream. It didn't cost you anything in your failed attempt at flattering me," *I snap back.*

"I was hoping for a bit of appreciation. I've spent almost two decades waiting for this moment. Do not make it anticlimactic for me, dear girl."

"How am I here?" *I echo once more, all the while ignoring the way his focus meanders from my lips to the deep cut of my black gown.*

He moves to my lips again and murmurs. "Epiales is not the only immortal desperate for my help and gifted with dreams. Although, it was Epiales who found the one treasure I asked of him."

"That's what I am to you?" I inquire, with unmistakable anger in my voice. "A treasure that you've found?"

His power within this dreamworld brings me a step closer to him. I can smell the waft of his essence, a combination of copper and cinnamon, as it swirls around the both of us like rope keeping us together. I glare up at him while his fascination remains on my scowled lips.

"The greatest treasure the Fates could ever find," he susurrates, but when he tries to lift his hand up to touch me, I smack it away. This only insights a laugh that disquiets the clouds between us. "I've imagined this moment a thousand times since I realized you existed, but I've been gifted only with disdain. Why?"

He cocks his head, feigning confusion, but I do not trust a single breath that he does not need to breathe.

"Why not?" I counteract.

"Epiales has never spoken ill of me, and he was your only access to information for two years, while my informants in Hermes's home tell me you haven't learned a single thing about me either. Yet, you stand before me without knowing me, and you've already condemned me. Why?"

Fighting him is futile in this dream world, not with swords or the foreign power that surges through my body, and I cannot run. My feet stay planted upon the ground of clouds, unable to waver without his permission. I stare at Kronos, and my mind cautions me to stay far from him.

I answer his question with honesty. "My entire life, I grew up in the prisons and learned that the gods are evil incarnate, and they will be my death. But I've met several gods and goddesses and none of them has incited such fear in me as I get when I stare at you. You say the pleasant lies, and your smile could lead any man or woman into blind obedience, but I know you're the one to fear. My blood turns to ice in your presence, and I know it is because you're the villain to each human's story in a way worse than any god or goddess who enslaves them."

I expect fury in response to my truth. I expect roars of ire to spew out of him, to break the silence, but my expectations for Kronos never come to fruition. He allows the world to silence around us, with only the three individual ticks of his clocks as company. Kronos no longer stares at my lips with hunger. He draws them to my brown eyes for the first time since I entered Mt. Olympus.

And he delivers the cruelest grin I've ever witnessed.

He kicks himself off of the column he leans against, and the scene around us changes. We are no longer surrounded by ornate supremacy, but truism seeps through the exterior like a thicket of fog. The authenticity of his soul erupts from his chest, and Mt. Olympus becomes shrouded in a rusted shade of gold that nears brown. The clouds turn black beneath my feet, the columns crumble to the ground. Debris kicks off into the air, burning me with cruel factualness, and before I grasp my new surroundings, Kronos's hand is around my throat.

The ticking of his watches pounds against my ear, screaming into my eardrums until they bleed both red and gold. Colosseums decompose like deceased bodies, and they drop around us in a circle of agony. His fingers tighten around my throat, but he doesn't break my airway. He applies just enough pressure to enliven my fear and remind me who is most powerful.

Kronos thrives off of pain and hates defiance, but he needs me alive. More than that, he needs me scared enough to comply.

He holds me with my head tilted upwards and our lips a breath apart, then he reveals. "You're right, my dear treasure. I'm the villain in every story ever concocted. Every sinister thought that went through a person's mind is derived from my words and actions. I am the destruction that crumbles cities and worlds. I am the titan of time and, therefore, life itself. You have every right to instinctually fear me because I am the manifestation of terror, and while my plan was for you to see the gorgeous face and perfect words and see them as the truth, I'm fine with having you see the monster that I am but have no choice but to obey."

"You might have tricked Epiales, but I am not so easily fooled," I gasp the words.

His hand stays wrapped around my throat, squeezing enough to still supply airflow but show his power in his dreamworld. He wants me to know that he is stronger than me, but his words contradict his actions. With his hand around my throat, I am the weak one; yet, when he calls me his treasure and weapon, I am the strength that he is incapable of possessing. The strength that can take down an immortal.

"Whatever you expect from me," I sneer with an inch of that power. "I will never do. I will be your ruination, not your salvation."

"You will not be my salvation." His thumb slides across the center of my throat as his bottom lip grazes mine. "You will be my weapon that I wield to destroy all the gods once and for all. The power living in your veins will be the last tool I need at my disposal to eliminate the children I never should've let enter this world. The gods will crumble, and you'll be their demise."

I push both of my hands against his chest, and I'm separated from him solely because he allows it. His glare threatens to smite me down, to turn me into nothingness, but then he gives me that wicked grin one last time. I stagger backwards, avoiding the carnage he manifests, but before I can tip over the clouds of Mt. Olympus and return to the waking world, he has one last parting sentence.

"Until the day we meet in person, my treasured god-killer."

THE TWENTY-SIXTH CHAPTER

I sit up in the bed and reach for my throat in frightened readiness for tenderness. Yet, my unscathed neck is smooth against my touch. I run my fingers across my throat, waiting for bruises to bubble to the surface, but all that remains from my dream is deliriousness.

I can still hear the sounds from my dream: from the crumbling of the columns; to the ticks of each clock around Kronos's wrist; to the words of enmity leaving his lips with the same rough accuracy as the fallen debris.

The gods will crumble, and you'll be their demise.

The bedroom door springs open without a knock, and I drop my hand and stare awestricken at the intruder. Hattie stands in the doorway, a folded set of sheets in her arms, but when she sees me cowering in bed, confusion crinkles her dark brows. She says nothing to me, but the droplets of blood from the basement floor are replaying in both of our minds.

We're both frozen in uncertainty.

"Why are you in Hermes's bedroom?" She asks, breaking the thorny silence.

"I am?" is my immediate response, then I see the fluffy, white blanket around my body that isn't in my bedroom, and I quip. "Oh Gods, I am in Hermes's bed. I slept in his room last night. Oh Gods."

I fling the blanket off of me, eager to leave the bed I found myself comforted by last night, but stickiness clings to my inner legs and stops me from leaving. With the blankets now flown off of me, I glance at the stickiness, and fear paralyzes me.

A large pool of blood sits in between my legs, the colors unmistakable. Crimson red makes a circle around the place in between my legs, but there are sprinkles of gold throughout. The abundant truth of my deformity is the wedge between her and I.

"Oh my Gods, I'm dying. He's making me bleed to death," I gasp as I search my thighs for any wounds.

I do not remember Kronos touching my thighs in Mt. Olympus, but perhaps that was his plan. To distract me in the dream world so that he could bleed me out while I slept in Hermes's bed. Tears build up as I'm unable to find the source behind all the blood that stains his once white sheets.

"You're not dying," Hattie says, now beside me.

She is frozen in disbelief as she stares down at the solidifying proof of what she saw downstairs yesterday. Her dark, monolid eyes stare at the proof once more, and as I bleed to death on Hermes's sheets, she stares in mortified realization that she saw two different colored blood yesterday.

"Please don't let me die." The words seep out of my lips in the midst of sobs and confusion.

Hattie pulls her gaze away from the sheets, then back at me. "You will not die," she extends a hand for me. "You're just having your period. Let me help you."

I take her hand, but as she helps me up, I ask. "I thought you hated me. Why are you helping me?" Neither one of us looks at the blood on the sheets, but I say. "My existence could get me executed. You could finally get rid of me, but you keep helping me. Why?"

Hattie presses her lips together. An inner battle rages in Hattie's mind as we sit in front of the blood-soaked bed, with my life resting in her hands. Shattered breaths fill the silence of the room, and just when I'm certain she will not answer my question, she walks me towards the bathroom door inside his bedroom.

"I didn't know why you were so special to him." She is both smaller and skinnier than me, but she takes most of my weight as my mind dizzies with the heaviness of my blood loss. Hattie guides me towards the bathroom and explains. "One day, we were all equals underneath Hermes's house, and the next, you're stolen from another god and you're everything. You're the one he comes home to see. You're the reason we aren't getting intensive studies like we used to. The rest of us work, but you have no job at all within this house except to play board games with him. We were all once coveted by him, but now you're his everything and we're just humans."

She opens the bathroom door, and we walk inside. She is careful with me, lifting the top of the toilet and setting me down on top of it. Then, she's rummaging through the bathroom cabinets until she produces a white cloth.

Hattie informs. "When we were in the prisons, the goddesses in charge of the prison cells took away human girls' fertility. So on the slight chance we could have relations with another human, none of us would get pregnant. The moment we leave the arena, our fertility returns, and with it is a thing called periods. It's a lot to explain to you right now, but girls bleed once every month. It's normal."

I look at my ruined leggings, sticky with blood, and I ask. "So, I'm not dying?"

She lets out a breathless laugh, which is the closest to amusement she's ever had with me, and shakes her raven locks. "No, you're not dying. Now, get out of those clothes and take a shower. When you get out, those sheets and leggings will be hidden from anybody else, and I'll teach you how to put on a pad."

"A pad?"

"Laborers not only produce children but other supplies the gods desire." Hattie explains. "After the modern world was overrun by the gods, the gods decided that males and unpregnant female Laborers would work in factories to create some of their favorite items. It's why we have these things called pads, which stop the period blood from going everywhere."

"Oh," I rise to my feet, and Hattie turns to leave the bathroom. Yet, before she does, I say. "I have one more question."

She turns to face me again. "Yeah?"

"I get why you hated me, but why don't you still?"

"Because I didn't know why you were so special to him before, but now I do," Hattie opens the bathroom door and says before departing. "I'll be waiting for you out here. Hermes shouldn't be back home until late tonight."

"Thank you, Hattie."

She nods her head and leaves the room.

I let the shower beat down upon my skin, the water scolding hot to ignore the thoughts pounding against my head with the brutality of a thousand cudgels. The same four words filter through my mind, neither term comforting to the longevity of my life nor the anonymity of my secrets.

Demi-god, whispers in my ear from the left.

God-Killer, whispers in my ear from the right.

My pale flesh threatens to break as I scrub my body until every trace of my golden blood is gone. I try to clean off every part of me that isn't human, anything Kronos could want as his weapon to wield to his own desires. I try to rub at that large vein on my arm that shows me the golden lines of my divinity, but nothing ebbs away with the soap and the water.

When the shower turns cold as ice and I turn it off, I am still the same demi-god; the one destined to kill. No amount of showering can diverge me from who I'm destined to become. Except, now I do not have my blood as visible for others to condemn me for.

Just as she promised, when I leave the bathroom with a towel tight around my body, Hattie is still there. She's sitting on the edge of Hermes's bed, where new white sheets replace the ones I destroyed, and the former are gone. In one hand, she holds a pair of underpants, and in the other she holds the pad that she took from the bathroom cabinet.

We glance at each other from across the bedroom.

"Why are you holding my underwear?" I ask.

While at first, she is teaching me about how to use a pad and the commonality of periods, it drifts to more than that as time progresses. The same laughter she had with Lamb is now directed my way, and somehow, we've found ourselves in my bedroom with her putting my hair into two twin buns surrounded by thin, intricate braids and she's telling me about the time she singed off Pyro's brows.

"I told him I couldn't help in the kitchen, and I'd mess up somehow," she says in between bits of laughter. "But he didn't listen and the next thing I know, I blew up the chicken on the pan and the fire went straight for his face."

I can barely breathe, much less stay still as she does my hair, while I'm imagining Pyro's expression as the fire swarmed towards him like their meal of choice.

"So, was it both of them or just one?" I ask, to which she chuckles louder.

"That's the best part. It was one and a half." She explains with joy evident. "One was completely gone, but the other one was only the front part. He looked demented, and of course Aphrodite came to our house the next day and nearly passed out in fear over the sight of Pyro. Can you imagine walking in and seeing his goofy face with those beady red eyes and only half of a pointed brow?"

"Oh my Gods," I wheeze out, now clutching my chest. "I never thought I'd say this, but poor Aphrodite." From the mirror's reflection, I can see Hattie's laughter leaving and an unfamiliar expression illuminating her face. "What?"

"It's the first time you've said a god's name, other than Hermes, without their formalities." She looks back down to my hair that she's braiding as she adds. "I guess all it took was for you to think you were bleeding to death to realize that you don't have to use formalities anymore."

"I guess there are bigger things to deal with right now than adding the word lady in front of a goddess's name."

"Like the fact that you think Hermes wants to kill you," Hattie adds.

"What? I don't think he wants to kill me."

It's her turn to frown, even as she continues to braid my hair. "When you first saw your blood, you cried that he tried to kill you. If it wasn't Hermes, then who were you talking about?" She snorts and asks. "Was it Pyro? You can be honest. Pyro is terrifying the first time you see him."

Kronos's scent wafts back into my mind. That distinct smell of copper and cinnamon makes bile rise to my throat. I shake away my thoughts with urgency, but they do not waver. I'm reminded that Kronos is out there and waiting for the moment I fall asleep, so he can terrorize me with threat-laced promises of using me as his weapon. His sinister words do not cease, no matter how desperately I want to forget for a little while longer.

I look at Hattie through the mirror's reflection and am quick to lie. "I was in a crazed state, and I thought it was Ares. When I calmed down, I remembered Hermes has that protection spell against any god who has killed slaves, so I don't know what I was thinking."

She presses her lips against each other again, in deep thought. I know she doesn't believe me. Hattie has this innate ability to read through a person's lies, to look into a person's soul and tell if they are telling the truth or hiding from their own secrets with deceit. She sees me and knows I haven't been honest.

Yet, she doesn't say anything.

"China should be in the kitchen waiting for you for your training, and she hates when people are late. Which you are, by a lot."

Hattie steps away, my hair finished, and I look back at her with gratitude. "Thank you," I say. "Not just for the hair, but for everything."

"My favorite stories Hermes has taught us were about demigods. I'm excited to see what stories you create along the way."

She's almost to the door when I ask. "Where did you put the sheets, anyway?" I snort as I add. "Did you burn them like Pyro's brows?"

Hattie laughs but shakes her head. "No, I just put them inside Hermes's dresser. I'm sure he can take them and throw them into the depths of Tartarus or something. They'll never be found down there."

She opens the bedroom door, but I exclaim. "You need to get them out of there now."

"Why?" she asks, once again shutting the door and turning to face me.

"Hermes doesn't know, just you."

And Kronos, Ares, and Epiales, I think in my head, but never dare say out loud.

"Yes, he does," she counteracts without hesitation. "He saw you bleed when you were given your scarification mark."

This time, I frown and shake my head. "No, he said I didn't bleed. It's some new needle or something. He said Hephaestus made it so that it wouldn't heal on immortal skin and wouldn't puncture it, either."

"Wow," Hattie draws out her disbelief as she scoffs. "The first part is true. The scarification mark will never heal because of some type of ink that Hephaestus made to track us, but it still bleeds. It's a needle, it absolutely bleeds."

My heart slams to a complete stop.

"So, Hermes knows," I conclude.

"And he doesn't want you to know that he knows." Hattie opens the bedroom door again and as she walks out of my room, she quips. "Good luck with that."

THE TWENTY-SEVENTH CHAPTER

"This is the letter S," China explains as I trace her scribe for the fifth time. "It goes after the letter r and it's the first letter in your name."

When I'm learning my letters with China, it's the only time of day when I do not think of anything else.

I realize with a spurt of awe. "I can spell my name now?"

China nods her head and prompts. "Yes, do you want to try?"

Excitedly, I nod my head, but she drifts away from where I sit across from her. She looks behind me, and when I turn my head, Hermes is leaning against the kitchen doorway. He's watching the two of us, flickering from the paper covered with the alphabet, and then the pen in my hand.

He looks at peace, his arms crossed over his chest and untidy wisps of brown locks fallen across his forehead. His messenger satchel, which is more often strapped around his shoulder than off, is absent, along with his feathered sandals. There is no sign he is working today, although a day off for him is as preposterous as a human free of their servitude.

"Good morning, girls."

"Morning, Lord Hermes," China responds, but I remain silent.

"Do you mind if I borrow your pupil for a few minutes?" Hermes asks China.

"But I want to learn how to spell my name," I murmur, but I speak too quietly and only China hears me.

China replies. "Of course you may," then she looks to me. "We'll start with spelling your name first thing tomorrow morning."

"Promise?" I ask, my pinky outstretched, and China's normally unflappable expression cracks like a hammer upon glass.

Her expression softens, her lips slacken, and she wraps her pinky around my own, and vows. "I promise."

My smile is bright, but as I rise to my feet and let our pinkies pull apart, the giddiness dissipates because I look to Hermes, and I hear Hattie's words. I stare at Hermes, whose head skims the top of the doorway, and I want to scream at him. I want to open my mouth and let every secret tied around us to cut away.

But I don't say a word.

I walk over to Hermes, and I let him obliviously look down at me as if I were just his human concubine and he were my kind master. "I have a surprise for you," he says, his elation elevating his cadence as he holds out his hand. "Let's go."

His hand is much larger than mine, nearly twice in size, and as I place mine within his, it disappears from sight. His long, thin fingers curl around mine, and he pulls me towards the double glass doors at the end of the kitchen, which leads outside to the backyard.

Rich fragrance from the multitude of flowers blooming and thriving in the expansive garden is nearly overpowering. Yet, when the sunlight gifts its radiance upon the tips of the flowers and the white gazebo in the center of this backyard, it is impossible to deviate away. I've seen the regal darkness of the Underworld's throne room, the excellence of alabaster gild upon Mt. Olympus, but I stare at the boundless array of multi-colored flowers and there is nothing in this world that is more gorgeous.

Panda waves to Hermes and me as we walk towards the gazebo, her white elbows darkened with dirt and arduous work, yet the pride she has in her gardening is evident from over a hundred feet away. Pyro stands beside his soulmate, watching with fascination and enamor while she plucks dead petals from otherwise vibrant flowers and waters each square inch of soil. Their love, even from far away, is the second brightest note to this splendorous garden.

Hermes leads me up the two steps, decorated with purple petals, into the gazebo. The few times I've been to the gazebo, there's been a table inside, with two chairs that Panda and Pyro sit at each evening for dinner. Today is different; there is emptiness and fallen purple petals. Hermes leads me into the middle, my hand still coiled in his, and slows us to a stop.

Hermes—a god created eons ago with endless powers upon his disposal—looks down at me with a small portion of his bottom lip caught underneath his teeth. His gaze moves from my face, then to the flowers on the ground, and to the circular lights hanging from the ceiling. His fixation does not stay in the same place for more than a few seconds, and the realization brings laughter to my lips.

Hermes watches me as the joyous sound escapes my lips and evaporates any other thought, and he finally asks. "Why are you laughing?"

"You're an immortal, who has seen everything in this world that I could only dream of, but you're scared right now." Once my laugh dissolves, a relaxed smile remains as I retort. "You must've faced more terrifying things than standing here with me."

He falters, the captured portion of his bottom lip slipping from his teeth. "I may be much older than you, but there are many things that I still fear, and you're one of them."

"Me?" I inquire, but I drift to that damn vein on my arm and the proof we both know but refuse to acknowledge.

The secret is pressing against my closed lips, demanding freedom from its confinement, but before I can confess the truth, he breaks the momentary silence and says. "Yes, you. I don't think I've ever been so nervous about asking a girl on a date in all the eons I've existed."

I look at his bare, wingless sandals. "A date?" I sputter out the word. "Like the food Pyro had me try yesterday?" I scrunch up my nose at the thought. "I didn't like them that much. They're not as bad as syrup, but they're not great."

When Hermes lets out a breath, it's one filled with amusement. Forest eyes glimmer with entertainment as he explains. "No, there are two different dates. One is the food, but the other is when two people interested in each other romantically spend an evening together. Like how Panda and Pyro spend dinner out here together each night, that's a date."

"Oh," I say, but then I realize the question he asks me, and once more I reiterate with emphasis. "*Oh.*"

"I'm not asking you to eat food that you don't like, by the way." Hermes's voice is laced with humor as he says. "I'm asking you to come to a symposium with me at Dionysus's house next week as my date."

"The romantic one, not the food one?" I double check.

He laughs once again, but this time nods his head. "The romantic one, yes," there is only a beat of silence between us, but he uses this time to elaborate. "It's the five hundredth year since we arrived on Earth, and Dionysus believes celebration is essential instead of mourning what we've lost. My nephew, Eros, and his wife will come over the day of to ride on the chariot with us, but if you do not want to go, then all you have to do is tell me and I'll understand. Few gods bring their concubines as dates, so I get it if you-"

"You're rambling, Hermes," I mention with slight hilarity.

He lets out a sigh. "I am, aren't I?" Nervousness pulls out a laugh, and he bites onto that small corner of his bottom lip again. "So?" He asks. "Will you go with me, Saffron?"

"Will Ares be there?" I ask, hating the wobbliness of my voice.

The previous time I saw the god of war reemerge in my mind; his face burning with rage, lips snarled in disgust, and his blade glinted with my blood. The thought of Ares destroys the tentative balance between my sanity and hysteria.

With the image of Ares poisoning my thoughts, the terse night he and I shared returns, too. The tales of a broken man frightened of the possibility of cherishing another, the tip of a blade against my heart that he feared would beat for him, and the moment his knife bled gold and we realized I was not mundane.

I try to forget I'm an anomaly, a creature not meant to exist in this world of serfdom and chaos, but everything reminds me I'm neither a god nor a human. The mention of Ares's name, of seeing him again, is one of a multitude of truth-ridden tokens I've collected over the past week.

Hermes's hand slips from mine, the coldness of its absence reminding me too much of the cool touch of the cell bars. Only a moment later, warmth replaces the chill. Both of his hands cup my face, tilting my head back to stare into Hermes's kindness.

"Yes, Ares will be there, but there's a reason Eros and Psyche are riding with us." As Hermes talks, my immersion shifts to one of his thumbs that skims the side of my cheek with such gentleness. "Eros has arrows with powers. Has China taught you about them at all?"

"No."

Epiales didn't tell me about the arrows, either.

"Eros has two types of arrows he plans to use against Ares that night. One of them, when he shoots Ares, will make him fall madly in love with the first person who he sees. The lead arrow, however, will make him fill with rage at the first person who he sees," Hermes explains. "Eros will shoot Ares with the love arrow when he's around some water nymphs or Aphrodite. He'll be so blinded by affection that he won't even realize you're there. If you want to go, that is."

"He won't speak to me?" I ask, but that isn't the crucial question circulating through my head.

Will Ares tell others about me? Will he tell the truth about my blood and condemn me to death? These questions remain unspoken.

"I won't let him get the chance," Hermes swears. "I promise. Will you come with me, Saffron?"

He drops one of his hands from my face to extend a pinky. There is hesitance across his face, with a crease of his forehead that's partially hidden by a few rebellious brown strands of hair. He never looks away from me, as if he fears I will deny him if he moves away or blinks.

"Why do you want me to come? You said that gods almost never bring their human concubines, so why are you inviting me? What makes me so special?" I ask the questions with a vague knowledge of the answers, but I want to hear him say the words.

He is holding his hand in the air, pinky finger extended. I mutely plead with him to say the correct answer, the one that he and I both know as truth but have been too cowardice to admit.

"Because I enjoy your company more than I ever thought I would. When I'm around you, it feels like all the problems of the world leave me alone and I can breathe," he says the words with the wind, the tone quieted but honest.

My heart skips a beat, even if they were not the words that I yearned for him to say. My cheeks burn, while my lips spread into a sheepish grin. "As long as you promise not to leave my side," I officiate my acceptance with a curl of my pinky around his. "Then yes, I will be your date."

Relief relaxes his face, and he looks younger than the eons he's lived. His cheeks tinge gold, the blood rushing to his skin, and the sight makes my heart skip. With his grip of his pinky finger around mine, he pulls me forward until my chest brushes against his.

The gazebo is silenced, with not even the whistling wind for company. The garden is stilled in anticipation, both inanimate and animate objects watching our interaction with rapt fascination. His fingers are delicate, cloud-like upon my skin, as he moves down my shoulder, across my arms, and around my round hip.

He holds my hip, while his other hand encompasses mine that once only held his pinky finger. We both stare at our intertwined touch, and the fingers that slide into their natural place. There are no words, but we stay in suspension between friends and another realm that I've never entered before.

"What are we doing, Hermes?" My voice is quiet, almost drowned away by the considerable tension thickening the open, flowery expanse.

When he looks back, he isn't looking at me. The forest hue of his gaze, which is sparkling underneath the setting sun, is on my lips. His lips are parted with shock and something foreign but welcomed. Time pauses in anticipation of his next move. It is only the two of us, but my body tingles in a way that makes me feel as if a thousand people are watching how he stares at me and the response my body has to him.

"There are many things I want to do that I have no right to do," his voice is heavier than usual, his cadence grave with bottomless starvation. "I want to do so much more with you."

I don't know when I shift my fascination to his lips' movements and the formulation of each grainy word, but I can't bring myself to look away. The color is pink as petals, and they're closer to mine with each unspoken confession. We're gravitating nearer to one another, unaware of our actions but unable to stop ourself. All that it will take is one of us to eliminate the suffocating tension and create a new feeling that I've never gotten the opportunity to experience before.

"I need to teach you to dance for the symposium," Hermes says.

Hermes pulls his head away from mine and takes one retreating step from me. A ping of disappointment hits me, but I ignore the emotion with a convincing smile that tells him everything is alright. We're still holding hands, his other one resting on my waist, but our chests are no longer pressed together. Our lips are not a breath apart, and the chance to get rid of the tension is cut apart by cowardice once more.

THE TWENTY-EIGHTH CHAPTER

Before, there was silence.

Thickened muteness clogs my lungs, but Hermes snaps and music fills the gaps of unspoken confessions. A golden instrument materializes in the far left corner, strings playing a wondrous tune without the accompaniment of a person's faithful guidance.

He asks. "Have I ever told you the story about the lyre?"

Colorless lights hang from the gazebo's ceiling, which once swayed with the wind, and they illuminate in shades of pink and orange. The gazebo I've walked past several times before is reconstructed into a dream too magnificent to be anything but reality. A golden lyre plays its indulgent melody, while Hermes and I sway back and forth.

"No, you haven't," I answer.

"I'll tell you the tale, if you'd like, but first," he looks to my free hand, which lays limp at my side. "Put your hand on my shoulder."

I obey him, my fingers curling around the back of his shoulder, my arm outstretched to its limit. "I think I'm going to need you to shrink when we dance together."

ICHOR

He snaps again, and my once bare feet are warmed with shoes that cause my height to increase. I once had to crane my neck in order to see him, but now I am leveled with his collarbone. My dance slows to a stop, and I look down at the shoes with long, pointed edges at the bottom.

"They're called heels," he answers my muted confusion. "Some women wear them. Aphrodite requests heels to be manufactured for her own benefit."

Once again, we sway.

We start with stepping left, then right. He integrates more steps into our movement. He is seamless with his teachings, and our movements become languid after only a few minutes. As we dance, he distracts me with the tale of him and Apollo fighting as children.

"While I created the lyre with a tortoise shell," he explains, gliding me across the ground with quickening speed. "I have a talent for stealing; a talent of mine that I enjoy using every chance I get."

"You don't say?" I tease, my presence in his house stemming from his thievery apparent to both him and I.

His mischievous smirk makes a reappearance. "My favorite things in life are the ones that I've stolen," he leans in a little closer, and his warm breath brushes across my lips as he confesses. "And I'd steal you all over again."

He spins me away from his body, our arms outstretched, and I ask. "So, what'd you steal from Apollo?"

He brings me back to him, my body undergoing endless twirls before I'm propelled back into his body. "His cattle," he says. "Fifty of them. I would've gotten away with it too, if it wasn't for this old man working at Apollo's vineyard who told on me."

There's laughter in my tone as I gasp. "How dare he?"

"Right?" Hermes outcries. "I was only a child, but Apollo was furious. He brought me to Mt. Olympus to talk to our father, who told me I had to tell Apollo where the cattle were. I knew my lies weren't working, although I consider the art of spinning untruthful words a talent of mine, and so I gave the lyre to Apollo and promised to never steal his possessions again."

"Well, did you?" I ask, our movements seamless until I step on his foot and wince. "Sorry."

He grimaces and fibs. "You're fine. It didn't hurt at all."

"Liar," I laugh.

"Did I what?" He inquires, our dance resuming with Hermes's suffering a slight limp in the first few steps.

"Steal from Apollo again?"

His grin is pure mischief. "What do you think?"

Hours come and go as the two of us are gliding across the grounds, but our dance is timeless. My feet burn, I'm out of breath, and I'm starving, but I do not stop. My feet never stop moving, and all I can pay attention to is him and the gentle sway of my hips.

The sun begins its descent, and the sky matches the flowers below in shades of pale pinks, purples, and blues. A breeze returns once more, caressing my arms with ginger affection, but it isn't until the thunderous grumble of my stomach that Hermes slows us down to a stop. Both of our ragged breathing fills the emptied backyard, and our bodies are once again flush against one another.

I migrate towards him, unable to pull myself from the endless green. "How long have we been dancing?" I ask.

His hand slips out of mine, and just like I can't look away from him, he is drawn to a piece of my hair that fell from its bun.

His index and thumb catch the wandering brown lock, playing with the strand as he hums. "I do not know."

My fingers curl into his shoulder, hyper focused on the fact that he is pressed against me. Every hidden muscle, every brush of skin against mine. My gaze drifts, moving towards his lips that are close to mine once again. We always seem to gravitate towards this pose, his head tilted down towards me and our mouths daring to play a game for which I do not know the directions.

"Saffron," Hermes murmurs my name like a prayer, his head dipping a little closer to mine. "I shouldn't be doing this."

"Why?" I ask once again because I am incapable of uttering more than a single word with our bodies this close to one another, but another reason is to see if the truth will come to the surface.

"Because you deserve a relationship where the person sees you for your magnificence and nothing more. You and I would be more complicated than that," is his vague, hushed response.

"Why would it be complicated?" I push for more, needing the words of truth from the gods of lies, but he stays transfixed on my lips with gnawing contemplation.

For a regretful minute, I think he is going to kiss me. To forgo all his words and press his lips against mine. He stares at me like a man starved, and I press myself against his chest. My wanton expression tells him to kiss me, and I garner hope that it will come true.

Until Hermes pulls away.

He drops the stray piece of hair and my waist, then looks away from my mouth. He retreats, just as he had hours before, and turns to exit the area of possibilities. Any elation I had today dissipates from the clear slap of rejection. Hermes is quick to move out of my touch, and he moves through the garden in a clear path for the house doors, but I storm after him.

Or, I try to.

Every step with these gruesome contraptions around my feet is wobbled, my soles burning after hours within these torture devices. He is nearly at the door when I throw the shoes that never reach their intended target. They drop a few feet in front of me, but the anger that rips from my throat reaches his ears with perfect accuracy.

"This isn't fair!"

Hermes is at the front of the backyard now, his hand in range of the door, but he freezes upon my words. He doesn't turn around, but he does not need to look at me to feel the rage steaming off of me in heated waves. The once frigid sundown is sweltering with my fury, and he can feel it a hundred feet away.

"I know," he says from where he stands, his back still turned.

While I walk barefoot down the gazebo stairs, I stammer. "I may not know a lot of things, not like you, but I know you can't lead me on like that because I don't deserve it."

As I walk past them, I kick the heels on the ground, but I can still hear him. "I agree. You deserve so much better."

"You can't leave petals on the floor, you can't surprise me with a date, and you can't say these sweet words to me only to walk away a moment later." I seethe, with the newly formed clouds thundering in alliance with my anger. "You can't surprise me with dance lessons or spend time with me for hours with that look on your face like I mean something to you. You can't spend almost every night with me, playing board games and telling me how beautiful I am, and making me feel like I belong somewhere for the first time in my life, but then you pull away and say that we are too complicated. It isn't fair."

The sky was once a beautiful array of colors in the world's sweet goodbye to the sun, but the clouds heard my screams and came to my aid. Thick, gray clouds cover most of the sky, and plump droplets of rain fall onto the ground. Steady streams of rain, along with clamorous thunder and the clashing of far-off lightning, join me in my angry walk towards Hermes.

He has speed on his side. He could open the door, slam it behind me, and leave me to the rage and the rain. But he doesn't. The distance he created between us is broken by my angry advancement, and he stays still. My hand curls around his shoulder, and I spin him so he is looking down at me once again.

Steady streams of rain crash upon our heads, making his hair fall upon his forehead. The water gets into my eyes as I look up at him, but I do not steer away. Anger keeps me solid in my stance, even as the bite of the cold creeps to the surface.

"Why, Hermes?"

"I wish for little in life," he says, voice cracking with an onslaught of truth after days of lies. "I've only ever wanted two things; happiness with a woman who I could love, and I've wanted to be seen for my worth and power. Most of my siblings are revered on Mt. Olympus, but I'm not. I'm just the messenger, and I hate it. Hate it more than almost anything else in the world."

"How does that pertain to this? Us?" I ask.

Hermes continues. "But more than anything, I want a moment of peace in the destruction of worlds I've witnessed and abhorred. I want to stop running and flying and scouring the world for others, and I want to settle down. I've never been married, and I've never been able to stare at somebody and know that they could be my forever, and it's all that I want from my endless life. Freedom and the happiness and sense of worth that comes with it. And when I look at you, I can see the potential of it all."

My hand drops from his shoulder, but he breaks the distance. Rain spits in between our faces, but Hermes tilts his head down until he is shielding me from the onslaught. His forehead presses against mine, while one hand cups my cheek and the other finds its place on my waist. His stare impales me as I stand shivering in the storm, waiting to hear words I fear will never come.

Hermes's voice cracks as he admits. "I can see the possibility of you being my future, of spending each night with the last sound in my ears being your laughter, but I look at you and know that you deserve so much better than me. Aphrodite was right; I'm a selfish god because when I look at you, I know I'll steal and lie and do anything I can to never let you go. Do you see now, Saffron? I'm not meant for you because I don't want you for just you; I want you for my own personal, selfish endeavors."

He takes another step. Our bodies are molded together by the rain and something stronger, more tangible. His fingers dig into my waist, and his warm breath is ragged against my lips. I used to ponder the reason behind the thoughts fluttering through my chest. I used to let my mind wander to Epiales, to his words that foretold danger wherever the gods walked.

But Epiales vanishes from my mind.

Not just him, but all of his words leave too. I once correlated Epiales with being the center of knowledge. He was my storyteller; but with Kronos's presence and the ice that enters my veins upon his arrival, Epiales blurs from my vision. Now, standing beneath the rainfall with Hermes, whose kindness wraps around us like a warm blanket, I can't see Epiales. The only person I can see is Hermes.

I reach my hands up and catch both sides of his face as if they are a prize I've won. With my grip on his face, I try to bring his face towards mine. To break the minimal distance between us. I've never been kissed, my lips bare from another's, and I'm yearning for Hermes to become my first.

My lips are so close to his that I can taste the exchange of words between him and me as I plead. "Kiss me, please."

I rise to my tiptoes, but where his mouth is, there is now distance. His hands rest on top of mine, and they are prying my touch from his face. When I wasn't looking, Hermes opened the door that leads inside, and with each step he retreats, he moves to the house and the absence of possibilities.

"I only know how to trick and thieve my way towards my desires, but I forbid myself from doing that to you. No matter how much I'd gain from you, I won't steal you anymore than I already have," he says, secrets deeper than the color of my blood laying wake in his words. He drops my hands, leaving me standing limp and defeated. "I'm sorry, but we can't do this."

He's almost completely inside when I announce the truth that the storm almost drowns out. "You're keeping secrets from me. So many secrets." I look up at him, the raindrops coating my lids, and I ask. "What color is my blood, Hermes?"

The god of mischief and lies, of trickery and thievery, lets the façade crumble. For just a second, his mask dissipates, his face slackens, his eyes widen, and he can't bring himself to appear godly in my presence. He's a boy, stricken with disbelief by a girl's brazen words.

I take a step closer to him, but this time, it's devoid of passion and desire. This time, my advancement is with ire. "Why did you steal me from Ares?" I take another step, and another question spills from my lips. "Why do you talk in riddles regarding our feelings for one another?" Another step, another question. "Why do I receive dreams when no other human does?" Another step, and our bodies are flush together without an inkling of desire for more. "Why does Kronos want me, and you want to flee from me?"

"Kronos?" Hermes's hand wraps around my bicep to keep me in front of him. When he talks again, his voice quivers with petrification. "What do *you* know, Saffron? It seems as if I'm not the only one keeping secrets."

"You first," I grit out. "With your hands off of me."

Fear replaces amour when he lets go of me. He looks at me, the human girl once cowering on the arena ground, and he sees what Kronos did in our dream world. He sees a darkness inside of me, and he takes a step away.

"We will talk in the morning," he no longer says with confidence and strength.

He doesn't steer his gaze away from me, but he retreats backwards. I stand in the doorway's threshold, in-between the grim storm and the pleasant home, and I'm divided between two worlds I do not belong in.

"Goodnight, Saffron."

He's gone, and I'm standing in the doorway with a revived sense of loneliness and confusion. I glance down at the vein in my arm once again, the golden strips laughing in a cadence identical to Kronos's, as they repeat the same two words on endless repetition.

God-Killer.

God-Killer.

God-Killer.

THE TWENTY-NINTH CHAPTER

Hermes may be the god of trickery, but we both are the masters of secrets.

Our nightly game of Monopoly has vanished, gone with the storm that destroyed so much more than Panda's daisy garden. He's almost never home, the wispy flaps of his wings ringing louder than any of his words. Many days have passed, but when the sun sets and the stars come out to dazzle in the nighttime's darkness, I sit in my bedroom with my hand around a Monopoly dollar.

I wait.

And wait.

I receive nothing in return for my patience. He never walks into my room to break the silence and lies with an inkling of truth. Instead, I can only hear his fluttering wings from his sandals as he travels far from his home.

Each night before I fall asleep and realize he's not coming to my room for a game of Monopoly and truth, I see his fear during the storm. I see his slackened jaw, rigid stance, and widened eyes as he looks at me and recognizes me as a monster. When I do not see Hermes's fright right before a dreamless sleep takes me away,

I see Medusa's decapitated head above Ares's fireplace, and his words about a woman who dared to love. Who was later detested as a monster for her foolish act of compassion.

Five nights have passed since the lessons in the garden, and the argument with Hermes, and each night was without dreams but minimal sleep, too. My body is more sluggish each morning, trekking down the steps to where China waits with a warm cup of tea and a new set of three-letter words to write on a piece of paper.

On the sixth morning, as I stumble into the kitchen with tiredness, China has a feast waiting for me. Her dark hair's silver streaks shine underneath the morning sun that drifts into the kitchen, making the beauty of her age enviable. Her typical bun is absent today, as well. For the first time in my two weeks inside of this house, China's hair falls into natural waves down past her shoulders.

The older woman pours two cups of hot tea. "Morning," she says. I take in the vast array of foods across the small, circular table, and she explains. "It's been a long while since I've cooked, and I felt the urge. Hopefully that's alright."

My stomach grumbles at my immediate response. I sit down and I ogle at the breakfast China made. Buttered toast sits closest to me while my mouth waters in famished anticipation.

As I reach towards it, shoving a majority of the bread into my mouth, I ask. "What words am I learning today?"

"None, my dear. I have a story instead. If you'd like," China says as she takes a sip of the glass of water next to her steaming cup of tea. "Afterwards, we can go over how to write some words from my story."

I nod my head, taking another bite out of my toast. "Sure, I like stories."

"You once asked me why Lord Hermes named me after a China doll, and I'd like to tell you the story now," China sips her water, but she watches me, following each piece of toast I bite into and each time I raise the cup of tea to my lips. "When I was won in the arena by Lord Hermes, I came into his home and began picking up everything inside. I was a curious little girl, and I held an ancient China doll in my hands when I saw the face of my soulmate walk down the staircase."

"Your soulmate?" I ask with a wave of giddiness. "What was his name?"

Her words are tinged with a broken heart. "Falcon," she says with a mournfulness to her voice. "His name was Falcon, and I knew he was the love of my life from the moment I saw him as children in our prison cell. I thought he was dead when he left the prison to be chosen in the arena, but he stood on that staircase, and I saw a second chance at loving him."

I take another sip of my tea, the swirl of mint and lavender melting upon my tongue. She has both of her hands, wrinkled with age, around her glass of water. Her pinkies tap on the glass, almost impatiently, as she talks about her soulmate.

"I dropped the China doll I was holding, and I half-expected Lord Hermes to become furious with me. I waited for my death to come as swiftly as I assumed my life was beginning, but he laughed. Lord Hermes saw how I stared at Falcon, like he was a gift from the Fates meant to enliven my days, and he decided we should immortalize the moment with a name that reminded me of seeing him once again."

My eyes grow heavy, either with fatigue from my poor sleep the night before or sadness for the grief that is imminent in her story, and my toast falls from my weighty hands. I still centralize on China, but I lower my head down upon my upright hand while I rapidly blink in a fight to stay awake.

China picks up her water glass and takes another sip; the click, click, click of her pinkies worsening with each new sentence she utters. "Lord Hermes allowed us to be together, to defy the rules of the gods without restrictions or rules. For six glorious months, I was with Falcon, with the closest inkling towards life as a free woman. The Fates gifted me with a soulmate when most humans weren't fortunate enough to experience a love that was half the magnitude of ours. Even as my belly became swollen with a baby, I was not afraid. I was happier than I thought possible."

She takes another sip of her glass, but her pinkies abruptly stop tapping. Stoic in nature, it is rare to see emotions on the older woman's face, but today she looks at me and I see decades of hatred on her wrinkled face. I no longer see the woman who spent hours each morning teaching me the alphabet and simple words, but a broken soul manifested in rage sits before me.

"That's when the explosion happened," she confesses. "When I was at my happiest."

China's eyes shimmer with tears as she relives the past through her words, but she does not cry. She uses her hatred for the gods to transform any remnant of sadness into rage. Behind blurred and heavy lids, I almost miss the knife she lies on top of the rounded table, hidden behind a stack of pancakes and a bowl of blueberries.

"King Poseidon and Lady Athena were fighting, an argument so inconsequential to them now that if you'd ask them the origin, they couldn't answer. When the explosion of two pure gods fighting against one another crashed through this kitchen, Falcon grabbed my hand, and we ran. Almost a dozen human bodies lay in the wake of their rage before Falcon hid me in the wardrobe, but he had no time to save himself."

I struggle to keep my head up, the back of my neck baring the weight of a thousand suns, but I ask. "What did you do to me?"

She ignores me and continues the story. "*King* Poseidon," she sneers the term with pure hatred. "Threw his trident to hit *Lady* Athena, but it impaled Falcon through the chest. He died within seconds, as I cowered in the wardrobe, but that was all it took to change my entire life. One mis-aimed weapon and three seconds before death claimed the one I adored most of all."

A single tear falls, but she wipes it away before it could stream down her pale cheek. She lives in front of me, with a beating heart and years of anguish in her thoughts, but I stare at China and see a corpse whose heart died alongside Falcon's many years ago. The only residuum of life that clings to her body is rage, which reeks like a disease eating away at what remains.

"*Lord* Hermes found me in the wardrobe after both gods were kicked out of his home, but the damage was irreversible. The Fates gifted me with a second chance at happiness, only to watch and cackle as I broke into a thousand terrible cracks, and there was no longer gleefulness. The child in my belly must've tasted the sourness of my sorrow because it came into this world without a pulse."

"What?" I lick my lips, fighting the numbness that overtakes my body and inhibits me from running from a woman fueled by revenge. "What did you-"

"King Kronos came to me in a dream one night, soon after, with a proposition that I could not refuse," she says. "He's getting rather impatient. The king wants you to join us now. No more waiting."

The story has been festering inside of China since Falcon's death, and telling her past distracts her from the rest of the world.

She does not realize who emerges from the garden doors because of either the engrossment of the story she tells, or her poor hearing, but she is oblivious to Hattie's stealthy entrance. She stands in between the opened back doors, a garden fork clutched in her hand, and disbelief slackening her features.

Hattie stares at the woman who she's seen as a mother figure, and she finally sees her for who she truly is—a monster.

There is turmoil brewing inside of Hattie, whether to save me or the woman who she sees as a mother, and it paralyzes her. She holds onto the garden fork, unable to advance towards us or run for help. She only watches the transaction with confliction and an onslaught of tears.

"What proposition?" I force the words out, the drowsiness slamming into me.

China flickers down to the half-drank cup of tea, and she says. "You need to finish your cup of tea, Saffron. You'll want to be asleep for the rest of our trip, and I had to kill far too many to get enough drugs to incapacitate you."

"Kill?" I ask as my eyes flutter shut.

"Panda became such a nosy little thing," as soon as China says Panda's name, my stomach curdles in disgust. "I had to dispose of her before she told you what she knew."

Panda?

Panda's gaped tooth smile burns in my mind. Her laughter, the nasal but carefree sound, taints my ears. I hear China's words, registering Panda's death, but I do not accept the fact that she's gone. With as much strength as I can muster, I shake my head at the familiar sting of sadness that another lost soul incites.

I look up at where Hattie stands, and tears stream down her cheeks and off of the tip of her chin. Where there was once hesitance, there is now only determination and sorrow. Each step

Hattie makes, both silent and lethal, is in honor of Panda. Hattie raises the garden fork into the air, and just as China turns around to face my line of vision, Hattie's weapon slides downwards.

China watches as the garden fork slides through her chest and impales her. The three prongs stick out of her back while rich red blood spills from her pale flesh. China tries to open her mouth, but crimson cessation slips from the corner of her lips.

She falls from her chair but does not fight her death. China does not wrap her fingers around the handle of the garden fork, but she lays her arms outstretched and watches her blood pool around her body. China is staring upwards at the ceiling, refusing to pay attention to anything but her own looming demise.

When her soul leaves her body, the truest smile graces her lips.

I am fighting the poison coursing through my body, but I will myself to stay awake long enough to check on Hattie. She stands over China's corpse, her hands vibrating and her body swaying. She cannot keep herself upright when the waves of distress crash into her tiny body. I trip and tumble my way out of my chair, but I stumble to Hattie fast enough that when she collapses, I am there to catch her.

When she screams, the walls tremble. With the lingering strength in my legs, I distance us from China until my back hits the kitchen counter and my arms are wrapped around hers. Hattie won't look away from China's corpse, the woman who she loved but murdered for Panda and me, but I intertwine our hands to stop them from shaking.

As the drug ebbs away the overbearing desire to slumber, I unveil the truth. "You saved my life."

"I'm a murderer," Hattie gasps, tears slipping from her cheeks and wetting my arms and hands. "I killed her."

"You saved my life," I reiterate. "You are a hero."

The garden doors are thrown open, and Hermes stands in the threshold with Pyro behind him with a knife in his hand. Hermes only wears a pair of shorts, his chest slicked in sweat, but his mighty *caduceus* is gripped in his hands as he looks around the room. Hermes expected a battle, but when he looks at China's corpse upon the floor, his grip on *caduceus* lessens.

"Are you alright?" Hermes asks, staring at me but then migrates his focus to Hattie's sobbing, bloody, and inconsolable form. "What in the Underworld happened?"

I migrate to Pyro. "I'm so sorry."

"Sorry for what?" Pyro asks, and he looks back with befuddlement, but I can't bring myself to say the words out loud. There is a long expanse of muteness, our words spoken within the lines of frightened silence, and Pyro knows. He takes a wobbling step forward, noticing Panda's absence, but refusing to believe the truth. "What are you sorry for? What happened?"

Anybody who lives in this mansion would've heard Hattie's scream as she murdered China, but Panda is nowhere in sight. She isn't here, and the tears that stream down Pyro's cheeks confirm she will never be with us again. Hermes turns to Pyro and places a comforting hand on his shoulder.

"No," Pyro shoves Hermes away, still shaking his head as he stammers. "No, she's fine," he looks at me and probes. "Right? Panda is fine, right?"

"I'm so sorry," I recite once more, my tears building up.

"No, you're wrong," Pyro says, his hands tightening around the knife in his hand. "Panda is just sleeping. I'll go fetch her."

Pyro runs downstairs, searching for his soulmate, but what he will find won't be what he is hoping for. The kitchen is silent as we listen to Pyro's fading feet. There is a prolonged muteness in the room as we wait in terrible imminence for his own realization that Panda is no longer alive.

His screams pierce the walls until there is a distinct *thud* of a newly fallen body and then nothing at all. I do not have to run downstairs to see the blood-splattered truth. We are in the kitchen, numbed by the gnawing realization that both Panda and Pyro are gone from this world, leaving behind nothing.

Nothing but the death of love ricocheting through the walls.

Hermes sheaths *caduceus* and walks towards China's corpse. As I hold Hattie tight in my arms, Hermes picks up the dead body of the woman who was betrayed by her own mind and agony. But another creature stumbles into the kitchen.

Panda's red panda, Roscoe, walks into the kitchen soaked in the blood of his owners.

THE THIRTIETH CHAPTER

In the same spot where Panda's favorite tulips grow in the garden, she and Pyro are buried side-by-side. The sky cries in mournful remembrance of their devotion for one another, the gentle petals of rain hitting our hair, face, and emotions as we watch Hermes lower their bodies into the graves that he dug.

They become a part of the Earth that was never kind to them, while only the three of us will remember the story of their life. None of us have spoken a word since that dreadful night, not when Hermes lifted China's body and disposed of it far from where she started the seed of betrayal and hatred. Not when Roscoe's stomach began its horrendous grumbles of hunger, his beady eyes looking for Panda or Pyro before he could eat a morsel of food.

Hermes lays each shovel-full of dirt upon their corpses, and with each slap that hits their faces, I see Kronos. I feel the icy spike of his presence, reminding me again and again that I could've avoided this if I told Hermes the truth about Kronos upon our first encounter. I watch as Pyro and Panda's faces leave this world forever, hidden behind six feet worth of soil, and I hear China's words.

The king wants you to join us now, no more waiting.

Sweat rolls down the sides of Hermes's face as he stares down at the new graves he's created, and then he swivels to me. Hattie stands behind me, mute since the day she killed China to protect me, but she stares at the graves without a glance at Hermes or me. Tears that do not shed but build. The suffering is burning with more intensity than the sun.

I do not ponder my action, but I wrap my hand around hers. At first, she freezes. Her body tenses upon contact, but within a few seconds the tears fall down her cheeks and she squeezes my hand in a tight grip.

"After the dance," Hermes says with conviction, drawing me back to him. "I promise I'll tell you everything. No more secrets or lies."

I nod my head, my words hushed but genuine. "After the dance."

Hermes lets out a deep breath, a fraction of his tension disappearing, but he centralizes on the graves once more and the sadness returns alongside a wave of guilt. "I'm going to take their souls to the Underworld," he tells us both before adding. "No matter what, I'll make sure that Panda and Pyro end up in the Fields of Elysium with Roscoe by their sides."

Roscoe's little form materializes in Hermes's arms, and the red panda stares at Hermes with confusion. He lets his feathered sandals fly him into the air with Roscoe, and within a fraction of a second, he is gone with the souls of our friends who invisibly soar beside him. I watch each flutter of his wings until he leaves my line of vision and the possibility of seeing Panda and Pyro depart with him.

Hattie must've been watching, too, because when Hermes's form drifts into the clouds, she collapses to the ground. With my hand intertwined with hers, I fall beside her. The ground is cold, but Hattie is burning with anguish. Sweat dribbles down the side of her face, intermingling with the tears of her sadness, but her hand remains coiled around mine.

"I almost didn't save you," Hattie says as her first words in nearly ten hours.

With a solemn nod, I admit. "I know."

"Did I ever tell you how Hermes won me in the arena?" Hattie asks, but she does not look at me. She stares at the two freshly dug graves which are decorated with Panda's favorite tulips. "Three gods fought for me, but Psyche was quickly defeated and only Heracles and Hermes were left. I found out later that Heracles required all of his slaves to take part in a smaller scale version of his twelve labors to see if they were worthy to live, but almost all of them die. I would've died if I were with him, I know it."

"How did Hermes beat him?" I ask, both because of curiosity and a need for the squelching silence to subside.

"He threw a little piece of candy onto the floor of the arena, right in front of Heracles's feet." Despite the sadness, Hattie lets out a laugh similar to a sob. "Heracles was so confused by the thought of having candy thrown at him he didn't see Hermes strike until it was too late. He bested Heracles over a small piece of candy, and I have lived eight years longer than I thought I would've. All because of a god and a piece of candy."

"Hattie, why did you choose me over China? Was it because of Panda?"

"Partially, but it was also because you saved the god who saved me," she responds. "You saved Hermes's life when you came into this mansion. He was not about to face the twelve labors, or have his throat slit for existing, but he was withering away in his mind. I didn't understand why in the beginning, and for that I hated you, but the god I care for saw you and no longer found a reason to hide himself in his work. He is eternal, but he started living because of you, and I would let nobody take that away from him. Not even China."

We drift into the silence again, but the tears have subsided. We are back to the torment of our inner thoughts, but our hands stay intertwined. As if we are each other's strand to sanity, we sit on the ground in front of the two graves, hands together, and we stare ahead at our own unknown future.

I whisper. "Regardless of who you saved me for, thank you for saving my life."

"I told you once and I'll say it again," Hattie ensures I am staring at her, our eyes almost identical in color but polarizing in size and shape. While mine are round yet petite, similar to an almond, hers are downcast and always narrowed in critical analysis of surrounding people. "Your presence is the turning of times. I saved you because of Hermes, but I'll keep saving you because you're the closest chance humanity will get to freedom, no matter if you choose the side of the gods or Kronos."

I look at her, shock causing my jaw to drop onto the floor as I ask. "Kronos?"

She nods her head once more but does not look away from the graves. "China was not the only human he found and tried to promise the world to. Not even close to it."

"Did he ask you to…" I ask, but fear stops me.

Did he ask you to kidnap me? Is what I was going to say.

Hattie finishes what I was too frightened to, and she says. "I told you I'll always save you. Just because a pretty face came to me in a dream doesn't mean I'm going to fall for it. Plus, I've seen far prettier faces in my time than his."

"Thank you, Hattie."

"Don't get all sappy on me, demi-god, or I'm going to rethink his decision just to keep you away from me."

"What did he offer you in exchange for kidnapping me?" I ponder aloud. "China was promised revenge against Athena and Poseidon, but what did he try to persuade you with?"

While she stands in front of me in the present, her mind and soul reverberate to a time when sadness ravaged her. "I had a twin sister, and I don't know if his words are true or not, but Kronos said she was a dispenser and died her first night out of the arena." She is quiet for quite some time, but when she speaks, her voice is distant. "He promised me revenge just like China because revenge is the only bargain he needs against humans who have nothing else."

Her hand slips from mine as she rises to her feet, and I do not stop her as she leaves the garden in search of a void of nothingness my company does not provide. When the back door closes behind Hattie, I'm alone with death and flowers. I sit upon the garden ground, my dress and skin covered in wet soil, and I am infused on where Panda and Pyro permanently lie.

"I'll kill him for you," I vow to where their bodies lie, but their souls are miles away. "If it is the last thing I do in this world, then I will kill Kronos."

And what about Epiales? My thoughts cry for an answer, the contemplation bringing an aching to my chest. What about the god who helps the titan responsible for such terror?

I can't answer my question.

Night arrives, Hermes with it, before I leave the garden. When his feet land upon the ground, he does not question by wet, fatigued state. He walks over to me, picking me up in his arms, and steers me away from the burial ground that lays two premature souls.

We are halfway up the staircase, nearing our bedrooms, when I ask. "Is this how life will always be? Full of death where there was once beauty?"

"I keep praying that the right hero will bring change."

"How, though? How will it change?"

He opens my bedroom door with a nod of his head, never once moving his hands from holding my body, and walks into the room. Hermes doesn't immediately answer my question, but he sets me down on the corner of my bed and wraps a materialized towel around my shoulders. He ensures that the thick material is snug against my body, before my wet clothes disappear with his magic.

Hermes assesses my trembling bottom lip and the steady drips of water from the bottom of my hair and mutters more to himself than to me. "With the right prophecy and the destined wielder, I think change will come sooner rather than later."

He pulls away from me fast, as if my skin were the center of a flame, and he migrates back towards the door he just entered.

"Hermes," a question is ready to leave my lips, but he is already closing the bedroom door behind him with a parting request.

"Rest well, Saffron."

THE THIRTY-FIRST CHAPTER

This dreamworld I'm catapulted towards is neither ostentatious, like Kronos's utopian view of Mt. Olympus, nor is it a room of spiraling smoke and ambiguous promises, like the Underworld's throne room. Ice-like wind prickles at my skin as darkness drowns any fabric of happiness. My chest tightens and my throat burns with an overwhelming suffocation of loneliness.

There is only one stream of light, but not in the traditional golden gleam from the sun. It's gray like a glimpse of the moonlight on an otherwise cloudy midnight. This shred of moonlight shows me a hunched figure, his arms wrapped around his hiked-up knees. He's shirtless, allowing anybody within this frigid nightmare access to a myriad of jagged scars and a spine that presses against his back, threatening to rip through the skin.

He doesn't look up from his hiding spot between his hunched knees, but I would recognize the raven curls anywhere. Even as Epiales stews in his dungeon of disparity and anguish, I can make out the tattoo upon the top of his hand. I still see him beneath the decrepit nature of his prism. I wade through the frigid emptiness until I am standing above my storyteller's seated form.

"He's coming for you soon," Epiales's voice no longer holds the strength of a thousand worlds. He's more fragile than the tiniest hu-

man. "You need to get ready for when he takes you back with him. I'll be freed when you join him."

Quieter than I've ever heard my voice, I respond. "I'm not joining him. Not today, or tomorrow, or even a year from now. He's evil."

Epiales lifts his head from its solitude between his knees. When his eyes meet mine, the silver is dulled. Its normal sheen is taken. Tartarus's darkness is a thief of what I've found most beautiful about my storyteller.

"Everybody is evil," he says, an undertone of rage deepening his otherwise fatigued tone. "Every god, every monster, and every human who sees adoration in those gilded beasts. They're all evil."

"Not all of them," I respond, with Hermes's boyish smirk filling my head. "They're not all as bad as Kronos, and he wants to condemn them all."

He scoffs at me, anger and desperation intermingling as he bites out. "So what if Kronos is evil? So what if he is not as perfect as that messenger scum you spend time with and forget that I'm dying in the depths of Tartarus?"

Epiales tries to stand up, but the strength he once possessed has long abandoned him. His knees did not have the chance to straighten before he is tumbling onto the prison ground again. Tears burn, but he doesn't let his fear for his own mortality slip.

Instead, he glares up at where I stand and sneers. "I will work with the greatest villains in the world if it means Zeus is taken down, and I am freed from certain death." For a moment, Epiales looks around the darkness of Tartarus, recoiling in fright at creatures I cannot see within the abyss. "Do you know what it means for me, the personification of nightmares, to stay within Tartarus?"

"No," I answer.

"Then let this be my last story for you, my queen," as soon as my nickname leaves his lips, so does his rage. At the reminder of who

stands across from him, and what I mean to him, the anger dissipates and only sadness remains. "Our powers have no outlet here, so they travel through the endless cave of imprisonment. I am the personification of nightmares, so my worst nightmares cover the walls and torment me as I slowly wither away into nothingness."

When I take a step towards him, that familiar tingling sensation returns. My body is magnetized to his, drifting me closer until I am sitting in front of him. My knees brush against his while my hands reach out.

His tatted hands grab mine, our fingers intertwining. Despite where we are and the opposite views we have for an imminent war, I'm at peace. When he holds me, and I him, the sadness and anger and desperation leave my mind. And from his deep exhalation, I know that the weight of his circumstances is momentarily released.

"I hear you in Tartarus," *he admits almost painfully.*

"Me?" *I ask, to which he nods his head.*

"You're screaming in here. A soul shattering scream that becomes a part of the wind and permanently terrorizes me. I beg to Tartarus to grant me a reprieve from the sound of your heart breaking with that ear piercing yell. I will it to go away for even a second, but it never does. Even now, I can hear you and that terrible shriek, which begs for death to swallow you whole."

"Why would I scream like that?" *I ask, but he shakes his head.*

"I do not know, but I have never heard a sound as excruciating as that one. For eons, I've existed and created nightmares. I've heard fear in its truest form, but there is still nothing as terrible as your agony ripping through the wind and finding its home there." *He continues to shake his head.* "Nothing is as terrible."

We are silent for a while after that.

Our bodies migrate closer to one another, the one beacon of illumination within the disparity of Tartarus. My body is in between his legs, our chests facing one another's. While one of his hands is still in mine, the other is running through my chestnut locks. His fingers glide through my hair, scratching my head with ginger care, while my free grasp is tracing the sword tattoo on his neck.

"What if there is another possibility?" I ask. "Not the Olympian's side or Kronos's, but something right in the middle? Where humans are freed, but the gods have a choice to change their ways. A way where everybody can be in a world of peace?"

He leans forward, forcing his last inch of strength to kiss the top of my head. "There will never be peace in this world, my queen, and when I get out of this place, I won't want peace. I want to watch Zeus burn and every god he cares about to burn with him."

"Then you're no better than the ones who kill their slaves. Perhaps worse, it makes you no better than Kronos." I look at him now, and the maliciousness that darkens his once ebullient silver irises. "Did you know Kronos tried to kidnap me? He had another woman in Hermes's house kill another and put drugs in my tea. The girl Kronos had gotten killed was barely any older than me and she had a boy she loved. When he saw she died, he killed himself. Two lives, happy in Hermes's mansion, murdered for Kronos's chance to get me."

I wish I was surprised, but there is no shocked expression on his face.

He knew.

"We have to do what's necessary to get rid of the gods," Epiales swore. "They're parasites to the world."

I stumble out of his grasp. His touch no longer electricity in my veins but the same coldness that I get from Kronos. I scramble up to my feet, trying to put as much distance as I can between Epiales and me. He tries to stand up again. His hands smack against the back of the wall, and he propels himself up into a standing position.

Epiales is still hunched over, his body weakening with each passing day, but I fear for his sanity the most. A scowl rests where a smile once had. A sense of safety I once felt from him is replaced with a vengeful creator of nightmares.

"I was a good deity before they imprisoned me," he snarls, unable to near me even as I retreat away. He can tell he is scaring me, but his ire discards my wellbeing, and he outcries. "Although I gave people a glimpse of their worst nightmares, I was benevolent. I never tried to kill or cause permanent harm to humans. Even as the enslavement began, I protected humans from the worst of the gods by winning them in the arena."

He smacks the wall behind him, making me flinch.

"I was good before Morpheus left with his soulmate, before Zeus saw it fit for me to become the punishment for my nephew's love. I was good for eons, but where did being good get me? Huh, Saffron?" He sneers my new name like a curse. "Being good was the worst thing I could ever do to myself. Being good meant I was selfless, but I'm tired of being good. I'm tired of letting a pompous monster call himself king and decide I deserve to die because I cared for my nephew more than myself."

I trip while making my distance away from Epiales, and I fall to the cold, unforgiving ground. Frigidness carries to my soul, but I stare up at him and the heat from his rage warms my skin from over twenty feet away. There isn't an ounce of my sweet storyteller in his current stance. Anger and desperation transformed him into something worse.

So much worse.

"There's only one monster I see, and he's staring right back at me." My honesty silences his heavy breathing and causes him to fall back to the ground.

He sits there, across the land of Tartarus and farther from me than he's ever been. "You are always the best part of my days in this darkness and sorrow. Your smile, in particular. I might even love you, but if I have to break your trust in me and your freedom to free myself and kill Zeus, then I'll do it without hesitation." He leans his head against the wall, exhaustion aging his handsome features, and he pledges. *"I'll be seeing you soon. Hopefully, willing to the cause."*

"But if I'm not willing?" I ask, with the demise of trust between us evident.

"It'll still be a beautiful sight. Watching Zeus's secret child kill him and all the other Olympians, whether or not it's against her will. Until then, my queen."

The dream shatters, like the pounding of a hammer against my glass heart.

I wipe away the burning tears that slide down my cheeks because of my nightmare, which confirms everything I once knew is a lie. Epiales was once the epicenter of my sanity, but he has become another cause of my unraveling. The bedroom door opens, and Hattie leans against the doorway. Her gaze is on my tear-stricken face.

"Tonight is the night," she says. "Are you sure you're ready? You're about to enter the field of gods."

No, I'm not.

I fake pleasantness and lie. "I can't wait."

THE THIRTY-SECOND CHAPTER

Hattie sees the tears drying on my cheeks and distracts me from tonight's endeavors. She sets a thick tome on top of the bed and right in between my legs. I look up at her with confusion, then at the book. Leaning forward, my fingers graze the four golden letters on the front.

"Z…" I go to the next letter and stammer. "E… U… S."

"Zeus," Hattie says, and she flops onto the bed and takes the book from my hands. "I'll take over your studies, and today you're going to learn everything about Zeus. If you can pronounce a word right, then…" she bends backwards, her hands leaving my line of vision, but a few seconds later a bowl of cut strawberries sits adjacent to the book. "You'll get a strawberry as a prize."

"Strawberries?" I squeal with excitement, and she nods her head.

"Let's get to reading about Zeus before Psyche and Eros show up and pamper you for the ball," Hattie says. "I think we have about two or three hours before she storms in with her butterflies," she shivers and adds. "Those things creep me out."

It'll still be a beautiful sight. Watching Zeus's secret child kill him and all the other Olympians, whether it's against her will or not.

ICHOR

Epiales's words come back into my head, burrowing its way through my sanity. Once again, I look down at Zeus's name written across the top of the booklet, and his words are screaming back at me.

Zeus's secret child.

Zeus, the king of the skies, is my father.

"Can we learn about somebody else today?" I ask.

Hattie counteracts with another question. "Why? Zeus has some pretty wicked stories. There was one time he was so scared of a prophecy about his second born chi-"

"Hattie," I snap her name, interrupting her story with my trepidation. "Please? Anybody else?"

She mumbles. "You're lucky I brought a book about Apollo, too," she bends over, and while switching books, she mutters. "I knew I should've brought brownies laced with laxatives instead of strawberries."

As she sets down the book with new letters on the top, I ask. "What are laxatives?"

Humor laces her dark eyes as she smirks. "Chocolate."

"Would it taste good with strawberries?" I ponder aloud, and her smirk widens.

"Delicious with strawberries," Hattie drawls, then opens the book on Apollo and asks. "Where do you think we should start? With the story about his birth or his story with Daphne?"

⁓

"A t-tr," I sigh, staring at the four-letter word Hattie told me to read aloud. "Trah."

"Tree," Hattie corrects me, then reads the rest of the sentence. "Her father, Peneus, took pity on his daughter and turned her into a laurel tree. Just as Apollo went to grab her, she began her transformation into the laurel tree."

"Tree," I sound out the word on my tongue, my finger tracing the four-letter word on the page. "Alright, I'll get that right next time."

Hattie turns the next page and says. "Alright, the next story about Apollo is about his friendship with a man named Admetus. Do you want to read the first line?"

I stare at the words, which float and turn across the page as if they're possessed by some powers to propel confusion. I try to stop the words from twisting and contorting themselves, but they do not listen. All the letters continue their distortion, which only furthers my disorientation.

Each letter swivels, but I still read. "Apollo saw in-"

"Was, not saw," Hattie corrects me. "But keep going."

I sigh. "It's like the d and b again," I elaborate. "When China was teaching me how to write the letters, I kept switching those two."

"Learning how to read and write isn't easy," Hattie explains. "You're fine. Just keep going and do not give up. Even when you want to throw the book and scream, keep reading."

I take a deep breath and try the sentence again. "Apollo was in big," I pause, staring at the seven-letter word. "Trewdell. What is a trewdell?" I look at Hattie and ask. "Is that a kind of food?"

"The word is trouble," Hattie points to the word and explains. "Trewdell isn't a word, but you're right, if it was a word, then it'd sound like food. I'm thinking of a pastry."

"Right." I look down at the page once again and repeat the sentence for a third time. "Apollo *was* in big *trouble* with Zeus. Zeus ex... ex..." I stare at the word a little while longer, trying to sound out each letter as Hattie told me to, and I test out the word on my tongue. "Exiled."

"You got it!" Hattie yells, a grin encompassing her face, and a joyous laugh escapes from my lips.

"I did?" I exclaim, my smile wide.

Hattie nods her head with obvious excitement. "Yup." She digs into the half empty strawberry bowl and throws me a piece. "Another new word down."

I pop the strawberry into my mouth with a newfound burning to my cheeks. Each sentence takes me several times, but Hattie surprises me with her patience. Hattie used to be the first to grow impatient with my confusion, but she's a better teacher than China ever was.

I periodically mess up the d and the b, as well as the p and the q, but Hattie never yells at me. She quickly reminds me of my error, and I try again. A few times, I am half-tempted to close the book and throw it across the room, but I don't. I take her advice and I try again, mess up, and then try again.

"Apollo saved his fr." I stop, take a deep breath, and finish the word. "Freb."

"Friend," Hattie corrects me.

"You don't know what the word 'friend' means?" A new, nasally voice outcries.

Hattie and I turn towards the opened door. Live butterflies rest upon her onyx hair, which is braided around her head like a crown. She is almost as beautiful as Aphrodite's forms, yet there is a childlike roundness to her face that makes her appear older, yet younger than me at the same time.

There is a youthful glow to her naturally tan complexion, which contrasts with the other goddesses I've come into contact with. While other goddesses have an archaic sophistication to them, Psyche glides across the room with a skip in her step, which reminds me of all the toddlers in the prison cells.

The butterflies never deviate from the top of her head until she and I are standing face-to-face. Then, the largest purple butterfly soars off of her head and lands on top of my shoulder. Psyche's eyes, which are squinted and in a rich multitude of browns and greens, watch the butterfly that sits on me.

"You're a purple soul. How exciting," Psyche's cheerful voice outcries. Her attention meanders towards the opened book on the bed and she giggles. "You are clearly not a green soul. When did you learn how to read? Yesterday?"

"She just started two weeks ago." Hattie slides off of the bed and glares at the goddess of soul. Her tone is clipped as she snaps. "You've had eons, so what's your excuse for all that air in between your ears, Psyche?"

I turn to look at Hattie, my brows raised in disbelief at her brazen attitude, but Psyche laughs. "Your wit will one day get you killed, little viper."

Hattie snaps back. "Yet undeformed, unlike your little butterflies."

"Until Hermes finally accepts one of my trades. You'd look beautiful with a red butterfly right here," Psyche points to her right eye, and Hattie recoils from the goddess. Amused, Psyche turns her attention to me. "You must be Saffron. It's a pleasure to meet the woman Hermes whisked away for the sake of love."

I look over at where Hattie once stood, but she is gone. She fled from Psyche, who claps her hands and demands. "Bring me all the purple dresses!"

Five female slaves scurry forward, purple dresses draped across their arms, but I focus on the woman on the far left, and I gasp.

My shower-mate, who was once the prettiest human woman I'd ever seen, stands amongst the slaves holding purple gowns.

Now, her right eye is permanently shut with a scarification mark. A butterfly, large and in a shade of amber brown with two white stripes, covers the entirety of her once important organ.

I glance around at the other humans, and they are all blinded by the scarification of a particular butterfly, too. I stare at the dehumanizing sight, unable to pull away.

"You mutilated them," the words slip out of my lips before I have the common sense to stay silent.

"The quickest and easiest way to a man's soul is through a woman's eyes. I did them a favor," Psyche says, her voice deepened in seriousness. "They should thank me."

"In case you've forgotten, *Lady* Psyche," I turn to face her, and my words are venomous as I sneer. "Mutilation isn't a favor, it's torture, and only monsters look upon torture and see something beautiful."

Psyche takes a threatening step closer. She expects me to balk, to fear the ground her immortal feet glide across, but the familiar pit of power deepens within my chest. I stare at the goddess of souls, and I see an opponent I could defeat.

My chin is raised in the air.

"I saved them from the dangers of men who do not accept no as an answer," Psyche snaps back.

I point at my shower-mate, who flinches with brutal anticipation for a punishment. "Did you know I grew up in the same jail cell as this girl? She is the same age as I am and grew up in the bastille right across from mine. She was sold in the same arena I was a little over two weeks ago, yet here I am, ready to be pampered and adored by you. Here I am, about to attend a symposium with you as Hermes's date, and here she is, suffering without an eye because you made decisions that impacted the rest of her life."

Psyche gapes at my shower-mate, who cowers in fright that today is her last day alive. Yet, the goddess looks at her and sees the mutilation. For a moment, I fear that I've cost my shower-mate her life, but Psyche glances back at me without malice.

Then, Psyche explains. "I was not born a goddess like many of the immortals, but I was a human girl Aphrodite disapproved of. She tried to decide disappointment was my fate. Aphrodite saw my beauty as a threat and wanted Eros to set me up with the ugliest man he could find. Yet, my Eros fell for me. If Eros didn't love me, then I would've lived a putrid life Aphrodite orchestrated without my say. If I didn't find a god's affection, then I would've been married to a repugnant man and died a forgettable life, but the world has changed since I first found Eros."

"The world didn't change enough to make mutilation acceptable," I snap.

"Yes, it did," she insists. "Because a relationship between a god and a human girl equates to demi-gods, and a swollen belly on a woman is a swift death sentence. You see a sadist when you look at my girls, but I see the marks as shields from a short life expectancy. My slaves live long lives, and-"

"Are they happy?" I interject.

The question confuses Psyche. "Excuse me?"

"You say they live long lives under your sadism," I say.

"Protection," Psyche sneers back, interrupting me.

"But are they happy with the life you chose for them?" I gesture to the girls, who tremble as they hold purple dresses, none of them showing a glimpse of gratitude for their master. "Do they look at you as their savior with their limited vision? Do they look at you and see a happy life in store for them? I wouldn't. If I looked into the mirror each day and saw mutilation after years of waiting to see the beauty of my reflection, then I might want to die a little more than I already did in the jail cells."

In my peripheral, I see tears sliding down the girls' cheeks. Proof of my words that neither Psyche nor I can ignore. The goddess looks back at her slaves. Some of their movements are tentative while they touch their scarification, but all wear mortification on their gorgeous yet mutilated faces. Others, like my shower-mate, cry with dismal remembrance of their deformed state.

"Glasswing," Psyche says, her voice no longer enlivened with confidence and jubilation. Her tone is fragile like glass with its first crack. "She'll wear the dress you're holding. Get Hermes's concubine ready."

The butterfly flees from my shoulder amidst its owner's rage. Psyche storms out of the room, and all the slaves scramble behind her except for one. Only my shower-mate, Glasswing, remains as the last girl slams the door shut behind her.

She murmurs. "Hi."

A sliver of my childhood returns, and I run towards her with my arms outstretched. She is frail, almost as malnourished as she was in the jail cells, and when my arms wrap around hers, it feels as if I'm hugging a skeleton. Glasswing hesitates for only a second, then she holds me with the same fervent need for comfort.

"I've missed you," I murmur into her shoulder.

"I've missed you too," when she pulls away from our hug, Glasswing reminds me of the past once more. "You told me I wasn't pretty."

"You said the same thing to me."

Her cheeks burn as she ducks her head. "It's clear we both lied. Gods, I wish we could've gone back to the days when we were kids worrying about our appearances."

"Those days were still unkind to us," I remind Glasswing. "Our entire lives have been one terrible thing after another."

She doesn't respond. Instead, she sets my dress down on top of the bed and walks to the makeup center. We were once equals, sitting together underneath the shower head and comparing appearances. We were once seen as two unfortunate human girls, pushing through adversity together.

Yet, as I sit down and she applies makeup to my cheeks, we couldn't be farther apart.

THE THIRTY-THIRD CHAPTER

Garnered in a goddess's clothing, I stare at my reflection in the mirror and no longer see a human girl staring back. I look at my eyes, a deep brown shade of endless swirls of chocolate and cinnamon, and they glow despite their dark tone. My skin, pale as the moonlight, is complimented by the light purple shade of my gown, which hugs every curve of my body like a second sheath of skin.

The gold within my blood sizzles as a creature of great divinity, who should not exist but does, stares back at the mirror's reflection. I know I am not human, no matter how desperately I wish to pluck away the gold within my veins. I am neither godly nor mundane, but this is the first time I see greatness within me without my blood spilling down my arm to confirm it. Miles separates me from the woman standing behind me, who I thought was my equal.

"Is the dress too tight?" Glasswing takes a hesitant step towards me, her one eye assessing me in the mirror just as I am. While I see a demi-god, who has not existed in hundreds of years, Glasswing stares at a woman unraveling. She is nervous as she quips. "I can try to loosen it."

Shaking my head, I fight away the thoughts roaming through my mind, but my voice is gravelly when I lie. "I'm fine, just tired."

Glasswing nods her head, but Kronos's words chant within my head. His moniker for me beats to a distressful, off-kilter tune I can't ignore. Two words are the dolor to any shred of happiness for tonight's endeavors. Glasswing is talking to me, telling me about her time with Psyche since she left the arena, but Kronos's chant is louder.

God-Killer.

God-Killer.

God-Killer.

"Saffron. Saffron, do you hear me?" the voice is in the faraway distance, so quiet compared to the discordant screams in my head, yet that bashful cadence persists, and I finally recognize it as Glasswing's. "Saffron. Saffron."

I pull away from the mirror, my head tilting back to stare at Glasswing. I look at my former shower-mate, and I can see the inquisitiveness brewing in her mind. Glasswing looks at me with concern speckling her face, but upon her stare, Kronos's words turn into a dim whisper.

I can relax enough to utter one word. "Yeah?"

She doesn't vocalize any of the thoughts written across her forehead; instead, she says. "They're ready for you downstairs."

I barely remember walking down the staircase or being introduced to Eros. I can recall riding through the sky in a golden chariot, but I know nothing passed that detail. My mind roars with one thought, one agonizing appellation playing on repeat and voiced by a man derived from the pit of hatred.

God-Killer.

God-Killer.

God-Killer.

Before I grapple with the fact that I will be in a room surrounded by gods, the chariot lands on the ground with a muted thud and Hermes is helping me out. My feet step out of the chariot, and the bright excellence of Dionysus's large alabaster mansion blinds me.

Hermes, with his hand on my lower back, guides me towards the beauteous sight. White marble columns wrap around the exterior of this home, which are decorated with green vines ripe with purple and red grapes. At least fifty steep steps lead to the two double doors twice a person's height. Twice, I trip, but Hermes always catches me.

On the far corners of each fifth step, there are twin fountains designed as a naked man or woman. Either their mouth or hands are spouting wine, which falls into an intricate creation on the steps that slides, curves, and lands in its designated place within the magnificent fountain in the middle of Dionysus's front yard.

The fountain, filled to the brim with red wine, is the size of two chariots and takes over a quarter of his illustrious front yard. The statue in the middle of the fountain is of a man draped in ceramic grapes. While almost completely nude, he wears the grapes and vines around his neck, hanging off of his mouth, and slithering up his legs to cover his most private spots.

"Dio has always been one to flare the dramatics," Hermes says, with both humor and annoyance lacing his voice. "You'll get used to it one day."

I say nothing, but I let him guide me up the rest of the stairs, where Eros and Psyche wait for us. The doorknobs are shaped like an animal without arms or legs, with a forked tongue that juts out. As Eros slams the doorknobs against the door, I swear the legless creatures slither in pain.

A dark-skinned man opens the doors, wearing a purple tunic. He is human, but he speaks as if he owns this magnificent home. The middle-aged man announces. "Welcome." Then, he snaps his fingers, and two humans walk out on both sides of him, trays of white and red wine in their hands. "Thirsty?"

A man with the brightest shade of blonde hair takes a step forward, extending the tray full of white wine to anybody interested. With a blooming giggle, Psyche accepts.

The woman, with a light brown complexion and rich, dark red hair, advances next. Her eyes, a bright shade of gold, switch between the four of us before she extends the tray full of red wine. Hermes picks up two glasses, one for me and one for him. The woman's attention jolts to me for a second, then she tilts her head in unspoken confusion.

Even a complete stranger knows I do not belong.

"Let's go, Saffron," Hermes says, migrating away from the female slave as we walk into the symposium.

Everything is in painted marble, ranging from gold to a deep shade of purple. The steps that lead towards the ballroom floor introduce me to a chandelier of pure magnificence. It dangles from the ceiling, the sight more eccentric than either Ares or Hermes's homes.

Dionysus—the god of parties and wine—ensures his home remains the first choice for any celebration amongst the deities.

Levitating platforms lift nine women into the air while they sing. Their voices are too harmonic to be anything other than godly, and I recognize them as the nine muses—Calliope, Clio, Erato, Euterpe, Melpomene, Polyhymnia, Thalia, Terpsichore, and Urania. These magnificent women are in gowns which glimmer in the nighttime against their dark complexions.

There are around two hundred humans working in Dionysus's house for the symposium. They're all in tunics, either in white, gold, or purple. Their ages vary, and now I see China is not the exception to a human lifespan that reaches maturity. Yet, those who serve the wine and food are not solely here for their ability to pass around nectar, ambrosia, and wine. They are the desired treats for any immortal who wants to give them a second glance.

A man, who is as spellbinding as this home, stands at the bottom of the staircase. His stance is slouched, indicative of somebody with more than a few glasses of wine in their system, but he is beautiful. Round, button-nose, and tousled golden blonde hair that brushes the top of his shoulders. He has plump lips that aren't smiling but curve slight enough to tell the world he knows their secrets and delights in them.

"You've outdone yourself, Dio," Hermes says to the man at the bottom of the staircase. "I've never seen the place look better."

"I could say the same about you when you have this delightful little creature on your arm." Dionysus floats his attention to me, but he asks Hermes. "Why have you been hiding this one all to yourself? She's more gorgeous than all of my concubines put together." He laughs and adds. "If I wasn't so inebriated during your arena fight, then I would've fought for you myself. You would've been my most beloved concubine."

I take my first sip of the wine in my hand before deigning Dionysus a response. "With all due respect, I don't see that as a compliment. More like a punishment." I end with another sip of my wine.

Psyche, who I forgot was standing beside me until now, gasps and apologizes on my behalf. "She continues to forget her place as a-"

"HA!" Dionysus lets out an infectious laugh, silencing Psyche, and he turns to me. "You are such an interesting little thing, aren't you? Hermes, I've always tried to grab that angry slave of yours, but how about a trade for this one? I'll give you-"

Hermes interrupts him before he can offer a trade for me, as if I were cattle or furniture rather than a living person. "Where's Ariadne?" Hermes's green eyes zoom across the room, searching for Ariadne, and Dionysus's smile disappears. "It's not like your wife to miss your parties. She must be around here somewhere."

"I will not let you ruin my party." Dionysus may be eons old, but he is childish and sticks his tongue out at Hermes, then storms away from us to gallivant with anybody other than his wife.

Eros looks to Hermes, who has a deep-set frown on his face, and chides. "You make it so easy for him to get under your skin, dear friend."

I take another sip of my wine.

"Go find that angry brute you call a father and get him distracted for the night." Hermes is sharp with his words, but he sighs a moment later and adds. "Please, Eros. It would mean a lot."

"It'll be done." Eros wraps his arm around his wife's, and while Psyche beams with amour as she stares up at him, he speaks in with hushed candor. "Let's go find my dad and distract him with endless nectar and talks about the Trojan War."

They drift away from us, becoming yet another blur in the tapestry of dozens of gods and goddesses, and for a minute I am blinded. The pure magnitude of this world's beauty, and those who inhabit it, stills me into a paralyzed state. I look around the room of laughing, joyous gods as they drink their wine and make their jokes.

I ogle at the creatures of true divinity in this room, but then I look to the slaves they brought with them and a terrible thought bubbles to the surface. How many humans would die if Kronos crashed through the ceiling right now?

I drink from my wine glass until it is empty.

"Saffron," his voice is somber, like wisps of clouds on a blue sky, and it pulls me away from the build-up of thoughts in my mind. Each worse than the one before it. His hand is nervously extended, yet a boyish smile grows over his pink-tinted lips. "Will you dance with me?"

I take his hand, and with it, my thoughts are replaced with his boyish features.

THE THIRTY-FOURTH CHAPTER

Hermes and I do not dance to elicit a sense of elation beneath the glittering chandelier. We do not hold one another beside the celestial radiance of the muses' hymns. Our bodies are gliding together as one to ease any tension that has built to a suffocating level over this past week.

Our lips never discuss the secrets or gaze at the prominent vein on my forearm that tells us both what we're aware of, and our ears never listen to the confessions of the other's lies. Even as the lights dim and the music drifts higher towards the ceiling, we let the dance become our escape once more.

I tilt my head back, letting the rush of air brush through my hair like tender, loving hands while Hermes twirls me towards the center of the dancefloor. He will stare at me with enough intensity to move mountains, but then look away a moment later. He will be present in our dance one second, then he is searching around the crowd the next.

We stop dancing for another sip of wine, another poison to drown my discombobulated mind. Then, our feet grace the floor again and we resume the endless game we play. Our game of make believe, where I am only his human concubine, and he is only my master without a mischievous thought in his head.

ICHOR

I let a smile grow over my lips even as Hermes searches the room for somebody else. I did not realize that I, too, was roaming the capacious expanse until I see navy eyes across the room staring back. He is far away from where I am with Hermes, his body almost completely shrouded by Eros's lanky frame, but I can see him despite the barriers between us.

Ares, who tried to murder me the last time he saw me, stares at me from where he stands, and traitorous jolts of electricity pulse through my body. He is nodding his head every so often in response to whatever Eros is saying to him, but he doesn't look away from me. Ares waits and plays nice with his son, while I dance and drink and try to ignore the world around me, but I know he will approach me if I'm alone.

Then, like the predator he is, he will strike.

Drawing my gaze back towards Hermes, I plead with newfound breathlessness. "Can we take a quick break? A drink sounds great right now."

I know I shouldn't. Remaining sober and of sound mind is the wise choice, but Hermes slows us to a stop and plucks two fresh glasses of red wine from the tray of a passing server. I do not fight what my trembling hands want, and Hermes does not comment on my heavy drinking tonight. We both fight back the words we want to say. Him with tight lips and me with endless glasses of wine.

"You look beautiful tonight," he says as we resume dancing, my feet more sluggish than they were at the beginning of the night.

My words are slurred when I respond. "Thank you."

His arm is still wrapped around my waist, but his other hand dares a change in movement. Fingers, callus from hard work, caress the side of my cheek. He is no longer searching the room for another; his attention is on me.

I stand beneath him, absorbed by the scent of the flowers from our garden that encompass him like a welcoming hug. Hermes brings me a step closer to him, flushing my chest against his, while he ogles down towards my parted, wine-painted lips.

"You told me that this was a bad idea," I vocalize the first glimpse of honesty between us all night.

He nods his head. "It is a terrible idea." He doesn't look away from my lips, even as he verbalizes. "I'm horrible for you."

"Yet?" I urge him for more.

His thumb slides across my bottom lip, teasing the sensitive nerves, and as I gasp, he discloses. "Yet, you're the most gorgeous woman I've ever seen. When I stare at you, this close but unable to kiss you, it feels like I'm being brutalized in the Fields of Punishments."

"Why are you unable to kiss me?"

"Because the Fates are as cruel to me as my own conscious is," he says, more to himself than me, but his thumb slips from my lips, then his hands join him in leaving me. He drops his touch from my body and takes a step back, muttering aloud. "I'll be right back."

"Wait," I say, but Hermes is already gone. Dejected and drunk, I finish my sentence for only my ears. "You pinky promised not to leave me alone tonight."

Joyous couples surround me, dancing and laughing and twirling around, but I'm alone in my disharmony. Standing in the center of the dancefloor, my shoulders brush the surrounding partygoers, but I'm ostracized once again. Then, like a glimmering ray of sunlight falling from the sky, a god parts the room and approaches me with an extended hand.

No matter what inebriated state I am in, or that I've never cordially met him, I know which god stands in front of me. The blinding rays from the chandelier's brilliance conceal a portion of his face, but I would always recognize Apollo.

Apollo is the god of prophecies and truth, healing and diseases, and music and dance. He is the brightest scintillant in a room of eminence. His hair is a part of the sun, blinding if looked upon for too long, but ever flowing. It's about as long as mine, resting upon the middle of his chest in natural waves and haphazard, thin braids.

Even his eyes have speckles of gold inside of them. Bright shades of greens and blues fight for dominance, but gold runs around the black pupil like a halo. Gold splashes his irises, but it's the most luminous in the middle. He's not as tall as Hermes, but his height is still considerable enough to cast a shadow over my shorter frame.

His cheekbones are sharp enough to split the Earth in half, and they are high risen when he smiles in amusement. "If you keep looking at me like that, then I might think you're attracted to me, ómorfo aínigma."

"What did you call me?" I ponder, my hips swaying as I stand before him, unable to keep still.

He doesn't answer my question; instead, he looks down at his extended hand, then back at me. "May I join you in a dance? It is a great sin to leave a beautiful woman alone on the dancefloor."

I search for Hermes amongst the crowd. I scour the ballroom for his tall frame, which towers over every other male and female in the vicinity, but I deflate each time a dark-haired and slender figure does not wear his face. Another server passes by us, her tray filled with white wine, and I pluck it for my own greedy ambition for obliteration.

In three rapacious gulps, the glass is empty. Only then do I accept Apollo's hand and ignore the stinging resurgence of Hermes's rejection. I let the golden god pull me to his brawny chest. His hand, the one that is not clasped in mine, glides to my waist.

Wine-gifted smiles are directed in Apollo's direction as we glide across the ground, my mind spinning with each turn, each press of our bodies when they dare to part from one another. He is infectious, a happy distraction from the stinging reminder of Hermes's dismissal, and with the surplus of wine in my system, I forget about the rest of the world.

"Are you enjoying tonight, ómorfo aínigma?" His voice is a deep bass, drumming through my body like one of the muse's instruments.

"That's a good question," I comment, but that's all I say because I'm not sure if I'm enjoying the night.

Would I still be enjoying this event if it were not for the succulent wine coursing through my body? The alcohol evaporates the fear and voices within my head, which tell me dastardly things about myself I'm not prepared to listen to. I enjoy the wine and the glimpse of freedom that comes with it, but am I enjoying myself? Or is this glimpse of freedom reminding me of all that I cannot possess? Epiales and Kronos's words burn in my head, causing the world around me to spin and the uneasiness in my stomach to worsen.

"I'm going to throw up," I garble.

Nausea churns my stomach, and bile makes its steady climb up my throat. Apollo, who has only known me for a few minutes, pulls me away from the crowd of immortals and rushes me towards the open air. He throws open two glass doors, which lead to a fountain in the backyard, where a naked figurine is spouting wine from their mouth.

I collapse onto the ground before the fountain, my knees slapping against the rough terrain, and all the wine I consumed spills out. Apollo's hands are in my hair, pulling it back as I heave. Ragged gasps leave, along with red chunks, but as the nausea subsides, Apollo's hands drop from my hair.

"Thank you," I gasp out as I wipe away the bile with the back of my hand. I stand to my feet, and as I turn to face Apollo, I explain. "That is the *last* time I drink that much."

The rest of my words die upon petrified lips.

Apollo is on the ground, gold ichor spilling from the side of his head, but his body is mostly concealed by the burly god who stands a foot away from me. Some of Apollo's blood is splattered across Ares's face, dripping into his dark scruff. Ares stares back at me with a calm demeanor, but I can only focus on the knife he has gripped in his hand.

The same knife he almost killed me with two weeks ago.

"I'm going to ask you one last time," Ares growls as he takes a step forward. "Who created you, *demi-god*?"

THE THIRTY-FIFTH CHAPTER

Since I first saw Ares on the arena ground, beneath the veil of fright, I found him to be the most handsome god. There has always been something about Ares, which makes some instinctual part of me yearn to gravitate closer. It could be the pout of his lips, the prickle of facial hair across his sharp jaw, or the sharp intensity in his eyes.

But right now, I stare at Ares, and I can see my own brutal demise staring back. The end begins with him and that blade, and no amount of alcohol can make the realization ebb away. I take a retreating step, only to trip on my own wayward feet and tumble downward. I land on the rim of the fountain, and my hands curl around the edge.

My nails dig into the material, but I do not deviate my focus away from Ares's advancing form. Not even for a second.

"I've had a few weeks to think about you," Ares says. "When the shock went away, and you were no longer around to answer my curiosity, I searched for my answers."

He takes a step forward, and as he does, the knife in his hand grows into a mighty sword. Its sharp blade glistens underneath the stars, promising me a swift death. With each step he takes, the tip of the sword screeches on the cobblestone.

"In order to create you, your mother had to be the very definition of perfection," he says the words as if they were not a compliment, but a mere fact. "I thought she was a goddess, so I went through and tried to remember the deities who didn't attend the arenas eighteen years ago. Who might've hid a pregnancy from the rest of the world."

His feet pound on the floor, making the ground beneath me shake. Stray rocks jump from their resting place, trying to flee from his mighty steps as he advances nearer and nearer. My hands tighten around the fountain's rim, the smallest crack forming beneath my fingertips.

"One day, I went and saw Hebe and Thetis." He takes another step. "Then, I met with Dione and Eris, Nyx and Achlys," another step, and another list of goddesses. "I stared into the eyes of Pasithea and Oizys and Lethe, but none of them were your mother. Each one of them weren't half as radiant as you are."

He kneels in front of me, and the tip of his sword finds its victim underneath my chin. He stares up at me with fastidious fascination, but I remind myself that he is my executioner, and I must expect the death he has wished to exact since we met on the arena ground. The sword will slide through the underbelly of my chin and kill me. I am certain the next time the faraway clock chimes a new hour, I will be within the Underworld. Charon will stand at the bank of the river, his wrinkled hand outstretched for currency, before taking me to my afterlife.

Ares does not cease to tell his journey towards my lineage, never once applying pressure on the sword he uses to dangle my life. "Some of them had brown eyes like you, but theirs did not sparkle the way yours do. Most had brown hair, but theirs did not have the shimmer that yours possesses. Two of them have round cheeks like yours, but when they smiled at me, they did not raise into the highest cheekbones I've ever seen. Not like yours. I saw dozens of goddesses, and you were too beautiful to be their children."

Ares hesitates to kill me, the woman he vowed to eliminate for the sake of his own heart. He hates the words he spews to me, but he cannot stop them from reaching my ears. This god, who prides himself on the lives he has taken with brutal savagery, kneels before me with a quivering sword pressed to my skin.

He does not realize that his words, laced with an undertone of dubiousness, are the sweetest compliments I've ever received. I've been called beautiful by him and others over the past few weeks, but he does not just see a beautiful face. He sees the uniqueness in the common color of my eyes, and at the risk of hubris, sees me grander than dozens of goddesses known for their beauty and charm.

But now is not the time to awe at my potential murderer. I do not have the chance to fawn over his words, to see them as more than just compliments. The blade is still against my throat, and murder is still Ares's aim. His words, which bring electricity to my veins, are meager compared to my skin threatening to break upon the sword's kiss.

Ares growls his next words. "Then I thought back to the human women in the arena nineteen or twenty years ago. Between the quarterly arenas, there were hundreds of human women who came onto the grounds to be sought after by gods. But if those goddesses paled in your perfection, then I did not know how I'd remember the ordinary appearances of a common mortal girl."

I should speak, to beg him for my life, but the words never spill out. I can't bring myself to cry, plead, or scream for Hermes's name. Apollo, whose forehead is healed but still lays unconscious on the floor behind Ares, wouldn't stir even if I bellowed his name. The crack of the fountain beneath my fingertips grows, little by little, as I stare at Ares, who does not know whether to praise me or kill me.

"That's when I remembered her," Ares says. "Round cheeks that hid high cheekbones, shimmering brown hair, and round sparkling eyes. Standing so meek in the arena ground, hugging her tiny body in the winter cold. A diamond amongst pebbles thirty years ago."

Ares does not let his sword deviate from my throat as he rises to his full, imposing height. Something foreign flickers across his face, making his lips turn into a deep frown as he stares down at where I sit on the fountain's rim. Maybe it is guilt for the murderous act he is about to commit, or perhaps it is a resolution that he must go through with his homicidal promise to himself.

The fountain's small cracks fall to the ground in muted cries. I refuse to glance at the growing carnage, but I stare into the depth of Ares's sharp features. I look at Ares as if I can pierce into his soul.

His frown worsens, and when he speaks again, his cadence is fracturing like the fountain around my gasp. "I remembered the scared, timid girl who looked identical to my father's first wife, reincarnated into a human woman. Zeus took one look at her, the mirror image of his only wife who he ever respected and cared for, and he jumped onto the arena ground. The entire room erupted in lightning bolts, and he promised to throw any god or goddess into Tartarus if they dared to fight him for her. He was so mesmerized by her beauty, and nobody tried to battle him for what he yearned for more than life itself. Not even my mother, his current wife, said a word as he left with the human in his arms."

He applies the tiniest pressure against the sword on my neck, and one trickle of blood falls. It's pure gold as it stains his blade, and I watch as Ares's face contorts with bloodshed. Desperation clings to my chest, and I can't die yet. Not when answers I've been searching for are within my grasp.

"Before you kill me, answer your question for me, Ares. Please, *please* answer your question." I beg for the truth Hermes has known, but he has refused to tell me. I peer at the last person I expected honesty from, and I let my answers spread through the outdoors like a burning toxin. "Who created me into this thing the world hates? A weapon to some, but a monstrosity to most? Who created this? Who hated me so much that they spawned such a creature?"

The sword wavers and with it, Ares's motivation to end my life. There's a shatter without the world splintering around our feet. An internal switch in both of us crumbles, transforming into debris. His desire to kill me is diluted when he sees the hatred for my existence staring back with blurry vision.

Meanwhile, Kronos's words scream in my head once again.

God-Killer.

God-Killer.

God-Killer.

"Put your weapon down, Ares." An unfamiliar, feminine voice pushes through the tense, cursed air around us.

I forgot about the party inside, where laughter and drinks are exchanged without anxiousness. I let the world outside of Ares and I disintegrate. My mind is so engrossed in his words and his actions, and my response to them, and I omitted the party from my mind.

Apollo is now up to his feet, a golden-edged sword pointed towards Ares, but he is not Ares's biggest concern. A petite woman with the same narrow yet upturned nose as Apollo stands in between two huntresses with their bows and arrows raised.

The one huntress, who stands to her goddess's right, is Sika. I glance at her leg, which is completely healed. My gaze drifts toward her face, and Sika gives me a sad smile. Sika, who was brash and wise, looks uncharacteristic with sympathy splattering her long face.

I look away from Sika, hating her expression, and I stare at the second huntress with a gasp escaping my lips.

The stories of Artemis and Willow are effusive in the jail cells, like a secret the other gods could not know. Humans do not have dreams when they slumber, or knowledge of the outside world, except for Willow and Artemis. Every human in my jail cell knows who Willow is because she is the greatest huntress to exist. As Artemis's favored huntress, Willow has been alive for nearly five hundred years, and has fought beside her goddess as an equal.

When humans dream, it is while they are awake. Each girl dreams of becoming Willow, a human with the quick speed of a goddess, and immortality to finesse her skills. With blazing blue eyes and blades wrapping around her biceps like a badge of honor, Willow is the exception to the fragility of humanity.

Ares sees Willow standing beside Artemis, and he drops his sword.

Artemis takes a step forward and she snarls. "Good afternoon, brother."

He should leave and count himself fortunate that he can escape without an arrow lodged in his chest, but Ares looks back at me once more. He stares at the tears I've refused to let fall, and the effect the secrets of my life are having on my mental state. Ares ignores the huntresses with fingers twitching on their bowstrings with excitement.

"Your mother's name was Metis," he says this, but by the time the arrows fly, he disappears from thin air.

Once Ares is gone, Apollo rushes towards me. Just as Ares did before, but with none of the magnetism, he lowers himself down onto his knees in front of me. I can't look at Apollo, who is as much a stranger to me as all the others in the ballroom. He almost touches me, placing his hands on my knees, but stops himself.

Instead, he holds his hand out once again in a voluntary invitation. "Let's go, ómorfo aínigma. We're going to take you home."

"Home?" I ask with hope swelling my chest, and I accept his hand.

When I stand up, the entire fountain collapses, red wine gushing across our feet like spilled blood. Apollo looks at my fingertips, which are healed, but specks of dried red and gold blood remain. I'm not surprised when there is no incredulity marring his face, but then we disappear in a bright ray of the long-fallen sun.

The party leaves my vision, but Hermes's mansion does not materialize when the light disperses. We're no longer in Dionysus's backyard, around the shattered fountain and overflowing wine, but we aren't in the place that I've called home these past two weeks, either. There are no tulips resting in a vase in the kitchen, or Hattie's faraway quips of anger. Books aren't haphazardly strewn around the house, open on a random page.

There's only darkness.

Only the Underworld stares back.

THE THIRTY-SIXTH CHAPTER

The Underworld's throne room is identical to the one Epiales created in our dream world. Both thrones are the same, regal in blackened jewels. I can see my tear-stained expression through the clean floor. It's so similar, but when Hades and Persephone rise from their seats as king and queen of this land, it is so different, too.

There aren't black feathered curtains that cover the window, and now the stretch of the Underworld is visible from clear glass. Smoke doesn't slither around the ground, greeting me in cold yet welcoming comfort. There is no Epiales, no matter how much I stare at the shadowed corners of the room, waiting for him to emerge.

This is real life, and that makes this experience more confusing.

Apollo's hand drops from mine, and he takes retreating steps back. He now stands with Hermes, Artemis, Willow, and Sika. My attention is solely on the Monopoly loving god, who kneels into a bow before Hades and Persephone. He won't look at me.

Although he is bowed, he tilts his head upwards and stares at Hades. Apollo, Artemis, Sika, and Willow are bowed next to

Hermes. I stand in between the two groups of gods, a handful of steps ahead of where Hermes kneels but behind the king and queen of the Underworld. I lower myself on wobbling knees, ready to bow just as they do, but Persephone breaks the drowning silence.

"Not you, my dear. Do not bow to us."

Persephone's voice is a hushed sound, but she commands respect with each heeled click of her shoes against the smooth, obsidian ground. Her gown reminds me of her eyes, both dark with a tinge of purple. She glides, and the dress follows behind her in a circular trail. The dress's train reminds me too much of the disgorged wine from the fountain, which I shattered with strength I was not aware lived inside of me.

Her hand is stiff as it cups my cheek, but I gaze up at the queen of the Underworld. The knowledge that gods bow before her, and I do not, speaks more than words. I remember the day of my arena with her. I remember the kindness she displayed, and the devastation that wrecked Persephone when she and Hades did not defeat Ares.

"Who am I?" I ask the Queen of the Underworld, and while Hermes shrouded me in secrecy, I look up at Persephone and see the answers within my reach.

"That is a loaded question, but I will answer it with only two requests."

"Anything," is my immediate response.

"First, you must wait until we are finished with our story before you can ask us questions," Persephone says, her voice quiet yet firm. "Secondly, and this is the most important one, is that you do not blame us for the terrible actions we made along the way. There wasn't a perfect option amongst the terror of our current world, and we did what we thought was the best we could with our circumstances."

"I just want to know the truth," I say with a weakened strain to my voice. "I'm sick of the lies and the secrets. People run from me when I just want to know who I am, and I'm so tired of it." I say these words to Persephone, but they are a bladed stab in Hermes's direction.

Persephone nods her head. "Very well."

Hades deviates from the four beings behind me. "Thank you for bringing her back to us. You may all leave with my deepest gratitude."

I look around the room, which is familiar only in my dreams with Epiales, with the certainty that I've never been here while awake. My waking life was within the prisons, the arena, Ares's mansion, or Hermes's home. I've never ventured further away from the land of the living, but Hades's words ring in my ear.

For one second, I hesitate to turn around and see him one last time. That's it. Just a second slips by before I whip my head behind me. I yearn to see his boyish smirk again or hear his laughter always brewing with an undertone of mischief, especially if this is the end to our story.

Yet, when I look back, only Apollo remains.

He's no longer kneeling on the ground before the king and queen of the Underworld, but he's standing and looking only at me. My forlorn expression speaks words I never will, and Apollo knows this. He stands taller than me, my presence shadowed beneath him, and he knows I wish he were somebody else.

The golden god lowers his head. "Until we meet again, ómorfo aínigma."

Then, he too, is gone.

When I look back at Hades and Persephone, their focus is not on me, but one another. Tension once filled this onyx throne room, but when Persephone stares up at her husband, the smallest smile peels over her lips. She stares at her husband and all of her anguish vanishes as if he were the peace amid a storm. When they behold one another, it is a private event, for their love is all-consuming.

Hades is the first to deviate away; he looks at me and then asks. "Would you like to go somewhere where you can sit during this conversation?" He hesitates for a minute before he adds. "This will be a long story."

"I'm fine where I am," I say.

I stared at Hades in the arena and saw him as the rest of the answers to the mystery of my life, and I was right. He leads Persephone and me back to the thrones that remind me too much of Epiales, but instead of taking a seat himself, he lets me sit in a chair meant for a king. I follow his silent request, and I lower myself onto the plush seat.

Hades stands at the second step closest to the chairs. His absorption is on me as he begins. "Eons ago, there was a war that cemented a deep-rooted hatred between the gods and the titans for the rest of eternity. My father, Kronos, fought against his children for possession of the world as its sovereign ruler. This war, to the humans, was titled Titanomachy and we were victorious."

Persephone starts where her husband pauses. "The gods who fought in the war threw Kronos into an impenetrable prison deep in the Earth, even lower than the Underworld. Every single titan who joined Kronos in the fight against the gods joined him in Tartarus. It's where Kronos was for eons, along with his followers."

"Nobody has ever escaped from Tartarus," Hades emphasizes. "It is an endless well, so far down into the Earth that nobody can crawl themselves out of its abyss. Even if they could climb out, magical bars block the exit, and Thanatos is waiting at the top with his scythe and an imperial duty to guard the prison from any daring to escape."

"Yet, somehow, Kronos escaped," Persephone says with a purse of her lips. "Magic blinded Thanatos for only a minute, maybe two, but when light returned, there was a crack in Tartarus. The bars were deformed, as if hands pulled them apart. We were fortunate in the sense that not everybody within Tartarus escaped, but all the titans fled from their eternal imprisonment."

"Thanatos closed the bars before other nefarious immortals could venture towards freedom, but the damage was irrevocable. Kronos, along with all the titans and cyclopes who fought alongside him, were free in a world unlike the one they left eons prior." A sigh breaks through Hades's explanation, silencing the room once bubbling with newfound information. "And with their freedom, the second round of Titanomachy began."

Persephone interjects. "The world the humans lived in when the second round of Titanomachy came was of learned helplessness and vapid beliefs. They thought they would never see strife in their life. They were given technology, medicines that could cure most diseases, and houses that had lights without the use of torches. They were spoiled, but when the war began, I felt an abundance of sympathy for those humans."

"Eighty-five percent of humanity died in this war, casualties of a battle they should've never had to witness. We should've protected them. We should've kept Kronos and all of his titans imprisoned for the rest of time, but we failed in our mission, and we failed the humans." Hades says these words with a bitter bite to his cadence, his hands curled into tightened fists. "But the titans had surprise on their side and all the monsters, who never died by a demi-god's hand but were thrown into Tartarus instead, joined the titans in the fight. Typhon almost killed Zeus in the battle, and Kronos's army was winning."

"They were going to kill humanity," Persephone's words are a mournful promise. "There are only two ways that an immortal can be killed, and Kronos was killing the entire human race because he did not want to defeat us in battle and imprison us. He wanted all of us to die by his hands. So, he started to kill humans in mass quantities."

"Have you ever heard of a god named Pan?" Hades asks, deviating from the conversation.

Confused, I shake my head. Epiales taught me about countless gods, ensuring I knew every detail about them. I knew which god was married to which goddess, which animals were symbols to specific immortals, but Epiales never told me about Pan.

"Pan was a fertility god and a sweet man, but forgettable to the humans. It took a few eons, but the humans forgot Pan existed. Because they no longer prayed to him, he disappeared from the world. The first god to truly die," Hades whispers the last sentence, almost afraid to utter the truth. "The humans in the modern world were egotistical creatures who barely appreciated the beauty of the world outside of their cell phones, but they prayed to us in their own particular way. There were countless poems and television shows written about us. Songs were sung in our honor and movies graced their theaters."

"They saw us as mythical creatures," Persephone admits. "But the humans prayed to us and let us live. They did not know it, but without them praying to us and remembering who we were, we would've faded from existence like Pan had. Kronos knew this, so he wanted to kill every single human who knew we existed."

I have none that pray to me. Epiales said to me on the night he brought Kronos into our dreamworld. *And I'm disappearing slowly and painfully.*

"Athena is both the goddess of wisdom and warfare. She looked out at the battleground and knew we were going to lose, and the death of humanity would join us, so she came up with a plan."

Hades moves to sit on the top step, his elbows resting on his knees and fatigue overtaking his appearance. The king of the Underworld, who sits on the floor while a girl takes his mantle, looks human. He's attractive in the same way the other gods are, but there's a sense of honest transparency with him that breaks the barrier of otherworldly attractiveness and shows human characteristics.

He rummages a hand through his shaggy, jet black locks, and divulges his tale. "Athena told Kronos that if the humans died, then all immortals would decease because every immortal needed to be remembered. Kronos and the other titans were included in her theory. There hasn't been a titan who has died from humans forgetting who they are, but she made an educated guess. It was an educated guess that Kronos believed enough to listen to her next plan of action."

"Zeus takes credit for the deal," Persephone says. "But it was Athena who came up with the idea of human enslavement. As if she were an oracle, Athena saw our deaths on the horizon and acted fast. She made educated guess after educated guess and spun a story where we did not end up in Tartarus and the entire human race did not die."

"Athena told Kronos that if he could escape from Tartarus, then so would they. She said that she knew how to escape from the impenetrable prison," Hades adds. "My father is a terrible man, but he also is smart enough not to test fate. Kronos and Athena sat at a round table on Mt. Olympus for fourteen days until they came to a mutual agreement. Both of them knew the other would break the oath the second there was an opportunity, but when we were looking at our deaths, this deal saved our immortal lives."

I want to ask, but Persephone answers before a word can leave my lips.

"Hecate was ordered to put a shield around Mt. Olympus, hiding the home of the Olympians from all of us. Then, we were cast aside and put on Earth with a sworn oath to Kronos that we would imprison the human race." When Persephone says the last sentence, she looks at her shoes rather than me.

"It was Kronos who enslaved people?" I ask, my jaw slacked, and thoughts I do not dare to express out loud blare in my head.

The same titan, who is promising freedom for the humans if they help him kill the gods, is the same monster who enslaved them to begin with.

"Yes, but we are no better in this situation," Hades said fast, but with a tinge of regret. "We agreed because of fear for our own mortality."

"But you saved the humans by agreeing to this," I respond.

"We were told we needed to own at least two slaves at a time," Persephone explains, diverting from my statement to finish their story. "But we weren't allowed to have any over two hundred slaves at the same time. We were given permission to have just enough slaves to keep us alive, as Kronos swore in his meeting with Athena, but not enough to give us our full strength."

"It was Zeus's idea to turn getting slaves into a game in the arena," Hades said. "And even if some of us hated the arena, most of us fought to keep ourselves alive. Then, as the centuries passed and some gods and goddesses' compassion for the humans withered away, many of us fought in the arena to save humans from gods who wanted to kill them."

"Some gods blamed our dependency on the humans for why we lost the war," Persephone said, her teeth gritted. "So, some began torturing the humans we gave up Mt. Olympus to protect. It took about a hundred years, but after all the humans who knew the truth died, the story changed. The vicious few who mistreated humans gloated, and their stories traveled farther than the actions of the benevolent masters. When the humans stopped hearing the tales of truth, they were replaced with the truth of horrors. We gave up our home on Mt. Olympus to protect them, but we are also the villains."

"Thank you for telling me the truth about how this all began," I say, but I look between them and ask. "But how does this connect to me? With the color of my blood?"

I mutter the last question with fear they do not know and will kill me for such an offense. The room is silenced by my question for a prolonged time. Persephone stares down at Hades, but he looks at me with a frown curling the corners of his lips.

"Earlier, Persephone said there were two ways to kill an immortal, and we only explained one of them. You, Saffron," Hades announces with great grievance. "Are the second way to kill any deity."

"How?" I'm struggling to breathe, much less produce one coherent word.

"It begins with a prophecy," Persephone says. "And a woman named Metis."

THE THIRTY-SEVENTH CHAPTER

Hades and Persephone do not hide under a sheath of pleasantries and amiable lies. They're honest, with their slouched stances and destitute expressions. As my world quakes, fracturing in half between what I know and what I'm afraid to discover, they do not cloak their grimaces. They do not use suave explanations to ease my mind.

"The prophecy was eons before you were born, but one cemented in every gods' mind. Especially Zeus's," Persephone adds. "Metis was a powerful titaness of good counsel, planning, cunning, and wisdom. She was wise, and she was one of the few titans who did not favor Kronos's side in the first Titanomachy. Instead, she aided us in defeating Kronos and all who dared to fight with him."

Hades's back is hunched over as he leans into his elbows, which still rest on the top of his knees. His bangs hang over his forehead, shadowing a portion of his face, but he does not shield me from this information. The king of the Underworld glances upwards, his thick black lashes intermingling with his shaggy locks, and he gifts me with candor.

"Metis was not just smart, but she was gorgeous as well. One of the rarest beauties that the world has ever seen," Hades admits. "She was so beautiful that both of my brothers, Poseidon and Zeus, fought for her hand in marriage. Zeus won, and she became his first wife. Many believe that Poseidon married one of Metis's sisters, Amphitrite, because it was the closest he could get to achieving the coveted titaness."

Persephone continues. "Zeus's entire world was Metis, who was his most coveted wife. Some insist she was the only wife he had never cheated on. Others say they've never seen the king of the skies as happy as he was when she was alive. Yet, many great romances in our world end in tragedies. Theirs is no exception."

When she falls mute, Hades fills in the space with noise. "Zeus called for one of Apollo's oracles to come to Mt. Olympus and tell him the gender of his first child with Metis. Yet, when the oracle came to the skies, her words did not warm Zeus; instead, rage and paranoia took siege."

"It was prophesied that Metis would bear powerful children," Persephone says. "The first child, who was prominent in Metis's belly, would be a mighty warrior on the battlefield. However, the second child they bore would become more powerful than Zeus. The oracle said that this second child would be a son. Before she could explain the prophecy, the oracle was killed because of Zeus's rage, but even oracles make errors in their prophecies."

Hades is leaning against her throne, his arms crossed over his chest, and continues. "Zeus, in a rage of paranoia, asked his wife to turn into a fly. Dutiful Metis obeyed her husband, and she transformed into a fly. Then-"

"Zeus ate her," I finish his sentence, my voice devoid of emotion as I regurgitate one of Epiales's stories.

Come to think of it, it was the first story Epiales told me in our dream world.

"Correct," Hades says. "Do you know how Athena was born, then?"

I nod my head, responding. "Zeus had a splitting headache one day and asked Hephaestus to help him. Hephaestus used an axe and cut into Zeus's head, and Athena sprouted from his skull in full armor."

"Hermes taught you a lot when you were there," Persephone commends.

I do not have the strength to correct her.

"Zeus thought the prophecy ended with Metis living in his stomach as a fly," Hades explains. "He thought his beliefs were cemented into fact when Metis was forgotten by the humans and died within his belly, and eons went on with Zeus unaware that prophecies always have a tricky way of resurgence."

Hades has a foot propped up against Persephone's throne now, and a passerby would assume that he's comfortable in the throne room, but his face tells a different tale. His forehead is scrunched, a row of imperfect wrinkles creasing his otherwise deific complexion. Then, every few seconds, his jaw twitches.

In a gravelly tone, Hades says. "After Athena struck the deal with Kronos to save us and the humans, the Olympians came together and agreed to a new set of laws while we lived on Earth. Our most important rule was to never create demi-gods."

I must've showed displeasure on my face because Persephone clarifies. "We feared the creation of demi-gods because we know the power they possess. Even a traditional demi-god of Ares's or Aphrodite's holds more power than a traditional human, and that kind of power is dangerous with Kronos living free. He is a master manipulator, and if a demi-god believed he was the benevolent one and we were the villain, then that halfling could change the balance that was created because of Athena."

"Yet, while I am not fortunate in this category," Hades says with a very uncharacteristic snarl in his cadence. "Most gods and goddesses are extremely fertile."

Persephone reaches out her hand, and Hades is quick to accept his wife's compassion after revealing his own infertility. A fact about him I realize is something he correlates with being deficient. The frown on his lips worsens until she squeezes his hand.

With their hands intertwined, Persephone turns to me and says. "Many immortals bed both female and male slaves, and terrible decisions were made on all of our parts when those humans would fall pregnant. Hundreds of humans lost their lives because of their pregnancies."

There is a long, guilty silence between the three of us as her words spoil the air. The pungent stench of regret sticks to the walls, the oppressive treatment of humanity screaming in a muted room. My gaze moves to my lap, to my nervous fingers that pick at the skin underneath my fingernail.

I do not look up, but Hades begins again. "One day, thirty years ago, there was a quarterly arena event. Nobody expected a different outcome than the previous thousand fights, but then we saw an anxious woman cowering behind a few rows of humans. She was thinner than Metis, by at least thirty pounds, but there was no denying whose face this human girl bore. Anybody who knew Metis saw her spitting image attempting to hide on the arena ground."

"Zeus wouldn't let anyone fight for her," Persephone explains, her hand still intertwined with Hades's. "He saw that tiny, fragile woman, and he saw his second chance to live with the only person he's ever loved. Zeus chose her without a standard arena duel."

Hades takes over, his voice roughened with growing emotions. "Metis was his great love, and no matter how many men and women Zeus spent his nights with, Metis never left his mind. When he had the human girl in his house, he named her after his fallen wife and gave her a scarification mark of a wedding band around her finger."

"Just as he had with the last Metis," Persephone says. "He fell for her. Hard. Zeus would no longer bed anybody else but her. He loved the human Metis as much, if not more, than his first wife, who he lost eons before."

"For eleven years, Zeus was careful not to impregnant her. Nobody could see her except for him, but he was happy. My brother, for the first time in eons, was elated to wake up every morning, and it was because of Metis. Yet," Hades says with a wave of sadness. "She became pregnant."

"Zeus never hesitated to kill his previous mistresses who fell pregnant," Persephone's voice wavers with an onslaught of emotions. "But not Metis. Except for Hermes, Zeus did not tell anybody that Metis fell pregnant, and he promised Hermes a promotion from his job as messenger if he helped protect his unborn child. Hermes would replace Dionysus as an Olympian, and he would become Zeus's child's betrothed as long as the child was a girl and could make it to adulthood. Zeus was going to keep his child and raise it with his soulmate, and with Hermes's help with the lies, he kept the pregnancy a secret from the world."

"That was, until Hera found out," said Hades.

I am still picking at the skin underneath my fingernails. They're talking, and as they explain this story of amour and loss, I know the direction it is going. No matter how valiantly I try to diffuse the thoughts, I know my involvement in this story. Their words scream in my head, telling me the rest of this tale that I need to hear, but don't know if my sanity can handle. So, again and again I use my thumb to scrape against the gold-streaked red, angry finger.

ICHOR

My skin is frayed, but I do not stop eroding the sore flesh. Even as gold and red blood bubbles to the surface, I listen to Persephone's hushed words and punish the body that holds so many secrets.

"Metis was nine months pregnant, ready to give birth, when Hera walked into the room and saw the truth that she long suspected. She killed the human Metis, and she left with the belief that the baby couldn't survive without its mother. Hera did not factor Hermes into the equation. Hermes came to the bedroom a minute later with a message to Zeus when he saw Metis. Her throat slashed and her hands around her swollen belly. A resilient foot kicking against the rounded stomach."

Tears drip onto my hand as I pick apart my flesh, centimeter by centimeter. Gold and red and the distraught liquid intermingle on the top of my thumb. There are screams in my head, but their words are audible beneath the steady stream of anguish.

Hades talks. "Hermes is the messenger of departed souls to the Underworld. So, when he took Metis's soul, he took the baby girl with him. That's where Persephone and I found Hermes on that memorable day. He was on the ferry ride with Charon, with the human Metis's spirit beside him and a crying newborn baby in his arms."

I know what I am, yet I do not stop their words. I do not announce my proclamation, and I let Persephone explain further. "Hades and I cannot have children together, but all I've ever wanted was to have a child that was both of ours. If I've ever prayed to the Fates for anything, then it was a chance to start a family with my husband, and Hermes gave us both that chance." Persephone wipes away her own tears as she hiccups. "When Hermes reached out his arms with the baby, I didn't hesitate. I took the first-born demi-god in five hundred years as my daughter, and I named her after the only flower sacred to both Hermes and me."

We both divulge my name to the air that listens with rapt fascination. "Saffron."

Hades, a god who is not biologically my father but took up the helm with pride, explains. "For almost two years, we could hold you and covet you as our first-born child together. Persephone has other children with other men, but you were our first, and it didn't matter that you had none of our physical features, or that you were my niece. I saw you for the first time, and I loved you as your father."

I didn't realize that Hades moved until his hands curl into mine, separating my finger from brutalizing my skin. He does not force me to look at him, or to accept his affection. He curls his fingers underneath the palm of my hands, and he waits to see if I will pull away or accept his embrace. My sight is blurry with tears, but I look at Hades, who wants to be my father, and a fragment of my sadness wanes.

He murmurs. "We both knew who you were and what prophecy you brought to life, but we did not care. We were going to train you to control your powers that came with being Metis and Zeus's second-born child, and you were going to become the princess of our land."

"What happened?" I squeak out the question.

"We wanted to announce on your eighteenth birthday that we conceived a child. You would ascend to a goddess, and you'd run the Underworld with us. Most immortals are too focused on themselves to question it, but we made a mistake." Hades runs his thumb up the top of my hand and informs me. "Hera frequently visited the Underworld to make sure Zeus's mistresses, who she killed, were dead. We were typically careful and quick enough to hide you before she would put the pieces together, but you look so much like Metis, and we weren't fast enough one day."

"We thought we talked our way through Hera's skepticism." Persephone rises from her throne, and she moves to where Hades kneels in front of me. She falls to her knees with him, and her voice trembles as she recounts the past. "But she told Athena everything. While we might've been able to fool Hera, Athena was too wise to trick. She was the strand keeping the oath between us and Kronos intact. When she realized the prophecy came true, Athena looked at you, her only true biological sibling, and she saw the ultimate weapon that Kronos needed to kill us all with."

Until the day we meet in person, my treasured god-killer.

Kronos's words send unwanted chills down my spine, his chanting promise intermingling with Persephone's next words. "She ordered that we kill you, our daughter, not by birth, but by love. If we didn't kill you, then Athena would make the sacrifice. Death was all that seemed to await you in your brief life, and we were both trapped."

"How-"

Am I alive? Was the continuation of my question, but I do not have the strength to finish the sentence. Hades's hand squeezes around mine, and although I did not end my sentence, he understands.

"Hermes came to the rescue yet again. He told Athena and Hera that he started this trickle of deceit, so he should be the one to end it. He asked for privacy to kill you, but while Persephone and I wept and Athena and Hera waited with us, Hermes took you to a prison that you could blend into. A child just died in the same cell from sickness, and he put you in the place of this child."

"When he came back to the Underworld with the already dead child, he used magic to make the dead baby look like you. Nobody within the cells knew the difference between you and the other baby, and Hera believed the glamor and left with no question." There is an embellished frown on Persephone's face when she adds. "Athena, however, was far wiser than Hera."

"We were going to take you back from the jail cells after they left, but Athena said that she would periodically check in. To preserve the peace between the titans and gods, Athena checked on us in the Underworld twice a week at random intervals, without warning, for the next fifteen years," Hades adds with unbridled sadness. "Each time we thought she was going to stop visiting and we could steal you back, she would make another resurgence."

"Compared to the Underworld, you were safe in the prison," Persephone says. "At least, until we could win you back in the arena."

"But you lost," I say.

They both lower their heads.

Hades speaks next, with a voice thickened in guilt. "Hermes came to save you yet again, just as he had his entire life, and once the wave of suspicion lessened, he always planned on returning you back to us. To your home."

Suddenly, every secret behind Hermes's words bled through.

He was never meant to be the god who fell infatuated with a slave, but he was the guard protecting the prophesied child he always saved. The child who would free him from the binds of his strenuous job and ascend him to the title of an Olympian. A chore of his, who he'd marry and used to elevate to new heights.

Aphrodite and Hermes warned me of Hermes's selfishness and eagerness for more in this world, but like a fool, I thought otherwise. I thought he only cared about me, but I should've believed the truthful lines in between his blasphemy.

"Do you have any more questions?" Persephone inquires.

I shake my head. Instead of questions, I have confessions.

"I think it's time I tell a story." I wipe at my tears that streak my cheeks, and I look at what I never thought I'd be fortunate enough to have—parents. "It begins with a dream two years ago with a god of shadows and nightmares."

THE THIRTY-EIGHTH CHAPTER

Fatigue tickles the back of our lids by the time I dispel my edge of truth. I've never spoken out loud about Epiales to anybody except from my jail cell best friend, but this is the first time my words aren't laced with a fantastical view of excellence. I no longer see Epiales as my hero, whisking me away from the mayhem of my restraints in the prisons, but I see him for who he is.

A broken god, who is desperate enough to join the villain for freedom, thus turning into a villain himself.

They ask me questions about Kronos's plans, and I answer them all. Only once my words cease and their curiosity disintegrates, do the screaming chants in my head disband. Tranquility empties my mind from a raging storm of thoughts, even with the influx of information Persephone and Hades had given me.

I look at the vein on my forearm, and the strips of gold throughout no longer frighten me. According to Persephone and Hades, I am the precipice of power in a world that I'm just now understanding, but the reality has not leveled. My brain refuses to accept their cautionary words of my powers, but I can only accept that the secrets have been revealed.

They lead me into the royal quarters of the prodigious obsidian mansion that is twice the size of Hermes's. I try not to flinch as skeletal guards patrol the hallways, nodding their appreciation to the three of us. Persephone will tell me brief stories about some of the skeletal warriors, but when we pass by a malnourished man on a bench, she tells me to never look at the humanoid monster.

As we stand in front of my new bedroom, the door a silvery sheen that counteracts the darkness of this home, Hades says. "If you need anything, then Atalanta and Achilles will always guard your door. We are in the room right down the hall." There's a small smile when he adds. "Just look for a three-headed dog wagging his tail, and we will be nearby."

Persephone walks forward and presses a motherly kiss to my forehead. "Goodnight, darling. I'll see you at breakfast in the morning."

With three guards behind them, the king and queen of the Underworld exit. They allow me space within this new home, a true form of freedom I grew up believing was an impossibility. It's with elation on my face that I wrap my hand around the doorknob, opening the entry towards my new world as a princess and a daughter, when I once thought I'd be inconsequential and void of family.

I take two steps into the bedroom before halting, my body paralyzed by the sight awaiting me. Hermes is an imposing figure, matching the door in height. He's so tall that the flowers in his hands seem miniature, as if they were shrunken before he brought them to the Underworld.

He is a god who has existed for eons, but when he greets me with that boyish smirk, I forget he isn't human. For a few seconds, as I stare at the nervous smile, the bouquet of saffron flowers, and the nervous shuffling of his feet, I misremember Hermes's godly status. I see a human boy who taught me how to become more than a slave.

"Hi," his voice is weakened by the gravity of this small word.

That single utterance destroys the image I had, that he was human and innocent. When his cadence enters my mind, the way he manipulated me reemerges. I take a few more steps into my new bedroom, but I do not make an immediate response. I let the silence pulse through the air, acting as a heartbeat. A third party to our interaction.

The bouquet in his hands lowers, and the first sight of defeat intermingles with the silence and tension. "I almost told you so many times," he sighs. "When I'd walk downstairs, and you'd be scrunching your nose while trying to figure out a new letter of the alphabet with China, I wanted to scream to you everything I knew and then more that I was too afraid to say out loud to anybody else. When you'd smile at me after winning Monopoly, or when you'd steal a few dollar bills when you didn't think I was noticing, I wanted to share what wasn't mine to express."

"But you didn't," I say, my words sharper than a blade as they slice into him. "You left me ignorant of the truth. You'd think you would tell me you were my betrothed, but no. Even the secrets that were yours to tell me, you didn't."

The flowers lower some more as the sharpened end of my sentence reaches him. "No," he admits. "I didn't tell you."

I take a step forward, and I glare at the man who I once trusted. One who I saw as a friend and possibly something more. He is standing in front of me in the Underworld's depth, but I see the pleasant moments we shared.

The dance in the gazebo.

First time I tasted strawberries.

A starry night when I laid my head on his shoulder and slept dreamlessly for the first time in two years.

"Instead of telling me the truth, you spent nights by my side playing board games and gifting me with compliments," I speak, and I hope he hears my anger and disappointment.

The tears slip, burning streaks of fire down my cheeks, but I do not push them away. I make sure his eyes trail the expanse of the clear liquid, and he feels a fraction of my betrayal.

I snarl. "Instead of telling me we share the same father and I'm a demi-god. Or that I was promised to you, and I was your ticket to a promotion; you danced with me and stared at me as if I were the most important person in the world. Rather than telling me you knew the answers to the questions I've had, you kept me in the dark while distracting me with feelings I knew better than to have for you."

"Saffron," Hermes whispers my name like a prayer, but when he moves to advance towards me, I place a hand forward and halt him in his movements.

"I don't want to hear your words. You always trick me with them."

The bouquet falls from his grasp, the soft *thud* against the black carpeted ground solidifying the end of something that never should've begun. Any trace of nervous jubilance is replaced with the somber truth that I will never forgive him for his lies and treachery.

"I know we aren't biologically anything. Hades and Persephone explained we share as much familiar ties as Hattie or Panda. That is not why I am mad." The purple petals are mocking me as I look at the fallen flowers. "I trusted you when I grew up learning to trust no god."

I abhor the way my legs can't stay still and the burning behind my cheeks worsens with each agonizing second that silence and tension squeeze in the space between him and I. My tears are not a sight of weakness, but a fabric of truth he never gave me. And I never gave him by omitting my candor about Epiales.

"Each night, when I fell asleep, I was tricked by an immortal who I thought cared about me. I found my storyteller, who spun tales about how loathsome the entire godly race is, and I believed his lies until I met you. Until you showed me he was what was wrong with my life, and the lies he weaved were for his own purpose and not my well-being."

I scoff at my roaring thoughts, wishing they'd disappear into incoherent whispers. Tears angrily spit upon the floor, staining the room with my bubbling ire. I refuse to look at him, centralized on the discarded saffron flowers that signify every coil of deceit he manifested.

"You may be the god of mischief and trickery," I say, while tasting the saltiness of my tears on my bottom lip. "But I trusted that you would never lie to me. You showed me your kindness, and with each passing day in your home, I believed everything you said to me. I believed I was beautiful to you, that I was special to you as nothing more than a human girl."

He tries to take a step towards me, but I take two more backwards. His hand was outstretched, but it drops when a curl of hatred ensnares my lips. My eyes are on the flowers, but he is examining my face for any sign that I could forgive him.

My next words refute his hope.

"But you were just like him. Worse, even," my throat is raw as more tears decorate my face. "You spun your own secrets to get what you wanted. My storyteller saw me as his freedom from certain death, and Kronos saw me as his treasured weapon. But you? I was your precious damsel and your ticket away from a job you hate. A key that unlocked your title as a hero and an

Olympian. With me as your prized wife, I would elevate you to new heights and make you viewed as a god to envy. I thought I was valuable to you because of my personality and the feelings you had for me, but I was just another object for you to steal for your own successes."

"Saffron, that is not-" he says, but I do not care for more of his words.

"I was the greatest story ever written about you." I admit. "The god who orchestrated the safety of the prophesied second child of Metis and Zeus. Forget about the tales of Heracles and Athena. Yours was going to trump theirs. The tale of a male who denied the orders of Queen Hera, who stole and saved a demi-god with the power to kill all enemies. Immortal or otherwise."

"I promise that is not what I want," Hermes says, but he is nervous as he skirts around the bedroom, unable to look directly at me.

"Was it the plan to have me fall in love with you, too? You already had my biological father's permission to become my husband, but did you want me to choose to marry you? To become your willing, pathetic fool? Was your plan to gain my trust, my fascination with you next, and then swoop in with some flowers once I learned you protected me my entire life?" He wanders to the fallen flowers the moment I look at him, and a scoff leaves my lips. "I may be young and naïve, but I was not dim-witted enough to feel anything but lust and temptation. Now, get out of my bedroom before you see the true depths of my powers."

"I wanted-" Hermes begins.

"I don't care. You have ten seconds to get out of here before I scream loud enough to let everybody in the vicinity hear me and rush to my aid."

"Ten seconds?" He asks.

I nod.

"Alright," he strides towards me in one fluid step. "That's one second." He wraps an arm around my waist and flushes me against his chest. "That's two."

Hermes's free hand grabs the curve of my chin and hoists it upwards so I can only look at his face. His scent wraps itself around me, ready to torment me worse than his façade has these past few weeks. He leans in closer, his nose daring to caress mine.

"When you were nothing but a babe in your mother's growing womb, I saw you for who you were. The prophesied child who would defeat Kronos. I saw you for what Zeus promised me. The hand of the single most powerful deity to exist and the freedom from my job as a messenger, which I've hated since the day I was cursed with it. "

"Three," I remind him.

"Everything was strategic to get you to kill Kronos then marry me, so I could get back home with the title of an Olympian on my shoulder. I knew Hades and Persephone wanted a child badly enough to ignore who you were, and I was certain they wouldn't ask why I cared about you living. They were blissfully clueless about my plans, and I used them to raise a powerful child. I was going to bring you back to Zeus on your eighteenth birthday and show him you were alive. Persephone and Hades thought I was being kind, but I have and always will be a selfish god."

"Four," I say.

"I had a plan, clear cut and perfect, my flawless trick. I was going to have you, a child of Zeus's and Metis's, and Hades's and Persephone's. You would be wanted by all single gods as a wife. The most powerful wife to exist. And you'd be all mine. When you ascended into a goddess, I was going to train you until you were ready to kill Kronos and free us from our ties to Earth. I wasn't going to do this for fame, though. I did not care about that."

"Five," I murmur, although I'm certain the ten seconds have surpassed. Still, with his body flush against mine and his version of the truth spilling from his lips, curiosity keeps me from screaming for the guards.

"I wanted to become an Olympian. To no longer be a messenger, a job that is below a child of Zeus's. I'm powerful and I wanted my family to finally acknowledge that, and I was going to use you to get that strength. I was going to use you to escape Earth and go back to Mt. Olympus as an Olympian and hero, but then I saw you on the arena ground."

"Six," I say.

"I hadn't seen you since you were two years old, after I dropped you off in the prison. When I saw you in the arena, hidden behind your friend, all of my plans disappeared. I thought I was the one in charge and you were mine to control for my gain, but I saw you and realized that you were going to be my undoing. Not the other way around."

"Seven."

"I lied to you a lot, but the way I felt for you was never false. Each time I called you beautiful or almost kissed you was as real as anything in this world. I could've continued my plan to seduce you and make you become exactly what I planned, but I couldn't. Each time I stopped myself from kissing you was because of the gnawing guilt that ate me alive, bit by bit, when the secrets still existed between us."

"Eight," I count aloud.

"I know you do not believe me, but it's the truth. I'm selfish and everything wrong with this desolate world, but in your company, I can't be those things. For the first time in eons, I care more for another's wellbeing than my own. My plan to marry you and use you was before I knew you, and before I fell in love with you. Now, I'd be a messenger, a lowly god, or a tormented soul in the Fields of Punishments, as long as it'd mean you are happy and safe."

"Nine," I remind him.

He breaks any bit of distance between us, and he presses his lips against mine. My first kiss, stolen by the god of thievery, momentarily freezes me. His lips are warm and smooth, and they glide across my mouth with lethargic desire. He isn't rushing through the embrace, and he isn't consumed by passion as Panda and Pyro were every time they kissed.

This is a parting entwinement, and when that realization enters my mind, I kiss him back. My lips part, and I accept his version of a goodbye. For a single second, I run my lips across his before pulling away.

When his warmth leaves my body, and I am left only with my dried tears and clamorous thoughts, I look up at where he once stood to see a single saffron flower left behind.

THE THIRTY-NINTH CHAPTER

Two female skeletons, who are dressed in tattered gray garbs that always flow regardless of the stilled air, dress me for the start of my day. Regardless of the dark shroud outside of my bedroom window that mirrors nighttime, my morning has begun in a world anew.

The silent, dead women style my hair in intricate braids and place a pale pink gown around my curvaceous build. A crown of braids and a headpiece of tangled white and silver thorns are woven into my chocolate locks.

Lipstick in the same shade as my gown accentuates my prominent lips, while kohl is placed around my almond-shaped eyes. I entered the Underworld as a confused monstrosity, peppered with both godly and human blood, without an inkling of its origins. However, I leave my bedroom with the two women and my two guards in tow as a princess.

A demi-god.

I believe Hades and Persephone when they told me the story of my life, their words too vivid to be anything but the truth, but I still haven't processed the discovery. I know I am the child they spoke about—the second born of Metis and Zeus destined to become stronger than any other immortal—but my mind comprehends each bit of information one step at a time.

Right now, I have come to terms with the fact that I am Hades and Persephone's adopted daughter, a demi-god princess of the Underworld. There is no way I can deny this part of my life, not as skeletal beings bow as I stroll the halls. I can't dissuade myself from the truth when the few beings with the ability to speak call me *Princess Saffron* or *my lady*. This aspect of my ever-changing life has cemented in my mind as I wear a tiara on my head.

Achilles, the guard to my immediate right with blood still seeping from the wound that killed him, opens the door to the dining hall with a black-teeth smile. I nod my head in appreciation, and I walk into the room with the assumption that only Persephone and Hades would be my company for breakfast.

However, two more seats are filled with familiar faces. One guest, beautiful but mangled by a butterfly tattoo, nibbles on a piece of bread as her single eye darts between where I stand and the two gods who sit nearby. She wears a green dress styled identically to mine, and her hair is spun into dozens of small braids, which trail down her back.

The other guest looks to me with her ochre skin blemished with splotches of food. She wears a blue gown similar to Glasswing's and mine, but just like her face, it's stained with the red, mushy food on her plate. A gold headband pulls back her raven locks, and a widespread grin shows pieces of food in her mouth.

"The cooks may be deader than a doornail, but their food is top-notch," Hattie says, and with further emphasis, she puckers her lips and throws a kiss in the kitchen's direction. "I think I found my soulmate in a three-thousand-year-old chef."

In bewilderment, I stare at my two friends and ask. "What are you both doing down here?"

Hattie snorts. "Missed you too, *princess*."

"Hermes didn't tell you?" Hades inquires, one bushy, black brow raised. He takes a bite out of the food on his plate, waiting for an answer from me I am too stunned to make. When silence responds to him, he answers my confusion. "Hermes purchased Glasswing from Psyche, then freed them both from slavery. To the rest of the world, both Glasswing and Hattie died, but only Hermes and we know the truth. Other than Artemis's huntresses, they are the first freed humans in over two hundred years."

The last sentence Hades says is in amazement, his astonishment at Hermes's actions laying in between his words. I think to Hermes, whose lips still linger upon my own, as I stare at Glasswing. She plays with the piece of bread on her plate, but she doesn't attempt to eat the food. While Hermes assured me that Psyche never harmed her slaves after the scarification mark, Glasswing's mind was dying in Psyche's mansion. Hermes's decision to free her from servitude undoubtedly saved her life.

"Why did he do it?" I ask everybody.

Hades and Persephone share a look, words spilling from the stare, and then she looks at me with knowledge on her ageless face. "Take a seat and eat, darling. We have a busy day ahead of us, and you'll need your energy."

Hattie, with a mouthful of food, is nearly incoherent as she mumbles. "You should try the strawberry jam and biscuits. It's delicious."

"Strawberries?" I inquire with audible excitement.

I sit down with thoughts of Hermes. I eat the strawberry jam that reminds me of his boyish smile and lanky frame. Hattie laughs, and I think of all the times she and Hermes would playfully jab one another with insults and that same laughter would fill our former home. The room talks, except for Glasswing, but all I can hear is him.

"Well," Hattie smacks her flat stomach as if it holds the entire world within it and grunts as she rises to her feet. "That bed made of feathers is calling my name once again."

She does not walk but hobbles out of the dining hall. Two guards, more ghostly than skeletal, follow behind her. Glasswing is close behind, saying her farewells. Just like Hattie, guards accompany my friend. Both of them, protected as I am, in a world where they are free.

We were born of shackles and serfdom. Since we were old enough to cry for the first time, it was in anguish for the life we were delivered. Since words were taught to us, we were begging for freedom that, even at such a young age, we knew was an impossibility. Yet, here is it. A world where we are neither slaves nor victims to the world's circumstances.

We are free.

I focus on Hades and Persephone, but he is no longer there. Only my adopted mother, Persephone, sits at the dining table with me. Her hands are folded on top of the furniture, the rings on her fingers glinting with dark light beneath the multitude of candles that surround us and illuminate the room.

This goddess of regality sits in front of me as my self-proclaimed mother. Persephone rules beside her husband as his equal in the Underworld: the largest expanse of land owned by any of the godly kings. Poseidon may have the seas, and Zeus may rule the skies, but both of their territories pale in comparison to Hades's land of the dead.

She rules with him as Hades's equal. A gift of equality that the other two queens—Amphitrite and Hera—are deprived of. They are queens solely in title and loneliness, but Persephone and Hades are dual leaders in the largest expanse of territory. She compeers with her husband, and she is before me as a monarch, who only the greatest fool would antagonize.

Persephone rises to her feet, effervescent in a flowing plum gown, and she nears me with hesitance and an inkling of uncertainty. A queen, a warrior, and a goddess stalls a few inches away from me. She looks at where I sit, unsure of her next steps, and I am just as hesitant.

"Can I ask you a question?" I ask, shattering the doubtfulness between us.

"Of course you can; you're my daughter and you can ask me anything."

"Did you know Hermes was in my bedroom last night, waiting for me with flowers?"

"Yes," she answers.

"Why did you let him?" I look away from Persephone, flittering towards my empty plate. "He was just like Epiales. He wanted to use me differently, but he still wanted to use me."

"For eons, men have thought they could take what they wanted from a female without repercussions or an inch of guilt. Gods like to believe they are impervious to mistakes, especially when their actions are accepted. Regardless of the terrible ways they used women."

Persephone lowers herself into a kneeling position to my immediate left, and while I can't bring myself to look at her, she stares at me as if I hold the stars and moon and galaxy. There's no ulterior motive, unlike Hermes and Epiales and Kronos; Persephone's only aim is to care for me how a mother would her child.

"Hades and I did not know Hermes's intentions with you when he brought you to us eighteen years ago. We were oblivious to the promise Zeus made to Hermes about your hand in marriage and his rise to an Olympian. He could've gotten away with deceiving us in the same way that he was tricking you. We would've been unprepared and unable to stop him in time if he gave you to Zeus instead of us."

She is silent for a beat before defending the man, who saw me as a prize instead of a woman with feelings.

"But while you were dancing with Apollo, Hermes sought us out and told us the truth. He admitted every terrible, archaic thought he had. He told us he thought he could possess you, but after he said everything, he asked that we take you home and far away from him. He realized his actions were monstrous and possessive, but he was not what his actions almost made him. Guilt read on his face from a mile away. We let him say goodbye before he promised to never see you again because he regretted his decision. Hermes punished himself more than Hades and I ever could."

"I think I hate him," I admit. "I think I hate him the same way that I think I hate Epiales."

"My dear, sweet daughter," Persephone says. "You are so young that you do not realize love and hate are two of the same coin. I do not think you hate either god. I think what you feel for both males is the opposite of hate, but that is your own journey to make. A journey that you no longer have to make alone."

I draw my gaze downward, to where Persephone is kneeling before me, and warmth fills my chest. When she holds out her hands, I accept, and they're my haven. Her embrace, her honesty, and her affection are a sense of comfort I haven't realized I've searched my entire life for until now.

"Can you take me on a tour around my new home?" I ask.

Raw emotion softens Persephone's features, an authentic mixture of elation and disbelief, and she squeezes my hands. When she answers me, her voice is broken by an influx of affection. "There's nothing I'd want to do more."

As Persephone and I stride out of the dining hall, Achilles and Atalanta are two steps behind us. Their boney hands are coiled around the handle of their swords, awaiting danger where it lurks, but they are not alone in our protection. A three-headed dog, its snouts bulbous and its body stout, licks the palm of Persephone's hand as it trots beside us.

Persephone giggles as one finger scratches one of its many ears. "The key to Cerberus's heart," she explains with a sideway glance towards me. "Is to scratch right behind the ear. Then he's loyal to you for life."

As if the enormous dog understands Persephone's words, two out of his three heads tilt in my direction. I swear the dog smiles, its tongue hanging out. While we walk through the obsidian mansion, Cerberus trots in an infinity loop around the two of us, and almost trips Achilles on one occasion.

The skeletal warrior is not amused.

At least one hundred steps separate the mansion's front doors to the floor of the Underworld. One hundred onyx stairs, where two guards are posted on every other with shields and spears tight to their chest. I once lived in Ares's house, which was guarded by malnourished and frightened humans who yearned for freedom, but the Underworld's guards are different from Ares's.

Here, in the Underworld, it is a fortress. With each guard we pass, Persephone nods her head in appreciation. Their soldiers are from the past, who died on the battlefield, Persephone explains. I do not mistake a few heartfelt bows we receive from the ghostly or skeletal men and women. Persephone is cordial to each guard and greets them by their first name, and the respect she has for them is as easily visible as the guards' passion for their jobs.

"Each guard who works during their afterlife decided without coercion. Neither Hades nor I approached any of the men and women who now serve as guards and warriors in our army, but all of them left their home in this afterlife and asked to join. They gave up their ability to speak, and they lived in their decomposed bodies to serve as they did in their living existence."

"Do you know why?" I ask. We are only halfway down the staircase, and already sweat is streaming down the sides of my face. My breathing is haggard as I elaborate. "Some of them were in Elysian Fields, right? Why would anybody want to leave the land of heroes?"

Persephone is quick to answer me. "All of our guards lived in Elysian Fields before joining our artillery. Each time we ask a deceased hero why they wish to become a sentinel, their answer is always the same. Happiness and peace bores the warriors who lived their entire lives on the thrill of war and battles. Some heroes become so disinterested in the Elysian Fields that they agree to become the skeletal remains of their former life; or worse, if your body was never given a proper burial, then those warriors become ghostly, faceless figures."

"Like the guards with Hattie and Glasswing," I conclude, and Persephone nods her head.

"Many live happy lives in the land of heroes, but champions like Achilles and Atalanta desired the fight that came with their previous life, which is why they stand behind us now. It's why these mighty soldiers stand on these steps. They wanted the choice to live a glimpse of their former life, and Hades and I accepted."

"Choice." I taste the uncommon word upon my tongue, and a smile lifts over my lips. "That's beautiful."

"No," Persephone shakes her head, purple-tinted brown hair streaming down her shoulders with the movement. "This world is so grotesque that choice seems like an unachievable beauty rather than an innate right."

We're almost done with the staircase when I stop. My hands are on top of my knees, and I hunch over, gasping for breath that slices down my throat like knives. I'm heaving, struggling to survive the downward trek, but Persephone stands beside me without a glimpse of perspiration.

"With your permission, Thanatos and Hypnos have offered to further the training you began with the huntresses," she looks down at me with amusement lighting up her face. "It might help you with a few stairs."

I gasp. "A few?"

Her laughter fills the air. "The trip to both the Fields of Punishment and Elysian Fields includes twice the amount of stairs."

"Oh, gods," I groan. "Where can we visit today that does not involve stairs?"

"We will see the rivers today, my sweet daughter."

She places her hand on my back and helps me down the last twenty steps. Better yet, when I collapse onto the floor and stare up at the black sky for ten minutes, she reins in the laughter that I can tell wants to burst at the seam.

THE FORTIETH CHAPTER

Cerberus zigzags between our feet, his tail wagging with enjoyment, when we visit the first river on the expansive journey through the Underworld. The Lethe is the river closest to the castle, and it's correlated with oblivion and forgetfulness. In the land of choices, the Lethe River is a chance for humans who suffered a slow, painful demise, or lived a regrettable life, to forget their earthly ties. With one sip from the dark blue water, most slaves do not remember their time with their barbarous masters.

"Your friends who passed away in Hermes's home." Persephone whispers the words that I'm almost too frightened to hear. "Are living in Elysian Fields, but their murderer chose the river before spending her afterlife in the Fields of Punishments. She is penalized for her acts of rebellion without recollection of her decisions that led to that point."

"Why?" I ask.

"Hermes found the punishment fitting, and Hades and I agreed," she answers.

"Can you take her out of the Fields of Punishment?"

We are walking away from the Lethe River when the question slips from my tongue. Persephone slows to a stop, and she looks down at me with an unmistakably confused expression.

"You are a princess of this land. You may decide anything you see fit, but why would you want that? She tried to kidnap you, and she killed your friends."

We are walking toward the next river, the Cocytus, where endless guilt-ridden souls suffer. Their wails live in the water, staining the air with a forlorn feeling. I frown as I stare at where the manipulated and tricked live. Those who listened to pretty lies, and whose greatest mistake was believing the trickery of another's words.

"It's easy to believe Kronos's falsity," I concede these words with Epiales on my mind and not China. "Especially when you think there's nowhere else to turn."

"Atalanta." Persephone turns to the female soldier, and she orders. "Go free the woman from the Fields of Punishment. She shall live the rest of her afterlife either in the depths of the Cocytus River or in Asphodel Meadows. The choice is the traitor's."

"Thank you," I hum when Atalanta runs off to complete her task.

"Please," Persephone implores as we begin our tour of the Underworld. "Do not thank me for listening to your wise words." We walk a few steps, then Persephone adds. "I can't free Epiales from Tartarus, though. Not without Zeus's knowledge."

There's a pinch in my chest when I am reminded of Epiales's predicament, and my words are hoarse as I murmur. "I may hate him, but I can't let him die in Tartarus."

Persephone nods her head, compassion written on her beautiful features. "Hades and I will speak to Zeus at our earliest convenience and see about lessening Epiales's sentence, but it's all we can do. This may be our land, but Zeus is the king of all, and he was the one who sentenced Epiales. We can't disobey his command without receiving repercussions."

I'm silent for a moment before I ask. "What can we do for him right now?" I hate the way my voice breaks when I admit. "He's dying, and I don't know how much longer he can survive down there."

Persephone thinks for a moment. "Do Hattie and Glasswing know about Epiales?" I shake my head, and Persephone says. "Tell Hattie and Glasswing about Epiales, and Hades and I will inform all the living humans in our castle. We have about one hundred former slaves in our home, and while it's not much, Epiales won't die if over a hundred humans know of his existence and pray to him."

"Thank you," I say, and I am quick to push away a single fallen tear.

"I want you to know that I'll do anything for you within my power. You are my daughter, and I'd move mountains for you."

"Daughter," I reiterate the word, tasting it on my tongue. "I never thought I'd hear somebody call me that."

"For eons, all I've wanted was to say that very word to a child that I had with Hades. You may not be my child by blood, but you are ours by love. You'll always have us, my sweet daughter."

We travel from the Cocytus River to the Acheron River, each one rich with stories and powers. The Acheron River is as black as the castle, reminding me of the wispy feathers of Epiales's crow in water form. She tells me of the Phlegethon River, which burns of fire and is a neighbor to Tartarus, but we do not venture near Epiales's prison.

I glance at the shrouded land, though, with a twisted ache of guilt.

When I look away from Tartarus and the Phlegethon River, I find myself staring at the largest river in the Underworld. In the far off distance, Charon is on his ferry and sails through the water with half a dozen newly departed humans. Persephone hasn't looked at the river once, I realize, but actively avoids the sight.

"We've passed this river a lot, but you haven't said a word about it," I say about the magnificent bulk of water, which both intrigues me and sends a chill down my spine.

The river is stilled, never moving like a stream the way the others have. Shadowy apparitions, screaming faces and twitching bodies move in the water, but not because of a current. They try to run away from their sentencing of eternal imprisonment within the black and silver depths. The deceased that fell into the river try to escape to no avail, and the despondency in their unblinking eyes stare back at me.

No longer believing they'll escape, nevertheless trying to breakout.

"No matter what you do, stay as far away from the River Styx," my mother was laughing with me just a minute ago. Now, fright deepens her voice as we stand side-by-side, two feet away from the edge of the river. "The titaness who lives within the water is the personification of hatred, and her river is the epicenter of her power. She is the scariest aspect of the Underworld, worse than Tartarus himself, but many immortals are too foolish and underestimate her power because she lives in a river. Never underestimate Styx."

I nod my head. "I promise."

As we carry on with our tour, Persephone asks. "Hermes mentioned you were learning how to read and write. How is that going?"

I look to the ground, and while I answer, my voice is mumbled and my feet kick at the dead grass. "It's alright, I guess."

"Can I confess something to you?" Persephone asks, and when I nod my head, she admits. "I'm not asking you this to embarrass you, but I want to give you a choice. I have some of the greatest scholars in Elysian Fields or Asphodel Meadows, and just like my warriors, these intelligent men and women miss teaching others. If you'd like to, then I found you a great tutor."

"Will they make fun of me?" I ask, still not looking up at her.

"Why would he make fun of you?"

"When Hattie and China were teaching me, I kept messing up a lot. It's like all the letters are in a river, moving around with the current."

We walk, but Persephone takes a second to ponder my words. "From what I know of humans, the difficulties that you have are quite common and it is nothing to be ashamed of. You've also only been learning how to read and write for a few weeks by other slaves who barely know the words themselves."

I ponder aloud. "Is there somebody you have in mind to teach me?"

"I do," Persephone answers. "He was a brilliant man when he was alive, but he made sinful choices that he's trying to atone for in his afterlife. Building the Labyrinth, for instance, was his greatest descension. He's offered to leave Asphodel Meadows to tutor you, and considering the mistakes he has made in his own waking life, there will be no judgement from him. And if there is, then I'll have Cerberus bite off a finger or two."

Persephone has a look of amusement across her face when I realize who she wants my tutor to be.

"Daedalus?" I ask, thinking back to the stories Epiales told me about the Greek scholarly architect responsible for the Labyrinth.

"He will tutor you every day after your trainings with Hypnos and Thanatos. I've already spoken to Hattie and Glasswing this morning, and Hattie will join you in the trainings while Glasswing will be there during the tutoring sessions."

"I never expected life to be like this," I admit.

"Like what?" She asks.

The land of death, where rivers wail and skies are as black as crow feathers, has become a home. Just as beauty does not equate to kindness, darkness does not equate to maliciousness. My place is within the obscurity, surrounded by skeletal guards and monarchs who covet choice, where respect runs as long as the River Styx.

I am truthful as I answer. "Beautiful."

After a picnic on the edge of the Asphodel Meadows, which Cerberus ate with us, we head back to the mansion. With each step we take back to our home, we learn about each other in the gap since I was taken away. Epiales told me about Persephone and Hades, but he only explained the stories that were told and glorified.

He didn't tell me that Persephone is terrified of spiders after an encounter with Arachne. Epiales did not know that Persephone's favorite fruit isn't pomegranates but peaches, but she is too nervous to tell Hades that and only enjoys the yellowish fruit when she visits her mother during the summer. While she learns about me, I discover Persephone's authenticity along the way.

I do not realize how much time slips from us until we are standing in front of the one hundred steps that lead to the front doors, and I groan. "Can't I just sit on Cerberus's back and have him race me up to the top?"

Persephone laughs, and Cerberus lets out a yelp of discontent.

"Consider the stairs your first day of training," Persephone jokes.

I stride towards the arduous sets of stairs before a gleam of gold blinds me. Wings that are miles long crash through the Underworld, and the petite goddess who owns them lands on the fifth step. With her blonde locks and golden armor, Nike contrasts the darkness of the land of the dead.

I see Nike, and my mind goes to my best friend. The only person I had growing up, who tethered me to the waking world. My protector and ally within the prison cells when I thought I had nobody. The first person to admit I differed from everybody else. One of the few people to never lie to me.

Nike bows in our presence, a fact that still sends an unwanted sense of strangeness through me, but she rises before I can tell her to stop. Her lips are in a firm frown, and I just know. Between the dried streaks of tears on her cheeks, and the red blood on her fingertips, I press a hand to my own stilled chest with a terrible knowledge smashing into me.

"What can we help you with, Nike?" Persephone asks, and her tone is laced with an undertone of clairvoyant, mournful knowledge.

"I have a request for you, your highness," Nike looks away from Persephone and looks at me. The sadness Nike wears on her face like a physical wound intensifies. "And an apology for you, princess."

"What happened?" Persephone asks, her cadence devoid of the previous jovial nature that it had only a minute prior.

"Titans," Nike says while fresh tears stream down her cheeks. Each silent click of a new tear upon the ground tells me whose blood lies on her fingertips. With each quiver of her lips, I flinch. "Two of them came into my home—Crius and Eurybia—and said their king needed to make an example out of my slaves."

She wipes away her sadness with the back of her hand, but a streak of his blood slides across her cheekbone. It's all I can stare at, the red smudge that I know belongs to him. My best friend, who warned me about my dreams. My loyal friend, who protected me on a continual basis at his own risk.

Gone because of Kronos.

Gone because I refused the titan of time.

Gone because of who I am.

Gone because of *me*.

"Most of my slaves are," Nike flinches from her own words and restates. "Were elderly. I tried to fight both titans, but they had a target, and I wasn't strong enough. Oh, gods, I'm so sorry, princess."

Nike's golden wings fold into themselves and she collapses onto her knees. She sobs for the humans she cared for as her equals within her mansion. Nike, who is the goddess of victory, mourns for the elderly men and women who she could not protect. Crumbling into herself, she yearns for my guy friend to live another day.

"He knew they were there for him before I did. I tried to run to him, to stop Crius, but I wasn't fast enough. Not with Eurybia fighting me. I tried, and I tried, and I tried, but I failed."

Nike was poised and regal when I first saw her in the arena a few weeks ago. She was immaculate in a way that most goddesses are. She was almost statuesque in her apathetic expressions, but today is the truth behind the façade.

I take the steps that separate Nike and me, and I sit on the same step with her. I take her hands, and I let a goddess press her body against mine. She rests her head against my shoulder, weeping for my friend until snot runs down her nose and she is gasping for breath.

Ares once told me a person's third love is your soulmate, the other half Zeus pulled you apart from, and I know with certainty that Nike was my friend's third love; his destined mate. I hold the goddess as she sobs over the loss of the one person who she was pre-destined to have forever. Her body trembles in my hold, inconsolable over the loss of her fated love. My thoughts return to my friend with a wry grin and blazing blue eyes, and I squeeze his mate tighter.

"What name did you give him?" I ask with tentative delicacy, as if the answer to this question will either unravel her or the fragment of rationality left inside of me.

"Angel," she can barely get the words out before sobbing once again. "I'm so sorry, I tried."

I'm numb as I sit on the staircase and hold a goddess as she cries. Persephone is gone, searching for my friend to take him to Elysian Fields as he belongs. The last time I saw Angel, we both subconsciously knew it was going to be an eternal farewell. We knew, just as I knew he was dead, that we would never see each other after the arena.

I hold Nike in my arms until her tears dry once more. She hiccups as she tries to plea. "Will he-"

I answer before the question can be uttered. "Yes, he's a hero, and that's where he belongs."

"I didn't know who you were to Angel until Hermes came to pick up his..." Nike stops, unable to finish the sentence.

"Soul," I say for her.

She nods her head. "Hermes recognized my Angel and told me of your friendship. I'm so sorry."

"Don't apologize, it wasn't your fault," I murmur, my thumb running up and down her fingers that tighten into a fist around mine.

It's my fault to bear.

"I'm going to kill them for this." I promise Nike. There is acrimony thickening my otherwise stoic voice, but the anger is laden with certainty that my words are destined to come true. "I'll start with Crius and Eurybia, and then I'll rip Kronos apart bit by bit until he realizes that his example for me was his own demise."

I don't know how much Nike knows of my existence, how much Hermes told her, but she doesn't question my abilities to kill the titans. Perhaps she is too distraught, or she does not care about words in the war of grief overtaking her body, but she is silent upon my declaration. Nike only has the strength to nod her head and cry.

THE FORTY-FIRST CHAPTER

Power buzzes through my body like an electrical current, zapping my skin and igniting me with adrenaline. Thanatos's scythe slices through the air, but I'm quicker. I duck and roll, avoiding the kiss of his blade with my sword raised.

I almost slash Thanatos's back, but Hypnos is there. The scar-littered god of sleep swipes his gray scythe down before I thwart his brother. Our blades clash against one another, vying for control in a room thickened with tension, pride, and sweat, and my smile is lethal.

An inkling of something dark and inviting plays in his gaze, and I pull him flush against my body. My chest is against his, and I can feel everything. The hammering of his heart, the wet sweat of his arms, the pronounced rigidness of his muscles, and the unspoken words of his desire as I stare up at him. Our bodies have never been this close except in his imagination, and our nearness brings me that much closer to victory.

I spin out of Hypnos's hold as Thanatos's scythe strikes downward. The blade is meant for me, but I whirl away from its trajectory. Hypnos isn't fast enough, though. In a state of disorientation, he does not realize Thanatos is about to accidentally defeat him until it is too late.

I am a foot away as Thanatos's blade sinks into Hypnos's shoulder and a terrible scream of vanquish ricochets off the training room walls. Thanatos yanks his scythe out of his brother's shoulder, then turns to me with the first smile that I've ever seen on his face.

"That was impressive," he says, all while twirling the five-foot long scythe stained with his brother's ichor. "Almost three months later and you finally find out Hypnos's weakness."

"Daedalus is teaching me about human desire right now," I inform my last opponent, and I white knuckle my sword and resume a fighting stance. "I'm a quick study."

Hattie, eating a bowl of walnuts in the background with Achilles and Atalanta, lets out a bark of laughter. "You? A quick study? That's a joke."

I turn to face my best friend, her hand wrist deep in a bowl of walnuts, and I stick my tongue out at her. For a second, I look away from my opponent, but Hattie diverts from my face to a spot behind me in silent warning. A smirk plays on my lips, and I continue to act unaware of Thanatos running towards me with his scythe raised.

Thanatos thought I learned only Hypnos's weakness, but he was wrong. Thanatos swings his scythe towards me, and as the familiar whoosh of his blade nears my ears, I fall to my knees. Once again, his scythe kisses the air and I spin a complete one-eighty on the floor.

He is ready for my sword, the blades meeting in disharmonious competitiveness, but he underestimates me. I expect each move my trainer makes, and while his scythe is pushing my sword downwards for the final blow, my free hand moves to the blade hidden in my boot.

Thanatos nears because I allow it. I let the curvature of his blade fog with my heavy breathing. When he thinks victory is in his clutches, I thrust my knife upwards until it reaches flesh. My lucky knife, gifted to me by my dad two weeks ago, slides into his shoulder in the same spot as Hypnos's injury.

Upon the realization that I defeated him, his face falls in disbelief.

For the first time since I entered this training room almost three months ago, I am victorious against Hypnos and Thanatos. Thanatos, still in shock, stumbles away from our previous position and staggers to his full, imposing height. Hattie is laughing in the background, her lewd comments about Thanatos being a sore loser loud enough to shake the walls and the aforementioned god's ego.

"I found your weakness, too," I tell him as I stand up to my feet.

"Which is?" Thanatos asks, and I do not mistake the annoyance in his voice.

"You still think I'm the same girl you started training three months ago, who tripped over her weapon," I wander to my blade, which is now sticky with Thanatos's defeat, and I gleam at my trainer. "You keep forgetting how well you trained me these past few months."

"Twice," Thanatos says after a moment of silence. "You tripped over your sword twice."

Hypnos barks out a laugh at his brother's comment, and he playfully smacks his back. "How does it feel knowing you lost in a fight against the girl who tripped over a sword twice? A little salty?"

Thanatos refuses to look at Hypnos, who looks identical to him except for the color of their eyes, their amount of facial hair, and the scars which litter the latter's skin. "You fought well today, Saff," he grits his teeth as he admits this. "But I'll be the winner tomorrow. I'd be a fool to let you underestimate me again."

"Just accept you lost," I coo. "And will continue to lose from now on."

"You've turned into quite the bossy princess," Hypnos teases as he props his foot against the wall farthest from me. A smirk grows on his lips as he adds. "I like it."

A second later, a walnut hits him square in the forehead.

"Don't make me barf all over the floor," Hattie snaps.

I pick up all of my belongings and I walk over to Hattie. She stretches her legs before standing, as if she's as exhausted as those who trained. While Hattie agreed to train with us, after two weeks of Thanatos's grueling workouts, she quit and decided to watch our sessions with a bowl of food each day.

Eventually, Atalanta and Achilles joined her.

Achilles, Atalanta, Hattie, and I walk out of the door when Hypnos's question cuts through the training room. "Are you sure you do not want to go?"

I freeze to the spot.

Every three months, on a season's solstice, the arenas are conducted. There are four prisons around the world, and the bastille I grew up in had their arena fights each summer solstice. Yet, another prison located halfway across the world has their arena today on the fall solstice, and as the proclaimed miracle child of Hades and Persephone, I am invited to take part.

To fight for a human to own, whom I can brand with a scarification mark and force their presence into the circle of problems with this world. Hattie, too, stills upon the mention of the fall solstice and the arena we were invited to. Just like me, she imagines the day she was fought for like a piece of property to obtain, which was the last day she saw her twin sister alive.

"I'd rather hangout with Tantalus in the Fields of Punishments," I say, and the four of us leave Hypnos and Thanatos.

Mom said that the one hundred steps to and from the mansion would be less grueling the longer I lived here, but it is the only time she's ever lied to me. Both Hattie and I groan as we stand at the bottom staircase and look up at the grueling hike that is ahead of us. They can't talk, but Achilles makes a sound similar to a laugh at the sight of us.

"Cerberus carried us up there once." Hattie looks at me and asks. "Do you think he will again if we promise treats?"

I frown. "My parents already left for the arena, and they took Cerberus with them."

Hattie groans. "Why didn't we steal any of Hermes's winged sandals before leaving?"

"I was too busy almost being killed by Ares," I turn to my best friend. "What's your excuse?"

Atalanta snorts.

Hattie glares back at the guard. "Whose side are you on?"

The skeleton smiles, showing an array of her blackened teeth.

Hattie groans. "Ugh, I want to grow wings. Not like Thanatos's or Hypnos's, but little ones that I could easily hide in my clothes but could use for moments like this," Hattie glares at the staircase, and as we ascend the torture device, she asks Achilles and Atalanta her daily question. "Was this the original Fields of Punishment? We're buddies, you can tell me."

I smirk when silence greets Hattie.

By the time we make it to the top of the staircase, my legs threaten to buckle from underneath me.

Hattie grumbles. "I need a nap."

After stumbling for the second time, Achilles leaves his spot beside me to help Hattie to her bedroom. Atalanta and I share a look, humor decorated on her decomposing face, and we head toward my bedroom, where the two maids—Myrah and Sasha—wait for me.

My days are pleasant and predictable. Myrah and Sasha are in my room, with a warm bath decorated in rose petals ready. A glass of champagne, rimmed in sugar, sits on the desk next to the tub, along with a bowl of cut strawberries.

I drop a few into my glass of champagne, and as the bubbly sweetness caroms my tongue, Myrah and Sasha help me pick out my outfit for the day. Everything is routine, from the braided crown upon my chestnut locks to the guards who lean against my doorway when I begin my descent to Daedalus's home.

Today, I'm in a sheer, pastel blue gown that is both sleeveless and uncorseted. Instead of a tiara Mom once insisted I wear, golden beads weave in-between my braided hair crown. Minimal makeup decorates my face, and I see my favorite version of myself in the mirror every day.

Just like every single day, Glasswing is waiting for me at the front of opened double doors. She is in a red gown, a color I've never seen her wear before. A gold eyepatch covers her scarification mark, an atrocity that no amount of healing medicines could lessen, but she's gorgeous. Glasswing, to me, has always been one of the most naturally beautiful humans.

When my friend turns her attention to me, there's a painful twist in my stomach that tells me something is awry. She stands beside her ghostly guards—Benjamin and Swiss—but doesn't register their presence. Glasswing is eerie today, her body's stiller than usual. This is odd for her; typically, Glasswing is fidgeting with something. Whether it is her morning plate of food, a piece of wayward fabric on her gown, or a piece of her hair.

Yet, today, she is still.
Relaxed.

"Ready?" I ask her, to which she nods her head.

Benjamin and Swiss are two steps in front of us, while Atalanta is two steps behind. At first, the adjustment of constant guards around me was daunting, but as time elapsed in the Underworld as its princess, the more accustomed I've been to my new role. She and I do not complain about the staircase or talk on our way to Asphodel Meadows.

Since Daedalus is dead and unable to communicate when outside of his place of eternal rest, Glasswing and I travel to him in the Asphodel Meadows. This is the farthest location, except for the Fields of Punishment, from the castle. We pass by all the rivers, Tartarus, and Elysian Fields on our way.

Glasswing is silent the entire time.

I will glance over at her, assessing her for any injuries like a bump on the head; however, she is unscathed. I try to spark up a few conversations, but each time, she is unresponsive. While she and I are not as close as Hattie and me, I've known Glasswing my entire life. I've known her since we were children, sitting under the showerhead together and surviving a terrible world.

"Are you okay?" I finally ask.

We are walking in between the River Styx and the Phlegethon River, but I stop to a halt. I turn my body to face the waif woman. She has gotten skinnier, if possible, since we arrived in the Underworld. Now, with true freedom, she appears more troubled than ever before. Her cheeks are sunken in and nearly as skeletal as Atalanta's and Achilles's.

"I will be soon," she says in a raspy whisper.

"What do you mean by that?"

Glasswing's attention shifts away from me to her two guards, and in the same throaty intonation, she says. "It's time."

The guard on the left—Swiss—acts without hesitation. His ghostly figure is only shadows and speed as he runs towards

Glasswing. Confusion stuns Atalanta, Benjamin, and I long enough for their plan to work. Swiss is behind Glasswing with his blade to her throat, but he is a ghost who can't hold physical objects for longer than a minute.

He drops the handle of the blade against Glasswing's throat, but she catches it. Her one eye is on me as Atalanta unsheathes her sword and points it at Glasswing, then Swiss, then back at Glasswing. If Achilles were here and not assisting Hattie, then she could take one down while Achilles handled the other.

But luck is not on our side today.

"Glasswing," I say. "What are you doing?"

She has not smiled since I've known her. She's been correlated with fear or hatred, never happiness. When Glasswing smiles, it isn't with elation. Insanity darkens her irises, and her hand is steady around the handle of the knife against her throat. She stares at me, unblinking, as she applies pressure to the blade.

A trickle of crimson blood spills down the long expanse of her throat, and I step forward. "What are you doing? Put the blade down."

"You are the symphony and victory, you are the fated in the tomes of history, but for the ruler of time you bring misery," the more Glasswing talks, still unblinking, the more she presses the knife against her throat. I try to take another step forward, but she snarls. "If you move any closer, then I'll slit my throat from ear to ear. Tempt me, the chosen treasure, and see the carnage that leers."

I freeze as realization crashes into my chest with such brutality.

Treasure.

Ruler of Time.

"Kronos," I seethe his name with acrimony poisoning my tongue. "You're working for Kronos."

"Swiss and me both. He brings the peace with each god whose life must cease. He is the release from the monsters that derive from Greece." With her free hand, Glasswing pokes at the side of her head, her maniacal smile growing to eerily large proportions. "He is the king, and you are the treasure that makes time sing. It sings with relief for the death of the gods, which begins with the thief. The thief who stole and tricked, then the dead that gripped-"

"You're not making any sense. Put the blade down," I order.

I do not peel my eyes away from Glasswing, even with the fighting grunts behind me. Atalanta and Benjamin fight for the Underworld, but Swiss battles his former allies because of a manipulative titan.

With one hand on the handle of the knife, the other pointed finger presses on her temple again and again, and I no longer recognize Glasswing. Kronos stripped any inch of sanity within her, resorting her to a rhyming, unblinking version of herself.

"Your allies are not meant to be gifted with life and lucidity." When she laughs, it's empty and chilling. "Your loved ones are the treasure's vulnerability. They are not meant for infinity, but for un-survivability. They are your weakness and liability. It began with an angel, but the next is the most ungrateful. All who the treasure adores will die until she is shameful. Death will taint her until the king of time finds her faithful."

Behind Glasswing, around one hundred corpses crawl and run towards us. Their allegiance has switched to Kronos's side, and they rush to Glasswing's aid with swords in their boney grasps and misguided hope in their hearts. Still, I stare at Glasswing, and I want to save her from Kronos, who has distorted her mind.

A body crashes against my valiant efforts.

Atalanta pummels my body into the ground, and an arrow dipped in an unfamiliar dark-green substance narrowly avoids my neck. Glasswing won't blink, but she laughs. A chaotic guffaw taints the once-pleasant air, and my home is distorted into Kronos's diluted image. Atalanta jumps off of me, two swords within her grasp, and I am up on my feet again. We watch the leader of a small army of traitorous dead souls as she laughs and laughs and laughs.

Benjamin is holding Swiss against the ground, and only Atalanta and I remain in a standing position. Atalanta looks around at the army doubling, then tripling in size, and I can see the defeat clear on her decaying face. Glasswing walks past Benjamin and Swiss, and she stands at the banks of the River Styx with her arms outstretched.

"It began with an angel, but the next is the most ungrateful." She repeats this line, and with wide eyes burning red with anger and insanity, she cries out. "The fiery one who denied the king of time will lose her spine."

Her laugh is derived from nightmares.

Ten sword-clad corpses flock to Atalanta. She lets out a roar as she swings her blades, decapitating two heads. Between fighting an influx of bodies rushing to capture me, Atalanta garbles a single word. Whatever she is trying to say is incomprehensible, but desperation clings to her bones. I stare at her, my mind foggy with confusion and betrayal, and she makes sure I am staring at her and nobody else as she repeats the same word again and again.

Finally, I follow the movements of her lips and read the three-letter word.

"Run," she says.

Atalanta's attention shifts, and I follow her focus. There, passed the fiery Phlegethon River, a man with curly black tresses and gray eyes identical to Hypnos's stare back. I know who this god is, who stands on top of Tartarus, sword raised in the air, without ever seeing his face before today.

The god of dreams screams from across the Phlegethon River. "Long may time reign!"

Morpheus, who left this world with his human soulmate over two hundred years ago, strikes his sword upon the cells of Tartarus and the Underworld splinters. Hands emerge from the cracks in Tartarus, and Atalanta still jumbles the same word.

"Run, run, run."

When a scarred hand, decorated with a black tattoo of a crow, sprouts from Tartarus and stabs into the Underworld's ground, I listen to Atalanta. I turn to sprint across the dead grass, but one sentence from Glasswing's psychotic rambles reemerges.

It began with an angel, but the next is the most ungrateful.

My mind rewinds itself, bringing me back to the day of Pyro and Panda's funeral. I do not reminisce about my friends' deaths, but I perseverate on Hattie's words when we talked about Kronos. About her rejecting Kronos's offer to join him.

Just because a pretty face came to me in a dream doesn't mean I'm going to fall for it, Hattie said. *Plus, I've seen far prettier faces in my time than his.*

"They're going to kill Hattie," I realize. I turn to Glasswing, who still stands in front of the River Styx with arms held out wide, and I growl. "Where's Hattie?"

"Let us see how pretty the treasure is when she cries," Glasswing responds. "Oh, and how loud she screams."

I look back at the castle, where Hattie was napping when I left her.

At least a dozen creatures are sprinting towards the castle with materializing weapons in their malnourished hands and homicidal thoughts in their minds. They're closer than I am from the castle, with a speed that doubles mine, and a scream of anguish and desperation claws at my throat. I can survive Angel's death, but can I escape here and leave Hattie behind?

Without pondering the question, I know the answer.

I look at the largest river in the Underworld. I stare at its black and silver tresses that twinkle with death's kiss. The fear I should have towards this expanse of deadly water is replaced with a need to save my best friend. The journey through the Underworld is five times as long because of how much we avoid the River Styx, but more titans and monsters from the depths of Tartarus run for the castle.

I'm certain they will reach its stairs before I do, unless…

One choice is left in a land ridden with war, and I move towards the river. "Hey, Glasswing?"

She doesn't respond. Only stares back, unblinking.

I advance until we are chest-to-chest, and I know she thinks I'm surrendering to her king. She sees my proximity and does not see my plan until my arms are around her thin body and our feet teeter off of the edge.

As we begin our fall, I whisper into her ear. "I'm sorry this world failed you."

Before we make the fall into the River Styx, I see two things. One, a shred of humanity etches Glasswing's fearful face. Two, Epiales stands beside Morpheus on top of Tartarus's border, and watches as I fall into the river with one word leaving his terrified lips.

"No!"

Then, I see nothing at all but the plunging darkness of the River Styx.

EPILOGUE

A desperate, selfish part of me thought Saffron would be at the arena today. An even dumber, more desperate part of me wore my favorite outfit and took twice as long to style my hair. I ascend my line of vision towards Hades and Persephone's private balcony, where they sit with Cerberus, but a third chair is not present.

Still, I hold hope until Thanatos and Hypnos arrive without her. From where I sit, several pews away from the two males, they look at me and shake their heads. Confirming she isn't accompanying them today.

These past three months have been a misery. Some of my many duties as the messengers of the gods are to travel newly departed human souls to the Underworld. When Saffron's friend from the cells died, I tried to run to her. I pushed past Charon to steal his ferry and sail to her, but then I saw her sitting on the mansion steps with Nike and I stopped myself.

Saffron was holding on by a thread, and I would've been the scissors. I would've changed the strength she clung to, so I left before she saw me. Since then, each time I brought a soul down to the Underworld, I would ask about Saffron and receive the same response each time. Whether it was Thanatos or Hypnos or Hades or Persephone, they had the same rehearsed line for me.

"She's not ready to talk to you," they said.

Today was supposed to be my chance to try anew, but a prickle of guilt re-surges when I remember the last time she attended an arena day. She was not welcomed as a surprise child between Persephone and Hades or placed as a princess in a throne, fitting her virtue. No, the last time she was at an arena, she was on the fighting ground as a frightened, quivering human girl.

"You look like you need a drink," an all too familiar voice says before plopping down in the seat next to me.

Based upon the reddish tint to his teeth, Dionysus has already had several glasses of wine. He holds out a chalice for me, and before I utter a single word to my little brother, he clinks our cups together and chugs his in three fluid gulps. He lets out an exaggerated gasp of enjoyment, dazed with inebriation, while his glass fills back up.

"Drink up, Hermie."

I frown. "Don't call me that," still, I take a sip.

"That nickname is solely for Aphrodite?" Dionysus asks.

My frown worsens. "She listens as little as you do when I ask her to stop calling me Hermie."

He leans back with a newly filled wine pressed against his lips. "I hate these events, so dreadfully boring."

Dionysus tilts his glass back, gulping the contents until it's empty, and I know the truth interwoven with his lies. He hates the arenas like I do, but his abhorrence is not directed towards their amusement level. We hate the way terrorized humans wobble to the arena, with tears streaming down their cheeks and occasional urine in their pants and gowns. We hate how we began human enslavement to save the race from Kronos, but some of our company became hungry with the need to inflict pain.

I take another sip out of my glass.

When Boreas, Priapus, and Circe materialize with a flock of terrified humans, my guilt becomes more than just a pinch in my chest. It covers the expanse of my body, snakes underneath my ribs, and pierces my lungs with a virulent bite. I stare at the thirty mortals, who are barely adults, and I see Saffron in each of their faces.

I finish my wine; wordlessly, Dionysus refills it.

Boreas—the personification of the north wind—takes a seat beside his wife, Oreithyia. And Priapus—a low-level god of vegetable fertility—saunters off of the arena grounds and finds a place to sit in between two other fertility gods, Aphaea and Phanes.

Circe, who is a low-level goddess of magic, remains on the arena ground. This woman, whose scorn matches her radiant beauty, was supposed to leave the arena when Boreas and Priapus did. I can't begin the announcements until all the prison masters have left the grounds. For five hundred years, this has been the law.

Circe, tall and lean with prominent freckles that can be seen at great distances, turns her attention to me. Her eyes are not as large as her mother's, Hecate, but hers brew with the same begrudged rage. She stares at me from at least a hundred feet away, and her heated glare speaks about the night eons ago where I helped a heroic demi-god, Odysseus, escape her clutches.

Green smoky magic, several shades darker than her mother's, coils around her arms and above her biceps. Her mist resembles snakes, slithering up the expanse of her pale flesh. Zeus rises to his feet, his lightning bolt smacking against the floor of his pew, and he glares at Circe with agitation.

"Why are you still on the arena floor, witch?" He outcries with obvious annoyance. "Let us start the games."

Circe does not look away from me. "Have you ever heard the story of the thief who was caught with sticky fingers?"

"I've never enjoyed your riddles," is my cool response, which hides the hesitance that follows with her words. Words that sound similar to Kronos's when he dared to visit me in my dreams two weeks ago.

You are a thief with sticky fingers. You may have returned the treasure where you thought it belonged, but thieves who get caught always pay the consequences.

Small, star-shaped orbs levitate off of Circe's magic. They rise in the air and follow the direction of the wind. The rest of the immortals are staring at Circe, surprise littering their faces, but I fixate on Athena from across the room and she unsheathes her sword.

Stall her, Athena mouths.

The star-shaped droplets of magic land on Dionysus's skin, right on top of his hand, but he does not notice. Dionysus stares at Circe as she circulates around the humans, who are supposed to be enslaved to their master today. Her hand caresses the shoulder of one boy, and I expect him to flinch away in fright. He doesn't, though. The human boy turns his attention to me.

While he opens his mouth, it's Circe's voice that flutters out. "The thief thought the worst consequence for stealing what was not his was a stern conversation with Daddy Dearest."

Next, Circe touches a girl's shoulder. She is a petite redhead, who reminds me too much of Panda, and the young female continues the story. "The thief was wrong. He stole more than cattle from his brother this time. He stole the king of time's precious treasure."

Circe lets a fingertip slide across a brawny, dark-skinned boy's bicep, and he growls in her voice. "He stole the king of nightmare's queen."

Another boy, with long hair in two braids, says next. "And Daddy Dearest won't be able to save the thief with sticky fingers this time."

"Because," a girl's mouth opens, and Circe's words flutter out. "The king of time is coming for you, thief, and nobody can save you from his wrath."

All the slaves in Circe's possession stand in perfect formation. Their shoulders are an inch apart, their stance rigid, and when spears materialize in their hands, the humans are ready. Athena shoots off two arrows, killing two of the mortals before they can throw the spear, but the other three throw their weapons towards where I stand.

One of them impales the foot of a god a few feet away from me, but I catch the other two. I glare down at Circe, whose widespread smile mirrors the humans in formation in front of her. I throw the spears to the ground, which immediately disintegrate into ash and mist.

"Beautiful show, Circe, but is that the best-" I stop talking and shift my focal point onto my hands.

On the palms, at least a dozen star-shaped bits of dark green magic embed itself in my skin. I never thought to look at Dionysus, who was hit by the stars, but I do now. He, and everybody around me, is unconscious. Their heads are leaned backwards, and their eyes are closed, while little bits of Circe's magic cling to their skin.

I stumble around, but my valiant fight to keep myself standing is futile. With a fresh wave of tiredness, I tumble onto my pew and search for hope in the slumbering crowd. That's when I see Athena. She is slicing at the stars that come for her, cutting them in half before any can reach her skin. The rest of the arena is incapacitated, but not her.

Not Saffron's sister.

With only one chance between Saffron's safety and Kronos's defeat, I scream the truth. "She's alive, Athena!"

Athena does not turn to face me. Her primary concern is destroying any of the stars moving towards her, but she hears me. "Who is alive?" She asks.

I do not answer, and Athena is intelligent enough to put the pieces together. My voice is drowsy because of the effects of Circe's magic, but I imagine Saffron's face and force myself to speak. To explain her existence to the only person who can save her.

"She's in the Underworld as Hades and Persephone's miracle child, and she's in danger. You may have tried to stop her life from starting, but it's here and she's our chance at surviving. Get out of here and save her."

Athena does not idle around for questions. As my lids lower and Circe's powers overwhelm my senses, Athena transforms into an owl and soars out of the arena. The stars try to race after her, but Circe's power isn't as magnificent as her mother's, and they fail in their race for Saffron's best chance at escape.

"Neat trick, huh?" Circe is no longer on the arena ground, but she is sitting on the ledge closest to my pew. Her freckled face beams with pride as she adds. "There's a perk to having Morpheus and Epiales around. They've taught me a lot about my powers."

I try to laugh, but the sound is strained. "Kronos won't be happy with you," I manage to say.

"And why is that? I incapacitated his children and the thief. He'll be thrilled."

"Some of his children," I correct her gloating statement as unconsciousness threatens to steal me away. "And only most of his grandchildren."

I'm still awake, fighting against the powers that will become victorious. Oblivion is nearing itself, inch by inch, but I hear Circe's response once she notices the empty balcony where one of Kronos's sons should've been.

I pass out as Circe curses one name.

"Poseidon."

My eyes burn as I peel them open, but once I take in my surroundings, I wish I could stay unconscious and avoid witnessing the catastrophe of a defeated effort. Shackles are tightened around my families' wrists and ankles; ichor spills from every direction, staining the alabaster floor beneath my kneeled position, and I wish I could ignore that this is my reality.

Kronos is standing a few feet away from the row of immortals he laid out in the throne room within our former home of Mt. Olympus. For five hundred years, I have yearned to see my land's excellence and its phosphorescent supremacy. I've fallen asleep with the image of Mt. Olympus waiting for me, but over the decades, the vision I remembered had lessened.

Now, I am back, but only as its prisoner.

Circe stands to Kronos's left, but the man to Kronos's right gains my attention. Epiales, Saffron's Storyteller, stands to the left. He was on the cusp of death because the world forgot his existence in Tartarus, but he survived and now stands victorious in front of me. His skin is horribly scarred by Zeus and Hephaestus for his crimes with Morpheus, but now both gods are at his mercy.

Zeus wanted the hideousness of Epiales's scars to match his atrocious actions, but black ink hides most of the torment inflicted upon his pale flesh. Instead of white, shockingly jagged lines, tattoos bring out the lethal blaze of his vengeance. The worst of Zeus's inflicted mutilation is now a sword on his neck, a crow on the top of his right hand, a detailed image of the Minotaur turned into stone on the top of his left hand, and a snake biting into a strawberry curling around his left shoulder.

"Impressive ink," my voice is groggy but coherent. "How'd you get that in the pits of Tartarus?"

Infatuation blossoms on Circe's face as she stares at Epiales. She coos several octaves above her natural tone. "I gifted them to him."

He refuses to look at her, but his silver eyes are glued to where I kneel. His gaze has always unnerved me, even before he was an enemy. They were akin to a sword under the sun, glimmering and dangerous.

"If it wasn't for her, then I'd peel your skin off inch-by-inch," Epiales snarls.

Her being Saffron, not Circe.

I surmise. "That would take a very long time, and I heal fast. Are you sure you're ready for that kind of commitment?"

"Your chance of surviving is already looking dreadful," Morpheus says, who has risen from the dead and stands beside Epiales. "I'd shut up if I were you."

"I've never been one to stay silent," I coo.

"Shut-up, Hermes," Artemis, who stirred awake a few feet away from me, growls.

I clamp my lips shut.

Kronos has been quiet, standing in the middle front of his impressive army of monsters, titans, and vengeful gods. His victory is speaking the prideful words that he does not need to. We are his prisoners of war, and there isn't a necessity for words when you are the champion.

He looks at Circe and finally speaks. "Retrieve my wife for the presentation."

Circe, with excitement, disappears in a plume of dark green smoke.

Kronos glances at one of his brothers, Crius. "Heracles is still unconscious at the end of the line. Transport him to Mt. Atlas. He will take Atlas's job holding the Earth up."

Obediently, Crius nods his head and walks to the end of the line. Heracles lets out an inaudible groan as he is lifted and thrown over Crius's shoulder. A moment later, they are both gone.

Next, Kronos looks at his brother, Coeus. "They said she died in the River Styx. Prove it and kill any human you see in the castle. I want her body, or there's no proof she's dead. You come back with a body or not at all."

"Who died?" I snarl, and Artemis doesn't try silencing me.

We both look at Kronos, who is smirking as Coeus obeys his command. He and two dozen members of their army dematerialize. Fear unlike any I've experienced before threatens to rip my heart from my chest, and I shift my gaze to Epiales.

"Who is dead in the River Styx?" I repeat.

My fright triples when Epiales flinches at the question. The dried, silver streaks of tears are now visible on his cheeks.

"No," I murmur. "She's not dead. You're wrong."

"We saw her jump in ourselves." Morpheus answers me, and he glance at Epiales with a mournful expression. "We know how slim the chances are that she survived the plunge."

Epiales wipes a tear away before anybody else can see, but he says nothing.

"I have faith my little treasure will emerge victorious." Kronos coos, then drifts his attention to me and smirks. "Hello, thief."

"Hello, cannibalistic child-eater." I snarl in a brutal effort to conceal my own overwhelming fear.

The smile on Kronos's face falls. Artemis, who is the only other immortal awake, snorts at my comment. Artemis and I are given a few seconds of amusement before the world crumbles. In those few seconds, we look at each other and say goodbye with a nod of appreciation. She tells me without words her hope that Saffron is alive, and I look back at her with a fear I can't afford to feel as my life hangs in the balance.

Several moans fill the air, and when other gods and goddesses awaken, Artemis and I look away from one another. I focus on Kronos, but Artemis looks to the floor to open up and swallow her whole. Zeus, who is to my left, lifts his head and sees Kronos for the first time in five hundred years.

Kronos's face turns into a scowl. "Son," he snarls.

Kronos says this one word in a taunting, vengeance laced cadence. Zeus is chained up and forced into a kneeling position, but Kronos watches his youngest son and dares him to fight the restraints. Kronos's fingers are twitching at his side, eager for a fight without magical spells and lightning bolts.

Zeus doesn't move an inch, but he glares up at his father with hatred that spans several eons. "Father," he responds.

Circe reappears, with Rhea in her grasp. Rhea—my grandmother and Kronos's wife—stands in front of us in more chains than the rest of us. Golden bondage tightens around each square inch of her wraith build, securing her as a vital prisoner in Kronos's plans. Once he sees his wife, there is not a look of fondness that crosses his face; instead, he looks at her the way one would glance at their favorite pair of shoes.

A preferred necessity.

Circe takes a step back, and all of Kronos's allies watch as he unsheathes a dagger. It's small enough to fit into the palm of

Kronos's hand, but power radiates off of the miniature weapon. It's bronzed, and in a vertical direction, Latin inscriptions rest on the blade.

Deos timere et catenam.
Fear the gods and the chain.

Rhea flinches at the sight of the weapon, and she murmurs for mercy. She tries to run, but with all the chains on her body, she collapses to the ground. Kronos approaches his wife with his knife in his hand, and Rhea's murmurs turn into helpless, incongruous screams.

She tries to kick her husband as she lies on her back, but he overpowers her. He is sitting on top of her lap and turns his attention to Zeus. "Do you know what this weapon is?" Kronos asks.

Tears of helplessness stream down Rhea's face as she kicks, screams, and tries to wiggle out of Kronos's hold. Zeus flinches at the sight of his mother in this state, but he can't help her. Zeus can only glare at his father and shake his head.

"I don't recognize it," Zeus says.

Kronos spits in disgust. "You are a disgrace, my son. Are you so vain that you do not research the weapons that humans have created over the years?" He scoffs and moves his attention from Zeus, narrowing it onto me. "Do you know the blade's importance, thief?"

I don't, but I do not say that.

Artemis answers a beat after the question is directed my way. "It's the Dagger of Chains."

"Very good." Kronos drags the tip of the blade down Rhea's chest, and the contact makes Artemis flinch. "Why don't you be a dear and tell us what the dagger does?"

Kronos wants her to play his game, but she stays silent. Artemis bows her blonde head, submitting to the titan of time. My resilient sister, who fears nothing and no man, trembles because of the dagger in his hands.

"What about a presentation?" Kronos asks the crowd, but none of us respond.

None of us have time to.

Kronos raises the weapon into the air, and Rhea lets out a terrible outcry. She looks at Zeus and sobs. "Save me. Son, please."

But he can't.

We all watch as Kronos drives the dagger into the center of her chest. She stares at Zeus, fear manifesting in her expression, but when Kronos removes the blade, Rhea is gone. Not dead. Not bleeding out on the floor.

Just gone.

"What did you do?" Zeus stares at where his mother once laid, and he looks to his father and lets two tears slip as he repeats. "What did you do?"

"In Ancient Greece, there was an architect who blamed the gods for the death of his son, Icarus. He was so infuriated that he created a blade, which could trap an immortal in a prison that sucks the power out of their bodies. Poor old Daedalus created a masterpiece that only needed an inscription on the side to activate." Kronos caresses the Latin words across the blade, then looks at us and inquires with wickedness on his tongue. "Who wants to go first?"

Kronos's face remains unsurprised when nobody raises their shackled hands to volunteer, but this does not derail him. The titan of time rises to his feet and chooses his victims with a stride in his step and pride illuminating his face. He presses the blade against Zeus's neck, right underneath his thick, white beard, but hesitates. Kronos stops himself from driving the blade into Zeus's throat because he wants his last sight of Zeus to be slackened in fear.

"Get on with it," Zeus growls.

"When you get out of this dagger, it will be with your second prophesied child with Metis readying your execution," Kronos's smile triples its size when Zeus's face pales with fear.

"The child is alive?" Zeus asks.

Kronos never answers.

He drives the dagger into Zeus's neck, and he is gone a moment later. One after another, Kronos stabs my siblings and aunts and uncles and cousins until only Ares, Hephaestus, Hecate, and I remain. Kronos lowers himself into a kneeling position in front of me, and I ready the pain and imprisonment that comes with the prick of his blade.

But the pain never comes.

Kronos sheathes the dagger, and when the realization that I will not be imprisoned in the blade settles, my fright multiplies. I do not have to glance at the three immortals who are chained and seated beside me, to know that the unknown torment that awaits us is going to be more frightening than the blade.

Kronos says with cruelness on his tongue. "I told you that thieves will always face the consequences of being caught stealing what does not belong to them. Oh, I'm going to have fun breaking every will you have to live, little thief."

Made in the USA
Monee, IL
06 January 2025